THE RUSSIAN

A top official in Russian intellegence, Viktor Denisov headed the conspiracy to establish a new and more powerful U.S.S.R. In three days, he and his comrades would reshape the map of the disintegrated Soviet Union—and forever change history.

THE AMERICAN

One of a handful of men who knew that the leaders of Russia and the United States were secretly meeting, Commander T.C. Bogner was responsible for protecting the presidents. There was only one catch: how could he perform his duties when everyone was out to double-cross him?

RED TIDE

In a heart-stopping race against time, Bogner had to outwit the Russian agents who were determined to destroy the new political order. It was a deadly game of international intrigue—and the stakes were world domination.

RED TIDE

R. KARL LARGENT

LEISURE BOOKS **NEW YORK CITY**

A LEISURE BOOK®

December 1992

Published by

Dorchester Publishing Co., Inc.
276 Fifth Avenue
New York, NY 10001

Printed in the United States of America.

To B.J. Elsner and Matt Clemens,
many, many thanks.

PART ONE

BASE HOUR
SEVEN–TWO
2100 NEGRIL LOCAL 10:5
0600 MOSCOW LOCAL 10:6
0200 GREENWICH (Z) 10:6

Base Hour
Seven-Two:
ZERO ZERO . . . 0000ZULU

Datum: 10:5 . . . Moscow, 0600MLT

Viktor Denisov had been awake for several hours, troubled by an unending turbulence of chaotic thoughts. Yet each of these transitory thoughts were examined like an irritating curiosity, given an evanescent examination and discarded without resolution.

Beyond the windows of the darkened room he could hear the raw October wind claw at the masonry walls of the seven-story Zaratsna Tower.

The Tower had been built as an accommodation for students attending what was now being called the New Russian Institute of Foreign Languages. But, as with everything in the new Russia since Zhelannov had been named President, the old ways were changing. The newly appointed Commissioner of Urban and Central Housing had been forced to recognize the growing plight of the capitol's homeless and the city-wide shortage of housing. Because of these problems, he was required to allow both students and faculty to take up residence in the Tower, students on the first four floors and select faculty members on levels five through seven.

For Viktor, the gnawing question was, how did the woman lying beside him, an entry-level instructor in English at the Institute, achieve the status of select faculty? He assumed, of course, that it had something to do with Ruta's former lover, Nikolai.

There were indications that he was a man of influence, but, other than that his full name was Nikolai Ilichev Kerensky, Viktor had been unable to learn much about the man. Even more surprising was the fact that what little he had been able to uncover about Kerensky was information Viktor considered to be from unreliable sources. Even the former GRU files on Kerensky were sketchy.

In the darkness, he scowled as he recalled his conversation with the young files officer in the new militia personnel section. The lieutenant had been reluctant to give Denisov what had once been classified information over the telephone. It was true, no one trusted anyone in the chaos that followed the dissolution of the union.

"Give it to me, damn it, I am General Denisov," Viktor had thundered.

Relenting, the young officer's voice became a monotone. "Nikolai Kerensky. Birth date: 5/23/50 Citizenship: Yugoslavian. Affiliation: former Yugoslav Communist Party, affiliation forfeited 12/12/91. Height: 5' 11". Weight:185

pounds. Married: wife, Akrina, one daughter, Meliva. Passports: None. Occupation: Engineer. Present address: Unknown."

Viktor slammed the phone down. "Unknown" was simply the designation the militia used in acknowledging former GRU and KGB agents. The Party had purged the records before turning them over to the militia. Viktor was certain of one thing: Kerensky had not been affiliated with the directorship. All this caused him to wonder if Ruta was aware that her former lover had been a KGB agent. If so, she said nothing about it.

For the time being however, Ruta and her former lover was a subject that had to be set aside. On this day, Viktor had other, more important matters to think about. Even with this awareness, he found his thoughts, like those of a lusting youth, returning repeatedly to the woman lying beside him. He had almost as many questions about her as he did Nikolai Kerensky.

What did he know about Ruta Putilin for certain? Only that which was verifiable. She was from Vladivostok, 29 years-old, and a former apprentice ballerina with the Bolshoi before finally earning a diploma from Suslov in foreign languages. He had met her on a flight from Vladivostok to Moscow when she was returning home after visiting her ailing mother. They had talked briefly at Domodovo airport, and he had waited a whole three days before he called her. If she had been a KGB plant, would she not have called him to make certain the liaison continued?

She was, in Viktor's opinion, an attractive woman—tall, slender, and possessing the stylishly muscular body of a former dancer. Still, her most appealing feature was her deep-set haunting and melancholy eyes—eyes that somehow searched and probed Viktor's very soul when they made love.

Now, next to him in bed, her long, fawn-colored hair tangled in the folds of her pillow, she slept. She stirred so little that Viktor marveled at the depth of her sleep. He was reminded of the old Russian saying that only the innocent sleep without reservation. He knew now that he could refute that. Ruta was not an innocent.

Perhaps that was the reason that Viktor found her so appealing—the gutsy way she embraced life, the way she communicated with fiery passion and made love with abandon. Over the years, General Viktor Denisov could boast that he had been intimate with a great many women, but none with the impassioned licentiousness of Ruta Putilin. The previous night alone they had made love three times only to have her feign anger when he was unable to accommodate her for a fourth.

In the filtered reflections of street light that invaded the darkness, he rolled closer to her and traced his blunt finger up her long slender arm, pausing for a second at the juncture where her arm melded into a smooth white shoulder. The coarse cotton blanket had fallen away to reveal her small soft breast, and he traced his finger down to draw an imaginary circle around the nipple, much as an inquisitive boy would in the course of experiencing his first love affair.

Despite the coarseness of the skin on his own ungainly hands, Ruta did not stir. Her sleep continued deep and untroubled. Youth, he laughed to himself, how often they sleep that way. But was it the slumber of someone without a conscience, or the sleep of the satiated?

He rolled away from her again, angry at allowing himself to be occupied with thoughts of her at a time when his energies should be focused on other matters. He was aware now that the cloak of wall-to-wall blackness in their room was being more frequently violated by the head lamps of cars on the streets below, and he glanced at the clock to check the time.

This was the dawn of the first day. The beginning, he was convinced, of a 72-hour period that would again reshape the map of the disintegrated Soviet empire—three days that would establish a new and more powerful Union of Soviet Socialist Republics, three days until his beloved Russia regained center stage among all world powers. The mere thought of this monumental undertaking sent a mercurial shudder rampaging across his broad shoulders.

Viktor Denisov had as many credentials as he did muscles. In the autumn of his sixtieth year, unlikely as it seemed, he could claim to be both the son of a common *kolkhoznik* and a graduate of the Kiev Higher Command School.

Posted to a regimental reconnaissance detachment after his matriculation, he had endured the rigors of military service as first a platoon commander, then a company commander, and finally, commander of reconnaissance before receiving his long awaited appointment to the Frunze Academy.

From the outset it had been a period of prudent endurance. Like the scions of the military aristocracy he cavorted with, he too had been able to avoid the reality of combat throughout his career.

After the Frunze, Viktor had made his choice. Unlike his battery mates, he chose to join the GRU instead of what was then known as the Committee for State Security, the KGB. Even in those days he passionately believed that the consummate threat to his beloved Russia was from within and not from beyond the borders. His beliefs had been vindicated. As proof he cited the preposterous and socially corrupting policies of the fools Gorbachev and Yeltsin and their now equally infamous and inept successor, Yevgeny Zhelannov. A *commonwealth*, he spat upon it. Outsiders and imperialists had influenced Russia like a cancer. That awareness fanned the flames of political dissidence that radiated inside him. Zhelannov had to be stopped, and the Union reunited.

Viktor's string of disjointed thoughts turned to his wife, Alima. If it was the fifth day of the month, she would be somewhere near the Turkman-Afghanistan border with the academy research team. He wondered if it was at all possible that her thoughts of him were as infrequent as his thoughts of her.

He depressed the tiny illumination button on his watch and checked the time. Was it the same as the clock on the stand beside the bed? This checking was merely one of his many precautions. There was no need to hurry, but he had to be punctual. Today of all days, there must appear to be nothing out of the ordinary. Today must be no different from the 100 days that preceded it, and only a small handful of men now realized how significantly different would be the 100 glorious days that were to follow.

Ruta stirred, and Viktor glanced down at her. She reached out for him in the darkness, searching for the man she called her "Bear." She did not use the Russian word for "bear" but carefully enunciated the word in her clipped version of Americanized English. At first the practice annoyed him, but now Viktor appreciated the fact that she talked to him in English. It helped him become more familiar with what he considered to be the confusing and harsh-sounding language of the decadent American imperialists.

He leaned over and placed his finger on her soft mouth. The tip of her tongue darted out and she began to suck on his finger.

"*Nyet*," he admonished her.

"Why? Are the fires of my bear's passions still quenched?" she teased.

"Do not make fun of me."

"I will call you anything I want, anytime I want," she said laughing, "and none of your pompous military friends will know what I am saying."

She was wrong of course, and they both knew it. Even the lowest ranking official in the vast and largely still-intact GRU intelligence network had a passing proficiency with the English language.

Viktor, who had stood up to look out the window, sat down again on the edge of the bed. The woman's hand snaked out from under the covers and over the hairy matte of his well-muscled leg. She began to fondle him, setting up a primitive rhythm, sensuously moving her hand back and forth with her lips parted in invitation. "Perhaps you would care to grace your Ruta with a going-away present." Her voice was husky.

Viktor stood up again. "*Nyet*."

"That was a most unflattering thing to do," she pouted.

He began to apologize in Russian.

"Speak English," she reminded him, as she sat up. The tone of her voice did not betray her. As usual there was no trace of admonition or stress in her voice. She knew all too well that Viktor was adroit at catching the slightest altered pattern in a person's voice. It was his edge in negotiations, a skill at which he considered himself a master. The voice, Viktor was fond of saying, is the window to an adversary's emotions. Yet even with her control and even though she knew he could not see her face in the darkness, he would know that she was frowning. Negotiation was his forte; the delights of the bedroom were hers. Rejection displeased Ruta.

"There is not time for passionate," he said clumsily.

"There is no time for passion," she corrected, leaning her head on her elbow and smiling.

He fumbled on the nightstand for a cigarette, lit it, inhaled and handed it to her. It was a Winston, a peace offering. He was reminded of how frequently Ruta expressed her displeasure with the quality of Russian cigarettes. He watched the tip of the cigarette glow in the darkness and mumbled an apology. "There is much on my mind."

"My dearest Viktor, you are indeed a bear, a very uncompromising bear."

Viktor stood up and turned to the window again. The sheen of a night-long sleet glazed the nearly deserted streets. It displeased him that she was making an already difficult process even more so. The whole routine of parting was something he dreaded. Perhaps it bothered him because it did not seem to bother her. Why? he wondered. Had she found it equally easy to take her leave from her other lovers?

"There is something bothering you," she said. "Can you tell me about it?"

"*Nyet*," he said. Then he corrected himself. "No! You know I cannot talk about these things."

"Are you afraid I will take your little secrets and run to my friends in the new Russian Security Bureau?" she asked laughing. She was standing beside him now, playfully tracing her finger down the length of his arm.

Strange that she would say that, Viktor thought. That was precisely his concern. He would be the laughing stock of Moscow—a former GRU directorate and a ranking Party official sleeping with an RSB informer. His thoughts returned again to the information he had been able to verify. The files had been purged, so he could not be entirely certain. The RSB now had the maddening authority to doctor even the files of a former GRU Director, a Lieutenant-General who once headed up the Electronic Intelligence Directorate. Because of that, he measured his response. "Of that I am not suspicious." Viktor was convinced that he had used the right words, but he was not at all certain however that he had used them in the proper sequence.

"Light the candle," she said, "so I can see your face."

Viktor complied, took the cigarette from her hand, and snuffed it out. Then he lit the candle. When the room became faintly illuminated, he saw that she was pulling her hair back and tying it in a loose bun. The pupils of her eyes were large and penetrating as she studied him.

The face that Ruta Putilin saw in turn was broad and furrowed, jowled by the years and etched with an expression of concern. It was a complicated mosaic that included a crop of thinning reddish brown hair worn somewhat long for a military man, large ears that, when combined with the teeth yellowed by an endless succession of cigarettes, constituted the face of the prototypical Bolshevik. From the neck down, he was brutish and bulky, covered with a thick mat of wooly and wiry red hair. There was no other word she could think of that more accurately described him than bear. Little about Viktor Denisov suggested finesse.

"Something is definitely wrong," she said. She was not questioning but was making her usual, accurate observation.

"I am occupied."

"Preoccupied," she corrected.

The teacher-like response brought a fleeting half smile to his thick full lips, and for a moment erased the scowl from his face. On impulse, he leaned over to kiss her. Then he straightened up as if to be caught in such an act of tenderness would be an embarrassment.

"Will I see you tonight?" she asked.

Viktor shook his head. "Not tonight." He did not want to tell her that he would be away for three whole days. Perhaps she would become bored and seek another lover. Nor could he tell her that he would be at the barracks throughout the period. She would know that something was up. If he said nothing, she would imagine the worst;

she had done that before as well. He turned and looked out the window again.

"Sounds clandestine," she teased. "Is my General Bear playing war games again?"

"Yes, war games. But I can no talk about it."

"Can't," she corrected. "The Americans call that a contraction, a shortened combination of the words *can* and *not*. Can't."

Viktor nodded his understanding and moved across the room. Ruta allowed the covers to fall away, issuing one last invitation. It was now 0630; he had exactly 30 minutes to shave and tend to his toilet, before he had to be downstairs in front of the building to meet his driver.

"Do not wake me when you leave then," she said. Her voice was flat, and Viktor knew that she was trying to punish him for his trenchant behavior.

He went into the small bathroom and closed the door. When he had finished, he walked back into the sleeping portion of the two-room flat. Ruta had extinguished the candle, pulled the covers over her head and gone back to sleep. The only sound in the room was the sleet pelting against the window.

Viktor finished buttoning his tunic, adjusted the epaulets, picked up his overcoat, his hat, his attaché case and left, locking the door behind him.

The elevator was inoperative until 0700, so he had to walk down seven flights to the spartan communal entrance.

There was a sign in the lobby. "THE NEW BEGINNING—THE COMMONWEALTH." The sign irritated him. How quickly, he reflected with a frown, the fundamental Party values were being swept under the rug.

He stepped out on the curb, inhaled deeply and surveyed the opalescence of the ice-coated Moscow streets.

It was precisely 0700.

His limousine was waiting.

Today, he thought to himself, will be a most memorable day.

Datum: 10:4 . . . Caribbean: USS Madison, *2117LT*

Commander Charles Evans Peel poured his second cup of coffee and scrutinized the watch change on the bridge. Satisfied, he went out on the fly bridge to assess the weather before heading below to the COM-CON center. The newly assembled crew of the *Madison* was finally starting to function like the unit he had hoped it would become when it was assigned. Peel, age 47, had just taken command of the Virginia class cruiser after a complete retrofit. Shakedowns completed, the routine and placement of things were finally becoming familiar to both him and his crew.

He scanned the sky, sipped his coffee and smoked what he figured would be his last cigarette of the day. All things considered, it was a fine Caribbean evening. Too bad Marcie wasn't there to see it. He checked his watch; she would be putting Skipper and Kristy to bed just about now. Then she would study; Marcie was finally back in school. When she graduated, she wanted to teach, and he would retire, go back to school and maybe become a teacher himself. Charley Peel, acknowledged pessimist, had to admit the prospects for the future were looking better all the time.

"Fine evening, Captain," Brubaker assessed from his watch post. The CWO2 had been with him on the *Hurley*. Peel liked and respected the man from Georgia, a good sailor. "Last cigarette tonight, sir?"

Peel knew Brubaker disapproved of his habit. "Some day I'm going to wise up and quit these damn things," he grumbled.

"Good forecast, sir; calm seas, no clouds. Just the way we like it."

Charley Peel grunted, ignored the double meaning of Brubaker's response, dropped his cigarette into the butt can and started below. He could hear Brubaker saying goodnight as he started down. Brubaker was right. With the exception of a barrage of a perplexing string of messages from CIN-ATL, the night watch should be a cakewalk.

On the way to the COM-CON, he poked his head into the radio room and checked the electronic voice board for messages; nothing since 2000ALT, 2300Z and that had been nothing more than a coded confirmation of his orders. "SURVEILLANCE POSTURE, COORDINATES DETAILED, POSITION FIX, ENTRANCE TO NEGRIL BAY." As Vice-Admiral Sannon had put it, "Get yourself in position, Charley, turn your monitors on, keep your eyes open, ears up and assume all the precautions of a second level standby." In other words, be on your toes. All of which would have been a little perplexing if the order had come from anyone other than Sannon. To Sannon, even dolphins were a threat.

The ears Sannon had referred to consisted of the *Madison's* sensors, tracking and surveillance radar and her oversized bow sonar. The *Madison's* enhanced bank of onboard computers could process in the wink of an eye anything her dual system electronic gear could ferret out.

In point of fact, Charley Peel, a 23-year veteran of duty tours in both the Atlantic and Pacific, mostly aboard ships with considerably less sophisticated gear than the *Madison*, was still somewhat awed by his ship's capabilities. The *Madison* was a nuclear powered, super-sophisticated, technical arsenal in every sense of the word. During her retrofit, the navy had installed third generation SPG-60-A radar. The SPG-60-A could acquire a target at a range of 150 miles and track it automatically. Not only that, it could track eight targets at once. The radar was backed up with six primary SPG-51EE missile control trackers with a two channel auxiliary. The *Madison* was a far cry indeed from Peel's days aboard the *Albany* when she covered the mine-laying operation in Haiphong Harbor or his days on the *Lansing* in the Persian Gulf.

From the radio room, he went out on deck, down one level and snatched one last look at the razor-thin slash of orange on the western horizon. From there he descended to the COM-CON level. The duty roster plates on the bulkhead above the entrance indicated two of his personal favorites were on duty.

Charley Peel divided men into two basic categories: good sailors and everyone else. Good sailors gained his respect by being dedicated, efficient, hard-working and sea-loving. Anything less and a man summarily fell into the second category.

Leonard Simons, Sonarman Second Class, was a last minute addition to the crew of the *Madison* when Peel lost one of his original choices to a failed physical. Simons came by way of the tech school at Groton where he had been schooled on the hardware of the second generation Aegis defense system. The *Madison* was scheduled for the 2g-ADS retrofit in January. Peel had been around too long to ask why the *Madison*'s total refitting hadn't been accomplished all at the same time. He knew he would have gotten some kind of bureaucratic response about the fiscal budget. "Bush bullshit," he called it. Seaworthiness and readiness had no place in the bureaucratic beancounter's train of logic.

Nevertheless, Simons was already aboard, and his superiors were already acknowledging that he had all the attributes of an excellent sonarman. He had an ear for what he was listening to, and he was rapidly teaching others the same skill.

The duty officer in COM-CON was Lt. Melvin Campos. Campos was an ROTC graduate who had opted to go regular navy after his first hitch. Peel had served briefly with Campos on the *Hurley* when Campos was a raw ensign. Despite the trio's mutual respect for each other, there was no greeting when Peel entered.

There were banks of monitors, some with black screens and sweeping green-yellow lights, others with gray fields and blinking red targets. Leonard Simons sat in front of a bank of six displays, his hands dancing over the control panels, tweaking maximum performance from each. There was a yellow-orange glow to both men's faces generated by the RXR-77 sweep displays. Campos was whistling a country and western tune.

Peel scanned the cluttered message board and noted the time on the last transmission. Then he switched on the auxiliary monitor and began punching out the values on the keyboard. In that fashion he could observe sequentially all COM-CON monitors and obtain a digitized situation analysis.

"What are we looking at?" Peel asked. The question was almost nonchalant.

"We're getting latterals, sir," Campos said. The Texan began pinpointing specific targets on the SD grid. "That close one there is a Russian Yankee class. Obviously a nuke and noisier than hell. We're picking up cavitation noise out the old bung hole."

Peel altered displays and isolated the blinking red light in quadrant three-three.

"I think she must be having some kind of reactor problems. She sprints then she stops, sprints then stops."

Campos leaned forward. "Those things scare the piss out of me. Who the hell knows who's got their finger on the trigger on those things anymore."

Simons looked up from his display. "If I was guessing, I'd say she was having trouble cooling her shaft."

"Bearing?" Peel inquired.

Campos squinted at the monitor. "Ought one seven one, Captain, same as ours. We altered course at 2300Z according to the SPAC log, and our noisy friend back there altered her course ninety seconds later. She's been sucking our wake ever since. Just to play it safe, I put it all on tape and notified control."

Simons reached up and hit the playback button. Peel watched a replay of the entire sequence on tape while noting the time intervals indicated in a small insert digital readout in the lower corner of the tactical display. He replayed it twice, lit a cigarette and asked the duty officer, "What do you make of it, Campy?"

"Weird. If that's a Yankee class sub down there, and the micro processors on the shore units have confirmed it twice already, that means we got a gray on our tail that could be packing twenty-four SS-N-8 Sawflys. But what makes it even weirder is she doesn't act like she cares if we know she's back there."

"Maybe she doesn't," Peel offered. "We're all supposed to be one big happy family in the world community these days. Maybe the skipper wants to catch up with us and have some good old-fashioned American ham and eggs for breakfast."

Campos smiled.

Peel replayed the tape again and snuffed out his cigarette. "Who the hell knows. One thing for certain, she knows we know she's out there on our tail." He looked at the sonarman. "What's the SAT-RECON profile?"

"SAT-RECON reports this same sub passed through the GIUK Gap eight days ago. ICON plotted her on true course to Havana. Yesterday at 1344Z, according to an AWS report, she altered course and started heading our way. She locked on to us at 1847 ALT last night."

Peel leaned back in his chair, frowning.

"You don't suppose there's any chance she intercepted Sannon's message?" Campos speculated.

"Not if she changed course at the time indicated. ASW doesn't make mistakes about things like that." Still not satisfied, Peel altered the display, enlarging the grid area. "She came from Murmansk?"

"Affirmative, Captain," Simons said.

Peel slowly traced his finger down through the Greenland-Iceland-United Kingdom gap and mentally-calculated a 190:00° course toward Cuba. "Holy shit," he exclaimed. "Do you realize how many miles that baby covered in the last six days?"

"Maybe that's why they got reactor problems?" Simons speculated.

"If you ask me," Peel speculated, "I don't think she intercepted Sannon's orders. I think she was instructed to alter course."

Campos got up from his station and poured himself a cup of coffee. "I think—"

"She's sucking up water again," Simons interrupted. He handed his headset to Peel. "Listen to that racket."

"Think she's playing games with us, sir?" Campos asked.

"I doubt it, not if she's got problems. She's got to know we're watching her."

"Could they have some kind of war games going on that we don't know about? That's the only thing that sounds logical to me, sir." Simons took the headset back and sat down again.

"Logic and Russian sub captains don't go hand in hand," Peel scoffed. "Besides, since the Soviets split, they usually play their games a little closer to home."

Campos took a long sip of coffee. "Well, if it ain't games, they got something else up their sleeve. There's too damn much going on out there." His fingers danced across the keyboard of his console, calling up an immediate proximity display. "Take that target right there. That's a Kiev class. She's about forty nautical miles off our stern, like she's following the Yankee. She's been there for the last five hours. According to SAT-COM she's got a Hormone B sitting on her deck."

"Kiev's carry a Yak-36 Forger VTOL," Peel reminded him.

"Not this one."

"Confirmed?"

"Yes, sir," Campos said. "An EC-130G Hercules spotted and verified her last night. The GI-CO channeled a PIREP through the ground station at Cayman Long. A couple of hours later we got a confirmation from the low frequency observer on Cayman Brac."

Peel hit the ELF code 6^6 >:bb and watched the repeat verification. He snuffed out his cigarette and lit another.

Suddenly Simons's hands flew up in the air in a halting motion. "Oh shit, look at this. I think our Yankee just took a nose dive."

Peel leaped out of his chair and bent over the display. "You don't suppose that silly bastard tried to purge that tub over the trench?"

Simons' face took on a worried look. "I've lost contact. We're getting nothing."

"Confirm on backup," Peel ordered.

Campos began typing commands. The screen flashed, and the blinking red dot was gone. "No contact. How deep is that goddamn trench?"

Peel snatched up a second headset. "Surely we're getting something." He looked at the screen again and depressed the intercom to the bridge. "All stop. Go passive. Deflate the buoyancy on the trailing antenna. Drop the blanket, Simons. If a mouse moves on that fucking submarine I want to be able to hear it."

Campos grabbed the phone to security. "The Captain wants somebody down here that can speak Russian. Find him and get him down to COM-CON on the double."

"The Captain ordered us to drop the blanket," the bridge reminded him.

"Never mind that. We've got to find a way to communicate with that damn Kiev about forty knots off our stern. Somebody better tell their captain that they've got a Yankee with eighty or so men laying at the bottom of the Cayman Trench."

Datum: 10:4 . . . Los Angeles: Shirmark Hotel, 1807PST

When the shadow fell over the table, Toby Bogner looked down at his watch. Twenty minutes late—just fashionable, never outrageous. Typically Joy. It occurred to him again that Joy was a helluva name for an ex-wife.

"Hi," she said. The smile was predictable but still disarming. "You know me. I was never very prompt." As far as Joy was concerned she had just defused the inevitable, because the Toby Bogner she had known in the past was not a patient man.

"How are you, Joy?" he said. From the tone of his voice she could have believed he really cared, but it was just as easy to believe it was the only opening line he could think of. Typically Tobias, she thought to herself; he just wasn't very good at small talk. The quiet type appealed to some women—but not her.

"Judge for yourself," she said, placing one smoothly contoured leg in front of the other, a hand on the hip and the other hand extended at just the right angle. He knew it had cost her a small fortune to learn to stand that way—her or the network—but in watching her, he decided it was worth it. It was intended to remind Toby of all the appealing and intimate feminine delights he was now deprived of. You can sit down now, he thought to himself, mission accomplished.

She settled into the chair across the table from him. She was still wearing her luxurious crop of sable-colored hair shoulder-length or maybe even a little longer. For the occasion she had selected a matching ensemble of jacket, skirt and camisole that appeared to be a feminine version of herringbone tweed with discreet threads of gold woven into the fabric. The makeup, as usual, was flawless. The earrings, oversized knotted gold ropes, came across as slightly extravagant. But what the hell, he told himself, no one is perfect— not even Joy.

She admitted to 40, was actually 45 and some- how still managed to look 30. To his surprise, she wasn't as worn around the edges as he had expected her to be after seven years. After all, Toby consoled himself, an ex-husband has a right to expect a little wear and tear after not seeing her for seven years. Then the thought occurred to him—if this show is all for the benefit of an ex-husband, what the hell was her current lover getting?

He nodded approval. "You look good."

"Admit it, I look great." She smiled and looked down at the drink in front of her. "For me? Scoresby? You remembered."

"Over shaved ice. I wasn't always asleep."

"You weren't always home, either," she purred, "but then that's all in the past, isn't it?" She brought her anchorwoman's voice down so that he would know she really wasn't asking a question.

As usual, Toby Bogner didn't reply. There was no need to. Joy had rehearsed her lines, and the scene was just beginning. She tilted her head to one side and snatched a quick look at herself in the mirror behind him. Next came the adjustment of the watch, a casual fingering of the oversized diamond on the third finger of her left hand and finally the musical little clearing of the throat. Toby realized that for Joy Bogner—make that the former Joy Bogner—the high point of their little rendezvous was already over. She had choreographed and staged her grand entrance, and he had to admit he was duly dazzled. She had carried it off well.

"So," she said, "how have you been?" Joy had two opening lines: "How have you been?" and "Seen any good movies lately?" The latter, he figured that even she realized, was inappropriate for the occasion.

"So-so. How's Elmer?"

"Ernest," she laughed. "Ernest Baxter Carpenter—and he's really a very nice man, Tobias." She still called him Tobias, not Toby or T. C.—nothing that would indicate that their relationship had ever progressed beyond the superficial formality of one of the endless round of cocktail parties she was always attending.

It had occurred to him once, a long time ago, that her habit of calling him Tobias could be the core reason for the breakup of their marriage. To put it another way, she simply had never gotten to know the real "Toby." On the other hand, he always vacillated; maybe if she had, they would never have gotten married in the first place. Why didn't she get to know him? He knew the answer to that one, too. How could she? He was gone most of the time.

There was a strained silence while she took a sip of her drink.

"How long are you in town?" she finally asked.

"Between planes. I'm on my way to Boston." He glanced down on the congested traffic on Sepulveda. "I probably should be leaving in another thirty minutes or so."

"Boston?" she repeated over the rim of her glass. "Business or pleasure?"

"To see Kim. She has a long weekend. Next week she starts midterms. How long since you've talked to her?"

When Joy trailed her crimson-tipped finger around the rim of her glass to stall, Toby knew it had been longer than she wanted to admit. The gap between professional mother and academic daughter had grown even wider than Kim had let on.

The former Joy Bogner was uncomfortable with the fact that she had a 19 year-old daughter at Boston College. She seldom admitted it, her network played the fact down altogether, and he doubted if the folks who watched the news even knew it.

"Too long probably," she admitted. Maternal guilt had forced her into one of her infrequent fits of honesty.

"She claims she's doing well in school, and she wants me to meet some guy named Todd."

"Serious?" Joy tilted her head to one side.

"She thinks it is."

"Nineteen is too young to get serious. Tell her getting serious about somebody when you're that young can fuck up your life."

"In so many words?"

"Aren't we living proof?" she snapped. Her eyes were hard.

Tobias Carrington Bogner had married Joyce Ellen Baker two days after an Act of Congress had made him an officer and gentleman. He was commissioned, married and assigned to navy flight school in the space of 72 hours. He was 22, and Joy was 21. He had a degree in engineering from Cal Tech, and she was a late starting junior at Pasadena City College. They were like Ken and Barby, an officer and his lady.

One week later he shipped off to Pensacola for flight training. He left her in a one bedroom apartment in South Pasadena to continue her education, and although neither of them realized it at the time, the fairy-tale glow on their romance had already started to tarnish.

"There were some good times, weren't there?" He had to ask because he wasn't sure she agreed with him. Even Bogner had to admit that he had tried hard to put the memories behind him.

"You were a better lover than you were a husband. If we could have found a way to spend the rest of our lives in bed we probably would have made it."

Bogner took a sip of Scotch and nodded without looking at her. Why in the name of all that made common sense had he even called her in the first place? Hadn't he been in and out of Los Angeles hundreds of times before, watched her on the news and thought about her? But he had never bothered to call her before. Why now? Why here—where they used to meet when she got her first job with that stupid little public television station staffed by a bunch of liberal twits?

Maybe, he rationalized, it was the picture in People Magazine, her and a grinning Elmer or whatever his name was, playing tennis at some charity affair. So he had called. He was an ass. He was surprised when she answered his call and even more surprised when she agreed to meet him at the Shirmark for a drink. Now that she was here, what the hell was he planning to say to her? Most of it had been said when she paraded him into a Los Angeles County courthouse and untied a 15 year-old knot.

A bland-faced judge, weary of watching crumbling marriages, had methodically split everything down the middle, awarded Joy custody of their only child and hurried off to his one o'clock tee time. Four years later, Joy, her career on the upswing and tired of playing mother games, shipped Kim off to upstate New York to a boarding school and then made certain their daughter spent every summer in Europe.

"Where to after Boston?" she asked.

Bogner shrugged. "Who knows what Clancy has up his sleeve? Probably back to Washington."

"How is dear old Clancy? I haven't talked to him in ages."

"Clancy hasn't changed—just the times. Now that he isn't carrying the whole threat of a Soviet invasion on his shoulders, he's thinking about retirement."

Joy nodded as though she had heard what he said, but he knew she hadn't. She was busy finishing her Scoresby and extracting her car keys and sunglasses from her purse. As she stood up she smoothed her skirt. Then she bent over and brushed her lips lightly on his cheek. It was the kind of kiss Toby figured she reserved for her agent and her hairdresser—and her ex-husband. He laughed. What the hell should he expect?

"Give Kim a hug for me," she said, "and don't forget to watch the news."

He watched her walk out. Then he signaled the waiter for another drink. "Make it a double," he said. "I've got a shitty taste in my mouth."

Base Hour
Seven-One:
ZERO ZERO . . . 0100ZULU

*Datum: 10:5 . . . Moscow: Council of Ministers,
0700 MLT*

Viktor's schedule for the fifth day of October had
been scrupulously arranged to make it appear that
it was no different than any other Friday. Yet, he,
along with five others, knew that this Friday was
decidedly different.

The countdown had already begun.

The plot had been set in motion. The 72nd hour
of their plan was already history, and there were
71 more, just waiting to unfold.

Viktor was occupied—no, *preoccupied* with his
thoughts.

As usual the Volga was too warm, and he unbuttoned his overcoat. His driver, Slava, a young corporal from Byelorussia, was always cold and in
turn harbored the belief that his passengers were
the same. Viktor tried the intercom, discovered
that it still was not working and leaned forward
to tap on the window that separated the driver's

seat from the Volga's pretentious passenger compartment. He pointed to the heater controls and made a downward motion with his index finger.

A muttered apology, further muted by the glass that separated the two men, was accompanied by Slava's typical somnolent grin. As far as Viktor was concerned, the man was a parody and a buffoon; it was the militia's way of getting even, assigning him a uniformed incompetent. The new Russian military was a travesty. That too would be corrected.

Viktor switched on the small convenience light over the rear seat and opened the large courier bag of overnight dispatches. Slava's duties included a stop at Communication Central to pick up the previous night's messages before his scheduled seven o'clock pickup of General Denisov. The canvas pouch was emblazoned with the Russian emblem and carried the official Military Department, 44388 coded tape across the hasp. Directly below the tape was stenciled LIEUTENANT-GENERAL DENISOV.

Viktor slipped his key ring out of his briefcase and used the red and white key to unlock the top lock. Then he dialed in a three digit combination to release the second lock. With the pouch open, he lit a cigarette.

Anxious not to appear overly interested in the contents of the dispatches, he placed them on the seat beside him. Then he glanced up to see if Slava was watching him in the rearview mirror. The driver had a habit of keeping one eye on the general, like a dog always anticipating his master's next command.

When Viktor saw that the man was watching

him, he turned the light off and stared out the window. The sleet-blanketed streets were still dark and deserted except for the inevitable convoy of military trucks coming and going from the arsenal inside the Kremlin.

Viktor checked his watch again. It was the one Ruta had given him, a Rolex obviously obtained on the black market. He ran the blunt tip of his finger over the crystal. In some ways, the watch was like her former lover, Kerensky. Viktor knew that he dared not ask too many questions.

His attention was momentarily drawn to a minor collision between a Moskvich and a small Zaporozhet at a side street intersection. From the looks of things, the driver of the Moskvich appeared to have lost control of his car on the ice. Two militia officers were already on the scene, and the drivers were gesturing at each other.

Impatient, he put out his cigarette and turned on the light again. He glanced at Slava, but the dolt had his hands full keeping the car under control.

There was one dispatch, of course, that was of more interest to Viktor than the others. When he found it, it carried the code name "72". It had been forwarded from the former Fleet Deputy of Intelligence and his long-time friend, Admiral Feliks Osipov. Viktor unzipped the plastic envelope and placed it on top of the other reports. He read it, slowly and carefully. As he did, a small smile began to play with the corners of his stern mouth.

It was a copy of the coded report that had originated the previous day in Montego Bay. At first reading it appeared to be a wholly innocuous document containing routine field information from Jamaica. As he read it, Viktor congratulated himself on having the foresight to keep his team of illegals in place even though the GRU had been officially disbanded. He read the message in its entirety, then went through it a second time, underscoring every seventh word and the second letter of every second word. The pieces quickly tumbled into place. Then he glanced up to see if Slava's attention was still focused on the road before allowing himself the luxury of a full smile.

In truth, it would have surprised Viktor if Slava had any connection with the RSB, but under the circumstances, the man's affiliations, or lack of them, was not something he could take for granted. Since its establishment, when the RSB was organized to take the place of the disbanded KGB, the new agency had demonstrated a propensity to have only one criteria for its employees— the fact that the man or woman in question had never been a member of the Communist Party. As a GRU officer, Viktor had despised the KGB, but the new RSB was, in its ineptness, even worse. At least, Viktor was forced to admit that the KGB had been efficient. That was more than he could say for the new security bureau.

With his eyes still on his driver, he put the rest of the communiqués back into the pouch, folded the report from Osipov and slipped it into the interior pocket of his tunic. He would destroy it as soon as Parlenko had a chance to assess it.

On Fridays, when Viktor had his weekly meeting with Parlenko, Slava used the opportunity to drive past Mosfilm. The young corporal had expressed a hope of seeing some of the screen personalities on their way to or from the film studio's commissary. He never did, of course, but that did not dissuade him from trying.

Viktor's routine was slightly altered on Fridays. Instead of reporting directly to his section in the Kamzatran where the Moscow-based officers were quartered, he had his 0730 meeting with Parlenko who was the former first deputy of the GRU.

Vitali Parlenko's office was still housed in the great hall of the old Council of Ministers at the Kremlin.

It had been a stroke of good fortune for their agenda when Parlenko was appointed to the position of First Council Director after moving over from his assignment as Chief of Aeroflot. Vitali Parlenko, like Osipov, was an old comrade; the three men had been students at the Frunze together.

Slava inched the car around another collision and turned left on Pirogovska. The early morning precipitation was now turning alternately from sleet to rain and back to sleet again. He plowed the Volga through the slush along the curb and splashed an old man standing at his news kiosk drenching his copies of the two-day-old *Krasnoye Znamya* Siberian newspapers. Slava glanced in his sideview mirror and laughed.

Viktor lit another cigarette as they neared the Kremlin. In the post-dawn half-light, the imposing castellated brick walls of the Kremlin managed to look even more somber than usual. And even though a thin veneer of ice lingered on the square, Slava did not reduce his speed.

They passed Saint Basil's and the now darkened entrance to Lenin's Mausoleum as well as the State Historical Museum. Many of the buildings had not yet been renamed, and for that Viktor was grateful.

Normally the square was active at this time of the morning, but Viktor knew that would not be the case today; the weather was too foul.

The Volga turned left and headed for Trinity Tower. Slava knew that Viktor preferred that he park and wait in the lot east of Alexandrovski Garden so that the general could walk over the bridge to enter the arsenal from the north entrance. By doing so Viktor would be sheltered from the weather and could enter the former Council of Ministers at the west entrance. From there he would cut across the Island Garden.

At this time of year there were no flowers, and the haggard old babushkas that tended the garden in the summer would be gone. Viktor sighed when Slava was able to park within 30 meters of the Tower.

At the foot of the Tower, Viktor encountered his first guard, an aged member of the new militia. The man was either half-asleep or half-drunk. He was slouched back in a small protective alcove that protected him from the weather. A soggy blackened cigarette hung from the corner of his mouth. He waved Viktor through the gate without looking up.

The guard at the top of the stairs was regular army and much younger than his counterpart. Despite Viktor's gray-green uniform and the rank and insignia on the epaulets of his coat, the man insisted on identification. Viktor produced his new military identification card which the guard scrutinized. Behind the guard was a large banner with red letters. It read "THE COMMONWEALTH IS A MONUMENT TO LIBERTY." There were ice icicles hanging from the banner. Viktor looked at it and grunted.

From there Viktor crossed the bridge and entered the arsenal. He walked the length of the first floor, noting with dismay that nearly all of the offices were still dark. Under Zhelannov too many of his former comrades had become sloppy in their work habits.

At the end of the hall, he climbed another flight of stairs to the second floor, went out an auxiliary door and crossed the garden. The sleet now had turned to a wet snow.

When he entered the Council chamber, he was greeted by the predictable little man in the gray business suit and the soft-soled shoes. It was another case where there was a change in name only. This RSB guard was clearly a former KGB agent; the man's prototypical bland face and hollow eyes betrayed him. Once again Zhelannov had been deluded, Viktor thought. As far as Viktor was concerned, the RSB agent's sympathies would not have been more apparent if the organization's old initials had been stenciled across the middle of his anthropoidian forehead.

By the time the man had inquired into the nature of Viktor's business, his dialect betrayed the fact that he was probably Estonian.

"I have a seven-thirty appointment with Director Parlenko," Viktor said.

The man studied Viktor for a moment and then nodded. "Second floor, room two-sixteen."

"Your name please?" Viktor asked.

"Turgennev," the man responded. The slight change in his expression revealed that he was surprised by Viktor's question. Viktor repeated the name to himself and took the elevator to the second floor, emerging at the end of a long crimson-carpeted hall. Parlenko's office was three doors from the elevator. He checked his watch; it was exactly 0730. He knocked once and entered.

Vitali Parlenko's office was larger than most in the Council building. The centerpiece of the room was a large oriental rug and an oversized black walnut conference table. There were three portraits on the wall. The largest was of Zhelannov and was flanked by smaller portraits of Gorbachev and Yeltsin. Viktor regarded them as the deposed and soon-to-be deposed.

Their greeting was cordial but restrained. Parlenko appeared to be nervous, and Viktor wondered if his own face betrayed as much anxiety as that of the aging Director.

"I have it," Viktor announced.

Vitali Parlenko held his index finger up to his lips, walked across the room and turned on the radio. "They will expect it," he whispered. "I turn it on every morning at this time in order to catch the news."

Viktor realized what the Director was doing. The volume of the newscast was too low to make the words distinguishable but loud enough to create an irritating background noise on the monitoring tapes. The Director pointed to a bank of ivory and black vestukas and indicated the location of the monitoring device.

Parlenko lowered his voice to a whisper. "The

phones are channeled into a central taping device. They think I do not know it, but they are clumsy, like children. Ever since they discovered the KGB center in the basement they have been using it."

Viktor lowered his voice. "Is it safe to talk?"

The Director nodded.

Viktor reached into the interior pocket of his tunic and handed his colleague the coded message from the illegal in Montego Bay. As Parlenko began to read it, Viktor flashed the seven and two finger signal as a reminder of the code key. Like Viktor, Vitali Parlenko smiled as he read the message.

"At long last it has begun," Viktor sighed.

Parlenko nodded. "Soon we will begin to receive word of the American expressions of alarm at the thought that we have lost one of our submarines at the bottom of the Cayman Trench."

Viktor folded his hands behind his back and smiled. Osipov was a vital link in their plan, and the helpless Yankee submarine was the perfect diversion, an indication of the Admiral's genius. "Indeed, the Americans will realize they have been duped when they discover what is aboard—perhaps I should say, what is *not* aboard our little diversion."

Datum: 10:4 . . . Caribbean: USS Madison, *2233LT*

"Alter frequency back to ninety-five," Campos snapped. "See if we can still pick up that sporadic clatter."

Sonarman Simons dialed to the designated frequency, increased the volume and pointed to the G-scope. "That's not cavitation, sir. That's either override or downdrift on the trailing antenna. If I feed that kind of data into our hook-up with the mainframe at COM-CON, it'll burp a couple of times and eventually get around to telling us we've got a magma phenomenon. Anytime it can't figure out what we're feeding it, it calls the input magma phenomenon."

Campos scowled and increased the magnification scale on the Number 2 G-scope. He could feel Peel hovering just over his shoulder, waiting for the display to present the new data.

The trio of Peel, Campos and Simons had been joined in the COM-CON by the *Madison*'s senior electronic engineer, Lt. Paul Bellinger and another Sonarman First Class, Gerald Fields. Campos had stationed Fields at the standby console of the ESD.

The enhanced image on Field's unit flickered, blurred and went dark as the playback sequence confirmed and finished reviewing their first observation.

"Captain," Bellinger's gruff voice cut through the commotion, "the bridge advises that we don't have anyone aboard that can speak Russian. Brubaker says McGuire ran it through the personnel computer twice to make certain."

"What about that guy Korskef in the crew mess?" Simons asked.

Fields looked up from his darkened display. "I know him. He ain't Russian, he's Polish. Claims he only knows one Russian phrase—*ceevh ifn-nova*."

"What's that mean?"

"Loosely translated—pig fucker." Bellinger shrugged. "I thought everyone knew that one."

Campos grinned. "At least they'd know we're Americans."

Peel straightened up and turned away from the console. "Well then, those poor bastards on that sub down there better hope someone on that Kiev can understand English, because that's all we got to throw at them." He turned his attention back to Simons. "Picking up anything?"

"Nothing, sir. According to the DS we're trailing the ears right over it. Not a sound. That's the quietest damn eighty-man crew I ever heard."

"Fields, switch back over to the AQ scanner and try another upgrade," Campos ordered.

The sonarman's hand darted to the scanner switch and the AQ began to pulse out a signal. Fields adjusted his headset. "No feedback, sir. It's like the depth of that damn trench down there just sucks up the signal." He furrowed his forehead as he listened.

Peel took Campos by the arm and pulled him into the passageway. He offered his communications officer a cigarette and lit one himself.

Campos knew what to expect; he had seen the *Madison*'s captain in action before. First came the rationalization process—and then the order.

"Damn it, Mel, we can't just stand around up here with our thumbs up our ass while eighty men die down there."

Campos waited for the order.

"Well, what the hell are you waiting for? Get me through to Sannon. When you reach him, pipe it down here to the COM-CON."

Campos picked up the phone to the bridge, and Peel returned to the COM-CON where Bellinger and Fields were verifying the identification of each of the targets on the display grid.

"That's the Kiev there, sir," Simons confirmed, "ten degrees off our stern and coming around. The rest of the targets are all commercial. That big one is a Dutch tanker. Judging from her configuration, she's traveling light."

"Are any of them talking to each other?" Bellinger asked.

"Negative, sir. That's the quietist bunch I've heard in ages."

Peel exhaled a cloud of gray-blue smoke which swirled up into the ventilation system. "Wouldn't you be, too? A damn Russian cruiser on one side and an American on the other. And with all the noise our friend was making, they've probably figured out that there's a sub in the area, too. They're probably not talking to each other because they're too busy listening, hoping to hell someone says something so they can figure out what's going on."

Campos checked his watch. "It's going on sixty-seven minutes since we lost them, Captain."

Peel rubbed his eyes and nodded acknowledgment. "How about it, Mel? Have we been able to get through to Sannon yet?"

Bellinger picked up the phone to the adjacent radio room. "Any luck?" There was a pause. He turned and looked at Peel. "Can't locate him yet."

Charley Peel knew it was a mere technicality, but up until now he hadn't actually disobeyed Sannon's orders. Still, the intent was there, and the more than an hour-long delay was already jeopardizing his ETA at Sullyman.

"We've got to find some way of letting that Kiev know what happened. Why the hell weren't they monitoring their sub, too? They couldn't help but be aware of all the trouble it was having."

"Look, Charley," Campos said, "passive sonar is one thing, but radio contact with either Sannon or that Kiev out there is something else."

"What the hell would you do, Lieutenant? Stand by while eighty men die down there?"

Bellinger looked up from the bank of monitors. "Mel has a point, Captain. How do we know that Kiev isn't already aware of what happened?"

"Simons," Peel barked, "have you logged any kind of signal back and forth between those two?"

"We've got our ears glued to everything," Simons said. "As near as I can determine there has been no contact between the Kiev and the sub. In fact, if that Kiev stays on her present course at her present speed, she'll pass a good twenty nautical miles east of that downed Yankee."

Peel looked at Campos, then Bellinger. "Tell Fields to get ready to drop an RBS on them."

The senior sonarman moved to the auxiliary console. His hands glided over the panel as he repeated the readiness sequence. "ASM repositioned. Shut Down Monitor released. Signal Syncron activated." He turned to Peel. "RBS is ready, sir."

"Okay, sailor," Peel growled, "let's see how good you are at keeping my ass out of a sling, and how long you can keep Fleet Guard guessing. No time signal. No position report. Give me a code six-one, sub down. And under no circumstances do you give a source ID. I don't care if Jesus Christ himself asks for one."

"No source ID?" Bellinger repeated. "They'll hang your ass, Charley, if they find out."

"Look, it's a calculated gamble. It will take them awhile to figure out that it isn't some sub broadcasting it's own code six-one," Peel said. "Maybe by then the captain of that Kiev will pull his head out of his ass and start looking around for his buddies."

"It doesn't make sense," Campos said. "That son-of-a-bitch was making enough noise that they could have heard it back in Moscow. Surely someone will check into it when they realize they've lost the signal."

Peel studied his watch. "Seventy-seven minutes. The cheese is starting to get a little binding."

Bellinger could feel beads of perspiration start to trickle down under his collar. "I'd be damned surprised if that Kiev isn't monitoring us and picks up the first six-one."

"That Kiev is due east of us, Captain, and she sure hasn't slowed down any."

"RBS the six-one," Peel ordered. Then he turned to Campos and Bellinger. "Well, gentleman, we're about to learn something about the Russian value system. We're about to discover just how bad they want to keep us from learning what happened to that sub of theirs."

"And I thought we were all just one big happy family these days," Bellinger said.

"Admiral Sannon is going to have our ass on a platter," Campos shuddered.

The words were barely out of the Com officer's mouth when Fields, on a signal from Peel, pressed the D-1 button and the distress indicator light on the standby panel began blinking.

"If anyone knows a good prayer for a situation like this," Peel muttered, "now is the time to step forward. When Sannon hears what we've done, we're as good as dead."

Datum: 10:5 . . . Los Angeles Airport, 1941PST

Bogner leaned back in his seat, nodded affably to the elderly gentleman seated next to him and looked up at the stewardess. She was a young oriental woman with smiling brown-black eyes, well-defined cheek bones and a coquettish hairdo. Her lipstick matched her imitation ruby earrings. Attractive, Bogner thought—and much, much too young for you, Toby, my boy.

"Do you have any idea how long I've been looking for you?" the stewardess asked.

After his exchange with Joy, Bogner was feeling slightly less than agreeable toward the female gender. "Pretend you still haven't, found me," he growled.

"You're Commander Bogner, aren't you?"

Before Bogner could respond, the woman produced a passenger manifest, double-checked the seating assignments and looked down at him. "See, it says right here, Commander T. C. Bogner, seat 11A. That makes you Commander Bogner. So my next line is 'There is a man looking for you, Commander. He's waiting for you on the boarding ramp.'"

"Tell him to go away," Bogner said.

"It's airport security," the woman explained.

Bogner got up, threaded his way to the front of the DC-10 against the flow of boarding passengers and went out on the ramp where a man was waiting. He was wearing a non-descript blue gaberdine suit designed to blend him into the airport

R. Karl Largent

throngs, and there was a telltale bulge under his left arm.

"Commander Bogner?" He had a smoke-tortured voice and wore the expression of a man who was working too much overtime.

Bogner nodded, and the man produced a small palm-sized leather folder with a tarnished brass badge.

"Bennett, LAX Security. Will you come with me, Commander?"

Bogner stiffened. "What's this all about? I'm scheduled to leave on this flight to Boston."

"I've been instructed to escort you to the nearest security station, Commander." The voice betrayed impatience. "We'll hold your flight as long as necessary, sir."

Bogner followed the man back up the ramp into the boarding area, through a door marked "No Admittance," down an austere flight of concrete stairs and into a smoke-filled room with no windows. Two of LA's finest were slouched over a counter at the rear of the room drinking coffee.

Bennett headed straight for a bank of telephones along one wall, picked up the red one and made his announcement. "We've located him." Then he handed the phone to Bogner.

"T. C.?" the voice questioned. Bogner recognized the voice of Clancy Packer.

"What the hell is this all about, Pack? I'm on my way to Boston."

"Better rephrase that—you *were* on your way to Boston. If you want me to, I'll call your daughter and tell her you've been delayed."

"What the hell are you talking about? It can't be

52

a Colchin assignment; he's spending the weekend at Camp David. I was just watching the television down in the airport lounge, and I saw him and Betty get on a helicopter less than thirty minutes ago."

"Where are you now?"

"In some damn little security room in the American Airlines terminal. Why?"

"Can anyone hear us?" Packer's voice had taken on that old familiar ring of understated bureaucratic urgency.

Bogner's eyes darted around the room. "We're alone."

Even with Bogner's assurance, Clancy Packer managed to drop his voice a notch lower. "Negril is now—this weekend."

Bogner was silent for a minute. "They moved it up?"

"U-huh, change of plans. It's tomorrow. I just came from a briefing. I'll fill you in when you get to Washington."

Bogner pulled a battered black notebook out of his hip pocket and thumbed through the pages until he found Kim's address and telephone number. He gave it to Packer. "You call her. I don't have the heart."

Packer acknowledged and began droning out instructions. "There's a flight from LAX to Dulles leaving thirty minutes from now. You're booked on it. You should arrive here just after two. I'll have someone pick you up at the gate. You'll be brought back here for a briefing, and then we've arranged to hustle you out of Andrews on a flight to Montego Bay. You'll be there by seven tomorrow morning."

"Damn it, Pack, haven't you got anyone else you can send?"

"Colchin wants you. And while you're at it, you better be going over Colchin's schedule while you're down there."

Bogner hung up and looked at Bennett. The security officer was holding his hand out. In it was an airline ticket on the next flight to Dulles.

Base Hour
Six-Seven:
ZERO ZERO . . . 0500Z

Datum: 10:5 . . . Washington: ISA Offices,
0203EST

Clancy Packer took his receiver off the hook and closed his office door. Then he opened a small brown paper bag and took out two containers of coffee.

"Here, figured you might need this." He handed one of the containers to Bogner and dumped two packages of artificial sweetener into the other. He took a sip, grimaced and threw the rest in his waste basket.

"So much for the amenities," Bogner said, grinning.

"Let's get to it. We have to hustle your butt out to Andrews by three-thirty. That doesn't give us much time."

"Look, Clancy, before you start, I've got a question or two of my own. First, I was under the impression this meeting between Colchin and Zhelannov was suppose to take place in Madrid

55

on the nineteenth. Second, I heard the secret service people told Colchin that Negril was out because of the security risks."

"That's exactly what we wanted everyone to hear. Negril is where the meeting has been scheduled all along. The timing is the only thing that has taken everyone by surprise."

"There must be some reason."

"Ours is not to reason, etcetera. Obviously there *is* a reason, or the President wouldn't have complied with Zhelannov's request."

Packer's response was exactly what Bogner expected—no more, no less. Packer was a Colchin man through and through. He never second-guessed the President.

"As I indicated earlier, we were briefed only a short time before I talked to you in Los Angeles. So what you're hearing now is the latest any of us have on the matter."

Bogner leaned back in his chair, took a sip of the coffee and scowled.

Clancy Packer opened his desk drawer, removed a manila envelope, opened it and removed two pieces of paper.

"This situation analysis was distributed to select bureau chiefs in the Secret Service, the FBI, the CIA and the ISA. The briefing boils down to this. The Russians have one of their Kiev class cruisers south and east of Cuba, headed for Jamaica. We have been monitoring her transmissions, but so far there's nothing out of the ordinary, all fairly routine stuff."

Bogner nodded.

"Now get this," Packer continued. "It turns out that at the same time they also have a Yankee nuclear sub in the area. Jeff Stinson, the OIC over at Naval Intelligence, is coming unwrapped because that sub is wandering all over the damn Caribbean, and he can't figure out why."

"Hell, Pack, you and I both know that we could look at a situation display of the Atlantic any time of the day or night and we could locate a whole fleet of Russian vessels."

"Exactly—so that's not our quandary. The problem is, according to Stinson, the Kiev and the sub are acting like they don't know each other is there."

"And you're thinking that might have something to do with the rumors we've been hearing lately?"

"We're not sure, Toby, but we do know that Russia is the only member country of that new Commonwealth of theirs where dissident factions have a sizable access to the residual Soviet arsenal. These same sources are warning us that there is a nucleus of former Party hard-liners who are getting restless."

Bogner's scowl intensified. "Question—do you think this sub is headed to Negril for the meeting?"

"Good question. And unfortunately, one for which we don't have an answer. We've been tracking this particular sub since she came through the gap eight days ago. SAT-COM has been on her all the way. The first two days we didn't see anything out of the ordinary. Day three she set a course that appeared to be taking her to Havana. Yesterday she altered course and began what the boys over at NI term an 'ERRPAT.' That's 'erratic pattern', or their way of saying they don't know what the hell is going on."

"When was Colchin's last contact with Zhelannov?"

"Friday, the twenty-eighth. Exactly one week ago today."

"Then we know Zhelannov isn't on that sub if it came through GIUK eight days ago."

Packer reached across the desk, took a sip of Bogner's coffee and started to load his pipe. "Not necessarily. Who's to say that Zhelannov didn't make his call from that sub?"

"Have we checked that possibility out?"

"We've been trying. The official word is that Zhelannov is resting at his dacha in Minsk, but we can't confirm it. No one has seen him. He canceled two appointments earlier this week with American trade delegations, and he was a no-show at a scheduled parliamentary session with Yeltsin."

"Then you are guessing that Zhelannov might be on the Kiev or the sub, correct?"

"Possible. Or he could be flying in on Aeroflot for all we know. But that doesn't seem likely in view of the clandestine way this whole affair is coming off."

"And NI knows nothing about the meeting?"

Packer shook his head. He was shrouded by a thin cloud of pipe smoke.

"If your buddies over at NI ever discover you had access to all this information and didn't tell them, they're going to be slightly pissed."

Packer leaned forward. "I prefer to look at it this way. If I'm going to piss somebody off, it is far better to piss off our friends over at Naval Intelligence than the President."

"Okay, so at this point just exactly who does know that Colchin and Zhelannov are meeting this weekend in Negril?"

Packer closed his eyes. He was mentally counting. "Let me put it this way. No more than a half dozen of the President's top advisors know what is happening. If you ask me how many know on Zhelannov's side of the aisle, I'll tell you I don't know. But I'd be willing to bet my last kopek on the fact that he's kept it to a minimum."

"One knows, all know," Bogner commented, "especially in the Kremlin. They broke up the Soviet Union, but they didn't break up their damned military."

"Earlier this week, President Colchin received a note from Ambassador Yerrov at the transition embassy in Washington. He informed the President that he would be receiving a call from Zhelannov and stressed that the call required the highest degree of security. From what I hear, Yerrov was so paranoid about the security of that call, he arranged the secured transmission himself. It wasn't until the day before yesterday that the President learned that Yeltsin hasn't been informed of this upcoming meeting."

"Okay, then that tells us one of two things. One, Zhelannov isn't taking his signals from Yeltsin— or he and Yeltsin have their own problems. In either case, it makes sense that the call could have come from the sub. But then the question is, how do we know we can trust Yerrov?"

"That's the rub; we don't. With all the intrigue going on over there, it's a day to day situation. We're operating on the theory though that the call was monitored. We do know that Zhelannov didn't use an interpreter, but Colchin did."

"Who?"

"Me, you suspicious bastard," Packer growled. "Would you like to question my integrity, too?"

Bogner laughed. "Sorry, Pack, but if I hadn't asked, you would have wondered why."

Packer shrugged off the apology and continued. "For some unknown reason, Zhelannov wanted the date of the summit moved up to this weekend. Not only that, he also requested that the talks be confined. In other words he wanted even fewer people there than the last time the two of them got together in Paris. Bottom line—Colchin's cabinet doesn't know. We not only haven't informed the press, the President's press secretary doesn't even know. And we damn sure haven't told those clowns in congress. Even the Commander of the *Black River* where the President is spending the night won't know who his VIP guest is until Colchin gets there. He simply knows he's been ordered to Negril and told to take up position." Packer checked his watch. "It's two-thirty in Negril now. Assuming no problems, the *Black River* is probably already anchored at the mouth of the harbor."

"Any other support?"

"We're holding the *Madison* in backup at Sullyman."

Bogner got out of his chair, went to the window and stared out at the cold Washington darkness. "I don't like it, Clancy. I've been to Negril too many times. There's no way we can make that harbor secure."

"The very fact that you're familiar with Negril is precisely why Colchin wants you there."

"Hell, I'm familiar with Boston and Bakersfield, too. Either one of them would have been a hell of a lot easier to secure."

Packer smiled. "Grousing doesn't become you, Toby. During the briefing I was specifically instructed to see that you were there. Colchin wants somebody there he knows."

Bogner spun around. "Hey, wait a minute, Clancy. That sounded like a cover-your-ass statement. Is there something you haven't told me?"

When Packer cleared his throat, Bogner knew it was a stall tactic. "I may have overlooked one or two minor details."

"Like what minor details?"

"Both Colchin and Zhelannov are traveling with small entourages. Colchin is taking Hurley and Spitz. Hurley will serve as interpreter, and Spitz is handling everything else."

"When do I hear the words 'secret service?'"

Clancy stalled.

Bogner frowned. "Don't tell me you're saying what I think you're saying."

"No secret service," Packer confirmed.

"Is Colchin out of his goddamn mind?"

"I hardly think so. We've taken every possible precaution. In addition to the *Black River* and the *Madison* we will have a four unit Coast Guard security patrol in the harbor."

Bogner shook his head. "Not enough—too risky."

"Just getting up in the morning is risky." Clancy sighed and leaned back in his chair. "Look, Toby, I don't make the rules; I abide by them. I am following orders—that's all."

"How about my backup?"

"Morganthaller left Kingston earlier this evening. He'll have everything arranged by the time you get there. He will leave instructions at the check-in desk at Le Chamanade on how to contact him. Our new man, Koorsen, will be there, too."

"Great! Morganthaller is obsolete, and you back him up with a green ass."

Packer shook his head. "No wonder Joy divorced you. Did anyone ever tell you that you can be extremely difficult at times?"

"Leave Joy out of this, Clancy. You know damn well Morganthaller can't cut it anymore. He's been on active retirement for the last five years."

"Under most circumstances Simon Morganthaller is more than adequate for our needs in Jamaica. Besides, you'll like Koorsen."

"Who gives a damn whether I like Koorsen or not. Can he back me up?"

"I put a copy of Koorsen's fitness report in your briefing. Look it over. I think you'll like what you see."

"I don't suppose any of this has been cleared with the Jamaican authorities?"

"That is purely a state department matter. Off the record, I doubt it. And I think you should probably assume that there will be a few ruffled diplomatic feathers before it's over, but that's not your concern."

Bogner stopped pacing; he walked back to the desk and glared at Packer. "By now you know I think this whole damn thing sounds like it was dreamed up in a fantasy factory."

Packer's owlish face worked itself into a smile. "That's why you're good at what you do, T. C.

You anticipate the worst, and you prepare for it. Sometimes I think you're disappointed if the worst doesn't happen." He stood up, glanced at his watch and extended his hand across the desk. "You better get going."

As Bogner picked up his jacket he looked at the bulky file. "Fitness report, huh? Out of curiosity, what makes you think Koorsen is a good man?"

"Same attributes as you—overly cautious, suspicious, skeptical and cynical."

Datum: 10:5 . . . Washington: ISA Offices, 0259EST

Bogner had been gone less than five minutes when the phone rang in Packer's outer office. The ISA night guard intercepted the call, and Clancy could hear the man explaining that the office accepted only emergency calls between 5 P.M. and 8 A.M. As Clancy headed for the door, the man put his hand over the mouthpiece.

"It's for you, Clancy. She doesn't know you're here. I told her you'd be in the office first thing tomorrow morning, but now she's insisting I give her your home phone number."

"Who is it?"

"She says her name used to be Joy Bogner."

Clancy went back in his office, closed the door, cleared his throat and picked up the receiver. "This is quite a surprise, Joy."

"It's been awhile, hasn't it?"

To Clancy she sounded the same as she had some 20 years earlier when he first met his new agent's wife in a Los Angeles restaurant.

He remembered that at the time he thought she was the most beautiful pregnant woman he had ever seen.

"Why is it I get the feeling this isn't a social call?"

"I know it's late, Clancy, and I'd love to reminisce but I'm working on something. We update the newscast at sign-off, and I'm chasing a story. I've already checked with the wire services and the other three networks, and they haven't got anything on it. So I played a hunch and called you.

"Our affiliate in Mexico City is reporting that an unidentified six-one code is being received in Havana and Key West. Years ago Toby told me that was the international signal when a sub went down. The problem is I can't get any kind of verification from anyone. Do you know anything about it?"

Clancy Packer knew there was only one answer. "Haven't heard a thing, Joy." And he knew that if there was a sub down, there were a lot of things that had to be verified before he started talking to the press.

He could tell she was disappointed. He also detected something in her voice that made him think she didn't believe him. They exchanged a few brief pleasantries and hung up.

Within a matter of seconds he had dialed the access number at NI and punched in his ident code. A strained voice answered, "NI—Holmgren."

"This is Clancy Packer over at ISA. I'm hearing a rumor that you're picking up a code six-one somewhere down off the coast of Cuba?"

"Damn, word travels fast, doesn't it? It's no rumor, Clancy. We started picking one up a couple of hours ago. About the only thing we've been able to determine so far is that it isn't one of ours, and we're not even ready to verify that yet. We're still in the process of going through channels to see who it belongs to."

Clancy was muttering to himself as he hit the disconnect button. Without hanging up the receiver, he dialed a second number. A sleepy, familiar feminine voice answered.

"Sara," he said without explaining, "I won't be home tonight." He hung up and loosened his tie.

Base Hour
Six-Two:
ZERO ZERO . . . 1000z

Datum: 10:5 . . . The Swath Yacht Cuboc, *0713NLT*

Ilya Vasilevich inched his way through the intricate grid of stainless steel tubing suspended from the bottom of the *Cuboc*'s hull. Even in the design stage he had complained that it would be difficult for a man only half his size to accomplish the premission equipment checks, and now, with the way the Cubans had finally configured the rigging, it was nearly impossible. He was forced to perform all of his maintenance and conduct his inspection while crawling on his stomach.

A cautious man, he was made even more so by the oft repeated admonitions he had received at the Havana shipyards. "It will be necessary to scrutinize all external rigging and fixtures before conducting a launch and retrieval attempt," one man had told him. Another had cautioned, "The superstructure will vibrate in the open sea and the fittings can be easily damaged." Finally, the project supervisor had warned, "It is imperative that you double-check every device."

The Cubans were referring of course to the Swath's extensive hull modifications, changes made to enable Ilya to transport and launch and retrieve the miniature Mala submarine from the hull of the *Cuboc*.

Actually, Ilya believed that the preparations for their Negril mission had been going quite smoothly until the former resident GRU illegal in Havana had passed along the unsettling news that "72" had been moved ahead two full weeks. Only the intervention of Admiral Osipov had been able to pressure the shipyard supervisor into an around-the-clock effort to complete the Swath-Mala modifications in time for Ilya's Tuesday morning departure.

At the moment however, Ilya was focusing his attention on the cluster of apparatus forward of the conn tower. He checked the air-charging connection, the retractable capstand, the securing davits and was in the process of tightening the fittings on the combination lift and tow motor.

He pulled down the cover, folded the silicone lip over the metal edge of the enclosure, turned up the air pressure, spit on his finger, ran it along the edge and waited for the telltale air bubbles. Unable to detect any, he again tightened the four bolts to the enclosure plate.

Ilya could still hear the coarse voice of the Havana supervisor. "The advance of your departure date leaves us with insufficient time. We have no alternative other than to omit several of the features we had planned to install."

When Ilya questioned what was not being installed, the man made references to a standby guidance system and a backup or mechanical retrieval system support unit. "Without them," the man stressed, "you are totally dependent on the primary systems. In the event of a systems failure of either of these units, it will be necessary to work out an alternate recovery plan."

Ilya had devoted a great deal of time to that very aspect of their operation during the journey from Havana to Negril, and now the solution was carefully programed into the Mala's computers. But there still remained one problem; from his crowded second seat, Zhukov would be unable to operate the computer, rendering the solution useless if anything happened to Ilya at the primary controls seat. The Mala was barely large enough to accommodate two men, and it would have to carry three men to safety. Ilya sighed even though a failure in the primary lock-on was unlikely, but the thought of it disturbed him. Somehow he would have to make it work.

From the conn tower he worked his way toward the bow, paying special attention to the condition of the salvage air connection, port of the centerline. It looked fragile. He made a mental note to himself to sketch its location on the diagram above Zhukov's control panel. There was always the chance, he reminded himself, that he would be forced to use it if the three men had to stay aboard the Mala for any length of time.

He rolled back over on his stomach and crawled to the sonar dome on the bow to complete his inspection. He traced his finger around the bullet-shaped protrusion to check the integrity of the gaskets and tightened the four screws that secured the access plate.

Ilya glanced at his watch. The exterior inspection was complete. It had taken him exactly 67 minutes.

Like all former Russian Spetsnaz commandants in the midget submarine brigade, Ilya had received most of his training in the Yugoslavian-built Mala. Ilya, however, had been more fortunate than most of his comrades; he had captained both the AZ and AW configurations. This was to his advantage, since the AW was more versatile and slightly smaller than its predecessor.

The unit attached to the twin hulls of the Swath was an AW-M, an upgraded version of the former. The enhancement was most evident in the vessel's newly installed electronic surveillance and recovery equipment as well as the bank of computers designed to simplify command control procedures. That improved recovery capability factor, more than anything else, was the reason Osipov had chosen the Mala AW-M for Zhukov's mission.

Still, Ilya was concerned; the Cubans had a long standing reputation for shoddy workmanship. This awareness had been the motivation for his three pre-launch inspections. For the moment, he was satisfied. All that was left now was to go over the interior.

He opened the conn hatch, descended the ladder and eased his way into the forward control area. In both size and configuration, the AW-M was essentially unchanged. Only the aft controls had been significantly altered. The engineers in Havana had installed all of the second seat controls on a temporary panel above the number two pilot seat so that both Zhukov and Vsevolod could get into the tiny compartment. It would be uncomfortable, but it would accommodate them for their return to the Swath.

Ilya closed his eyes and began pointing to the cluttered clusters of instrumentation, naming them and calling out the function of each display and switch: valve vent control #1, valve vent control #2, full close device *on* to the right, full close device *off* to the left. Above the closing device were buoyancy activators one and two, both fore and aft. Upper right was another cluster of switches and their positions—ignition *on* in the up position, *off* in the down position. Next to the fore and aft trim indicators were the lubrication valves and the lubrication cooling controls.

Ilya wormed his way into the second seat, pulled Zhukov's auxiliary panel into place, activated it and sequenced the operations data. Then he flipped a small toggle switch and laughed; the Cubans had used a standard wall panel light switch to activate the second seat computers. From Zhukov's seat, he checked access to all manual switches. If anything happened to him, Zhukov, if he kept his wits about him, could guide them back to the Swath. For Ilya, *if* was the operative word.

All indicator lights worked, and Ilya went through the entire control sequence from the second seat. If there was trouble, their fate would be in the hands of Zhukov; Vsevolod would be of little help.

From the second seat, he lay down on the interior grid on his back and double-checked the position of all mechanical valves on the flood control ports, the vent riser and each of the 18 battery units adjacent to the main diesel power plant. The armament compliment had been removed and an additional bank of six batteries had been installed. After the ignition control check, he shimmied back into the personnel unit, took out his check list, went over it and put it back in his pocket. He was satisfied for the time being— or at least until a new concern cropped up.

Ilya worked his way back up the ladder, checking as he worked his way through the vessel. He resealed the access hatch from the outside and hauled himself back up on the gridwork platform between the twin hulls of the *Cuboc*. He came up through the floor in the master stateroom, bolted the hull hatch from the inside, sealed the hidden latch and repositioned the carpeting. As an extra precaution, he bent over, placed his ear against the floor and listened to the telltale sound of the engaging rubber seal between the hull plate and the platform. When he heard the satisfying *hssss* sound, he breathed a sigh of relief. Then he straightened up, and Olga applauded him.

"Now, my worry-wart husband, now that you have checked and double-checked your toys for the hundredth time, can we finally go topside and capture some of this glorious Caribbean sun?"

"Only a fool would trust the workmanship of the Cubans," Ilya grumbled.

"You are not even home yet," Olga said, "and already you are beginning to sound like a true Bolshevik again."

Ilya's face sobered. "You go," he said. "I do not want the American Coast Guard to be certain of how many people we have on board."

Ilya was just as mindful that the second stage of their mission would be as critical as the first. When Zhukov, Vsevolod and he returned to the *Cuboc* after completing their mission and the Mala had been jettisoned, there would be one more person on board than there had been previously. The Americans must never be able to verify that.

"Go ahead," he said. "Enjoy the sun. Take the boy with you. I have work to do."

Olga smiled, and Ilya watched while his wife of 27 years peeled out of her clothing and donned the brief string bikini she had purchased in Havana. The young Americans will appreciate the view, he thought to himself.

When she disappeared into the passageway outside of the stateroom, he heard her call their son, Thomas. The two were laughing as they went up on deck.

Ilya Vasilevich was, in fact, his real name—Commandant Ilya Pytor Vasilevich—but not many people remembered that. For the past several years, his neighbors in Oceanside, California had known him as Gorgi Mantovan, a displaced Russian Jew that the Lockheed Electric Boat Division had imported from Israel because of his acknowledged expertise in shipboard avionics.

Ilya had worked for Lockheed for seven years, living the so-called good life and waiting for an assignment. Only when the Union crumbled and dissolved into a montage of floundering republics had he begun to think about going home, even though he had never had the opportunity to serve his country.

Red Tide

Throughout, Ilya Vasilevich never forgot that first and foremost he was a Russian, a Party member, a former commander in the Spetsnaz and a passive illegal for the GRU.

Then on Christmas night of 1991, he had watched the television, in tears as the Soviet flag came down and Gorbechev's resignation signaled the end of the Union. There was no longer any reason to hope for a call—but a year and a half later, the call had come.

Four weeks to the day after receiving that call, Ilya was in a Galveston shipyard, purchasing a 30 meter twin-hulled Swath and preparing to sail the coastal waterways until he rounded the Keys and headed for Cuba.

In Havana, the Swath, now rechristened the *Cuboc*, after his grandfather, was retro-fitted to accommodate the tiny Mala submarine and the latest electronic technology.

Everything had gone smoothly, unfolding with the precision of a Tchaikovsky concerto, until he had received Osipov's unexpected message; the date of the Negril summit had been moved forward.

Suddenly there was cause for concern. There had been no shakedown of the Mala, the carriage between the *Cuboc* and the submarine was untested, and there had been no opportunity to test the seaworthiness of the hybrid combination.

Despite the hurried journey from Havana to Jamaica, they were now anchored inside Negril harbor, and the U.S. Coast Guard felt compelled to assure them several times a day that there was no reason for concern even though the American cruiser *Black River* was temporarily blocking the harbor.

"Sorry for the inconvenience, Skipper," one of the American officers had shouted from the deck of his cutter.

Ilya was amused; there was so much the naive Americans did not know. He had stood on deck, shouting greetings in a rusty Danish dialect, and the Americans didn't even know the difference. They were simply grateful that the crew of the *Cuboc* was not giving them a hard time like the Dutch couple on the Van Dam ketch or the Austrian couple on the ancient Durbeck trawler. That was another thing that Ilya had learned while he lived in California—smile, always smile. He constantly reminded Olga with the words, "American are never suspicious of foreigners who smile, only the ones who frown."

He stood for awhile, listening to his wife and son situate themselves on deck, then went forward to the master stateroom and retrieved his journal from a hollowed-out space he had discovered in a stanchon close to the bulkhead. He sat down on the bunk, opened the journal and reviewed his notes. He had promised Olga that he would keep a diary so that they would have a record of their small role in the ascendency of a great Russian leader to the position of Supreme Soviet and the reestablishment of the mighty Soviet Union. Like Olga, he knew none of the names of the individuals involved; for now, it was sufficient to know only that he would be part of this glorious event in Russian history.

Ilya began his entry with a notation of the time:

Red Tide

5 October: 0755 L
*All is ready. I have reviewed the procedures
again. I am confident there will be no con-
fusions. Commonwealth President Zhelannov
will board the American yacht at 2010 L. It
will be 0500 in Moscow. The American President is scheduled to board the yacht some ten
minutes earlier and welcome Zhelannov. His entourage will include Marshal Zhukov, who will
serve as council and first assistant, and Josef
Tcheka for an interpreter.*
*I have been instructed to position the Mala some
30 meters from the stern of the American yacht
and maintain observation depth. At Zhukov's
request, Vsevolod, if asked, will board the American yacht to assist in whatever way necessary
and then the three of us will return to the Cuboc.
After we reboard, the Mala will be rigged for jettison upon leaving the harbor. It will be towed
over the area known as The Jehovah Hole and
released.*

Ilya closed the journal when he heard Vsevolod
coming down from the bridge. Like Olga, Vsevolod knew only that he had finally been assigned
to a GRU mission; he did not know the nature or
importance of his assignment.

Younger than Ilya, and untrained to do any but
the most menial of chores, he was sunburned on
the face and upper torso. "Here, comrade," he
said, handing Ilya a white, blue and red aluminum
can. "It is Pepsi Cola, genuine American Pepsi. See
the label? It was made in Mi-am-i. We could not
obtain it in Havana."

Ilya took a long drink and smiled. "Reminds me
of California," he said.

Vsevolod, who had never been any further west than Cuba, slumped back against the bulkhead grinning. "Caly-forn-e-a," he repeated. "I like that name."

Datum: 10:5 . . . Washington: ISA Offices, 0731EST

Clancy Packer had just washed his face, shaved, donned a fresh shirt and was adjusting his tie when Miller entered his office. He was carrying a yellow dispatch envelope with a red stripe around the hasp end.

"According to the phone log you contacted NI last night. I checked with Rhymer who said you were inquiring about a random sixty-one being reported in the Caymans. This is probably a response; an NI courier just brought it over."

Packer ripped open the envelope and read the contents of the communique under his breath.

To: Packer—ISA-DC-7565
From: Stinson NI-DC-4134
Subject: Random 61: Confirmed:
Cayman Trench
Subject vessel believed to be Soviet Yankee III. Designation: ROZHKO. Ident unconfirmed. Repeat: Unconfirmed USS MADISON on site—passive under orders.
System AGSI, authorized, Stinson,
NI-DC-4134.

Packer read it a second time, then handed it to Miller. "Damnit, Robert," he muttered, "I don't like the way this is coming down. It's getting stickier by the hour."

Miller scowled. "How so, Chief?"

"Get somebody on this. Something's up. I don't like the way this smells. As near as we can tell, the Russians have lost a nuclear submarine, and twelve hours later they still haven't acknowledged it. As near as we can tell, they aren't doing anything about it. If you ask me I think they are trying to divert our attention from something. They've already managed to delay the *Madison*."

"Delay the *Madison* from what, Clancy?"

Packer looked up at his assistant and then at his watch. "Better sit down, Robert. Under the circumstances I think you had better be brought up to speed." He closed the door and began the briefing. "By nine o'clock this place is going to be crawling with field personnel. I'm going to need your help."

Base Hour
Six-Zero:
ZERO ZERO . . . 1200Z

Datum: 10:5 . . . Moscow, 1814MLT

The weather had not improved. From his second floor window, Viktor stared out across a bleak expanse of brick courtyard and continued to ignore the reams of reports and papers piled high on his desk. A relentless barrage of sleet pelted against his window, and even the normally busy chabost was deserted.

Viktor had returned to his office after his meeting with Parlenko and maintained a high visibility throughout the course of the day. By the middle of the afternoon he had tried to call Ruta twice, once at her apartment at the Zaratsna and the second time at her office in the Institute. She did not answer on either occasion.

At 4:30 he placed a call to General Meshcheryakov at what had formerly been known as the GRU Second Directorate but was now known as Administrative Support Agency. He was informed that Meshcheryakov had gone for the day, and he ended up speaking to the General's assistant, Lt. Drachev.

"This is Lieutenant-General Denisov. I am seeking information on a Yugoslav by the name of Nikolai Kerensky."

Drachev sounded almost hesitant to ask the inevitable question. "Does or did he have a party affiliation, General?"

"*Da*, I am told he was at one time a member of the Yugoslav Communist Party."

"Do you have his number, General?"

"I do not have it," Viktor said, slightly agitated. He knew Mescheryakov's section had been instructed not to pass on File 57 information without the party number. "I am calling because I have reason to believe that this man Kerensky is involved in subversive activities that may be detrimental to the welfare of the commonwealth. It is important. Is there no way of checking without the number?"

"*Nyet*, General. We are under strict orders to—" Viktor cut the young officer off. "I will obtain the information from General Mescheryakov. Have him call me."

"Yes, General," the young man said. Throughout he had been the paragon of military protocol.

Viktor slammed the receiver down just as a Chaika limousine came through the gate into the courtyard. The driver pulled into the visitor's parking lot, and a tall man dressed in a dark overcoat with his hat pulled down to protect him from the weather stepped out.

It was Moshe, and Viktor's pulse quickened.

Moshe would doubtless have news of the *Rozhko*.

Viktor turned in his chair to face the door and wait for the telltale protesting sounds of the ancient mechanical lift. When the elevator doors opened, he heard Moshe's footsteps coming up the hall. By the time the man had opened the door and entered the room, Viktor felt a chill of anticipation.

Hawk-faced, thin and bent with the years, Moshe looked even more unhealthy than usual. A nervous smile played on the corner of his crooked mouth. "Have you heard, General?"

Viktor shook his head.

"Six-fifteen is down. It has been confirmed."

Viktor felt elation and a tremor of excitement. He refrained from talking until he had taken a deep breath and regained his composure.

"All went as planned?"

"Even better than we planned, General. The Americans are the ones who reported it."

Viktor rocked back in his chair and threw up his hands. "Wonderful. Then it is even better than we hoped for."

Moshe reached in his pocket and extracted a wrinkled piece of paper. "We just received this communiqué from our resident illegal in Havana, General. Admiral Osipov relayed it less than an hour ago." He handed it to Viktor.

SHORTLY AFTER MIDNIGHT, A RANDOM INTERNATIONAL 61 (SUB DOWN) SIGNAL WAS BROADCAST. AMERICAN SOURCES (NAVY & COAST GUARD) ATTEMPTING TO VERIFY. STORY ORIGINATED IN A LOS ANGELES (CALIFORNIA-USA) NEWSCAST.

"Now the American television networks are carrying the story. They are of course denying that it is one of theirs."

"Are they attempting to contact us through channels?"

Moshe smiled. "But of course, General."

"Have we responded yet?"

"*Nyet.* As planned, we will not respond until five tomorrow morning. Even then we will say that all of our units have reported. The Americans will ask for verification, and finally we will admit that it is a test unit."

"But by then it will be too late," Viktor acknowledged. "Zhelannov is traveling under a cloak of secrecy, and he will already be aboard the American yacht and will have no knowledge of the tragedy until the Americans inquire."

Viktor laughed again, but this time the laugh was robust and unguarded. He lit a cigarette, revolved in his chair and looked out the window at the encroaching darkness.

"Excellent, Comrade, excellent. But what about our ships? What are they saying?"

"Admiral Osipov assures me that Commandant Ammirof will follow orders to the letter."

"He is an excellent Commandant," Viktor agreed.

"*Da.* Of course he has in no way responded to the frantic babbling of the American cruiser that reported the six-one."

"Then you believe the Americans are sufficiently distracted?"

Moshe put his hands behind his back and smiled. "They are distracted all right," he said. "We have created the perfect diversion. With only one American cruiser on the scene in Negril and a handful of small American Coast Guard units to assist it, Zhukov's escape should be guaranteed."

Viktor Denisov held up his hand. He was still looking out the window with his back to Moshe. "We both are confident that between our primary plan and the alternatives we have a fail safe plan, Comrade. But have you really thought about what would happen if the crew of the Mala was not recovered?"

Moshe Aprihnen was silent for a moment. He knew that Viktor Denisov was not the kind to ask rhetorical questions. "I am afraid I do not understand."

"Come, come, it is a very simple question, Comrade. What would happen if Zhukov did not survive this mission? Ask yourself, would it alter the outcome of our endeavor?"

Moshe studied his long-time compatriot. "If Marshal Zhukov successfully completes his mission but is unable to survive . . . ?"

"Precisely. Would he not still have the undying gratitude of certain members of the Party? Correct me if I am wrong, my friend, but it would appear that the only difference is that he would not be around to accept the warm accolades of his comrades."

When Viktor turned around, Moshe was still reflecting on what he had said.

"Have you ever heard the expression, 'Overt is often the most covert?' " Viktor asked. "It is a principle one should never forget, Comrade. I offer the *Rozhko* as an example. It is right under the American noses, and only when it is too late will they realize what we have done."

"Are the components of such an alternative plan in place?" Moshe asked.

Viktor walked back to his desk, opened the center drawer and took out a fresh pack of American cigarettes. He lit one and allowed a thin cloud of smoke to swirl around his bulbous face.

"Most assuredly, Comrade Aprihnen, the components are in place. It is merely a matter of setting the plan in motion. While our American friends and Russian bureaucrats are preoccupied with the downed *Rozhko*, we will proceed with our plan—with one slight revision, of course. Marshal Zhukov will unwittingly be making the supreme sacrifice, which will make the new Supreme Soviet all the more grateful to him."

"Who else knows about this plan?" Moshe asked.

"Only you and I, Comrade."

"Do you think we should consult with the others first?" Moshe asked.

"*Nyet*," Viktor thundered. "It is our plan; we do what we must do to assure success."

Aprihnen shivered involuntarily, and Denisov smiled.

Datum: 10:5 . . . Washington: ISA Offices, 0923EST

Clancy Packer paced back and forth until the four section heads took their seats. Robert Miller stood by the door. Gordon Taggert of the Chicago Bureau, Mike Henline from Atlanta, Peter Oskiwicz of the Los Angeles branch and Mildred Ploughman from the Denver Bureau had all been flown into Washington during the night. Collectively their eyes were red from a lack of sleep.

Packer leaned forward with his hands, palms down, on the conference table and cleared his throat. "All right. It doesn't take a mental marvel to figure out that something's up. The last time I called you in like this was during the August coup when they attempted to overthrow Gorbechev but that was after the fact. This time we're going to do it a little differently; we're going to try to avert a disaster instead of sitting around wringing our hands after it's too late. In case you're wondering, Miller has already advised your offices that you will be here for the duration, which could run at least the next three or four days."

"I've been hearing rumors," Taggert admitted. "Is it true?"

"I'll get to that in a minute, Gordon, but before I answer any questions, I want each of you to hear what Bob Miller has to say."

Packer's assistant walked to the front of the room and opened a manila file folder. "We have several issues to cover, so I'll get right to it. First, what you've been hearing since you got here is true. President Colchin is meeting with Commonwealth President Zhelannov later today in Negril, Jamaica. They are planning a series of meetings aboard the American yacht, *Codicile*, in Negril Harbor. The President has chosen to take a minimum entourage consisting of three people including himself. President Zhelannov is doing the same."

"What about the secret service?" Henline asked.

"None," Miller confirmed. "The closest thing we've got to security for this meeting is a military contingent; a cruiser, the *Black River*, is stationed at the entrance to the Negril harbor as well as some Coast Guard runabouts. A backup naval unit, the *Madison*, has been delayed. But more about that later.

"If everything goes according to schedule a Sea King will settle on the pad of the *Black River* at precisely sixteen-hundred Negril time. The President will be aboard the chopper along with Bob Hurley and Lattimere Spitz. The President will rest for an hour, attend a last minute briefing and then be transferred to the yacht *Codicile* at nineteen-fifty Negril time. President Zhelannov and his party are scheduled to board ten minutes later."

"*Codicile*?" Mildred Ploughman repeated.

"*Codicile*," Miller confirmed. He retrieved another document from his stack of papers. "It belongs to the President's former law partner, Amos Sparrow. For the record, it is a Baglietto design, shallow-drafted, water-jet propulsion.

"As you're probably already aware, our man on the scene during all of this is Toby Bogner. One of the reasons Bogner was selected for this mission is that he spent some time aboard the craft with the President and Mr. Sparrow last year in the Dutch Leewards. In anticipation of this meeting, President Colchin requested that the *Codicile* be moored in Negril Harbor over a month ago. By now the locals have gotten used to it. Also for the record, the *Codicile* has a crew of four, the Captain is a Texan by the name of Roger Network, an old friend of both Sparrow and the President. They met him a number of years ago when they chartered his fishing boat.

"Again for the record, we are being told that subsequent sessions aboard the *Codicile* will be scheduled as President Colchin and President Zhelannov see fit. In any case, they are expected to conclude their meetings by twelve-hundred hours, Negril time, on Sunday."

Clancy Packer looked around the room. "If there are any questions, now is the time to be asking them." There were none, and he nodded to Miller to continue.

"Second item. I'm sure each of you have been listening to the news. The American cruiser *Madison* lost surveillance contact with a nuclear-powered submarine, believed to be Soviet. Indications are that the sub went down somewhere in the Cayman Trench. The *Madison* was on its way to Negril as backup for the *Black River*. Through diplomatic channels we have been attempting to get verification from the Russians. So far, they have not responded. The OIC over at Naval Intelligence thinks they can't respond because some of their units are running ears down." He looked at Packer. The bureau chief nodded, and Miller continued, "Any questions?"

"Do you think there is any connection between the downed sub and the Negril summit?" Oskiwicz asked.

"At this time, we don't know. At first there was some speculation that President Zhelannov might be aboard, but judging from the way the Russians have responded, it seems reasonable to conclude that isn't the case. On the other hand, Oscar Jaffe over at the CIA indicates that Zhelannov has not been seen for eight days. Bottom line—we don't know where he is and we probably won't know until he shows up for the meeting on the *Codicile*." Miller turned to Packer. "Do you have anything you want to add, Clancy?"

Packer stood up again. "By now you're asking yourselves why the hell we brought you in for this. There have been other summits and it's been business as usual, but there are a couple of aspects about this one that are alarming. I don't like the way it's piling up. First, we've got the unconfirmed downed sub over the Trench. Of course this could be nothing more than an unfortunate coincidence, or it could be one of their typical goddamn diversionary tactics. Temper this with the fact that I don't trust the Russians nearly as much as President Colchin does. If it is a diversionary tactic, the question has to be why. Are they planning something? Is this whole damn thing a setup? By delaying their confirmation they've already succeeded in diverting the *Madison* from its primary mission of backup for the *Black River*.

"Secondly, why did Zhelannov insist on the limited entourages? I don't like it when the President isn't backed up by his normal cadre of support personnel. As I told Miller this morning, as far as I'm concerned, this whole thing is beginning to smell funny."

Henline held up his hand. "Miller indicated Bogner was down there. Is he part of the President's entourage?"

"No, Colchin wanted him there, but not as part of the official retinue. The President does not want to jeopardize the evolving air of mutual trust with Zhelannov. Colchin figures too many people already know Bogner."

Gordon Taggert shifted in his chair. "So what do we do now, Clancy?"

"We wait. If Toby needs backup, we provide it. If push comes to shove, I'm going to need all the help I can get—and that's why I sent for the four of you."

Miller turned off the lights and turned on the projector with the map displays. "In the meantime, let's make certain everyone is familiar with the configuration of Negril harbor."

Datum: 10:5 . . . Negril Beach: Le Chamanade, 0937NLT

Bogner walked through the flowered courtyard of Le Chamanade into the open lobby. The attractive young Jamaican woman behind the desk was trying to console a tourist whose husband had not come back to their hotel room the previous night.

He slipped around behind the desk, poured himself a cup of coffee and whispered a one word question in the girl's ear, "Bouderau?"

The girl turned and smiled while her eyes scanned the Le Chamanade dining room. "I have not seen him yet this morning, Commander," she said in her carefully cultured English.

The open lobby of the hotel looked out over a palm-sheltered, cabana-cluttered veranda which, from its elevation, overlooked the full expanse of Negril harbor. It was still too early for most of the guests to be out, and the only thing that detracted from the view of the tranquil Caribbean seascape was a handful of fishing boats and the still slumbering pleasure craft moored inside the reef.

The fishing boats were scattered across the

horizon, and the latter were clustered around the Negril wharf and lee of the reef near the Jehovah Hole.

Where the reef separated at the entrance to the harbor, the American cruiser *Black River* was anchored.

Colchin, an ex-Navy man, made no bones about it, the *Black River*, a ship he had once captained, was his favorite. It had been hurriedly modified so that the President's Sikorsky Sea King could land on it.

In addition to the *Black River*, Bogner could count at least four Coast Guard units stationed at various locations around the harbor.

Just below the flagstone veranda there was a narrow strip of beach populated by palm trees and an occasional deck chair. Bogner took his coffee down to one of the cabanas, sat down and began to mentally sift through his check list. Even while Packer was briefing him he had been aware that the harbor site was a security man's nightmare. Now he had to deal with it.

While Bogner sipped his coffee, he combed the harbor a second time. He had pinpointed the location of the *Codicile*, moored some 500 yards due east of the wharf. Knowing Network as he did, he knew that the *Codicile's* captain had thoroughly studied the harbor and decided that its present position was the safest location he could find for Sparrow's gleaming white jewel.

If Clancy was correct, Bogner reasoned that Network would be unaware of what was happening. In all probability, Network had simply been told to anticipate the arrival of Amos Sparrow and his entourage.

Still, as far as Bogner was concerned, the acid test of secrecy was whether or not Bouderau knew. If the Frenchman knew, all bets were off.

Bouderau owned Le Chamanade, but his real expertise was information and drugs. Information was sold to the highest bidder. He sold the drugs to anyone with money to buy.

Bogner was still consorting with his phantoms from the past when a heavy hand clamped down on his shoulder.

"So, *mon ami*, you finally arrived."

Bogner spun around. "Damn it, Lucian, you scared the hell out of me."

Bouderau's well-defined moustached and tanned face assumed a hurt expression. "We are edgy, are we not? Such a hostile greeting for such an old friend?" Bouderau's cognac-oiled voice was as smooth as ever. "The mere fact that I am still able to stalk the famous T. C. Bogner without him hearing me pleases me. I have not lost my touch, heh, *mon ami*?"

"You haven't lost your touch," Bogner assured him. The two men embraced, and Bouderau invited his long-time friend to sit down again.

"And how is the lovely Joy?" Bouderau inquired.

"Damn it, Lucian, you ask me that every time we see each other, and every time I remind you that Joy and I split ten years ago."

"I am first and foremost a Frenchman, *mon ami*. I live for love. I am always hoping you two will get back together again. Is that not a possibility?"

"Highly improbable, Lucian." Bogner didn't elaborate. "So what's new with you?"

"Same old thing. The tourists spend too little

money, and I am forced to live by my cunning."

"And just how cunning are you these days?"

"I have not lost my touch. I still pick up morsels here and there. For example, your friend Morganthaller reserved a room for you yesterday, yet you did not sleep in it last night. That means either you arrived this morning or spent the night elsewhere with Bouderau knows not who. Then when you checked in, you went to your room and made a phone call to West Mathews Properties, Limited. Enough?"

Bogner smiled. "Like I said, Lucian, you still haven't lost your touch."

"Now I have questions for you. Shall we take a little stroll along the beach—for privacy's sake?"

The two men got up and began to walk north along the sandy strip leading away from Le Chamanade toward the Yankee Drummer. Bouderau took out his cigarette holder and inserted a carefully rolled ganja.

"You realize that your presence only confirms my suspicions. Where my old friend Bogner is, there is always much intrigue."

"This time you're wrong, Lucian. I'm here on vacation."

The Frenchman laughed. "But of course—but perhaps you would care to explain then why it is you arrived carrying only one very small valise. It must be a very short vacation, no?"

It was Bogner's turn to laugh. "Hey, what could be better than a weekend in Negril?"

" 'No,' I say to myself. Something very important is happening. Two days ago the Ruskie weasel is here, pretending to enjoy the beach, but Lucian can see that his eyes are nervous. He assesses the bay like a lusty woman. Like most of them, he does not ask questions but checks everything for himself. He rented a small boat and spent most of the day out on the reef, pretending to fish. When he returned, his face was sunburned and he was green with the sickness."

"What Russian?"

Bouderau stopped and looked out at the bay. "His name is Andrakov. He is a Russian Jew; a former GRU agent. He has been in Montego Bay for many years. He thinks no one knows what he is, but to Lucian it is obvious. He is a very transparent but dangerous man."

"If you're so damned curious maybe you should have asked your friend Andrakov what was happening."

"He is nothing but a set of eyes and a messenger," Bouderau scoffed. "He knows nothing more than his superiors tell him." Lucian's eyes brightened. "But, now there is no need to ask him since you are here. That is all the confirmation I need that something is happening."

"Confirmation of what?"

Bouderau made a sweeping motion with his hand. "Look, *mon ami*, first the big American boat arrives and then the small boats. Now comes the famous Commander Bogner. Is that not confirmation enough?"

Bogner turned his back on the bay and ran a hand through his crop of thick, sandy-colored hair. "Suppose I needed a skiff a little later in the day . . ."

"I have one, *mon ami*, but I must tell you that I hope you come up with a better story than the Russian."

Base Hour
Five-Eight:
ZERO ZERO . . . 1400Z

*Datum: 10:5 . . . Moscow: Chesnakov Compound,
2000MLT*

Following his session with Moshe Aprihnen,
Viktor had been driven to the Chesnakov Compound where the GRU Directorates had been
housed and the officers provided with auxiliary
bachelor's quarters during the transition.

During the course of the evening he again had
tried to contact Ruta at both her Tower residence
and her office at the Institute. On his second
call, an associate of Ruta's known to Viktor as
Pytor Tadzhik, an instructor in Germanic languages, informed him that Ruta had earlier in
the day mentioned the possibility of going to the
theater.

Determined to find her, Viktor called Intourist
where unsold tickets for various theaters throughout the city were brought prior to the evening's
performance. He was playing a hunch. Ruta was
fond of Chekhov, and Chekhov's *Marinska* was

being performed at the Krupskaya Theater. When he inquired the woman's only response was, "May we reserve a seat for you, General Denisov?"

"Is there any way of checking who has purchased tickets for tonight's performance?" Viktor pressed.

"Not unless the tickets were ordered by phone and then picked up," the woman informed him.

With visions of Ruta meeting Nokolai Kerensky, Viktor attempted to work off his consternation, first in the officer's sauna and then in the Chesnakov swimming pool. By eight o'clock, his anger at not being able to contact his mistress had subsided to the point that he went to the officer's club for dinner and his second meeting that day with Vitali Parlenko.

A carafe of his favorite wine helped him assuage his anger still further, and by the time Vitali Parlenko joined him, Viktor was again focusing his energies on "72."

The two men watched as the elderly waiter picked up Denisov's half-empty carafe and refilled both of their glasses.

"It is very good," Parlenko assessed, studying the wine through the candlelight. "What is it?"

"Antinori Chianti. I discovered it at a Milan Conference several years ago. I prefer it to the heavier, sweeter wines the club usually stocks."

Parlenko leaned forward. "You do know, my friend, that the former chief chef was a Circassian. He had no eye or taste for wine." Vitali's voice was always slightly less audible when he was gossiping.

"The strangest of all combinations," Viktor agreed, "a Circassian Jew. If he had not been a member of the party in good standing, I personally would have seen to his dismissal."

The two men laughed.

At dinner, they dined on escarole and red pepper cabbage with blackened salmon. When they finished they signaled for the club's traditional bowl of chilled berries and cream.

"You appear to be quite relaxed this evening, Comrade," Parlenko commented.

"The frustrations of the day are behind me. A good dinner, a good wine, a good smoke and a good friend—what more can a man ask for?"

"I am sure the news of the *Rozhko* pleases you?"

"If I embraced the philosophy of a higher deity," Viktor answered "I would at this minute be thanking him profusely for his divine assistance in the day's events."

Parlenko squinted his eyes. "Do you think the Americans really believe we have lost a submarine?"

"That is exactly what they believe. Can't you see them now, anxiously wringing their hands, wondering why it is taking us so long to respond to their verification request?"

Vitali lifted his glass in toast. "I have known you for over three decades, Viktor Denisov. You are a strategist without parallel. The sinking was a stroke of genius."

Viktor saw no need to acknowledge that it was Osipov's idea. He smiled over the top of his glass and accepted his colleague's compliment.

"But now I have even more important news for you, Comrade," Viktor said.

Parlenko arched his eyebrows. "News?"

"I have decided that it would be better if Marshal Zhukov did not return to receive the accolades of the Party."

Parlenko stiffened. His thin smile faded and his eyes hardened. "You have decided? What do you mean *you* have decided? I have been laboring under the impression that this was a joint endeavor. Have you consulted with the others?"

Viktor wiped off his chin, his guileless expression unchanged. "Only Moshe," he admitted, "but I am confident the others will go along with me."

"I am one of the others," Parlenko reminded him, "and I do not go along with any change in our original plans."

"My dear Comrade, you are also an incontrovertible pessimist. This is altogether different than administering the affairs of Aeroflot. You look upon any tactic that has not been studied by a committee for six months as being too risky."

"I look upon that as a fail safe dimension to all of my planning," Vitali countered. "What makes you think that you can change the plan without introducing an additional element of risk? Zhukov accepted this assignment because he knew he had more than one avenue of escape. I am told that even the *Rozhko* can be reactivated at any time."

Viktor held his response while the waiter placed a small saucer of strawberries floating in thick cream on the table in front of them. The old man stepped back and waited for some indication of the General's approval.

Viktor dismissed him with an abrupt wave of the hand and leaned forward again, ignoring the berries. His voice was reduced to a harsh whisper. "You will agree, Comrade, that Marshal Zhukov has proven to be something of a thorn in our side since the inception of our plan. Need I remind you that there are those who actually fear that Zhukov will not be content with his role in the new, revitalized Party. *If* something should go wrong and the Americans learn that our beloved President Zhelannov died by some other means than the blast that destroys the American yacht, Zhukov's duplicity in this scheme could be discovered. And if it is discovered, our friend, Zhukov, could prove to be—how do the Americans say it—a liability? We do not need the added burden of an international embarrassment as we institute the new order. I'm sure you agree that there are those in the Commonwealth, even the Party, that will not see the assassination of President Zhelannov as a heroic act."

Parlenko leaned closer, still cautious. "So how do you propose to remove Marshal Zhukov?"

Viktor spooned a large helping of berries into his mouth and swallowed them whole.

"It is very simple," he said. "After Marshal Zhukov and his accomplices return to the yacht, they will secure the Mala to the hull of the *Cuboc* and wait for the Americans to complete their investigation and lift the blockade. After they jettison the Mala and before their departure, I will instruct Admiral Osipov to have Commandant Ammirof make certain that the *Cuboc* does not make it back to Havana."

"You are leaving a great deal to fortune," Parlenko replied.

"Ah, my cautious friend, there are even alternatives to the alternative plan."

"Such as?"

"I have associates in Jamaica that are capable of handling the entire affair."

"Surely you are not talking about Andrakov," Vitali sneered.

"Andrakov is merely a formality, a puppet. I have other resources. Do you not have your own illegals for matters just such as this?"

"You are more confident than I would be under the circumstances," Parlenko hissed.

Viktor managed to lower his voice even further. "When the body of the new President of the Commonwealth is discovered, the Americans will conduct themselves in a very predictable fashion. First they will conduct an investigation to determine what has happened. Then they will operate on one of two premises. They will come to the conclusion that the explosion was either the result of an untimely malfunction aboard the yacht or the result of some kind of terrorist activity. If they believe the latter, they will spend a great deal of time searching the Negril area, both land and sea. If they act promptly enough, there is always the possibility they will discover the Mala before it has been properly disposed of."

The possibility that the Americans might discover the Mala while it was still tethered to the *Cuboc* had disturbed Vitali more than any other aspect of the plan. He took a deep breath. "Go on," he said.

"If the Mala is discovered," Viktor continued, "I can envision a number of highly disagreeable scenarios, the worst of which is the possibility that they might capture Marshal Zhukov alive."

"But we discussed that. Will not the Americans believe that it is the work of a single deranged madman?" Vitali sneered. "A latter day Oswald so to speak?"

Viktor sighed. "Is that a risk we are prepared to take?"

He paused, finished his desert and waited for Parlenko to respond. Viktor Denisov knew his comrade too well. If the plan worked, Vitali would claim that he had embraced it from the outset. If it failed, he would be the first to disassociate himself.

Vitali Parlenko leaned back in his chair and wiped his mouth with his napkin. Then he rummaged through his pockets until he found his cigars. He extracted one, cut off the end and lit it. As he exhaled, a smile toyed with the corners of his thin mouth.

"You are not only a superior strategist, my friend. You are also very devious."

Viktor Denisov bowed his head. "Thank you, Vitali," he said.

Datum: 10:5 . . . Negril, Jamaica, 1131NLT

Following his conversation with Bouderau, Bogner caught the shuttle bus from the beach area into the village of Negril. As the crowded Toyota van limped into the city with its cargo of 13 people crammed into space for no more than seven, Bogner decided that he would walk back to Le Chamanade following his meeting with Morganthaller.

When the pride of the West Mathews Provincial Department of Transportation came to a stop in front of a string of stalls selling tee shirts, fresh vegetable and religious artifacts, Bogner got off.

Bouderau had indicated that he would find the office of West Mathews Properties Limited directly across the street from Chicken Lavish, but the only building Bogner could see was a whitewashed and weathered two story house, cantilevered into the side of a sheer cliff that plummeted straight down to the water.

The entire area reminded him of an exclamation point. He had come to the place where the jewel known as Jamaica ended and the azure blue of the Caribbean took its place.

He followed a potash and sand path down to a flat stone deck that had once surrounded someone's concept of a tropical garden. He was already down one level from the street. Ahead of him was a large rambling porch with warped flooring guarded by decaying flower boxes choking with weeds and brilliant royal red poiciana. The flower boxes, like the rest of the West Mathews Properties office, needed a great deal of attention.

At the far end of the porch, a tall, angular black man, with muscles bulging through the strained fabric of his white linen coat, lounged in a cane rocker. A military-style automatic in a shoulder holster hung over the back of his chair. He glanced at Bogner and then went back to watching two girls sunning on the narrow strip of beach below the cliff.

Bogner entered without knocking. Inside the first room off the porch were two empty desks. A sign on one of them instructed the customer to ring the bell for service.

Bogner walked past it, through a second door and closed it behind him. An overhead fan made an irritating clicking sound each time it rotated.

Under the feeble rustle of air sat an enormous mountain of a man, more fat than muscle. To Bogner, the scene was reminiscent of an old Sidney Greenstreet movie.

The man laughed. "I knew they wouldn't try to pull this stunt off without getting you involved."

When he heard Morganthaller speak, Bogner remembered that Morganthaller wheezed rather than spoke.

"Colchin's idea, not mine. I had plans to spend the weekend in Boston."

"Encouraging, Bogner, very encouraging. It gives me confidence in my colleagues. I like to think that no one in his right mind would spend any more time in this godforsaken place than he had to."

The fan wasn't equal to its task, and Simon Morganthaller had large blotches of perspiration under his arms.

Bogner slipped into a chair across the desk. "From the looks of things, Simon, I'd say you haven't been keeping up with your jogging."

"Fuck you, Bogner."

Bogner had forgotten that the man was immeasurably better at grumbling profanities than he was at civilized discourse. He watched while the man opened the middle drawer of the desk, took out an envelope and threw it on the desk in front of him.

"Read it," the man said. "I'm in a hurry."

Bogner examined the envelope. "Is everything here?"

Morganthaller shrugged.

"The courier seal is broken. You're getting careless, Simon."

Morganthaller didn't flinch. "Curiosity didn't kill the cat, Bogner, stupidity did. Of course I read it. Who the hell do they think they're fooling? A goddamn ISA courier shows up at my office, tells me to book a room at Le Chamanade and make certain this envelope gets delivered. How deceptively clever! So the famous Tobias Carrington Bogner is going to be in Negril. So what? That, I say to myself, can only mean one thing—Colchin."

Bogner glowered back at the man whose disgusting manner and unmitigated gall hadn't diminished.

"You know what you can do, Bogner?" Simon wheezed. "You can kiss my ass. You've got your orders; now I'm headed back to Montego. Packer said nothing about sticking around to back you up. Apparently that is Mr. Koorsen's job."

The fat man struggled out of his chair and stood up, sweating profusely. He reached down into one of the desk drawers and produced a bottle of local rum, splashed a stained highball glass half-full, picked it up and walked toward the window. Then he looked back over his shoulder. "Well, read it, dammit. I can't leave until you do."

Bogner peeled open the envelope. It was a coded confirmation of everything Packer had told him the night before, plus two pages of minor items Packer had neglected to mention. He read it twice, wadded the paper up, took out his lighter and set it aflame. When nothing remained but a charred ball of carbon, he used the butt of his hand to grind it into black grains of dust.

Morganthaller chuckled. "You've been reading too many spy novels."

Bogner's expression didn't change. "You're off the hook, Simon. Consider the message delivered. Now go back to Kingston or Montego or wherever it is people like you hide from reality."

Morganthaller glared at him. "It is Colchin, isn't it?"

"You read it, Simon. You tell me."

"You know I'm not cleared to a four level code. I don't have access to the key. That's just Packer's way of rubbing my nose in it. I sit down here in this stinking hole for ten years and the first time anything big crops up they send you down to handle it. How the hell do you think that looks on my record?"

Bogner got up and walked toward the door. "Look in the mirror, Simon. Tell me what you see. What makes you think you could have handled the assignment in the first place?"

Simon Morganthaller glared at him.

"And don't worry about your record. I'll keep you updated," Bogner promised.

Bogner left, closing the door behind him only to find the black man standing on the porch waiting for him. He studied Bogner with a level, unbroken stare. Then he laughed.

"I thought legends were taller," he said.

Bogner stopped. "You're Zacariah Koorsen?"

Koorsen smiled. "And Clancy didn't tell you I was black, right?"

Bogner tilted his head to one side. "I've learned over the years that Clancy always leaves something out. I think he thinks it keeps me alert."

The two men shook hands. Koorsen, Bogner noted, was even more impressive when he was standing up. He judged him to be at least six-foot-four and probably a good 225 pounds, all hard muscle.

"You've had a chance to assess the situation. How do you read it?"

Koorsen hesitated and watched while Bogner looked away and scanned the bay. From this vantage point Koorsen knew Bogner could inventory everything in the harbor.

The mooring area was crowded. There were berths for 14, and they counted a total of 22 different vessels in the wharf area alone. It was anyone's guess which one contained their Russian counterparts, but both men knew they were out there.

"Well, *mon*, want me to give you the rundown?"

"*Mon*?" Bogner laughed. "The locals won't buy it. You're too damn big to be a Jamaican. Besides, I can still hear a tinge of Georgia accent."

"Just practicing." Koorsen grinned. "Packer is cool, *mon*. My dialect is better than that. A dollar to a dime says he gave you a copy of my fitness report."

Bogner nodded. "Zacariah Eugene Koorsen, born Atlanta in fifty-two, BS in Mechanical Engineering from Georgia Tech, MA in Languages from Capitol, two years with the navy SEALS and two years at the ISA Institute in Washington. Know what Packer says about you?"

Koorsen shook his head.

"He says you're cat-quick, mentally and physically. For Packer that's tantamount to beatification."

"Saint Zacariah Eugene." Koorsen smiled. "I like the sound of it. There's only one problem—I'm Baptist."

Bogner turned his eyes back to the harbor. "You never answered my question. You know this place; what's different?"

"Lots of stuff—stuff that isn't normally there."

"It figures. How much have you been told?"

"Like Simon says, it doesn't exactly take a four year curriculum in logic to figure out it has something to do with the President. I read the field reports. Judging from everything I read so far, you spend more time with the President than you do your family."

"That wouldn't be hard to do."

Koorsen shoved his hands in his pockets and looked out over the harbor a second time. "Well, to start with we have been monitoring all transmissions in and out of Montego Bay for the last two days. One of their former illegals has tripled the number of transmissions to the former naval directorate in the past week. Most of the messages have been directed to the Chesnakov Compound and coded seventy-two. I was able to break the code working backward on feedback transmissions."

Bogner walked down off of the porch and stepped out on a small rock outcropping jutting out in front of the house. Forty feet below him the water swirled and eddied, momentarily polished the face of the sheer granite wall and then sacrificed itself back to the sea again. To his immediate right was a little narrow strip of beach where a volleyball game was underway. It occurred to him that the bikini-clad lovelies were about the age of his daughter, Kim. That saddened him.

"First lesson," Bogner said. "Accept the obvious. One of those floating pleasure palaces out there contains every damn sophisticated piece of electronic surveillance equipment the Russians know how to build. I guarantee it. The question we should have the answer to and don't is, which one of those damn boats is it?"

Koorsen walked out on the point and stood beside him. "You're close to Colchin. Maybe you should tell the President his timing sucks. Two weeks ago this harbor was almost empty. The minute the leaves start turning up north, this harbor starts filling up."

"I'm more interested in the ones that have arrived in the last couple of days. Unless Zhelannov informed some one that he was moving the date up, they have to be scurrying around as fast as we are."

Koorsen began pointing. "We'll start with the big gray one flying the Union Jack. She's at least sixty meters, and they've got her rigged to look like it's a combination sun pad and skeet range. But if you look at the way it's reinforced, it's beefy enough to accommodate a chopper the size of a Seasprite."

"What about the old trawler down on the end?"

Koorsen laughed. "I don't think so—too obvious. Even the Russians aren't that bald-faced. If they've managed to slip anything inside the reef during the past couple of days, they were pretty cagey about it. What we do know is that they've had a couple of Kara class guided missile cruisers and a Kiev in the area for the past three weeks, but NI claims the Karas are out of the Cuban base and they think it is nothing more than routine. The Kiev is new to this area though. Late last night the Lockheed patrols out of Guantanamo reported the Karas were on their way home. Until Simon got that message from the courier and you showed up, none of it was making much sense."

"Does it now?"

Koorsen nodded. "It's starting to." He reached in his coat pocket, produced a pair of miniature high-powered binoculars and handed them to Bogner.

"Look where I'm pointing. That Alden Ketch came in yesterday. She's out of Fort Lauderdale, and according to the harbor master she's been here the last three winters. The Broward Flybridge and the twin Gulfstar are both Kingston boats. The Broward belongs to a local drug kingpin by the name of Parant. If the navy boys keeps her penned up in the harbor very long, Parant starts to lose money."

"What about that Swath?"

"New," Koorsen admitted. "Not many of them down in these waters. As twin hulls go, that's one of the bigger ones you're likely to see. She's flying the Danish flag. One of Stone's cutter crews checked it out yesterday. He says it's just an old Danish couple that smile all the time."

Bogner turned away. "Think we can get a closer look at our more recent arrivals?"

Koorsen nodded. "Whenever you're ready. Satisfied?"

Bogner nodded. "For the moment."

"Good. Then it's my turn. I've got a question for you."

"Shoot."

"Who's handling the security?"

"We are."

"Just the two of us?"

"To hear Clancy tell it, we've got the U.S. Navy out there and the Coast Guard. If Zhelannov is on the up and up, that's more than enough. If he isn't, then no amount of backup is enough."

"What's our schedule?" Koorsen pressed.

"The President lands on the *Black River* at sixteen hundred local. Another ship, the *Madison*, will be positioned about thirty minutes north near Sullyman Reef off the coast of Mercy Town. The Coast Guard is running an around-the-clock harbor patrol. Two of the four CG units are positioned near the fishing lanes at each end of the reef. The *Black River* will send a message up through channels if the CG is convinced that the harbor is secured. Only then will the President land."

"So what do we do until then?"

"In the meantime you and I are going to check out the security on the *Codicile* and take a cruise around the harbor."

Koorsen had a wry smile. "I figured that. Think it will work?"

"It better. If everyone does their job and keeps their mouths shut, it'll catch the world by surprise. The folks back home think Colchin is holed up at Camp David this weekend—and I wish to hell he was."

Base Hour
Five-Five:
ZERO ZERO . . . 1700Z

Datum: 10:5 . . .Caribbean: USS Madison *, 1410ALT*

In the COM-CON of the *Madison*, Capt. Charles Peel and his Senior Electronics Officer, Lt. Paul Bellinger, watched with apprehension while Campos, Field and Simons maintained their vigil over the downed submarine.

A weary Peel eased himself into the open chair in front of the COM-CON auxiliary control display panel when he heard the Exec Officer's voice over the intercom from the radio room.

"Captain, I've got Admiral Sannon on three three."

Peel leaned across the console and picked up his headset. He locked the chest mike in position to free his hands. "Peel here; go ahead, Admiral."

"What's the latest, Charley?" Sannon's voice sounded fatigued.

Peel scanned the bank of monitors. The cluttered array of static and active displays looked the same as they had for the last half hour. He hit the systems review key and watched the flashing red cursor measure the activity on all visual presentations. The data scrolled in front of him. "No change from the previous report, sir."

"Update me on the situation analysis board, Charley. We're catching all kinds of shit up here. The Russian Ambassador is indignant as hell. He wants to know why every time a sub goes down we start pointing fingers at them. The damned wire services and television networks are ringing the phones off the hook. Half of them think we've inadvertently sunk a Russian sub, and the other half think we've lost one of ours and are trying to throw a blanket on it."

Peel lit a cigarette. There was only one left in the pack. A good time to quit, he thought to himself, and just as quickly discarded the idea. He had tried too many times before, and Charley Peel knew he would have a tough time quitting even under the best of conditions—and this was a hell of a long way from that. He looked at the weary Simons and hunched his shoulders.

"The Admiral wants to know if we can give him some kind of assurance that the sixty-one is definitely Soviet. He's catching a lot of flack."

"What the hell does he want us to do?" Bellinger complained. "Swim down and take pictures of it?"

"Tell the Admiral we know it isn't one of ours because we don't have one that makes that much noise," Simons added.

Campos looked up from his console. "She's a Yankee class all right, Charley. Anyone who has ever had to sit and listen to one of those things cavitate for eight hours would recognize it. Tell him you've got an officer who would be willing to bet next month's pay on it."

Peel pressed the transmit button on his microphone. "We've got a consensus, Admiral. We're about as certain as we can be under the circumstances, but officially I'd have to report that verification based on available data is not possible."

There was a momentary silence on Sannon's end of the line before another voice boomed into Peel's ear. "Charley, this is Merle Lapley, the Chief of NMO. We think we might be able to assist you on the identification of your sub if your guys can give us some readings. We'll feed the data into our own computers and recalculate between you and the latest PIREP's from the two Charley-Cs we've got in the area."

Peel had heard of Lapley, but he had never met Sannon's Chief Meteorologist. He released the receive button.

"We're trailing gear. It's a 41DS, but we have reason to think we're getting distortion because they've got their damn Kiev sitting right on top of our target."

Lapley paused for a moment. "Okay, now listen. We've got an E-6A TACAMO with a four kilometer drop line antenna just out of ear shot of the Kiev. When we get your readings we'll interpolate between the two."

Peel leaned back over his shoulder. "Fields, get on line two and update all influence factors."

The sonarman scanned the readings on his instruments.

"Stand by for taping. Advise when ready." Fields waited until the line was open and the red light started to blink. "Current conditions; read and check. We're below the permanent microcline. We've compensated for diurnal effect with a standard deviation based on speed, wave height and water temperature. We could be getting some salinity effect because of the rapid drop in temperature, but it looks to us as if the pressure maximized at some undetermined level above the bottom of the trench. Drag allowance calculated. I used the following load factors—3.13 kg/cm 2 pressure impact, 35ppt salinity, estimated sound velocity 1.494 m/sec—and got a temperature read out of five degrees centigrade. Stand by to receive current readings."

Fields verified, transmitted and looked up at Peel. "Maybe we ought to tell the NMO officer it looks like we're fluctuating between 1090 and 1151 metres. We know the charts say the trench isn't that deep there, but that's our reading. I've had Simons verify the depth twice."

Peel stalled. He wasn't in any hurry to tell NMO his men thought their charts were wrong.

"Lapley, it appears that we've got some depth discrepancy," he finally volunteered.

"Reverberations?" Lapley questioned.

"We think we've taken all the bathymetric effects into consideration," Peel answered.

"Where are you trailing your antenna?"

Peel studied the ASD monitor. "192.1 off stern, speed two knots. The acoustic transmitter is below horizontal. The receiver is a vertical 180 without drag configuration. We're trying to circle the silly bastards and get some information without being too obvious. They're watching us like hawks."

Peel could hear Lapley explaining the situation to Sannon.

"Even with a water column depth as deep as we're dealing with, the propagation path hasn't bottomed out. The deep sound duct is being refracted." Then he was back on line to Peel. "Give me the position of your data transducer."

Simons fixed the point. "41.01 at 1733.42 Zulu. Mark!"

Peel, out of habit, double-checked. "Affirmative. Receiver is 750 metres off stern."

Suddenly Lapley was gone and Sannon's voice was coming over the headset again. "Charley, give me a visual profile on that Kiev."

"Roger. Bellinger has been studying it. He believes she has been stripped which may account for her earlier non-profile speed. No apparent armament. Nothing on deck and her SAML appears to be down. She's got some amenities we haven't seen before."

Sannon's voice went from probing to clandestine. "Are we secured, Charley?"

Peel wasn't aware of it but he had automatically lowered his own voice in response.

"All secured, Admiral." He glanced around the COM-CON. "They can hear me but they can't hear you, sir."

"Just listen then." The Vice-Admiral was choosing his words carefully. "We have a report through Cayman Long that your Kiev out there is sporting a Hormone B."

"Confirmed. The ident profile is Protivo Lodochny Kreiser."

Sannon paused again. "Charley, we are beginning to think there is a good possibility that the

113

Russian President is on board that cruiser."

Peel blinked. "Repeat?"

"Commonwealth President Zhelannov may be aboard that Kiev."

Peel temporarily forgot protocol. "Why the hell . . . ?"

"When are you scheduled to open your phase II packet?" Sannon interrupted.

"Thirty minutes off of Sullyman Reef at 1900 Zulu," Peel replied. The phase I orders expired at 1859Z, and he was nowhere near his mark. Surely Sannon realized that.

"Better open them as soon as we break off. Is there any possibility at this point that you can make RP-2 on schedule?"

Peel glanced at the chronometer over the main display panel. "Not a chance. At the moment the best I can give you is a rough estimate. There's no sign of it yet, but my weather officer tells me we've got some weather moving in."

Sannon was still weighing his words. "Don't estimate. Run it through your computers and give me an ETA for RP-2 at three levels. Now, the rest of this is for your ears only. President Colchin is on his way to Negril. Zhelannov is scheduled to meet him there. You're backing up the *Black River*. NI thinks it's possible Zhelannov is on that cruiser and that Hormone you see sitting on her deck is the way he intends to get back and forth to Negril. In other words, we think it's possible that Kiev is caught between the proverbial rock and a hard place. That commandant has to make certain we don't go snooping around that six-one and at the same time he has to get Zhelannov to Negril. They know the whole damn world is watching."

Peel looked up at the television monitor overhead. The camera was aimed at the Kiev. "At the moment she's just sitting there," he confirmed.

"She may be waiting for assistance."

Peel lit his last cigarette and crumpled up the empty pack. "That still doesn't explain why there isn't any attempt on their part to contact the sub. We're monitoring everything, and so far we haven't even picked up an attempt at contact."

"Hang in there, Charley. We'll get our heads together up here and see what we've got. Let me know if you hear anything."

Sannon didn't wait for confirmation. The line went dead.

Peel looked around the COM-CON. "Anybody picking up anything?"

Campos looked up at the elapsed time. "We're closing in eighteen hours, Captain. That's one hell of a long time to be lying at the bottom of that trench."

Campos leaned back in his chair, took off his headset and rubbed his eyes. "Anybody got a spare cigarette?"

Simons handed him one, and he lit it.

"Know what I think?" He exhaled. "I don't think there is anyone alive on that damn sub and our friends on that Kiev know it."

Datum: 10:5 . . . Negril Beach, 1441NLT

As Bogner worked his way back up the stretch of beach between the water and Le Chamanade, Koorsen tied up Bouderau's skiff at the pier. The Frenchman was there to greet them.

"Two observations, *mon ami*," Lucian said.

"One, you will never catch fish unless you bait your hook. Two, you neglected to mention the fact that you knew the owner of the American yacht."

"Very observant." Bogner grinned and waited for Koorsen.

"Bring your friend, *mon ami*. Come. Sit down with Lucian and tell him all about the fine craft flying the American flag. It is an Italian design, is it not?"

Minutes later the three men settled in the shade of the nearest cabana, and Bouderau signaled to one of Le Chamanade's white jacketed cabana boys. He held up three fingers.

"More specifically, Lucian, it's a Ballietto and it belongs to a man from Texas."

"Ah, these aging eyes are not so good as they use to be," Bouderau apologized. "I studied the name with my glasses, but alas, I could not quite make it out."

"*Codicile 1*," Koorsen said evenly

"*Codicile 1*," Bouderau repeated, rolling the name around on his tongue as though he was savoring his favorite brandy. "What is the meaning of this name?"

Bogner looked past Koorsen out over the sun-drenched harbor. It was the hour of the day when activity dwindled. The tranquility was such that he could have believed that neither the Russians nor the Americans were taking any special precautions for the upcoming meeting. The waiter returned, placed three lemon-rum drinks on the table in front of them and left. Koorsen scooped his glass up and downed half on the first swallow.

"Shall I explain to him that it's a legal term?" he said, looking at Bogner.

Bogner laughed. "You're wasting your time. My friend Lucian here has a habit of asking rhetorical questions. He knows full well what the word means. Not only that, he knows that the *Codicile* belongs to Amos Sparrow and that Sparrow is a Texan and David Colchin's former law partner. He can, I'll wager, also tell you when and where the craft was built and he probably has the names and birth dates of every member of the *Codicile*'s crew. Right, Lucian?"

The Frenchman threw his head back and laughed. "You flatter me, *mon ami*." Then he leaned forward and focused on Koorsen. "The truth is, I have not yet learned the birth dates of the crew." The admission unleashed another round of Lucian's robust laughter.

Even with their long association, Bogner found it difficult to pinpoint many things about Lucian Bouderau. His age, birthplace and background fostered stories up and down the beach, but no one seemed to know anything for certain. Bogner assumed he was in his late fifties but admitted it was only an educated guess; he could have been older. He was a robust man who pretended at being the local gossip. Yet he was a man of social graces, devious ways and some wealth. Only because Bouderau had revealed something of himself in an all night drinking orgy with Bogner many years ago did T. C. know more than the average man who came in contact with the Frenchman.

On that occasion he had confessed to being a salvage diver for a French oil company in his early days. He had come to Jamaica on a holiday and enjoyed himself so much that he decided to stay. That was, as Bogner recalled, 30 years ago. He had married a local girl, Sophia, who was wealthy, lovely and sick. She had died seven months after they were married.

Bogner knew him to be an opportunist, selling not what he had but what he knew and could learn. People talked, Bouderau listened, and he profited by it. He made it his business to know what was going on in Negril.

At the moment, Bogner was convinced his long-time acquaintance did not feel that he knew enough about what was happening in his own backyard. That was bad for a man dealing in information.

"I notice, Mr. Koorsen, that your Commander friend refers continually to his watch. Is something important about to happen?"

The black man slouched back in his chair and winked at the Frenchman. "New watch," he said. "He's very proud of it."

"I thought perhaps it might have something to do with the important meeting taking place tonight on the American yacht."

Bogner tried not to overreact. He studied Bouderau hard to see if the Frenchman actually knew something or was guessing.

Bouderau was still waiting for a response when a cabana boy approached the table. He carried a tray with a small, folded piece of paper. He stopped several feet from the table and waited until the Frenchman gave him permission to interrupt. Lucian Bouderau took the paper, and read it.

118

Red Tide

"You do not demonstrate the same mental agility you once did," Bouderau said laughing. "I will be anxious to see if you can come up with one of your patented clever answers while I tend to a small business matter."

Bouderau slipped the piece of paper in his pocket and looked toward the archway leading from the lobby into Le Chamanade's lounge. There, a short, stocky man with brown horn-rimmed glasses, wearing a wrinkled seersucker suit and carrying a battered, oversized leather briefcase, waited for him.

"See why Bouderau is always asking questions, *mon ami*? Now I have a client and he is in the buying mood. If you had revealed more then I would have more to bargain with." The Frenchman looked at Koorsen, "Let that be a lesson to you. Always strike while the iron is hot. Get your information while you can. With your taciturn friend, Bogner, controlling information, I fear I will not make much money today."

Koorsen lifted his glass. "I'll take that advice."

Bouderau moved around to Bogner's side of the table. "As you can see, *mon ami*, it is the season of the spy."

Bogner's eyes shifted to the man in the archway. "Spy?" he repeated. He tried to sound only half-interested.

"This costs you nothing," Bouderau said. "Would you like to meet him? I will be happy to introduce you. You would be surprised at how much you two have in common. He believes that no one knows he is an agent of the Soviet government, and you gentlemen choose to believe that no one knows you work for the American government."

Bouderau was pleased with the irony of the moment. He looked at the Russian and then the two Americans.

"Comparing the two," he laughed, "I must assume your government pays you a better wage for your services than his. His attire is rather unflattering, don't you think?"

Bogner assessed the stocky little Russian over the rim of his glass. He wondered what the man would do if he lifted his glass in a toast.

As Bouderau crossed the veranda heading for the lounge, the Russian agent stepped back into the shadows. The movement amused Bouderau, as did everything about Boris Andrakov, who masqueraded as a clerk for a Jamaican export firm by day and filled his nights feverishly filing the still required reports of a GRU illegal.

Bouderau's dossier on the soft-bellied man indicated he was 46 years-old, unmarried and a longtime resident of Montego Bay. In the margin of one of Bouderau's extensive files was the notation that Andrakov's perverse sexual appetites included young boys.

In exchange for Bouderau's often useless flow of information, Andrakov dutifully delivered the sum of 1000 American dollars to the Frenchman on the first day of every month. Bouderau, who would have cared only if the money stopped, never bothered to ask Andrakov if his contacts back in Moscow were pleased with the arrangement. If they were not, Lucian concluded, the flow of American dollars would have stopped long before now.

Bouderau stopped in the archway, where he knew the Americans could still see him. "Boris, to what do we owe the pleasure of your company twice in one week?"

Andrakov's fat creased face still showed traces of his sunburn. He bowed stiffly and promptly opened his briefcase to search for the envelope. He was nervous and checked repeatedly to make certain no one could hear them. As he handed Bouderau the envelope, he said, "I must talk to you—in private."

Bouderau opened the envelope, peered in and quickly shut it. It was the Frenchman's turn to smile. "But of course, *mon ami*, but of course. I always have time to talk to you. Let us see if we can find a quiet place more to your liking."

The Frenchman turned and started down the hall toward his office and Andrakov followed. When the door to Bouderau's office closed, Andrakov opened his briefcase again. This time he produced a large blueprint, opened it and spread it out on Lucian's desk.

"A colleague of mine has a small problem," Andrakov said. "It is a malfunction in a small mechanism under the hull of his boat. He is an amateur diver and the device captures and secures his miniature diving sled. Tonight, while he explores the floor of the harbor, he has asked me to solicit someone who knows about these things and hire them to repair it."

Bouderau studied the apparatus. "Your friend is very brave. Diving at night can be quite dangerous."

Andrakov forced a smile. ''Many things are dangerous, Monsieur Bouderau. My colleague has, how should I phrase it, a flair for adventure?'

"And when will your colleague be diving?"

"He plans to leave at 2000 hours, local time, of course." Andrakov straightened up and fumbled for a cigarette. His hands were shaking. "Are you familiar with such devices?"

"And you say I will find this mechanism under the hull of the Danish Swath?"

Andrakov nodded.

"Consider your colleague's problem solved, *mon ami*. I shall be happy to take care of it. You will leave the blueprint and the money, of course, with me."

Lucian's request took the Russian by surprise. He hesitated. "Is it necessary?"

Bouderau laughed. "It is not only necessary, but it is imperative. You would not want me to repair the mechanism improperly. If I did, your colleague might not be able to reboard his vessel, and you wouldn't want that, would you?"

Andrakov's smile was nervous but real this time. "Most assuredly, I would not want that." The Russian's attempt at another smile failed.

Bouderau looked at his watch. "Do you know the place called Apostle Point?"

Andrakov nodded.

"Meet me there," Bouderau said, "by the old fisherman's shed at the time your friend will be diving."

This time there was no humor in his velvet voice.

Base Hour
Five-Three:
ZERO ZERO . . . 1900Z

Datum: 10:5 . . . Washington: Arlington Hotel,
1603EST

With the passing of the years, Clancy Packer had come to the realization that little things annoyed him almost as much as big things. Being late for appointments, cold toast, cluttered desks and Washington traffic were little things. Colchin going to Negril without the security of the secret service was a big thing.

On this day when the flow of traffic forced him to drive on past the Arlington exit, he was annoyed with two things: Colchin's decision and being late for his appointment.

He found a parking place two blocks away from the Arlington and walked back. Jaffe had instructed him to enter through the alley.

As he turned the corner, an imposing looking black with a heavy beard, dressed in a dirty navy pee coat, turned-up collar and a black stocking cap pulled down over his ears, stepped from the shadows. The man cradled a brown paper sack in one hand while concealing the other in the slash pocket of his coat. From the bulge in his pocket, Packer knew the man was armed.

"Goin' somewhere, pretty boy?" the man grunted.

Packer hesitated momentarily then started to elbow his way past this latest annoyance.

The man planted a club-sized hand in the middle of Packer's chest and began to push him toward the wall. "You lookin' for trouble, whitey?"

Packer pushed him away. "You got a problem, boy?"

The man's wink was nearly imperceptible. He leaned closer to Packer. "Through the rear service door, across the kitchen, look for a door on the right. The sign says 'Employees Only.' "

He pulled his hand away, appeared to stumble backward, and before Clancy realized it, had disappeared into the alley shadows.

Packer smiled to himself, turned and started up the alley.

A plain brown LTD was parked near the door, and a man wearing a camelhair overcoat, smoking a cigarette and stamping his feet to ward off the cold, was guarding it. He watched Packer until he entered the building.

The kitchen was deserted except for two salad chefs preparing for the evening dinner crowd. Packer slipped through the kitchen, passed two busboys snatching a quick drag on a reefer and stopped in front of the door. He knocked twice before entering.

Oscar Jaffe was sitting in a straight-back chair

with his feet propped on a table. He was sipping coffee from a brown mug, his back turned to a pile of dirty linen in the corner. The pungent odor of kitchen grease saturated the room.

Jaffe looked up without smiling. Clancy had known the CIA chief for years. The curious thing about Oscar Jaffe was that Clancy could not remember ever seeing the man smile. He reasoned it was either because Jaffe never had anything to smile about or didn't know how.

"The head shed thought you ought to be aware of this," Jaffe said. He pointed to a greasy manila folder lying in the middle of the table.

Clancy took off his hat, unbuttoned his coat and sat down. "Who's the big guy at the entrance to the alley?"

"Burnsy? Like him, huh? He's my main man. I recruited him out of a theological seminary in Kentucky. He had his heart set on being a Baptist minister, but the money was too good to pass up. Damn near kills him that we make him carry that bottle of ripple around with him to make him smell authentic."

Packer opened the envelope. It contained a single piece of white paper. The word *Complexity* was written across the top. Below it were seven columns of tightly compressed numbers, five digits to a cluster. Miller would be able to decode it back at the office.

"I take it you've heard of Complexity?" Jaffe asked.

Packer nodded. "Who hasn't? Still active, huh?"

Jaffe always played by the rules. He neither confirmed nor denied. He took his feet off the table and leaned forward with his elbows on his knees. "Complexity is very, very reliable."

Packer scanned the report. It was date coded earlier that morning.

Jaffe drained the last of his coffee and wiped off his lips. "You know how these things go, Clancy. I give you the information and you decide what you're going to do with it. Complexity tells us there's a high level plot brewing with some of the old Party hardliners." Packer leaned back in his chair.

"When aren't they cooking up something?"

"This one has a mean little twist to it. We're told they are after the main man this time."

"Zhelannov?"

"That's what we're being told."

"When?"

Jaffe pursed his lips. "Before we get in to that, I take it you are aware of the doings this weekend?"

Packer sobered. Stinson had used the same code word. Colchin's secret meeting wasn't much of a secret. He nodded.

It was enough to satisfy Jaffe. "Complexity thinks it all comes down in Negril this weekend."

"What else does Complexity think?"

"Doesn't know when, doesn't know who, doesn't know how. But Complexity assures us there are several offices in the Council of Ministers burning the midnight oil and waiting for word that it's a done deal."

"Tie a ribbon around it."

"Complexity thinks the scenario plays out something like this. They knock off the main man and blame it on us. Their line is we can't be trusted, and the old Party hardliners step in and grab control. Apparently there are a lot of people who want Zhelannov tucked away in Novodevichii cemetery. When that happens, everything goes back to square one. Red Square."

Packer stuffed a stick of gum in his mouth. "Hell, Oscar, they can knock off Zhelannov any time they have a mind to and there's not a damn thing we can do about it."

"We know that, but the head shed figures you may want to take precautions to make certain Colchin isn't caught in the cross fire. The fact that Complexity believes they'll try it this weekend makes us think they're going to attempt to implicate us."

Packer grunted and rubbed his chin. "There are three separate sessions scheduled. The first one kicks off tonight at 2000 hours. Tonight's session is supposed to be more form than substance. If Complexity knows what he's talking about, we're vulnerable, because Zhelannov insisted on each side having only two aides present. We couldn't get Colchin to agree to let us plant anyone aboard Sparrow's yacht. He insisted on playing it straight. We couldn't go around him because he knows the crew personally. He'd spot a salt first thing out of the box."

"Who's on the team?" Jaffe asked.

"For Colchin—Hurley and Spitz. They're en route with the President. So how much does the President know about all of this?"

"He's heard rumors. We'll update him as soon as we're certain he is safely aboard the *Black River*. Our office will advise Spitz. He'll update the President. Who is your man in all of this?"

"Commander T. C. Bogner, hand-picked by the President."

"Who is his backup?"

"Koorsen, one of our best."

"Tell them to watch their flank," Jaffe grunted. "We understand that the field agent down there is a fellow by the name of Boris Andrakov, but Complexity insists that there is a twist in there somewhere. This guy Andrakov is said to be nothing more than a front for a heavyweight illegal that they've been keeping in reserve down there."

"What do we know about him?"

Jaffe shook his head. "That's what's worrying us. We haven't been able to learn a damn thing about him," Jaffe said as he stood up, "but we're not through digging either." He stuck out his hand. "Give Sara my best."

The meeting was over. Packer followed Jaffe out into the kitchen, waited until the CIA man got into his car and then left by the same rear door. This time, Burnsy was nowhere in sight.

By the time Packer got back to his car, the rush hour had begun. It was five minutes before five and the streets were congested; traffic had slowed to a crawl.

He looked at his watch. By now, Colchin was safely aboard the *Black River*. He wondered if they had traffic snarls in Negril.

He bullied his way into the traffic flow, picked up his car phone and began stabbing out the ten digit access code. Miller picked up on the first ring. "Anything new?"

"Yeah, Chief, we think we finally got something on that downed sub."

"Have the Russians confirmed it?"

"Not a word. But NI has come up with something. Does the term *Rozhko* mean anything to you?"

Clancy Packer rifled back through a webby maze of Russian code words. "Hell, yes. Wasn't that the code name they gave to an experimental Yankee III sub that was supposed to operate without a crew?"

"You got it," Miller confirmed. "NI has claimed from the outset that they had the technology to control the vessel from a surface ship."

"Which would explain the presence of that Kiev."

"And would also explain why we can't monitor any exchange between the surface and the sub. They aren't talking, for the simple reason there is no one down there to talk to. They're obviously sitting on top of it, trying to figure out what the hell went wrong."

"Or it's that damn diversion I've been talking about. How quick can you get me a profile on the *Rozhko*?"

"Henline's been working on it. Stand by." Packer could hear Miller's fingers laboring over the computer keyboard. "I'm bringing it up."

"Give me everything you've got."

"*Rozhko*, 615SSN, Yankee I with a modified III conversion April, 90. Modification done at Menshevik Shipyards. Length 329ft or 100 meters, range 1600nm or 2950km, active and passive sonar, mast mounted sensors. The computer uses a Cod Eye radio sextant for navigational accuracy. It says here that the remote operational electronics and systems were installed at Severodvinsk in the spring of 91. We have no data on any shakedown cruises. Maybe that's what this is—and something went wrong. Obviously we underestimated the range if that's what we've actually got."

"Bullshit," Clancy snapped. "Maybe that's what they want us to believe. Those assholes are up to something. The question is—what?"

Miller's end of the line was silent.

"Depending on the damn traffic, I should be back in the office by six. See if you can locate Bogner. He needs to know what the hell is going on."

"Where do I start looking?"

"Start with the bar at Le Chamanade."

Base Hour
Five-Two:
ZERO ZERO . . . 2000Z

Datum: 10:5 . . . Le Chamanade, Cottage 5,
1715NLT

The knock on the door brought Bogner up out
of a sound sleep. He looked around the room
trying to get his bearings. Koorsen was gone. His
Scotch and water, ice melted, was sitting on the
nightstand beside his bed. He had dozed off.

"Who is it?" he managed.

The response was a second knock, this one less
timid.

Bogner grumbled and looked at his watch. He
had been sleeping for over an hour. He managed
to get to the door and open it. A young Jamaican
boy stood smiling up at him. The lad, no more
than ten years of age, was wearing only a pair
of worn khaki shorts secured by a thin cotton
rope. He held a piece of paper out for Bogner's
inspection.

"Are you Bogner, *mon*?"

"You found him."

The embarrassed youngster thrust the paper at him and raced off through the hotel's courtyard. The message from the Le Chamanade switchboard was straightforward. "Packer trying to locate you." It was signed Morganthaller.

Bogner went back into the room, sat down on the edge of the bed and dialed. The Jamaican phone system was shaky at best, but to his astonishment, he got through on the first try.

Clancy Packer answered. There was no exchange of pleasantries.

"What's it look like down there?" Packer snarled.

T. C. leaned back across the bed and cradled the phone against his shoulder. "About eighty degrees, skies were clear an hour ago, no wind to speak of—"

"Damn it, Toby, what about Sparrow's yacht?"

"Squeaky clean. Cameron's security team from the *Black River* has been over it from bridge to bilge tanks. Everything has been checked and double-checked. Koorsen and I went through it after they did. Rest assured, even Sparrow would be proud."

"What about Stone's CG units? Have they checked out the transits?"

Bogner grunted. "Everything that we know to check has been checked, Pack. I rode shotgun on one of the cutters and they gave me a close up look at everything in the harbor. It looks clean. Koorsen went over the papers of every transit in the harbor. We boarded and searched anything that has papers less than a year old. Unless they were clever enough to anticipate a document check and forged their papers, we know who is suspect and who isn't.

"The *Black River* has the harbor sealed off and Colchin arrived right on schedule. I almost hate to say it, but at the moment—no problems. He's resting aboard the *Black River* right now."

"What are the locals making of it?"

"They're convinced we're in here to lower the boom on one of the local drug lords."

"Good," Packer grunted. "The way things are beginning to shape up, you and Koorsen are going to need all the breaks you can get."

"What the hell do you mean by that, Clancy?"

Packer cleared his throat, and Bogner braced himself for the worst.

"I just came from a one on one with Oscar Jaffe. The CIA received a transmission from their agent in Moscow earlier today. Our contact claims that there is a plot underway to dump Zhelannov."

"Full blown purge?"

"No purge. They are planning to assassinate him."

Bogner sat upright. "Assassinate?"

"According to Jaffe, his sources are telling him that the whole thing may be coming down this weekend, anytime in the next seventy-two hours."

Bogner swallowed hard. "How good is this source?"

"Jaffe assures me that this is solid. I learned all of this a little over an hour ago and less than fifteen minutes ago his office sent over a decoded version of Complexity's report. Supposedly one of the former GRU Directorates, a man by the name of Viktor Denisov, is behind this plot. There are five others involved, maybe more. Complexity has been able to identify some of them: Osipov,

Parlenko, Ammirof and Aprihnen."

"That's only four of the five. What about the others?"

"Obviously, one of them is the assassin. The problem with all of this is the assassin doesn't have an identity. Jaffe thinks it could even be someone in Zhelannov's official entourage."

"Doesn't seem likely. Zhelannov is supposed to be coming in with his own crew of hand-picked loyalists."

"That's where you come in. Jaffe also thinks it could be somebody on Sparrow's crew."

"Long shot. It's the same crew Sparrow had last year when the President and I were aboard. Besides, you told me yourself that Colchin kept his decision to use the *Codicile* in the freezer right up until the last minute. There wouldn't have been time for the Russians to get one of their plants aboard."

"What about a local?" Packer persisted. "Is that a possibility?"

"Tall order for the kind of talent they would need to pull it off here, but I'll check with Koorsen just to be on the safe side. The folks around here deal in ganja, not borscht. One of my contacts claims that the former GRU illegal in Montego Bay has been hanging around for the last several days, but he doesn't look the like the gun-toting type. He looks more like a wire man than a hit man."

"Jaffe insists that they've got a heavyweight in the area, but he doesn't have any names."

"Maybe I'd better get Morganthaller in on this."

"Leave Simon right where he is. We need him to monitor this guy Andrakov's transmissions. We've got Simon checking everything in and out of Montego Bay."

"How much does the President know about all of this?"

"He is being advised of Jaffe's report at this very minute. How he choses to handle it is up to him."

"Clancy, the way this thing is set up, I'm too damned far away from the President to assist him if there is any trouble."

Bogner could hear Packer fuming on the other end. "Damn it all, Toby, I don't like the way this whole thing appears to be falling apart. This started out low profile. Now it's anything but that. Every time I talk to Stinson over at NI we've uncovered something else."

"What's the word on that downed sub? The crew of the *Codicile* have been monitoring the *Madison*'s transmissions."

"We're monitoring the *Madison* up here, too. So far there's no indication that the Kiev cruiser has made any attempt to contact the sub."

Clancy had already decided not to complicate Bogner's situation by introducing NI's still unconfirmed theory that the *Rozhko* was a robot.

"That's the way they handled the *Podozoski* when it went down off the coast of Iceland back in eighty-five," Bogner reminded him. "Rather than have us learn anything about one of their subs they kept us at arm's length for four days until their own recovery ships got there."

Packer's voice softened. "Look, Toby, it may not be much of a consolation at the moment, but we brought in the heads of the field units and we're all standing by. We'll help you any way we can. From this end though, it's beginning to look as though we've cozied up to a real hornet's nest. I put in a call to Lattimer Spitz aboard the *Black River* less than thirty minutes ago. I asked him to make one last ditch appeal to Colchin not to go through with this. If they hit Zhelannov during one of these sessions and blame us, we'll have a major goddamn war on our hands within hours."

Bogner knew there was nothing to say. When Packer wished him luck and hung up, he was glad to see Koorsen standing in the doorway.

"We better hope your friend Bouderau wasn't tapped into that one," Koorsen said. "If he was, he'll have a whole lot more to sell and tell."

Bogner nodded. Beyond the towering figure of Koorsen, out over Le Chamanade's gardens, he could see the first splattering droplets of rain. The sky to the west had deteriorated into a dirty slate gray and he could see infrequent flashes of lightning.

Koorsen lumbered into the room and sat down on the edge of his bed. "Thought you'd be happy to know. I just checked with Cameron's security officer. They've got a crew installing the monitoring gear over at the wharf. I was thinking maybe you'd want to go over and check it out."

Bogner picked up what remained of his drink. "*Exceptio probat regulam de rebus non exceptis,* or do you prefer, *Exitus acta probat?*"

Zacariah Koorsen sprawled back across the bed and stared up at the ceiling. "Whatever you think is fair, *mon.*"

Red Tide

Datum: 10:O6 . . . Moscow, O119MLT.

The phone rang several times before Ruta answered. "Yes," she said, her voice thick with sleep.

"Ruta," Viktor grumbled. There was a twitch in his voice that he hoped the woman did not hear.

"Viktor, is something wrong?" she asked.

Suddenly he felt embarrassed. The anger that had grown through the evening hours when he was unable to contact her started to subside.

"Viktor," she repeated, "what is wrong?"

To Viktor Denisov, the woman's voice sounded mechanical, void of emotion, as though there was someone else in the room and she was speaking in guarded tones.

"Where have you been?"

There was, it seemed to Viktor, an unnecessarily long interval between his question and her response. Why was she finding it difficult to give him an answer?

"I have been here, my bear. Why?"

"You are lying," he groused. "I have been trying to reach you for hours."

"I went to the theater with Kontesha earlier. We saw the ballet, *Kiskatem*."

"Who is this Kontesha?" Viktor demanded.

There was another pause before Ruta answered, this one longer than the first. "Kontesha Voska-vich, like me, teaches at the institute. She had tickets and asked me to accompany her."

"You are alone now?" he demanded.

The question elicited a muted laugh that Viktor interpreted as derisive. "Ah," she said, "now I understand. These questions are spurred by jealousy. You could not contact me, so you thought

I was with another man, true?"

Viktor choked on his answer. It was impossible for him to be totally honest. If he did, he believed it would demean him in her eyes.

"That is what you thought, isn't it, my bear?"

In the darkness of his bachelor's quarters, sitting on the edge of his bed, the sensation of embarrassment eroded until now he felt as if he had made a fool of himself. Still, he reminded himself, she had not denied his charge and confirmed that she was alone.

His own infidelities over the years fostered pictures of Ruta, her lithesome body intimately entwined with that of another man.

"Is it so difficult to admit that you want to be with me?" she said. Her voice was fluid again—the voice of a lover—and he knew she was teasing him. "Would you like me to come to your barracks and show you how much I miss you?"

"*Nyet*," he said. "That's impossible."

"Will you come here then?" she teased.

Viktor knew that she was offering alternatives that he could not accept. He fell silent.

"Did you not tell me that you would be gone for three whole days while you consorted with your general friends playing war games?"

Viktor did not answer. Instead, he placed the receiver back in its cradle and lay back across the coarse sheets of his barracks bed. In the darkness he was convinced that he had heard the voice of a man in the room with Ruta. Could it have been Kerensky?

Base Hour
Four-Nine:
ZERO ZERO . . . 2300Z

Datum: 10:5 . . . The Yacht Codicile I, *2010NLT*

Zhelannov's entourage was on schedule. Colchin could hear the Commonwealth President's launch before he could see it. He glanced at his watch. It was precisely ten minutes after the hour and the first vague outlines of the tan and cream-colored craft were beginning to materialize out of the mist.

Colchin, his advisors and the crew of the *Codicile* watched the approach through binoculars. Despite being swaddled in foul weather gear, Zhelannov was still recognizable.

As the launch approached, Colchin's thoughts returned to their first meeting at the Yalta conference earlier in the year, a time when both men were still reeling from the bizarre events that had catapulted them into the forefront of world affairs. Colchin termed it a *cruel blow*.

It was, however, President-elect Chester

McMurtry that had been dealt the cruelest blow. The Kansas senator had been elected to the nation's highest office by the narrowest of margins in what had been termed the biggest political upset of all time. Then, in a perverse twist on the night before his inauguration, he was robbed of his moment in history when he succumbed to a heart attack.

As a consequence, David R. Colchin, a Texas lawyer and financier and Chester McMurtry's reluctant running mate, was suddenly thrust into the awesome responsibilities of the office of the President of the United States.

Seeing Zhelannov's launch approaching, Colchin's recollections of that frigid Washington night rushed back at him. Recollections of being awakened by the Secret Service, of the hurried drive from his hotel along the frozen shores of the Potomac, of the subsequent series of meetings in the White House, and finally his realization along with that of a stunned nation that the President-elect was dead.

David Colchin still remembered the haunting early hours of that gray dawn when the chilling reality finally set in; in a matter of hours he would become President.

Now his thoughts shifted back to Zhelannov and the series of bizarre events that leveled the once mighty Soviet Union—the departure of Gorbachev, the establishment of the Commonwealth of Independent States, and the night he first sat across the conference table from the man.

No one, Colchin was convinced, had ever looked less like his concept of a world leader. Sergei Zhelannov had not impressed him. He was a man of average stature, average weight and an unpreposing appearance. Only a carefully trimmed silver-flecked moustache and goatee distinguished him, a distinction that Colchin felt gave the man nothing more than an aura of great sadness.

Sergei Yevgeny Zhelannov, however, had emerged as a man with a sharp intellect and an enormous appetite for life. As a consequence, David Colchin had learned to both like and respect his Russian counterpart.

As Colchin watched the launch plow through the veil of encroaching fog and darkness, Lattimer Spitz's hurried and cryptic summary of the Complexity report played over and over in his mind.

At first, Colchin had been unwilling to give the report any credence, yet he knew it was a disturbing possibility. Every situation analysis he had read indicated that Zhelannov was surrounded by dissidents—frustrated, power hungry and ambitious. Then he remembered a professor in law school who termed assassination as the despicable tool of weak men.

David Colchin, son of a pacifist minister, found the concept of one man taking the life of another totally incomprehensible. And to his dismay, he had already witnessed it too many times—Ghandi, the Kennedys, King, Aquino. The list was far, far too long.

As Zhelannov's launch moved closer to the *Codicile*, Colchin struggled with the disturbing premise of the Complexity report. Stripped of its political ramifications and left to his own devices, he would have openly discussed it with his counterpart. But Jaffe and Spitz and even Hurley, each for different reasons, had warned him to avoid the subject.

"Every world leader lives under the shadow of assassination," Jaffe had theorized. "It goes with the territory."

"Zhelannov has one of the most effective internal police organizations in the world," Spitz had assured him. "The RSB has probably already taken the necessary steps to defuse the plot."

"Don't embarrass him," Hurley cautioned. "It makes it sound like we're giving credence to the dissident factions in the Commonwealth. We wouldn't want him listening to the dissident voices in our country."

Still Colchin hadn't made up his mind. He wondered if it was possible that Zhelannov was unaware of the plot. And if he did know, could he protect himself? What did the names Denisov, Osipov, Parlenko, Aprihnen and Ammirof mean to him? Jaffe had indicated that Complexity report implied that as many as eight people could be involved. Who were the others? For that matter, could he name his own enemies? Had Jack Kennedy ever heard the name Lee Harvey Oswald?

"The launch is moving alongside, Mr. President," Spitz informed him.

Colchin looked around at the *Codicile*'s crew. They were standing at attention, waiting for the Russians to board. Then he peered down into the launch. Zhelannov was sitting midship under a canopy, out of the weather. He had already discarded his raincoat. To his right stood a much larger man, coarse-featured and grim-faced, wearing a military uniform with his arms folded defiantly across his chest. Colchin mentally rummaged back thru the dossiers prepared by the Secret Service. The big man would be Marshal Ivan Evseyevich Zhukov. Hurley referred to him as the only former Soviet military man who had gotten close to Zhelannov. Hurley recalled meeting the man years earlier at the Geneva SALT talks; his assessment—an out and out son-of-a-bitch.

The third member of the Russian entourage was a smallish man who chose to stand immediately behind his leader. He was dressed in a plain blue suit and held his raincoat tightly folded over his arm, as though he was concealing something. His name was Josef Tcheka. Colchin had met him before. He had owl-like features, but now his large eyes were partially concealed by large horn-rimmed glasses. He was wearing the prototypical expressionless face of a Bolshevik.

Spitz had warned Colchin that Tcheka was believed to be an RSB agent, but after three thorough searches, they had found nothing in the CIA or NI files to confirm that fact.

Finally, Zhelannov's launch sputtered into position near the *Codicile*'s port side boarding ramp. As Colchin watched, he felt Lattimer Spitz move in beside him again. Spitz was reciting the last minute protocol and leaned closer to the President.

"The *Codicile*'s crew will assist Mr. Zhelannov's party aboard, sir. Then they will retire to their quarters for the duration of the session. I have instructed them to board President Zhelannov first, then Marshal Zhukov and finally Mr. Tcheka. You will step forward and greet the President the moment he steps on deck."

Colchin nodded. Everyone was aware that the new President was a great deal more comfortable with affairs of this nature than he was the pomp and ceremony of official state ceremonies. Even his wife had criticized him for his Texas approach to politics.

"It worked for LBJ," he liked to remind her.

As Zhelannov stood up and started for the ramp, Spitz continued to vie for the President's ear. "All of the recording devices in the stateroom where the meeting is being held have been situated so that they can pick up any conversation located anywhere in the room. The recorders are all voice activated."

"Did Bogner check . . . ?"

Spitz nodded. "Captain Network informed me that Commander Bogner went over the *Codicile* from stem to stern, Mr. President. He indicated that he was satisfied."

Colchin smiled. He knew bringing up Bogner's name would irritate Spitz. By the same token, Colchin knew that Bogner wasn't completely satisfied. Toby Bogner was the eternal pessimist when it came to security, no matter how extensive the precautions.

Spitz's voice droned on. "Each voice monitor carries a backup in the event of a malfunction in the primary unit. By the time the launch takes us back to the *Black River*, the computer will have converted the digitized voice impressions to hard copy."

"Are we certain no one else will be able to pick up the transmissions?" Colchin asked.

Spitz smiled. "Yes, Mr. President. We're transmitting back to the *Black River* in cluster bursts of sporadic five word parcels on random alternating frequencies."

Colchin realized now that the reason for Spitz's uneven smile was that the communications arrangements had been his baby; in effect, the way Spitz viewed things, it put him one up on Bogner. At the same time Colchin was aware that Zhelannov probably had his own method of capturing a verbatim record of the night's conversations.

That thought brought a smile to the President's face. During one of their previous meetings, Colchin had considered showing his counterpart the clandestine recording devices and asking the Commonwealth President to compare it to his own systems, a gesture he knew would have driven Spitz into a cold sweat.

"In addition," Spitz went on, "there are passive sensing devices on the platform, along the corridor and at the entrance to the main lounge where the meeting will be held."

"Sergei wears a prosthesis below the knee on his left leg; it won't embarrass him, will it?"

"No alarms, sir. The sensor processes a digital image on monitors in the H Center on the *Black River*. The SO will advise us if anything looks out of the ordinary."

As Zhelannov started up the ramp, Bob Hurley went forward to the *Codicile*'s bridge to notify the Security Officer aboard the *Black River* that the Zhelannov party had officially boarded. The SO had been instructed in turn to relay the word to Stone's CG units who were under orders to freeze all traffic inside the harbor for the duration.

By the time Hurley returned to the stateroom, the introductions had been completed and the crew of the *Codicile* had retired to their quarters.

Zhelannov was conducting a robust description of his flight earlier in the day and punctuated his oratory with gestures and loud laughter. Zhukov, on the other hand, was his antithesis, stiff and formal, forcing a smile. According to Spitz, he was uncomfortable in the company of the Americans. Tcheka, still sober-faced, remained in the background.

Colchin moved to the bar and began fixing drinks.

"I have been looking forward to one of your famous Texas martinis, David," Zhelannov said laughing.

"That's a Washington drink, Sergei. Down where I come from, we drink bourbon—straight. Come on down to the ranch and try it sometime. Believe me, it tastes a whole lot better than this gin shit."

Spitz winced, and Hurley forced his own version of a smile. Colchin raised his glass.

"Gentlemen, here's to progress—and getting rid of the chill in the air."

Datum: 10:5 . . . The Swath Yacht Cuboc, *2031NLT*

Ilya Vasilevich turned to his comrade. "Are you ready, Vsevolod?"

His sunburned companion nodded, but Ilya detected nervousness in the man's demeanor. It was to be expected; he knew how Vsevolod felt. A training mission was one thing, but a real mission spawned gnawing anxieties.

Embarrassed, Vsevolod reached out, embraced Olga and quickly lowered himself through the escape hatch in the flooring of the *Cuboc's* stateroom. Ilya waited while his comrade opened the exterior hatch on the conn tower of the Mala and began easing himself into the second seat.

Then it was his turn. He reached out and pulled Olga to him. She circled her arms around his thick neck.

"Am I allowed to say that I am frightened?" she asked.

Ilya held her close, kissing her on the eyes, the nose and finally the mouth. He could taste the saltiness of her tears. He would have lingered longer, but she pushed him away.

"Enough," she said. "You will be back soon enough."

Ilya knew there was nothing to say. He let go of her and began lowering himself through the opening in the hull. Then he motioned for her to seal the access plate behind him.

"When we return, you will hear the mechanism engage. When the system is locked into place, the red light on the control panel on the bridge will begin blinking. Make sure there are no prying eyes before you come below to open the hull hatch."

Olga nodded. Her eyes were closed. He knew she was listening, but he also knew she was praying.

Ilya lowered himself past the grid guard, through the conn access into the forward cockpit and began sorting through his pre-dive check list. He could see Vsevolod's anxious eyes in the rearview mirror he had rigged over his console.

"Ready, Comrade?"

Vsevolod nodded. The gesture was too vigorous, and like his eyes, betrayed him.

"Indicate on or ready," Ilya ordered. The tone of his voice had changed. "Battery bank one on, primary and secondary on standby, fore ballast purge, aft ballast purge, fore trim, aft trim, flood valves closed, pressure air open, vent riser closed, all compression seals engaged."

He knew the sequence by heart.

As he went through each item on the pre-dive check list he made eye contact with Vsevolod for confirmation.

Ilya began the second list by activating the small map light on the primary console. The illumination cast an eerie glow in the confines of the cluttered compartment. He began comparing the readings on the gauges with the values indicated on the chart. When he looked in the mirror again, he could see Vsevolod smiling, holding his thumb up. The smile was a lie. Anxiety had given away to fear.

"You will feel better when we get under way," Ilya assured him.

He reached up, gripped the D ring that served as the release lever, pulled down, turned off the com assist and felt the submarine lurch forward, disengaging itself.

There was the momentary sensation of an undulating downward drift as the air rushed out of the ballast tanks. A montage of red and green pinpoints of light began to flicker and dance in the maze of gauges on the panel in front of him.

He flipped the toggle switch and activated the fore bank of batteries.

He depressed the AP button on the F-X-L,

saw the green triangle appear on the scope and watched as the Mala's computers took over to trim the dive.

Datum: 10:5 . . . Apostle Point, Negril Beach, 2042NLT

Lucian Bouderau and Boris Andrakov stood in the middle of the misty beach, watching the fortunate turn in the weather. The mist had enveloped the harbor in a gray blanket.

They had been waiting over an hour.

While they waited, Bouderau had changed into his wet suit and unloaded the gear from the trunk of his aging Simca. The array of diving gear and a spare air tank was spread out on a rubber blanket in the sand in front of them.

"You are quite certain that no one knows we are here?" Andrakov asked.

Bouderau ignored the man's question and buckled the battery-powered propulsion pack onto his tanks. Then he slipped into his buoyancy jacket.

"How far would you estimate that Coast Guard cutter to be, *mon ami*?"

Andrakov squinted into the dampness. "I cannot tell," he admitted.

"And that is why you pay me the money you do—because I know these things. From where we stand to the opening in the reef and the location of the American Coast Guard unit is slightly more than a half of a kilometer. We cannot see them, and they, most assuredly, cannot see us. Besides, they are much more concerned with what they expect to come through that opening in the reef.

They guard against that which has already happened, right, *mon ami*?"

Andrakov, uncertain how to answer, stiffened. Instead he asked, "How long will it take you to repair my friend's craft?"

Bouderau chuckled. Even a Russian should not expect him to believe such a poorly constructed story.

The nervousness in Andrakov's voice became more apparent as the barrage of questions continued. "You are certain you have a way of getting to my friend's boat and repairing it without being discovered?"

"I find it curious that that is important to you, *mon ami*." Bouderau laughed.

He could no longer assess the man's expressions because of the darkness. The Russian was now little more than a faceless obligee to whom the Frenchman owed a performance in return for the money.

"I have explored these waters many times, my Russian friend. No more than twenty feet from the shoreline is a rapid fall away, dropping perhaps thirty meters before it levels off again. From that depth I can make my way to the reef. Then, by staying close to the reef, I can avoid the American detection devices. Their vertical sonar will isolate me, but they will think I am just another large fish night feeding on the reef."

"But surely the size of the signal you project on their screen will arouse suspicion."

Bouderau laughed again. "Your concern is curious. I thought it was your friend that you did not want to know. Your thoughtful gesture for your friend is of no concern to the Americans." He continued to play games with Andrakov. "The signal will arouse no suspicions. The Americans are well-aware of the size of the sharks that feed along this reef."

"Sharks?" Andrakov repeated.

"Very large sharks, six gillers. Many of them are uncataloged by even the most prestigious maritime universities. They are known to frequent the place known as the Jehovah Hole in large numbers."

"The graveyard of ships," the Russian acknowledged. "I did not know whether this so-called Jehovah Hole actually existed or whether it was a figment of native superstition."

Bouderau's voice sobered. "It exists, *mon ami*. It exists."

Andrakov watched as Bouderau finished putting on his gear, tested his tanks and started for the water. At the water's edge he paused, pulled his mask into place and within seconds disappeared beneath the surface.

A nervous Andrakov stood there for several minutes and then began mentally composing the report that he would send back to Osipov.

Datum: 10:5 . . . Negril Wharf, 2047NLT

Bogner and Koorsen had taken up their watch in a small wooden shanty at the end of the Negril wharf. The dilapidated old structure had once served as the harbor master's office.

A bank of electronic surveillance and monitoring gear from the *Black River* had been installed, and they could audit all security communications between the *Black River* and the *Codicile* as well as between the mother ship and the four Coast Guard units.

Koorsen, his binoculars scanning the wall of mist stretching over the harbor, stood outside the shanty while Bogner stayed inside, standing sentinel over the array of instrumentation.

Chilled by the clammy fog, Koorsen leaned against the doorframe and rubbed his hands together. "And to think I use to envy guys like you who came to these tropical paradises for your vacation."

Bogner looked up from his bank of instruments. "Don't lay that deprived black kid from the ghetto routine on me, Koorsen. Five will get you ten that you've never even been inside a ghetto."

Koorsen grinned and turned his attention back to the harbor.

"It's getting worse, Commander. Forty minutes ago I could pinpoint the bridge on Sparrow's tub. Now the only thing I can see is a couple of lights on the stern."

"Yacht," Bogner corrected. "Anything that costs twelve million bucks is a yacht, not a tub."

"All the same, if it wasn't for those two running lights on the stern, I would have lost it altogether." He put the glasses down and looked at Bogner. "Are you picking up anything?"

"The security signal is strong. No dialogue. About every thirty seconds or so they are transmitting a digitized cluster back to the COM-CON on the *Black River*. The computer is alternating frequencies, and they are using a burst code."

"What about the Coast Guard patrol units?"

"No activity at the moment. Stone has one unit at the south end of the reef and another up at the north end near Apostle Point. The third unit has the beach secured. Stone's command vessel is situated about four hundred yards off the bow of the *Codicile* between the mouth of the harbor and the *Black River*."

"What about our Russian friends?"

"One of them must be wired," Bogner acknowledged. "It's either a recording device or a transmitter. I'm not picking up anything specific, but I'm getting some background clutter that would indicate some other kind of signal is leaving Sparrow's yacht."

"If we knew where Zhelannov and his entourage were being put up between sessions, we could probably trace it," Koorsen speculated.

"They're working on it. One of the Charley-C's out of Guantanamo claims he trailed a Hormone B in from the Kiev sitting over their downed sub. The Charley kept his distance, but he was able to determine that the Hormone slipped in through the back door and met an unscheduled Aeroflot flight at Montego Bay. We've since been able to confirm that Zhelannov was on that flight, traveling incognito."

Koorsen leaned up against the plotting table with his arms folded. "Then it's reasonable to assume that Zhelannov is staying aboard the Kiev. But that still doesn't explain why that Kiev hasn't responded to the downed sub."

"It's like any Russian puzzle. If you pick at it long enough, it still may not be logical, but you'll finally begin to see how the pieces fit together."

Koorsen sighed, hunched his shoulders against the dampness and scanned the harbor again. "It's still getting thicker out there."

Bogner nodded. "Yeah, and I don't like it. If there really is someone out there with plans to knock off Zhelannov, this weather has to be to their liking."

PART TWO

BASE HOUR
FOUR–SEVEN
2200 NEGRIL LOCAL 10:5
0700 MOSCOW LOCAL 10:6
0100 GREENWICH (Z) 10:6

Base Hour
Four-Seven:
ZERO ZERO . . . 0100ZULU

Datum: 10:5 . . . The Yacht Codicile I, *2244NLT*

Zhukov's dispassionate eyes moved from face to face as he assessed the situation. For the past 30 minutes or so, both Zhelannov and their American host had been showing signs of growing weary with the proceedings. Both men were in their late sixties, he reminded himself; it was to be expected.

He was convinced that the discussions, for this session at least, were about to be concluded. Zhelannov's eyes had grown heavy, and Zhukov had twice caught the man the Party viewed as an inept compromise between Gorbachev and Yeltsin glancing at his watch.

Zhukov excused himself as he had done twice earlier in the evening on the pretense of having a cigarette, but in reality he was making another check of the layout of the American yacht.

So far at least, there had been few surprises;

the illegal's sketch of the schematic obtained from the Baglietto factory's files had been surprisingly detailed and accurate. Now, after this third excursion, he was confident his mission would be successful.

For Zhukov, the time had come.

On the aft deck he lit a cigarette and studied his surroundings. The curtain of undulating mist had reduced the visibility until the harbor was now completely obscured. He could see only the vaguest indication of the well-lit Negril wharf and, beyond that, only an occasional muted light.

There was the mournful sound of a buoy in the distance and the infrequent protest of a disturbed gull. He checked the compass on his watch. The American cruiser was directly off the bow, but its precise location was concealed by the weather. He would have to estimate.

He walked slowly around the entire deck, measuring distances and again carefully making note of the location of the crew quarters to the bridge and the proximity of the engine access area to the lounge where the meeting was taking place. From the crew quarters he heard the occasional sound of laughter and intermittent profanity. From the sound of their sporadic conversation he decided they were playing cards. Satisfied, he put out his cigarette and returned to the meeting.

Colchin was leaning back in his chair, his hands on the table. "You're a better man than I am, Sergei. I'm bushed."

Zhelannov laughed. "Bushed? You make joke. I see no resemblance between you and your predecessor."

"Bushed—talked out," Colchin clarified. "Down

where I come from they say, 'I feel like I've been rode hard and put up wet.'"

Zhelannov's eyebrows arched in a question mark.

"Just another way of saying *bitoostalim*," Colchin replied. He enunciated the word carefully.

Zhelannov laughed and slapped the table. "You are learning, David," he said, as he stood. "The arrangements for tomorrow's session are complete, *da*?"

Spitz leaned across the conference table toward the sober-faced Tcheka. "Please inform your President that we will reconvene tomorrow at fourteen hundred hours, Negril time."

Tcheka nodded. He was the antithesis of Spitz. During the course of the evening he had spoken only to his President and then only in hushed whispers. He jotted down the meeting time and handed it to Zhelannov.

"The same protocol will prevail," Spitz continued. "President Colchin's launch will arrive ten minutes before President Zhelannov's."

Again Tcheka nodded. As always, he avoided making eye contact with anyone at the conference table.

"Okay, Lattimere," Colchin said, "let's wrap it up. What's the procedure for departure?"

Spitz stood up. "I took the liberty of turning on the bow running lights about thirty minutes ago, gentlemen. The light is intense enough even in this weather for the launch crews to spot it. The first launch will take President Colchin back to the *Black River* and the harbor launch will pick up President Zhelannov to return him to the beach area."

"I trust the beach area is secured?" Zhukov questioned. There was an overtone of distrust in his voice.

"We have one of our Coast Guard units on the beach, Marshal." Spitz's response was equally icy.

Colchin was on his feet, walking around the conference table and shaking hands with the Russian delegation, when he turned to Spitz.

"I think it's time we invited Captain Network up so that Sergei and I can thank him for his hospitality, Lattimere."

While Spitz summoned the *Codicile*'s captain over the ship's intercom, Colchin led the Russian delegation out on deck and took Zhelannov to one side. Spitz could overhear him.

"You know, Sergei, if it wasn't for this protocol nonsense and patriotic paranoia on the part of both of our countries, you and I could probably get something accomplished. We'd do it the way we work things out down in Texas—pour ourselves a couple of stiff bourbons, set down across the table from each other and hammer away at these issues until we were making some progress."

Zhelannov threw his head back and laughed until he began to cough. Tcheka came to his aid.

Network arrived just in time to shake hands with Colchin and assist the President's entourage into the first launch.

Zhukov meanwhile positioned himself near the stern and casually searched the surface of the water for evidence of the Mala. He remembered Osipov's warning: "It will be difficult to tell if the Mala is in position even on a clear night." Now, with the heavy curtain of mist, Zhukov realized it would be all but impossible. He would have to trust the plan.

In the background he could hear Colchin's launch begin to idle away from the yacht, and while Zhelannov occupied himself exchanging gifts with the captain of the *Codicile*, Zhukov gave the signal. He lit a cigarette, removed a small straight pin hidden under his tunic lapel, inserted it in the small hole in the shield of his butane lighter and dropped it overboard.

From that moment, the timing became critical. He had exactly ten minutes before Vasilevich was scheduled to surface the Mala and take him aboard. At the same time he was aware that Osipov had instructed the former submarine commandant to wait on the surface no more than ten minutes before submerging again.

Zhukov reached down in the shank of his boot and pulled out the 45 caliber American automatic. From his other boot he produced the over-sized Russian silencer—a blunt, black, oblong-shaped object ringed with gas vents. He attached it, slipped it inside the front of his tunic and headed back to the lounge.

Zhelannov was still exchanging pleasantries with the captain of the *Codicile*. Finally Zhelannov turned to him.

"It has been an excellent evening, Marshal Zhukov. We have accomplished a great deal. Now, while Comrade Tcheka and I gather our papers, please escort Captain Network to the crew quarters and thank the gentlemen for their most gracious hospitality."

"Of course." Zhukov nodded and followed Network out of the meeting room. As the two men began their descent to the lower level, the Russian officer began to explain in belabored English that President Zhelannov had a small token of appreciation for each member of the crew.

At the door of the crew quarters, Zhukov slipped the automatic out of his tunic and whispered the captain's name.

Network turned just in time to feel Zhukov burrow the steel muzzle in the fleshy area just under his chin.

There was a sudden *phuut* sound and Network's head exploded.

The captain's body catapulted backward amidst a shower of fragmented bone and tissue.

From there, Zhukov stepped calmly into the crew quarters and squeezed off three more rounds. Two men died in their bunks, their faces still filled with surprise. A third was just coming out of the crew head. He was wearing only his underwear and Zhukov's shot blew away his face. His body flew backward, twitching and convulsing.

Zhukov felt nothing but the exhilaration of having completed the initial phase of his mission with unmitigated efficiency. He glanced at his watch. It had taken him less than 90 seconds to complete this phase of the operation and assess its outcome. The crew quarters of the *Codicile* had been transformed into a scene of carnage. For Zhukov, it was a moment of triumph. He removed the half-spent clip and inserted a full one. There was more to be accomplished.

He stepped carefully around the bodies of his victims into the tiny crew quarters and looked in the mirror. He straightened the collar of his tunic, smoothed his hair, tucked the American automatic back in the breast of his tunic and started topside.

As he stepped into the damp night air, he heard Zhelannov's launch approaching. He went to the railing and looked down. Along with the two Soviet airmen from the Hormone that had met their flight in Montego Bay, he saw a Jamaican harbor pilot. The launch had not yet tied up to the *Codicile*.

Zhukov checked his timing. So far he had used only four of his ten minutes. Then he checked to see if Zhelannov was still in the lounge. He was still there, arranging papers in his bulky leather valise. Josef Tcheka was standing in the narrow corridor between the head and the stateroom, putting on his raincoat.

Zhukov stepped out on the grid platform and motioned for the two airman to come aboard. "Come up," he said impatiently. "You will have to assist the President down these steps."

As the two men scampered up the ramp, Zhukov's hand darted inside his tunic to search out the automatic. Tcheka saw the Marshal's hand emerge with the automatic, and his normally expressionless face registered shock.

"Into the wardroom," Zhukov ordered, "all of you." He thrust the weapon at a retreating Tcheka. As they backed into the wardroom, Zhukov turned off the lights. Now the only illumination in the room was coming from the small fog-shrouded lamps on the aft deck and the refraction of the red and green mooring lights on the stern.

Zhelannov, his face contorted into a mask of

confusion and half-realization, stepped forward to protest.

"What is this all—"

Zhukov waited until his President was less than five feet from him before he fired. Zhelannov's body was rocketed backward by the impact of the bullet.

Even though he was unable to assess the damage in the surreal half-light, Zhukov felt a rush.

Zhelannov's face was transfixed in an expression of stunned disbelief. His briefcase tumbled to the floor, and his hands clutched vainly in an attempt to close the gaping hole in his stomach.

He managed one step back toward his assailant then pitched forward, blood spewing from his stomach.

Zhukov turned calmly toward the two young airmen who were frozen in fear. He studied them for a moment, looking into their eyes. "Some things are necessary," he said.

He fired twice. Neither man uttered a whimper as their violated bodies crashed to the floor.

Now, only Tcheka remained.

The owlish little man was cowering in terror. Somehow his glasses had been broken, and Zhukov wondered if Tcheka could even see his assailant well-enough to read the determination in his eyes.

"I have saved you for last, Josef," Zhukov hissed, "because you are even worse than Zhelannov. You are a puppet traitor. You relinquished your place in the Party to support this madman who whores our country. Now you know what is happening. You are witness to this event, former comrade. The Party will emerge from the ashes of what you called the Commonwealth."

Tcheka fell to his knees, his hands folded in front of him, tears etching their way into his gaunt face.

"Comrade . . ." he whimpered.

Zhukov raised the automatic and fired. He was less than three feet from his target.

Tcheka's face detonated in a paroxysm of destruction. The homely little man in the plain blue suit, his violated body concealed by a blood-drenched overcoat, rocketed backward, falling amid the bodies of his countrymen.

Zhukov paused just long enough to check his watch again; seven minutes and seventeen seconds had now passed.

He walked to the grid on the ramp, leaned over and called out to the Jamaican harbor pilot. The old man looked up, and Zhukov fired. The lifeless body tumbled backward into the oil-stained hull of his launch.

Two minutes left.

Zhukov walked to the stern and looked for the Mala. It had surfaced less than 20 yards from the *Codicile*. Vsevolod was standing on the deck in the darkness holding the tow line.

"Come here," Zhukov hissed. "There has been an exchange of gunfire. I have been hit. I need help."

Vsevolod hesitated. Ilya had cautioned him that they had a ten minute window, no more. From the outset they had reasoned that the sophisticated American surveillance gear would pick up the sound of the water being purged from the ballast tanks when they surfaced.

"Swim to me," Zhukov demanded. He said it as

loud as he dared, aware of how sound travels on the water. It was an order.

Vsevolod slipped into the water and within moments was at the platform on the stern of the *Codicile*. As he emerged from the water he was already asking questions.

"Where were you hit, Comrade? Can you make it back to the Mala?"

Zhukov brought the automatic up out of the darkness, crushing it against the young Russian's skull. Vsevolod staggered and slumped forward on the deck.

Zhukov wasted little time. He unbuttoned his tunic, took it off and put it on Vsevolod. Then he took off his boots and put them on the young submariner as well. As a final measure, he buried the muzzle of the silencer against the soft underside of Vsevolod's face and pulled the trigger. He fired a second shot through the side of the head destroying what was left of the jaw. Even the most judicious comparing of dental records would yield nothing now. The uniform, if it survived the fire, would be the only thing the Americans had to go on.

He checked his watch again. There were now less than 45 seconds to complete his mission. Barefooted, he threaded his way back into the stateroom and retrieved his attaché case. Inside, concealed under a sheath of papers, was the carefully wrapped packet of plastic explosives. Next to it was an electronic detonator no larger than a kopek. He unwrapped it, activated the miniature transmitter and adjusted the band to the narrow control frequency. Then he pulled the small disc from between the two charge layers. From that point on, only the steady interference generated by the frequency would keep the charge from detonating.

Zhukov shoved Tcheka's body to one side, pushed open the door to the wardroom head and placed the charge near the base of the small gas-fired water heater. Then he took out his knife and punched a series of pinpoint holes in the gas line. Instantly he could smell the pungent odor of gas.

The build-up of fumes in the tiny compartment would only add to the force of the blast. He closed the door, thereby trapping the fumes and increasing the intensity of the explosion.

Another check of the watch showed he was now a full 41 seconds behind schedule. He went to the porthole to see if he could still see the Mala. Instead he heard the distant sound of one of the American Coast Guard cutters. He reasoned that the American President had probably already arrived back at the cruiser and now the cutter was returning to escort Zhelannov's launch to shore.

He fumbled his way back through the darkened stateroom, placed his open briefcase on the table, gave the ghostly scene of devastation one final cursory check and went out on the aft deck. From there he lowered himself over the transom, holding the plastic-wrapped transmitter between his teeth, and making certain his head was sufficiently above the surface of the water, he began dog-paddling his way toward the Mala.

As he crawled up onto the deck of the submarine, he heard the American cutter coming closer. He shimmied his way through the hatch and dropped into the second seat. "It is done."

"Where is Lavrov?" Ilya demanded.

"He is dead," Zhukov said evenly. "The operation is in shambles, but our mission is accomplished."

Ilya Vasilevich did not question the senior officer. He reached up and manually began to rotate the hatch seal. Then he scanned the Mala's control panel and opened the valves to the ballast tanks. The small red light over his console began blinking.

"Secured?" he asked. He could see Zhukov's penetrating eyes in the mirror adjacent to the warning light.

"Secured," Zhukov repeated.

"We are now in a dive configuration," Ilya said flatly.

Zhukov closed his eyes and looked up at the Mala's chronometer. He was counting. In two minutes he would interrupt the frequency on the detonation device.

Base Hour
Four-Six:
ZERO ZERO . . . 0200ZULU

Datum: 10:5 . . . The Negril Wharf, 2329NLT

"Commander!" There was an urgency in Koorsen's voice.

Bogner, who had been out on the pier, stepped into the shed.

"I think you better give this a listen," Koorsen said. "I'm getting something."

Bogner blinked his eyes. "Listen to what?"

"Don't know what it is, but we're picking up something. The CG units are picking it up, too. I can hear them going back and forth. They've been trying to isolate it."

Bogner took the headset, held one of the receivers to his ear and looked out the window. "Damn," he muttered, "look at that fog."

Koorsen nodded. "I have been looking at it. I've been checking it every ten minutes for the last hour or so. The maritime frequency says this soup has most of the western third of the island socked in."

Bogner continued to search the wall of grayness until he found the muted pinpoints of the mooring lights on the *Codicile*.

"When did they turn the lights off in the wardroom?"

"Just a couple of minutes ago. The navy launch has already picked up the President's entourage." Koorsen looked up at the clock. "Seven minutes ago, to be exact. I'm monitoring the exchange between the launch and the *Black River* now. They expect to bring the President aboard in three minutes."

"Then Zhelannov hasn't left the *Codicile* yet?"

"No, but he must be about ready to leave. The harbor launch that's picking him up has been tied alongside for at least ten minutes now."

Bogner assessed the pall in front of him. "Then this noise you're picking up is the first sign of anything out of the ordinary?"

Koorsen nodded. "It's a pulsing sound. It was faint at first, then seemed to get a little louder and a little closer to the *Codicile*. CG-144 was picking it up, too, and they investigated. The signal faded, and the Commander reported back to Stone that they couldn't confirm anything."

"Maybe we're picking up some kind of shadow effect from the harbor launch?" Bogner speculated.

"I don't think so, Commander. We've got that isolated. You can't see your hand in front of your face out there, but you can see it here on the HSD. It shows up as an elliptical pattern on the scope. Probably an old Johnson or a Mercury. That's a pretty good indication it's a two cycle. The other signal was somewhat elongated. It reappeared for awhile then became very faint again. CG-144 thinks it might be the cable on the buoy off the stern of the *Codicile*, but all of a sudden it appears to be moving again—away from the *Codicile*."

"Anyone else picking it up?" Bogner asked.

"CG-217 thought they had something, but they lost it in that maze of transit craft moored over by the reef."

"Did they check it out ?"

Koorsen nodded. "They took a swing through there, but couldn't find anything, except that *Broward* is battened down for the night. Apparently there's a party aboard the *Broward*."

"I'm glad somebody is having fun," Toby muttered, rubbing his hands together. He turned up the volume and scanned for the signal. There was nothing on the scope. He had decided to tell Koorsen that they would give Zhelannov's launch another minute or two and then would tell the two CG units to go in.

Before he could however, the pervading silence was shattered by the sound of an explosion, followed immediately by a second one.

The second was bigger than the first. A brilliant flash of silver-white light ripped a hole in the smothering mist and the night was illuminated by a searing, churning ball of blue-orange flame. It spiraled up into the night, trailing fire and debris behind it.

The window in the old harbor master's shed exploded. The walls buckled, and the room was splattered with razor-sharp splinters of glass.

Bogner was knocked to the floor, and the HSD

unit toppled over on top of him, landing on his chest. The air was knocked out of him. Koorsen was propelled backward, slamming into the wall, his face peppered with tiny shards of glass.

Datum: 10:5 . . . Le Chamanade, 2334NLT

Bouderau, his assignment for Andrakov completed, had repacked his gear and left the Russian standing on the shore at Apostle Point. Now he languished across the bed watching Mulveea undress.

The slender Jamaican woman pulled the dress over her head and placed it carefully on the bed.

Lucian Bouderau delighted in the fact that she never wore any undergarments, and now he studied her tantalizing figure silhouetted by the fog-smothered security lights from the beach.

She was little more than an inviting gossamer shadow, swaying suggestively to the familiar strains of *Inside Moves*, an old Grover Washington tape Bouderau always played when he made love.

Just as Mulveea pulled the covers back and started to get into bed, the room was rocked by an explosion. The glass doors leading to the balcony overlooking the beach shuddered, and the interior of the room was momentarily bathed with an eerie yellow luminosity.

Bouderau leaped from the bed and bolted to the window. In the middle of the harbor, close to the place where the American yacht had been moored, he saw an angry tower of belching flame.

"What is it?" the woman screamed. Mulveea was still sitting in the middle of the bed with the sheet pulled up to conceal her nakedness. "What has happened?"

For the moment Bouderau was transfixed by the apparent calamity. The harbor in front of the wharf was on fire, and one of the American Coast Guard units was racing toward the devastation. The silhouette of the churning craft looked hopelessly insignificant and helpless against the backdrop of flames.

Mulveea crawled from the bed and went to the window. Terrified, she clung to Bouderau. He could feel her body tremble.

At that very moment, Lucian Bouderau began to piece together what up until now had been an oddly ill-assorted puzzle. His mind replayed Andrakov's unusual request. The task had been simple enough. He had surfaced under the hull of the Swath and pulled the spring from the engaging mechanism so that it hung loose, swinging freely in either direction. It would no longer lock into receiving position.

Bouderau had not deluded himself. He knew the Russians were up to something, but so what? How different was this from the drug king Parant's assignments to retrieve the jettisoned cargo from his *Broward*? A client was a client, he rationalized.

Still, as he watched the scene in the harbor, Andrakov's labored story about a diving friend dissolved into the reality of the situation.

"What is happening?" Mulveea shuddered. Her voice was thin, and she continued to shake.

"They are playing games," Bouderau said drily. "Our American and Russian friends are playing very foolish games."

"Must you go down there?" she asked.

Bouderau began to smile as he looked at the clock. "Not tonight. Tonight I have saved for you."

"Are you not concerned about what is happening?" The question was a lover's ploy, and Bouderau understood that.

The Frenchman folded Mulveea in his arms and pressed her body to him. "I see no reason to investigate," he said. "The dawn will reveal what has happened. A few hours will not change things."

He could hear the sirens in the background. He took her hand and drew her toward the bed. A pleased Mulveea giggled girlishly and allowed him to entice her down.

Lucian cupped her breast in his hand and kissed it. "Exquisite," he sighed, "how very exquisite."

The intense orange light of only a few minutes earlier had softened and now did little more than bathe the room in a muted yellow.

Bouderau kissed her and pressed himself down on her until she yielded. Her low, throaty moan pleased Lucian Bouderau, but he was not thinking about her. He was thinking about Andrakov.

Datum: 10:5 . . . The Swath Yacht Cuboc, *2337NLT*

Olga Vasilivich was standing on the misty deck of the *Cuboc* when she saw the explosion. She had been staring into the darkness, knowing only too well where the *Codicile* was anchored.

What she saw was an orange, terrifying, consuming ball of flame erupt into the overhanging darkness. What she heard was the deafening, sickening sound of a ship dying.

It lasted no more than a few seconds, and then all that remained was a wall of horrifying brilliant light reaching up from the ravaged harbor.

She shuddered, and an icy feeling of hopelessness engulfed her. Ilya had said nothing about an explosion. He would have told her. Something had gone wrong. She waited several minutes, listening to the wail of sirens, then walked to the stern of the craft to wait for the wake of the *Mala's* periscope as it maneuvered into docking position under the *Cuboc's* twin hulls. As she did, two American Coast Guard cutters darted back and forth among the transit vessels anchored along the reef, their probing searchlights slicing the fog like surgeon's scalpels.

She had followed Ilya's advice to the letter and put a housecoat on over her sweater to make it look like she had come up on deck to see what had happened. The cutter's searchlights skimmed along the hull of the *Cuboc* and disappeared into the darkness.

She could see lights erupting now on the other vessels near the mooring area along the reef.

Olga's eyes searched the surface of the murky water for the *Mala's* periscope until she spotted it some 50 meters off of the stern. It was headed straight at the *Cuboc* at engaging speed.

She waited, watching it slip in under the twin hulls, then felt the Swath shudder and the sound of the *Mala's* corrugated exterior as it engaged the hulls of the *Cuboc*.

But there was no capture, no locking of the retrieving device, and she raced to the port side to see the *Mala's* conn emerge at the bow and begin to maneuver for a second pass.

Again at the stern she watched the second attempt. The result was the same. As she fell to her knees, she heard the sound of the Coast Guard boats approaching again.

Datum: 10:5 . . . Aboard the Mala, 2338NLT

Ilya was positioned for his first approach. The Mala was located 100 meters behind and ten meters below the *Cuboc's* twin hulls. The submarine's computers had aligned him perfectly. He wiped a small amount of condensation off the cluster of instruments on the console and increased the volume on his receiver.

"What is the delay?" Zhukov demanded.

Ilya Vasilivich reminded Zhukov to keep his voice at a whisper. "The American Coast Guard units are all around us. They are monitoring everything. Currently they are right above us. They appear to be checking all the transit units along the reef."

"Have they given any indication of what has happened?" Zhukov demanded.

Ilya shook his head. "They have said nothing to indicate that they have any idea of what is happening at the moment. Judging by their transmissions, they are alarmed. They are assessing all possibilities. Anything that moves is being checked. There is obviously a great deal of confusion on their part."

As he reported, Ilya studied Zhukov in the mirror over the console. The Marshal was a coarse man with a wide, oval-shaped head with close eyes. They were the color of the spent sea when it hurls itself upon the beach. His ears were large and pinned too tightly to his head. The jowls were lardy, and the mouth was creased in stubborn determination. A few sparse strands of gray and white over his ears were all that he had to show for hair.

Zhukov's face was a montage of obstinacy and independence, Ilya decided. He was not yet ready to admit to himself what he felt about the man.

There was a change in the level of sound from above, and Ilya looked up.

"Are they moving away?" Zhukov asked. This time he kept his voice low, but it was flat, toneless and unemotional.

Ilya shook his head. Finally he asked. "How did Vsevolod die?"

At first it did not appear that Zhukov would answer him. His empty eyes were fixed on the electronic displays laid out in front of him. Finally he said, "I shot him."

The trenchantness of the response sent a chill through Ilya.

"Was that part of the plan?" Vasilvich asked. He kept his voice under control despite his anger.

Zhukov leveled his glare until their eyes locked in the mirror. "It was never part of Denisov's plan, Commandant, but it has always been part of my plan. It is simply one less person to worry about in the event our plan goes awry. Besides, Comrade Vsevolod has made his contribution. He has done all he can do for the Party. Would you not agree?"

Ilya continued to look at the Marshal without speaking.

"I asked you a question, Comrade," Zhukov said. "Do you agree?"

Although he suspected that this would be the case from the outset, Ilya had said nothing to Olga. For him it was enough that she knew this was a mission conducted by GRU operatives. Olga knew all about the GRU.

He closed his eyes and attempted to ignore the constriction in his throat. Loss of personnel was to be expected. Still, this was different. This was Vasevolod. There was no justification. For the first time Ilya felt anger at the cold staring man sitting in the Mala's second seat.

They sat in silence for several minutes with only the distant propeller sounds of the Coast Guard units to violate the stillness. For Ilya it was the music of an always familiar world of eerie, distant and nonconventional sounds—the hull of the Mala creaking and groaning, the ping of radar, the rhythmic sound of his own breathing.

The sense of being in an alien world only served to alarm Zhukov.

"They are going away," Ilya said. "The noise of their propellers grows fainter." With that news Zhukov straightened up in his seat.

Vasilivich waited, then pressed the purge button indicator on the aft ballast tank. The electric pumps engaged, and he could feel the Mala's stern begin to rise slowly, the hull mildly protesting the subtle change in pressure. Then he released the safety on the FBT, and the sound of the bow pumps hissed, bringing up the bow.

Zhukov stared stoically at his instrument panel. Ilya could see tiny beads of sweat clustered on the bridge of the Marshal's nose.

"What is your procedure, Comrade?" Zhukov asked.

"I will take us up to observation depth first," Ilya replied. His hands were already busy tweaking information from the displays at his fingertips.

Zhukov watched as the electrically driven periscope was elevated and Vasilivich plotted new values to adjust both the azimuth and vernier scales. Then he leaned forward putting his eye to the Obs Sant. The lens mechanism and the mast-mounted television camera were both driven by a light sensitive computer, and the cylinder rotated in a 360 degree sweep. The camera went to the light source, and Ilya inspected the entire horizon in sweeps from the CFP.

Zhukov studied the scene on the monitor in front of him. "What is going on?" he demanded, his voice no longer a controlled whisper.

"From the appearance of things, your mission was a success," Ilya evaluated. "The harbor is chaos, and there is no trace of the American yacht."

If Zhukov felt any elation, his expression did not reflect it. His lips moved stiffly, but his puffy face remained immobile.

The periscope came down, and Ilya urged the Mala forward. Zhukov felt the bow incline and then level. On the HSD in front of him, Vasilivich had the craft perfectly aligned. He felt the craft shudder, heard the harsh metallic sound of abrading steel and then felt the sub begin to settle again.

"What is wrong?" Zhukov demanded.

"The retrieval mechanism malfunctioned."

"Bring it around and try again," Zhukov ordered.

He watched the computers align the tiny submarine for a second pass, felt the sensation of being propelled forward and heard a repeat of the metallic sound. Again the submarine began to settle.

Zhukov's eyes asked the question.

"It is like threading a needle in the dark," Ilya explained. "We must engage the retrieval bolt for the hydraulic lift mechanism to be activated. Only that will lift the conn hatch above the surface."

"Can we not surface and swim to the *Cuboc*?" Zhukov asked. "Is it not feasible to surface, open the hatch and lock the ballast tanks in the open position as we escape?"

"It would be feasible if the surface were not swarming with American Coast Guard units," Ilya said. In the mirror he could see Zhukov sweating.

As the Mala's computers indicated that the vessel was in position for a third try, Ilya's sonar began picking up the signal of the patrol boat's propellers again. They were returning. He hit the flood port controls, and Zhukov heard the air being pumped from the tank. The red warning light began blinking again.

The Mala settled deeper.

Ilya dared not risk a full dive; the American sonar might pick him up.

"Have they discovered us?" Zhukov asked. His voice had become agitated, no longer a monotone.

"I do not think so," Ilya conceded, "but we cannot attempt another pass until they have abandoned their search."

"What will we do?" Zhukov demanded.

"We will sit on the bottom and wait," Ilya said calmly. "I have done it many times before."

He said nothing about the battery reserve indicator which was already showing a diminishing power source. The wait had been too long, and he had not anticipated the American's harassment on the surface.

If the Mala was forced to use her diesels, he knew the Americans would discover them in a matter of minutes.

Datum: 10:6 . . . Chesnakov Compound, 0841MLT

Viktor had lost track of time. What little sleep he had been able to get was fitful. He rolled over and looked at the clock.

Allowing for the time difference, the task in Negril was now accomplished. Until the news of what had actually happened in Negril broke to an unsuspecting world, there was nothing for him to do but wait.

In some respects he had stayed close to his original plan. His personal routine had been conducted exactly as planned. After dining with Parlenko he had returned to his auxiliary quarters in the barracks where it would be convenient for Slava to bring him the latest dispatches as soon as they arrived.

Viktor congratulated himself. It was going well. The world was waiting breathlessly for news on the downed Soviet submarine. By now, Ambassador Yerrov regretfully had informed the Americans that the downed sub was a robot nuclear unit and that his government had wanted to explore all possibilities for recovery before revealing the nature of their loss.

It was the perfect distraction.

The Americans, of course, would be outraged at the thought of a robot missile carrier, but at the same time they would understand why the new commonwealth government acted with such a lack of alacrity. No lives had been at stake. It would also explain the all too apparent consternation of the Commandant of the Kiev cruiser and why he took no action. Even at that, American outrage would be short-lived when it learned of the disaster that had befallen the Commonwealth President in Negril.

Viktor lit a cigarette and inhaled deeply. As his eyes swept the room, he took note of the time. All the better, he reasoned, for Slava to find him still sleeping, as though he expected nothing. If only he had been able to put thoughts of Ruta out of his mind, everything would be perfect. She—and she alone—kept him from savoring the moment.

He put out his cigarette and threw his legs over the edge of the bed to sit up. Just as did, there was a knock on the door.

"Enter, Slava," he said.

But it was not Slava. "Sorry to bother you, General," the young woman said. She was olive-skinned and attractive, proudly wearing the rank of corporal. She was carrying a dispatch envelope.

"Your name?" Viktor insisted.

"Corporal Achina Maslovaka, General."

"You are new?"

"I have recently been transferred from the Bureau of Strategic Affairs, General."

"Where is Slava?" Viktor demanded.

"I was sent to replace him, General. He was put on emergency leave last night; his mother is very ill."

Even though Viktor was sitting on his bed naked, the young woman made no pretense at averting her eyes.

Still suspicious, Viktor cocked his head to one

side. "What is your specialty?"

"Codes, General Denisov. I have been trained for three years as a crypto specialist."

Viktor leaned back, propping his back against the cinder block wall. "Ah, then I can assume you have already deciphered this dispatch from our naval intelligence sector?"

The young woman blushed. "Oh no, General. It is a four level dispatch. I am not authorized. The seal indicates it is for your eyes only."

Viktor studied the envelope for a moment and handed it back to the woman. "Let me see how good you are at your specialty, Corporal Achina Maslovaka. Demonstrate. Read it for me."

The perplexed woman took the envelope and opened it. "It is not a security four code, General. It is a conventional radio gram."

"Read it to me then," Viktor demanded.

"It is dated 0202Z this date. The transmission originated in sector three. It says simply, 'Project 72 continues on schedule. XXX Phase one complete. XXX. It is signed 12J'."

Viktor threw his head back and laughed. "Ah, you bring good news, Corporal Achina."

When she saw how pleased the news made him, she said, "I nearly forgot." She turned, went back to the door, stepped out into the hall, bent over and returned with a bouquet of roses in a crystal vase. "These were delivered early this morning. The OD knew that you had put in a long day and decided not to wake you."

Achina Maslovaka smiled and handed them to him.

Viktor opened the card which was signed by Ruta.

"The General has an admirer?" the woman asked.

Viktor nodded.

"What is the lucky woman's name, General?"

"Ruta," Viktor replied, "Ruta Putalin."

Achina Maslovoka's face erupted in a smile. "I know her. She was my instructor at the Institute. She is a lovely dancer, you know."

Viktor stared at the woman. "A dancer," he repeated. "Ah, yes, she studied at the Bolshoi for some years."

"Oh no, General, not the Bolshoi. With Officer Kerensky. I saw them dance many times."

"Officer Kerensky?" Viktor repeated, stunned. "You know this Kerensky?"

"Most certainly, General. Nikolai Kerensky was the chief of Secretary Gorbachev's internal security force."

Base Hour
Four-Two:
ZERO ZERO . . . 0300ZULU

Datum: 10:6 . . . Coast Guard Cutter Hensley, *0307NLT*

The *Hensley*, CG-217, was a 72 foot Coast Guard patrol craft under the command of Lt. Marion S. Nelson. In addition to its primary role as the Coast Guard command unit for Negril harbor security during the summit, it had been pressed into duty as the temporary command post of Lt. Commander Joseph Stone, Cameron's designee to head up the investigation of the *Codicile* explosion.

Stone, who was quartered aboard the *Black River* as Coast Guard liaison during the summit, now had a total of six units at his disposal—the *Hensley*, the *Red Fox*, CG-144, and the 4C2's *Rimfire* and *Benchley*, which had been stationed at opposite ends of the reef to deny harbor access. In addition, the *Black River* had deployed two high-speed inflatable dinghies to assist in the recovery effort.

At 0241 Negril time, nearly three hours after the blast, Stone was informed that the latest body recovered was that of a white male, age unknown, wearing the uniform of a Russian officer. That body, like the others, had been taken aboard the *Black River* and assigned morgue ticket 77A. Concurrent with that information, he was informed that the Jamaican authorities were demanding to talk to the OIC.

He ordered CG-217 taken to the Negril wharf where the Jamaican officials could board.

Colchin, meanwhile, had ordered Bogner to the *Hensley* less than ten minutes after learning of the explosion, and Koorsen was subsequently assigned to the *Rimfire* as part of the security contingent securing the beach area.

For Bogner, the President's orders were explicit. "Stay with Stone until he wraps up the first phase of the recovery effort, then report in." For that reason, Bogner was on deck when the harried two–man Jamaican delegation boarded the *Hensley* at 0310 local time.

The older of the two men introduced himself as Consul Avery Thomas from the government's Montego Bay Foreign Affairs Bureau. For Bogner, the man was an easy read; Thomas was white-haired, black-skinned and annoyed.

His colleague, somewhat younger, taller and taciturn, introduced himself as Deputy Consul Bernard Edwin. Both men spoke with clipped and decidedly British accents. From the moment the two men stepped on board, it was obvious there was going to be trouble.

"It's been a long night. May I get you gentlemen some coffee?" Nelson offered.

"This is not a social call, Lieutenant," Thomas bristled. The words came out in perfectly articulated but aggravated English. "I prefer to get right to the heart of the matter, and you can start by explaining why you did not contact the Jamaican authorities when you learned of the gravity of this situation."

Thomas' opening volley took Nelson by surprise, and the senior officer in the group, Stone, stepped forward. "I'm afraid we do owe you an apology, Consul Thomas, but the fact of the matter is that no one was very much concerned with bureaucratic protocol when that ship blew apart. We were all a hell of a lot more concerned with trying to determine if we had any survivors."

"We can appreciate your situation, Commander Stone," Thomas said icily. "But the fact remains that Mr. Edwin and I have been here for over an hour, and we are still unable to obtain anything but the most fragmented pieces of information about what occurred here. So far about the only thing that we have been able to verify is that there was an explosion, that it was aboard an American yacht and that it occurred sometime around midnight."

"What you've heard is correct," Stone acknowledged.

"We have also been told that a high ranking foreign diplomat was aboard the craft at the time of the explosion. Is that correct?"

Stone looked at Bogner then back at the Consul. He was becoming more agitated. "Your sources seem to know more than ours do, Consul Thomas. To the best of our knowledge, none of the victims have been identified."

Avery Thomas bristled. "Need I remind the Commander that this incident occurred on Jamaican territory and that you are here, sir, as the guests of the Jamaican government. Also, technically I have the jurisdictional prerogative to take control of this investigation and the legal right to demand that all information be handed over immediately." Thomas reached inside his coat pocket and produced a gold cigarette case. He opened it, extracted one and lit it. "Do I make myself clear, Commander?"

Bogner recognized what was happening and stepped between the two men.

"Consul Thomas, my name is Commander Bogner." He lowered his voice, took Thomas by the arm and steered the Jamaican official away from the group. "You'll have to excuse Commander Stone, sir. We've all been under the gun here for the last couple of hours. But I'm sure you can see that we have a rather delicate situation on our hands here." He pointed to the floating debris and oil where the *Codicile* had been moored only a few hours earlier. "The problem is that flotsam out there is all that's left of a yacht that belonged to a very close friend of the President of the United States. And we know for a fact that an important meeting was taking place there earlier this evening. Unfortunately, people at the level of Commander Stone and I are not privy to the kinds of information people like you and Mr. Edwin have. Now if you know for a fact that there was a foreign official aboard that yacht earlier this evening, we would like you to confirm it for us and then let us know how you came into possession of such information."

Thomas continued to glare. "We know, Commander, because we received a telephone call."

"If you want my help, Consul Thomas, you're going to have to be a little more specific. Who told you there was a foreign official on board that yacht?"

Thomas glared at Bogner. "To be specific, Commander, the caller said there had been an explosion aboard an American yacht in Negril Harbor. The caller also claimed that some very high ranking Russian diplomats were on board the craft at the time of that explosion."

Bogner took a step closer. "Now we're getting somewhere—but you still haven't answered my question, Consul. Who made that call, what time did he make it, and who is this Russian official suppose to be?"

Thomas cleared his throat. "Jamaica, Commander Bogner, is a tiny country. You must understand that we could find ourselves in an extremely delicate position if certain influential Russian officials were aboard an American yacht when it exploded in a Jamaican harbor. I feel certain that even the Americans would agree that we have all the ingredients here of a very unsavory international incident. If our information is correct, the Jamaican government could be found negligent— and the fact that we did not even know this meeting was taking place could be a source of extreme embarrassment to my government."

Bogner continued to lead Thomas down the deck, away from the others. "You look like a reasonable man, Consul, a man that understands the give and take at the negotiation table. So let's negotiate. You tell me who made that call, when you received it and what the caller said—and I'll see that you and your colleague are fully apprised of what happened here. Deal?"

Thomas eyed him before answering. "To be perfectly honest, Commander, I received the call shortly after retiring last evening."

"What time was that?"

Thomas rolled his eyes, "Around midnight. The caller did not give his name. His exact words were, 'There has been an explosion aboard an American yacht in Negril Harbor. At the time of the explosion, several high ranking Russian officials were on board.' Then he hung up."

"You're certain he used the words 'has been?'"

Thomas nodded. "Quite certain."

"No name?" Bogner persisted.

"No name," Thomas confirmed. "And frankly, Mr. Bogner, that is why I disregarded the call. However, when I received a call from the West Mathews Provincial police only thirty minutes later informing me of the explosion, I gave my taped record of that earlier conversation to Chief of Police Chastain in Montego Bay. He is attempting to follow up on it."

Bogner smiled. "You have the call on tape? Now we're getting somewhere. You asked me what I meant by a deal? Well, this is the deal. You give me your word that you'll let me know what you're able to uncover on your caller and I'll see that you get full disclosure on everything we have so far—plus anything we turn up later."

Thomas smiled and extended his hand. "We have a deal, Commander."

Bogner escorted the Jamaican back to where Stone and Nelson waited with Thomas' assistant.

He nodded to Stone. "I believe Consul Thomas and I have reached an understanding, Stony. So why don't you have Lieutenant Nelson give our friends an update."

Nelson glanced at his clipboard. "As near as we can determine, the blast occurred at 2341 local time. Our units CG-217 and CG-144 responded. They were the first on the scene. A harbor fire patrol boat arrived on the scene shortly after that. According to the log, the oil fire was extinguished at 0131 local time and the search for victims continued. We had recovered three bodies earlier, but since the patrol unit used a 4QA foam to kill the fire, we think the residue may still be hiding some of the victims."

"How many victims?" Thomas asked.

"Ten so far. No known survivors at this point.

"Were there any Russian officials among the victims?" Thomas pressed.

Nelson slipped the clipboard under his arm and looked at Stone.

Stone stepped forward again. "Excuse me, Consul, but have you ever worked a recovery mission such as this?"

Thomas shook his head.

"Because if you've ever had to pull a body out of the water after a shipboard fire and explosion, Consul, you'd damn well know there is no way to identify what you've got. They're covered with oil and they don't look much like people. They look like charred things—things that don't much look like anything you've ever seen before."

Both Thomas and his assistant stiffened. "Where did you take the bodies?" Thomas demanded.

"A temporary morgue has been established aboard our cruiser, the *Black River.*"

"Why did you not use the facilities here in Negril?" Thomas persisted. "If the victims were dead, they should have been sent to the local morgue. That is a point of international law."

"We didn't know what we had when we picked them up, and we thought it was possible that some of them might still be alive. The hospital facilities aboard the *Black River* are among the finest," Nelson argued.

Thomas scowled and closed his notebook. He looked at Bogner, ignoring the others. "And you will see that I get a complete copy of your report, Commander?"

Bogner nodded.

Thomas, with his assistant behind him, started for the gangplank to the wharf. At the last moment he motioned to Bogner and spoke barely above a whisper. "You are aware, Commander, that you have already confirmed one thing for me."

Bogner looked at the man.

"There were Russians aboard at the time of the explosion. Had they been Americans I could have understood why you took the bodies aboard your cruiser. Had it been anyone else except Russians, I feel quite certain that your people would have turned the victims over to the Jamaican authorities. Hence, since they weren't Americans and you didn't turn the bodies over to us, they are Russian. We Jamaicans can be quite logical, you see, and I understand now why it is so important for you to obtain the identity of the mysterious caller."

"You'll have to be discreet." Bogner cautioned.

Red Tide

"I will be discreet, Mr. Bogner, but you must also understand that I am not your problem. Jamaica is the problem. This is a small island. There are few secrets. Word will travel fast." Thomas extended his hand. "Good luck, Commander Bogner. Judging from appearances, you are going to need it."

Datum: 10:6 . . . Wardroom, USS Black River, 0359NLT

The crew of the *Black River* was well-aware of the fact that it was no longer considered a conventional Virginia class cruiser—and they took pride in it.

Five years earlier she had been towed into the Greystone shipping yards for extensive retrofitting and refurbishing. When she emerged, she was a hybrid, a combination Virginia class cruiser and all-operations support ship.

She was still capable of launching surface to air missiles as well as Asroc antisubmarine missiles, but Colchin, the former captain of the *Black River* during his Navy days, had found any number of ways to keep his old ship busy in a variety of other ways as well. Now, at the request of its Commander-in-Chief, the Navy made certain *Black River* was available when Colchin needed it. To the Secretary of the Navy's delight, it was the first close liaison between the Navy and the Chief Executive in years.

The *Black River* had been refitted with a variety of unusual amenities, among them a helicopter pad and hanger for what had become the President's personalized SH-3D-A Sikorsky Sea

King. David Colchin used Air Force One for the long hauls, but he was particularly fond of the Sikorsky's versatility and he called on the twin GE-powered, former antisub helicopter whenever the opportunity presented itself. It was obvious that Colchin regarded the Sea King with the same affection earthbound men display for the Ferrari.

It was shortly after the Jamaicans departed that an ensign had flown ashore and intercepted Bogner, hustled him aboard Colchin's Sea King and transported him to the *Black River*.

The Sea King chopped its way through the predawn soup and put him down on the brightly lit helideck on the bow, a bow that was butressed by four levels towering above the main.

The President, Bogner was informed, was sequestered in a stateroom immediately below the projecting wheelhouse. He looked around. Security, always tight, had been doubled. Everything, at this point, was considered possible, even a plot that could include an attempt to assassinate Colchin as well.

Bogner followed the young officer through a maze of passageways, past a door marked CRYPTO, two more marked RESTRICTED and finally into the VIP bay. The door to Colchin's quarters was guarded by a towering E3.

The President was in wardroom L-4 adjacent to his stateroom. He was flanked by both Hurley and Spitz. Despite the long night, Colchin still managed to look alert. Only Hurley and Spitz appeared to be worn-out.

There were two other men in the room, and Bogner recognized them both. One was Vice-Admiral Albert Cameron, a former Academy man and one of Colchin's long time cronies, part of what the press had dubbed the "Texas Connection." The other was Commander Peter Langley of Naval Intelligence.

"Sorry it took so long to get here, Mr. President," Bogner apologized.

Colchin looked up from a raft of computer reports. "Long night, huh, T. C.?"

Bogner nodded, and the President motioned for him to sit down.

"Peter here tells me that it looks like you were the closest one to it when the *Codicile* blew. Did you see what happened?"

Bogner paraded Colchin through the sequence of events leading up to the explosion. "I was looking right at it. The only thing we noticed that seems in any way out of the ordinary is the fact that the lights went out in the main wardroom shortly before the blast. We were monitoring Zhelannov's launch, so we were reasonably certain he was still on board when she blew." He looked around the room. "Has his body been recovered yet?"

"His was one of the first," Spitz said.

"Peter also tells me Stone's CG units were picking up some kind of interference just prior to the explosion," Colchin said. "Did you pick it up on your monitors?"

"We were monitoring something," Bogner admitted, "but we weren't able to nail it down."

"Do we have it on tape?" Langley asked.

"We're trying to get a profile on it," Cameron said.

"Could turning off the lights have been a signal to the harbor launch?" Spitz tried.

"Or could it have been some kind of precursor to the problem itself? You know, something electrical, a short or something?" Hurley was doing his speculating from the end of the table. He had taken off his coat and was undoing his tie as he spoke.

"If it had been a shipboard electrical problem, Network would have been on the radio in nothing flat, especially with Zhelannov still on board," Cameron said.

Bogner was frowning. "I haven't had a chance to check it out yet, but Koorsen is the one that picked it up. He said one of Stone's units reported an unidentified wavering chatter. We knew it wasn't Zhelannov's launch because we knew it sounded like a standard two cycle. Whatever it was, Stone's boys picked it up again north of the *Codicile* just before the blast."

Colchin leaned forward and put down his coffee cup. "What do you make of what Toby is telling us, Peter?"

Peter Langley was a thin, somewhat awkward man with a crewcut and a penchant for wearing turtlenecks. He reminded Bogner of a slightly younger version of his own father.

Langley pursed his lips. "We're aware of what Commander Bogner is talking about. Both of Stone's patrol units were also reporting it. We haven't been able to come up with anything definitive from the audio so we're going through the infrareds frame by frame."

"Wait a minute," Bogner said. "Are you telling me you've got this whole thing on film?"

"I wish it was that simple," Langley sighed. "The night vision surveillance cameras were sequenced for long duration operation. As a consequence, we were only shooting one frame every half second on a one eighty sweep. Everything was fully synchronized with the audio sensors. So, when the audio picked up the chatter, the infrared camera acknowledged it, repositioned itself on the chatter and missed the whole damn explosion." Langley was demonstrating each sequence of the cycle with his big, expressive hands.

Cameron pushed himself away from the table, walked across the room and poured himself another cup of coffee.

"The more I hear us talk, the more I'm convinced we're overlooking something important. If we go back to the beginning, Jaffe's message came in at 1615. Peter and Lattimere then notified the President about Complexity's report. That means that the President was here on the *Black River*, Zhelannov was on the Aeroflot flight into Montego Bay, and everything else was already in place—and at that point we had secured the harbor."

"We thought we had secured the harbor," Langley interjected.

"Why didn't they just blow that damn Aeroflot flight out of the air?" Spitz asked. "It would have had the same net effect."

"Except if they did that, we couldn't be so easily implicated," Langley reminded him. "Complexity was right. They had to pull it off in our own backyard."

"But back to what I was saying," Cameron said. "Somewhere between 1615 and 1620, the bridge logged Langley's confirmation that the harbor check was complete. My own men went over the

Codicile this morning and Toby went over it this afternoon. In the meantime I had the CG units double-check every damn boat in the harbor. We reverified registry, checked papers, backgrounds, and most of them were even boarded for a search. Hell, we even profiled the local fishing boats. Let's face it. They pulled this off right under our god-damn noses."

"We'll figure it out," Langley said. "Before it's over, we'll know everything. We even know what the crew on that Hormone had for chow."

"Then how the hell could something like this happen?" Colchin demanded.

"What about the possibility of something being fired from the shoreline?" Spitz asked. "Have we considered that?"

Langley thought about the question for a moment and shook his head. "Possible, Lattimere, but highly unlikely. The way that damn thing disintegrated tells me someone planted something on board."

"Back to the logic," Cameron insisted. "If Complexity's theory is right and they intended to implicate us by claiming we blew up their President, they went about it all wrong. Because it was an explosion, we could claim it was a malfunction aboard the yacht—or even a terrorist attack. Hell, we've got a thousand outs if we want to use them."

"Damn it," Colchin thundered, "I don't want outs. I want answers. All hell is going to break loose in the next couple of hours if we don't start coming up with some."

"Well, if someone rigged a bomb of some sort aboard the *Codicile*, it was a goddamn suicide mission because there sure as hell wasn't any way for them to get off," Cameron said.

"Maybe the assassin intended to get off on the launch?" Spitz speculated.

Colchin got up, walked around the table and sat down next to Bogner. "How about it, Toby? You're a swimmer. Could someone have planted the bomb, dropped overboard and swam to shore?"

"It would be risky, Mr. President, but it depends on the variables—kind of bomb, how good a swimmer, knowing when to detonate the device."

"Could the bomb have been planted earlier in the evening and timed to go off after the President left?" Spitz asked.

"No one knew exactly when the President and Zhelannov were going to wrap it up," Langley reminded him. "But the fact remains, the Russians couldn't have accused us of anything if David here had still been on board."

"I should have scrubbed the whole damned affair the minute I heard the Complexity report," Colchin sighed.

"We're still overlooking something," Cameron insisted.

There was a knock on the door. When it opened, an E6 stepped into the room. The Petty Officer handed a message to Cameron. The Vice-Admiral read it and threw down on the table.

"Well, gentlemen, the plot has thickened. We just discovered how our Russian friends took all the risk out of their little plan. Forsythe reports that every one of the ten bodies we've recovered so far has at least one bullet hole in it. He wants us to come down to sick bay, Mr. President. He says it's urgent."

Colchin turned to Bogner. His west Texas face creased in a scowl. "Toby, my boy, it looks like the shit just hit the fan."

Bogner nodded. "Sounds like it. Now they can claim we shot their President and blew up the ship to make it look like an accident."

Colchin leaned forward with his hands on the table. "Well, gentlemen, let's see what Forsythe wants."

Datum: 10:6 . . . Crew Hospital, USS Black River, *0438NLT*

The scene reminded Bogner of something out of a surrealist nightmare. There were three sheet-shrouded gurneys parked end to end along the bulkhead and two more parked just inside the bay doors.

Colchin and his entourage were standing in the waiting room outside the surgery arena of the crew hospital. Forsythe had joined them. He was a balding middle-aged man with a drawn face and horn-rimmed glasses. His green scrubs were bloodstained.

Cameron handed the surgeon a cigarette. "The message said it was urgent, Sam."

Forsythe looked at Bogner.

"It's all right to talk," Cameron assured him.

Forsythe's voice was shaky. "I just came from C deck. I wanted to double-check before I sent that message up." He paused. "Zhelannov is still alive!"

"Say that again," Langley muttered.

Forsythe took his scrub cap off and twisted it between his hands. "I had Ensign Martin going over the bodies up in the morgue to see if there was anything we could use to help identify any of the victims. He called me about thirty minutes ago and told me I had better get up there. He didn't say why. When I got there I discovered they had just wheeled Zhelannov into the intensive care unit. It took some doing but we were finally able to get a pulse. He's alive, but I don't know how long we can hold on to him."

"How the hell could we have missed this when we brought him aboard?" Cameron demanded.

Forsythe was emotionally drained. He shook his head and shrugged. "I don't know how, Admiral. We had four recovery vessels working, and I instructed them to get the victims aboard the minute they located one. They started bringing them aboard less than thirty minutes after the explosion. I was up in surgery on standby. Ensign Martin was assigned the task of checking them in. We kept asking, but no one could even tell us for certain whether or not Zhelannov was on board when the damn thing exploded. At any rate, nobody recognized him. No one is at fault. There isn't a hell of a lot there to recognize on some of the victims. When Zhelannov was brought in, they brought a young man in a flight suit in on the same trip. The airman was still alive but died on the way up to surgery. Two hours later, I was in the morgue when I found the gunshot wound in the body of the man we identified as the harbor pilot."

"Who all knows about this?" Langley demanded.

"No one outside of the surgical area."

Langley turned to Cameron. "Seal this area off," he demanded. "Tell your men to make damn certain no personnel comes in or leaves this area."

Then he turned to Bogner. "Get this Ensign Martin in here. Then make certain no one in the bay talks to anyone outside of this area. I want this place totally muffled until we figure out exactly what we're going to do."

"Shouldn't we let them know Zhelannov is alive?" Hurley asked.

"That's the last thing we want to do," Colchin said calmly. "For the time being we want whoever it is that pulled off this goddamn stunt to think their plot is a success."

Base Hour
Three-Nine:
ZERO ZERO . . . 0900ZULU

Datum: 10:6 . . . Washington, 06111EST

Clancy Packer was still in the shower when Sara knocked on the bathroom door. "Honey, Bob Miller is on the phone. He says it's urgent."

"For Christ's sake, Sara, tell him I'm in the shower. Get a number and tell him I'll call him right back."

"He's on his car phone, and he knows exactly where you are. He said to get you to the phone, pronto."

Packer climbed out of the shower, toweled off, put on his robe and picked up the phone.

"This better be damned important, Miller. It's getting so I can't even have any time to myself in the damned bathroom."

"Chief, better you hear it from me than some half-assed reporter."

"What the hell are you talking about?"

"Turn on your television. Those crazy bastards

203

blew up the *Codicile* last night."

Packer felt his stomach churn over. "Oh, shit!"

"Look, Chief, I'm on the Parkland Expressway, close to the eight mile marker. With any luck at all, I'll be in the office in another thirty minutes. I've already called Henline and Oskiwicz and told them to hustle their butts in. Mildred and Taggert worked the night watch, so they're already there."

"Who was working the desk when we got the call?"

"Millie. She called me because she couldn't get through to you."

"I'll be there as soon as I can," Packer said. He hung up the telephone and turned on the television just as Sara walked back into the room. They could hear a woman's voice talking about the explosion long before the image crystalized.

"Clancy," Sara said, "isn't that Joy, Toby's ex-wife?"

"It sure as hell is. She called me two nights ago trying to chase down some official word on that downed Russian sub."

"She looks better than she did when—"

"For Christ's sake, Sara, I'm trying to listen."

The camera picked up Joy Bogner in the NBC newsroom. "One source informed NBC News that the blast occurred shortly before midnight, Negril time. The yacht is reported to have belonged to Texas millionaire and former President Colchin law partner, Amos Sparrow. Witnesses say that the luxury craft erupted in a ball of flame and disintegrated in an explosion that shook structures up and down the seven mile stretch of beach in this tiny Jamaican resort.

Red Tide

"Lyle Daily is on the scene in Negril and is standing by." The television went to a split screen, and the camera was picking up the image of Daily. "What's the latest, Lyle?"

"Joy, the U.S. Naval spokesman that we talked to is still refusing to comment on the persistent rumor that Commonwealth of Independent States President Sergei Zhelannov was aboard the Sparrow yacht when it exploded. We have, however, been able to confirm that an unscheduled Aeroflot flight did arrive in Montego Bay yesterday afternoon. Whether President Zhelannov was on that flight or not has still not been confirmed.

"Jamaican officials at the scene however are saying that both President Colchin and President Zhelannov were aboard the yacht earlier in the evening."

Sara put her hand on Clancy's arm. "How can that be? I thought you said Colchin was spending the weekend at Camp David. Did you know about this meeting with Zhelannov?"

Clancy nodded without looking away from the television.

The split screen dissolved and showed Daily standing next to a Jamaican official.

"I have with me now," Daily continued, "Vice-Consul Avery Thomas of the Jamaican Foreign Affairs office in Montego Bay." The backdrop was a foggy panorama of the Negril harbor. Thomas looked appropriately somber.

"Consul Thomas, we are told that you attended a predawn briefing with the American Coast Guard authorities."

"That is correct," Thomas said.

"As you know, Consul Thomas, there is still a great deal of conflicting information in the reports that we are receiving. My question to you, sir, is—during your briefing, did the Coast Guard spokesman reveal who was aboard the American yacht at the time of the explosion?"

Thomas, mindful of his deal with Bogner, shook his head. "They indicated only that they had recovered the bodies of ten victims. At that time, they also indicated that none of the victims had been identified."

"We continue to hear reports that a high ranking Russian diplomat, possibly even President Zhelannov of the Commonwealth of Independent States, may have been aboard the yacht at the time of the explosion. Are you in a position to comment on that, Consul Thomas?"

Avery Thomas cleared his throat. "They neither confirmed nor denied it. And I would prefer not to speculate."

As the camera zoomed in a for a close up of Thomas, Packer caught another glimpse of the fog-bound bay behind him.

"So there you have it, Joy." The television went to a split screen again, picking up the image of Joy Bogner in the NBC studio. She was taking off her glasses. "The situation is still unfolding here in Negril and the facts are still sketchy at this time."

Daily disappeared, leaving Joy on the screen.

"Let me recap what we have been able to learn so far." Joy glanced down at a piece of paper and began to read. "Shortly before midnight, Jamaican time, an American luxury yacht belonging to Texas millionaire Amos

Sparrow mysteriously exploded and burned in Negril Harbor. At this time, NBC News has confirmed that ten people are dead, but U.S. Coast Guard officials on the scene have informed us that the identities of the victims will not be released until the next of kin have been notified."

The camera panned again, picking up the image of the local Washington anchorman.

"Thank you, Joy."

"Clancy," Sara said, "Joy is here in Washington. I recognized Paul Blain of the Washington bureau."

Clancy Packer was already getting dressed. Sara handed him his customary morning cup of coffee.

"My God," Sara muttered, "is it possible? You don't actually think President Zhelannov was on board, do you?"

Clancy Packer looked at his wife. Their eyes met in the unspoken communication of people who have lived together for years. He knew he couldn't answer the question—but he had.

Sara Packer now knew why her husband had canceled their weekend at the Vermont farm at the last minute.

"Is there anything I can do?" she asked.

"Yeah, call the office and tell them I'm on the way. And tell them to see if they can locate Bogner."

Sara's pulse quickened. "Toby is down there, too?"

Packer answered with his eyes.

The color drained from Sara Packer's delicate face. She was hesitant to ask the question.

"Clancy, there isn't any chance that Toby was on that yacht, is there?"

Packer looked at her. "I wish I knew."

Datum: 10:6 . . . Wardroom, USS Black River, *0618NLT*

His eyes glazed by lack of sleep, Langley sat across the conference table from Bogner in the wardroom. His face was stubbled and haggard.

Stone, equally disheveled and irritated, had been summoned to the same meeting. The *Hensley* had been left in the command of Lt. Nelson.

Admiral Cameron had come down from the bridge of the *Black River* with the news that Air Force One was now airborne.

The four men were breathing easier for the first time since the explosion. At last Colchin was out of the sector, whisked away by his Sea King to a rendezvous with Air Force One in Monitor Bay. There had been no indication that the plot included Colchin, but with him safely out of the area, the possibility was minimized even further.

Bogner reflected on his last minute conversation with the President.

"Look, Toby, I don't have to tell you that this is getting messier by the minute. I've instructed Admiral Cameron to put Peter Langley in charge of the on-site investigation. Stone has his hands full just keeping the harbor secured. I want you to find out how the hell this happened. Don't let anything get in your way. I've told Cameron to give you whatever you need. Whatever you do, don't let somebody drop the ball down here. Any questions?"

"Just one—what about Zhelannov?"

Colchin rubbed his eyes. "We're taking it one step at a time. I just came from the IC unit. He's alive—but barely. Forsythe doesn't know how much longer he can hold on."

"How do you want me to handle it?"

"If worse comes to worse, let me know. Right now we're buying time. I instructed Secretary Halsey at the State Department to have Ambassador Parker in Minsk request a meeting with their Vice-President Churnova. I've already received word back that the meeting is scheduled at 1630 Moscow time. That means they are getting anxious to know what the hell is going on as well."

"Will Parker tell Churnova about the plot?"

"No. Parker is being faxed a detailed report of what happened here as well as a medical update on Zhelannov, omitting of course any reference to the fact that he was shot. Complexity could be right. Churnova could be in on it. At this point, we intend to do nothing more than extend an invitation to a Russian medical team to come aboard the *Black River* to assist our doctors."

"No chance of flying him back to Walter Reed or some place like that?" Bogner asked.

"Forsythe assures me he wouldn't survive the trip."

Bogner shook his head. "I don't like it."

"Under the circumstances, I don't think we have an alternative. Like I said, Toby, we're buying time. It's up to you now to figure out what happened and how it happened. Langley estimates it will take them at least twelve hours to put their medical team together and fly them over here. He also figures they will request permission to put a couple of their observers aboard the *Black River* to keep an eye on Zhelannov until their medical team gets here."

"Any one or all of them could be part of the plot," Bogner reminded him.

"Calculated risk," Colchin acknowledged.

"What happens when one of them discovers that their main man is missing half his midsection?"

Colchin shook his head. "We can stonewall them only so long. This way it at least looks like we're cooperating. It gets even uglier though when we can't tell them who pulled the trigger."

After that, Bogner watched the President board the Sikorsky and disappear into the low hanging clouds. Now, less than an hour later, he was listening to Langley. The Naval Intelligence officer was pulling the projection screen into position. His voice was getting hoarse, coming at them in raspy scraps.

"Zhelannov is Forsythe's problem. We can't help him. Our job is to figure out not only how but also who pulled the trigger. The way I see it, the minute we come up with the attempted assassin and hand him over to the proper Russian authorities, we defuse the situation by a good fifty percent."

"What about those infrareds, Peter," Cameron asked. "Did we come up with anything?"

Langley turned on the projector and turned off the lights.

"We were filming with four different cameras when the explosion occurred." He depressed the button on the film feed. "What you're looking at is an edited sequence of the film shot between 2329 and 2354NLT. Position A is from the fantail of the CG-144. At the time, it was located about three hundred yards off shore from the Chupa airstrip where their Hormone was located. Position B was located at the northeast corner of the wharf and positioned so that it could record starboard activity on the *Codicile*. Position C was located on the second floor of the Yankee Drummer Resort Hotel up on the beach. It was programed to provide beach and stern surveillance. Position D was the all positions backup and was doing a syncron sweep of the entire harbor. Both positions A and B were programed to respond to audio sensors, but because of the sporadic interference Toby mentioned earlier, both cameras were distracted and missed the actual blast. As luck would have it, they were the ones in the best position to record the explosion. So the only record we have is what we were able to piece together from positions C and D. From that, however, you can see that there are two distinct blasts aboard the *Codicile*."

"Are you saying two bombs, Peter?" Cameron asked.

"Probably not. Our best theory at the moment is that the first explosion was simply a trigger mechanism. It detonated the second charge which was much larger."

Langley stopped the film, rewound it and played it a second time.

"As you can see—clearly two blasts, microseconds apart."

Cameron leaned forward. "Okay, Toby, there were two blasts. What does that tell us?"

"Well, it brings down the chances that it was an accident. In theory, you put a small device in a specific location, somewhere like the engine room, and let the stray fumes do the rest."

"Bogner is right," Stone turned and studied the map of the harbor, "but that means that whoever planted the device had to have some way of triggering it and getting the hell out of there. That brings us to another fork in the road. Either the one that planted the device was on Sparrow's yacht earlier in the day, after Cameron's crew and Bogner went over it, or was one of the President's contingent that left the boat—or it was a suicide mission. None of which sounds plausible if I was trying to sell it to the Russians."

"I think we overlooked one possibility," Bogner interrupted. "Suppose someone came aboard after Colchin left?"

"You tell me how they hell they could have done that when we had that harbor wired?" Stone demanded.

"Stony is right," Langley said. "We had infrareds shooting. The surface was squeaky clean. Even the audio, which I might add, is sensitive enough to hear a fish fart, recorded only one minor and unexplained noise the whole damn vigil. We had four static audio monitors. No way could someone have rowed out there, crawled aboard and pulled the trigger. I'd have to go along with Stony's theory that whoever shot Sergei Zhelannov was willing to blow himself up right along with Sparrow's yacht. Hell, it wouldn't be the first time."

Bogner got up from the table, turned on the lights and walked over to the harbor map.

"Stony, roll that audio tape back to the point where we picked up the distraction noise, the one that cameras at positions A and B followed. Doesn't that mean that both CG-144 and CG-217 picked up on the same signal? What would be the farthest intersecting point at which those signals crossed?"

Stone walked to the map. "Nelson said he lost it about here." He pointed to the spot.

"You won't get anywhere with that theory, Toby," Cameron said, leaning back in his chair. "Charley Peel over on the *Madison* has a top rated sonarman. We had him audit the tape. He thought it sounded like someone dumping a damn bilge tank."

Bogner spun around. "Of course—or blowing a buoyancy tank."

Cameron's head popped up. "Damn it, Toby, that could be it."

Stone frowned. "You aren't suggesting a damn submarine for Christ's sake. This harbor is too small and most of it is too shallow. Besides, we've had the harbor sealed off. If there had been a sub out there, we would have picked it up when we secured the harbor."

Bogner looked at the Coast Guard commander. "You're right, Stony. It's too small for a nuke or a conventional sub. But what about a sea sled or a midget?"

Cameron was smiling for the first time in hours. "Midget, mini, sea sled—any one of them could have been piggybacked in by any of the larger craft out there."

"If it had been a diesel, we would have picked it up," Stone argued, "but not if it was run on batteries."

Cameron looked at Langley. "Do they have anything like that, Peter?"

"Not that we know of," Langley admitted, "but that doesn't mean they don't have one. We know the Japanese have been testing a battery-powered mini, but it burns up its power too fast."

"Yes, but this one wouldn't have had to go very far." Cameron looked around the room for agreement. "Plausible, gentlemen—or better yet, possible?"

"I suppose," Stone conceded, "but how the hell did they get it out of the harbor? The *Black River* is riding drag over the entrance to the harbor with some of the best damned fixed position sonar money can buy."

"And," Langley reminded them, "Stony's units are positioned at each end of the reef."

"Maybe it didn't get out of the harbor," Bogner said. "In theory at least, it would only have two options. Either it goes out the way it came in or it sits on the bottom."

"It would be simple enough to check the hulls of the craft in the harbor if one of them actually piggybacked a mini in," Langley said. "If there is a carriage under one of those hulls we'd know what we're dealing with."

Cameron turned to Bogner. "You know this harbor, Toby. Is it practical to pursue this sub theory? Is there any place a sub could hide in this harbor?"

Bogner went to the map. "Here, inside the reef at the point they call the Jehovah Hole. It's a junkyard. According to NI there are at least three World War Two German warships down there. They scuttled them there at the end of the war."

"Size?" Cameron asked.

"The entire harbor can't be more than ten or eleven square miles. Most of it is no more than a hundred to two hundred feet in depth—except the Jehovah Hole, and no one seems to know how deep it is. Some of the locals claim the hole tunnels back under the reef and out to sea."

Cameron's smile turned to a frown. "Could a mini or midget get through that hole?"

"Hard to say, Admiral. First thing we'd have to do is determine that the hole actually tunnels through the reef."

"Well, damn it, let's find out," Cameron glowered. "If that son-of-a-bitch is still in the harbor, I don't want him slipping through our fingers just because there is a damn hole in the reef."

Stone stood up. "I'll have my units deploy hydrophones all along the lee side of the reef. That way we'll know if he tries to slip through."

"At the same time," Langley said, "we'll start checking the hulls of the transits."

Datum: 10:6 . . . Negril Harbor: the Mala , 0640NLT

Ilya Vasilivich tried to massage away the numbing stiffness in his legs and wiggled his toes to enhance the circulation. He could feel the swelling in his ankles and the stiffness that was settling through his knotted shoulders.

There was too little room, and he knew that the moment he stopped, his circulation would be restricted again and the aching sensation would return.

He glanced first at the brass chronometer over the control panel directly behind the Obs Sant and then in the mirror at the stoic, reflected image of Zhukov.

Ilya had observed much about the man in the

last few hours. Zhukov was a man who did not sleep, did not show his discomfort, and for the last hour or so had not communicated with Ilya. He stared straight ahead, giving indication of neither pleasure nor pain.

"They have started up again," Ilya felt compelled to explain.

Zhukov arched his eyebrows only slightly.

"The American Coast Guard units are making their rounds again. There is more activity on the surface than there has been for the past several hours."

"Are they working in a recognizable search pattern, or is it random as if mere comings and goings?"

Ilya inclined his head to one side and placed his ear as close as he could to the bulkhead. "It is random. But I believe there are even more of them than before. Perhaps the Jamaican patrol boats have joined them."

Zhukov fell silent again.

Ilya continued to massage the numbness in his legs until his hands cramped and he had to stop. He waited several moments before speaking again.

"I . . . I have been thinking, Marshal, about our alternative plan." He hesitated again, wondering if he should continue. "Admiral Osipov's charts indicate that there is a hole through the reef in the place known as Jehovah Hole. . . ."

Ilya's voice trailed off when he realized that Zhukov was not listening.

He reached up and turned the valve forward on the fresh water supply, sipping from the single strand of clear plastic tubing that hung down from the gravity flow device. The needle gauge indicated that there was less than half a liter remaining. He took a sip and attempted to capture enough of the precious fluid to run his tongue over his parched lips.

A bead of sweat traced its way down the side of his face. He wiped it away with the back of his hand and returned to massaging his legs again.

Ilya watched the second hand creep full circle around the face of the chronometer and wondered if he dared risk turning on the radio to monitor the communications between the American surface vessels. He checked the battery reserve indicator on the service pack and decided against it.

When he glanced up, Zhukov's eyes were open again. The brooding officer had been watching him.

Datum: 10:6 . . . Moscow, 1555MLT

The Chaika limousine, with Achina Maslovaka driving, hurried up the Suslov Way, carrying Viktor Denisov from the Chesnakov Compound to the Hall of Bureaus.

There was little traffic on this gray afternoon in Moscow, and Viktor was convinced it was because the citizens were hovered inside near their televisions and radios, waiting for further word of the shocking events being broadcast from Jamaica.

Would they weep for Zhelannov? Probably. Would they weep for his free market policies? Probably not. Most of them had suffered with too little for too long.

The Party would correct all of that.

Damn the Americans, Viktor fumed. How they infuriated him. Why did they refuse to acknowledge Zhelannov's death in the explosion aboard the American yacht? Why did they send their simpering idiot of an ambassador with the news couched in his courier's attaché case? It was a foolish time to be diplomatic. The Americans would soon realize that. They should have informed the world of Zhelannov's death.

How much more heroic it would have been if he, Viktor Denisov, could display his shock and outrage in front of the masses.

The Chaika turned on to the new Avenue of Patriots, recently rechristened by the Ministry of Revision.

What did the Americans hope to gain? The last report said that they had recovered ten victims; surely Zhelannov was one of them. Would they not have said survivors instead of victims if any of them had been alive? Was there some subtle difference between the two words? He wished that Ruta was there to explain the difference.

He settled deeper in the plush upholstery and allowed his mind to drift to Zhukov. He wondered how his old Party adversary had reacted to the Mala's inability to dock with the craft that had mothered it. Was the man such a fool that he really believed that Viktor had forgiven him for his years of opposition?

Viktor lit a cigarette and permitted a small smile of satisfaction.

As Achina turned off of Patya and headed up Mushlin Esplande, Viktor was mentally preparing himself for the next 39 hours. He envisioned how he would answer the call of the Party faithful and establish order out of the economic and political chaos caused by the renegade states that had deserted the Union.

Too staged?

Too melodramatic?

Was this not theater, the Russian theater, mother of brooding tragedy and father of triumph?

He applauded himself like a child and the Maslovaka woman's eyes met his in approval in the rearview mirror.

As the limousine pulled into the square, his thoughts turned away from his vision of triumph to the more disturbing reality of why the Americans had not yet reported the death of Zhelannov.

Base Hour
Three-Eight:
ZERO ZERO . . . 1000ZULU

Datum: 10:6 . . . Council of Ministers, Kremlin, 1630MLT

Viktor Denisov was relieved when he finally received Churnova's call informing him that the American Ambassador had requested a 4.30 meeting in the Vice-President's office. At last, he thought to himself, the Americans have finally come to the realization that it is folly to further delay their announcement of Zhelannov's death. Yet, until they made the announcement, he couldn't be certain.

It had been more than seven hours since Viktor received the initial communiqué forwarded through the naval intelligence sector of the former Fifth-Directorate. He found the Americans' prolonged silence and obvious consternation over their dilemma to be both amusing and maddening.

For the past several hours he had occupied himself with images of the confused and blundering imperialists trying to sort their way through their predicament. Who would inform the independent states? When would they inform them? How will the Russians react? The Americans were nothing more than pompous, bureaucratic dolts. What else could one expect from a country whose generals were castrated by a continually inept congress? He must, Viktor reminded himself, not permit such a crippling power check when he reestablished the leadership of the Party.

The impending confrontation with the American Ambassador had already been played out in Denisov's mind. He could play it two different ways—icy and suspicious acceptance of the American mouse, Parker, and his abhorrent announcement, or assume the posture of the crestfallen recipient of the news that would sadden all of the Commonwealth. "The reports are true," Parker would reluctantly admit. "President Zhelannov died in an explosion aboard the American yacht, *Codicile*, shortly before midnight last night."

Viktor envisioned the fat little man handing over the official document. How much outrage would be appropriate? How should he react? Should he embarrass the man by asking him to explain the inordinate delay? More than anything else, the delay was a waste of time. There was so much to be done, and nothing could be accomplished until the official word of Zhelannov's death was received.

But now, Victor was able to smile with anticipation; the moment was at hand. Parker had arrived in Churnova's outer office and was engaged in polite conversation with Dubreeno, Churnova's assistant.

Viktor chose his position in the room carefully. He was standing behind Churnova's desk with the official portrait of Zhelannov directly over his left shoulder.

The flabby-faced American who smelled of expensive cologne could not miss the symbolism. It was the image Viktor wanted the man to carry with him when he left the room.

Parker was ushered in, and the introductions were strained. Viktor stepped forward, bowing slightly, aborting the Ambassador's attempted handshake. Dubreeno, Churnova's aide, entered the room prepared to translate.

The American did not fumble with the latch on his briefcase as Viktor had suspected he would. He was amazed at how steady the man's hands were when he handed the envelope to Churnova.

The envelope contained the customary diplomatic accoutrements, Parker's credentials and the perfunctory greeting. Churnova grabbed the communiqué out of his hand, read it and suddenly slumped back in his chair. Finally he turned to Viktor, his eyes hollow, his face sobered.

"Secretary Zhelannov is alive," he managed.

Viktor Denisov refused to believe what he was hearing. He snatched the piece of paper out of Churnova's hand and read it himself. The words were a blur. "What does it say?" he demanded.

"My personal copy does not lend itself to an exact translation," Parker admitted. "It says simply that we are all very fortunate; somehow President Zhelannov managed to survive the explosion. He is in the intensive care unit aboard the *Black River*."

"You have the necessary medical facilities on

this ship?" Churnova asked.

"We do," Parker assured them. "Your President is under the care of some of our finest medical personnel."

"I hope," Denisov glowered, "that your military doctors are better than ours, Mr. Ambassador."

Parker knew any response would be inappropriate and waited before he continued. Finally he made the offer.

"President Colchin is prepared to make arrangements for your own medical team to assist and monitor Mr. Zhelannov's recovery."

"An overdue gesture on the part of your bungling President," Denisov snarled.

Churnova folded his hands on the desk in front of him. "I must assume, Mr. Ambassador, that your government would likewise not object to the placement of military observers from our Unified Forces until such a time as our medical team is able to be assembled."

"You will have our full cooperation," Parker replied.

Churnova turned to Denisov for the second time. "How long, General, do you think it will take us to assemble our medical delegation?"

Denisov knew that Churnova did not need to inquire. It was his way of letting the American Ambassador know who was really in charge.

"It will be necessary to consult with the Ministry of Medicine," Denisov stalled. He had purposely replied in Russian, forcing Dubreeno to translate for Parker's edification.

"Our state department has prepared a complete medical briefing for your medical analysts," Parker said, reaching back in his briefcase and withdrawing a second packet. He lay it on Churnova's desk. To his surprise, neither of the men reached for it.

Denisov's face had grown dark. For some reason the American Ambassador was too confident. He was certain now that Parker had not been told that Zhelannov had been shot. Why?

Now, for the first time, there was an element of uncertainty in Denisov's mind. Was it possible that Zhukov had failed? Had something gone wrong at the last minute? Was Andrakov's report in error?

Churnova stood up. "Need I remind you that this is a volatile situation, Ambassador Parker? The Russian people have been waiting too many hours for word of what happened. The American media is full of reports. We have been told that there were no survivors. You will understand if I request that you excuse us while I consult with General Denisov before replying to your truant communiqué."

Parker looked puzzled. Both Denisov and Churnova were reacting like men caught off balance.

"I feel compelled to tell you, Vice-President Churnova, that I am equally puzzled by your reaction to the news that President Zhelannov is alive. My government thought you would be relieved when you were informed that he had survived."

Viktor took a step forward, his peasant face flushed with rage. He spoke in brittle Russian fragments, spitting out his words.

"And I, Ambassador Parker, feel compelled to inform you that we are dismayed that the Americans did not take the necessary precautions to see that such an atrocity was avoided in the first place. I further confess that I view this as a typical example of imperialist bungling."

Parker stiffened as Dubreeno translated. He attempted a mild counter protest, but Viktor brushed the words away with a wave of his hand.

"You will protest nothing," Denisov glowered. "If there is any protesting to be done, the Russian people will do it. President Zhelannov was a progressive moderate, beloved by millions upon millions of his people. The people and governments of the Independent States will not take kindly to your pathetic response in their hour of crisis."

Parker, face flushed, stared icily at the pair while Churnova guided Denisov from the room.

"Are you mad?" Churnova hissed as the door closed. "We will accomplish nothing by provoking this man. We cannot afford to close doors. We must have access to President Zhelannov if we are to succeed."

Denisov turned away. Churnova could see the muscles twitching in the man's jaw.

"Damn," Viktor hissed, "it appears that Zhukov has botched the entire operation."

Churnova remained calm. "The plan can still be salvaged, but only if Zhelannov dies. If he recovers, he will identify the assassin, and then others of less commitment will reveal who is behind the plot."

"Do you think I have not thought of that?" Viktor thundered. "I must have time to think. I am convinced Zhukov believes he has accomplished his mission. It is quite apparent that the Americans have revealed only to us that the President is alive. The question, Comrade, is why. What kind of game are they playing?"

Churnova looked anxiously over his shoulder. "We cannot continue to delay our response, Viktor. Parker is already suspicious. We did not respond appropriately to the news that the President is still alive. You can rest assured that he will waste no time relaying that information to his superiors. Our only approach is to delay our formal response."

"There is even more wisdom in stopping him from reporting back to his imperialist superiors." Viktor insisted.

"You have a plan?"

Denisov thought for a moment. "We will tell him that we are putting together a medical contingent as their President has suggested. We will also tell him that we are arranging to have two representatives from the Russian fleet put aboard the ship where Zhelannov is being retained."

"I am more concerned about what he reports back to his superiors."

"Is it not customary," Viktor asked, "to give the American Ambassador a response while duplicating and transmitting the official response through electronic channels for text verification?"

"That is correct," Churnova confirmed.

"Then we have nothing to worry about, Comrade. We will prepare a response and give it to the Ambassador. We will tell him that we will follow the standard diplomatic procedure and transmit a verification copy to our embassy in Washington." Viktor paused just long enough to light a cigarette. Then he permitted himself a small smile. "While you are doing that, Comrade, I will tend to the more delicate matter of making certain Ambassador Parker does not relay the news of our unfortunate reaction to his message."

As Boris Churnova turned toward the door to his office, he was again smiling broadly and congratulating Denisov. "Excellent, General, excellent."

Datum: 10:6 . . . Washington: ISA Offices, 0759EST

"How long has it been since we've seen each other?" Packer asked.

Joy graced him with her best on-camera smile. "Clancy, that's not the kind of question you're supposed to ask a woman. It implies that a lot of years have passed, and no woman likes to think in terms of passing years. You're supposed to say something like 'it's been too long, Joy.'"

Packer laughed. "It was Toby they gave the official title 'officer and gentleman,' not me. At the University of Buffalo, I was damned lucky to get a degree, period." The moment he mentioned Toby's name, he was sorry he had done so.

She was sitting across the desk from him with her briefcase in her lap, wearing a dark blue suit and tapping her long fingernails on the russet cowhide surface. At the same time, Packer was pretending to ignore the press pool request that needed his signature.

"Since I don't have a security clearance, I thought I could prevail on . . ."

Miller brought in the coffee, and they both took a sip before Joy continued.

"So how is Sara?"

Packer rambled on for several minutes about Sara, the kids and even the grandchildren before he recognized that Joy had simply asked the question out of courtesy. He wrapped it up and asked how she had been.

Joy gave him a summary of her progress up through NBC outlets in the southern California market, culminating with her promotion to anchorwoman at KNBC. They bandied names of celebrities and finally got around to discussing some of the events that had led up to her call when the news of the downed sub had broken.

"As luck would have it, my co-anchor was sick that night, and the news director asked me to tape a couple of news breaks they use during the all-night movies. That's when I first picked up the story on the downed sub. If Toby hadn't described what a six-one code was one time, I might have missed it. It wasn't getting any coverage, just a capsule item in an East Coast summary."

"But you're headquartered in L.A.—and now you're here. Why?"

Joy smiled. "Simple. I asked for and received permission to follow up. Besides, it didn't hurt when I told them I had a few connections back east because of my former husband."

"Then you're on your way to Negril?"

She tilted her head to one side. "You're stalling, Clancy. Why else would I have made the request for the press pool approval? Besides, I know Vice-Admiral Albert Cameron; I met him back in what I call my Toby days."

"You're aware, of course, that we sent Toby down there?" Packer said.

Joy stiffened. "I saw him just two days ago. He said he was on his way to Boston to see Kim."

"We changed his plans."

Joy leaned forward. "Clancy, what's going on? First the downed sub, then Sparrow's yacht blows up—and now the persistent rumor that Sergei Zhelannov was on that ship. All of a sudden you tell me that Toby is down there. I know for a fact that the President leans on him. That could lead a thinking girl to two conclusions: one, Colchin is or was down there, and two, the ISA is involved. So what's going on?"

"You know I can't answer those questions, Joy." Packer picked up his pen and scratched his name across the press pool request. He pushed it across the desk to her.

"Pack?" Joy's voice had softened. "You know why I divorced Toby don't you?"

Clancy Packer could feel his face color. "Joy, I love you like a daughter, but you know that's none of my business."

"And you are very special to me, Pack. That's why I think you ought to know. It shouldn't have turned out the way it did. I know that, and I believe Toby feels the same way. We were young, and we were selfish. I didn't like sharing my husband with the goddamn Navy any more than he wanted to share me with a couple of hundred thousand TV viewers."

Clancy took a sip of coffee, set the cup down and leaned back in his chair. "Sara thinks you two will get back together someday."

"Sara is an incurable romantic," Joy sighed.

Base Hour
Three-Four:
ZERO ZERO . . . 1400ZULU

Datum: 10:6 . . . C Deck, USS Black River, *1104NLT*

Bogner followed Cameron down the corridor of C Deck into a well-lighted wardroom across from the *Black River*'s COM-CON. In the middle of the room was a narrow chart table. Seated at the table was a dark-haired woman Bogner estimated to be in her early to mid-forties and a frightened boy of no more than ten or eleven. The woman was stoic. The boy had been crying. Stone and Langley sat across from them.

Stone began the introductions in a weary monotone. "Admiral Cameron, Commander Bogner, this is Olga Vasilivich and her son, Tomas."

Cameron acknowledged the introductions with a curt nod of the head and took a seat. Bogner continued standing. "What have we got, Peter?" Cameron asked.

Langley had an array of photographs laying on the table in front of him. "This," he grunted. He slid the photographs across the table to the Vice-Admiral. "It looks like Toby was right. The lady here was taken off a Danish registered Swath out at the reef. She and the boy were the only ones on board."

Cameron began to sift through the photographs. They were underwater shots of mechanical rigging.

Langley reached across the table with a pencil and began pointing. "All of these shots were taken under the Swath yacht *Cuboc*. Look at the superstructure. Notice the clamping devices. There is a flanged securing plate at the bow and stern of each hull. Not a lot of detail but we can enhance them if we play with them. There is some kind of black box device rigged between the hulls that activates a hydraulic lift that brings the vehicle to the surface, levels it and allows the captain to secure it. Crude, but probably effective. They were able to get into the harbor with it. The securing cables appear to be on some kind of recoiling device that stows when not in use. It's pretty cluttered down there."

Bogner studied the photographs over Cameron's shoulder.

"But no sub," Langley concluded. "We got lucky. One of the divers off of CG-144 discovered the rigging during the last security check. He says the capture device is very primitive—a spring-loaded, oversized D ring that captures an insertion pin. The way he describes it, the whole recovery would depend on the seamanship of the submersible's operator; no insertion would take place unless the docking craft was perfectly aligned. In something this crude, there wouldn't be any subsequent hydraulic action unless the tanks were blown and the craft had been pretty well purged. A real touch-and-go operation. As soon as this meeting is over, I want to take these photographs down to the CAS boys in the computer room and see what I can come up with. But again, no sub. If there was a hen in this nest it sure as hell didn't come home to roost last night."

"We found these too," Stone volunteered. He laid a man's shirt and a pair of shoes on the table. "The shirt has an American label, the shoes were made in Russia. Dissimilar sizes or a oddly shaped man—can't tell which. My guess is that the clothes are for two different men. In either case, too big for the boy. And there was nobody aboard but the woman and the kid."

Cameron looked at the woman. "Do you have anything to say, Mrs. Vasilivich?"

Olga Vasilivich stared back at him, refusing to acknowledge the question.

Stone laid a cardboard envelope on the table. "These are the *Cuboc*'s papers. According to her registry, she's out of Kiel, Denmark. We're checking it out. Meanwhile we're towing the *Cuboc* in from the reef and mooring her at the Negril wharf. Langley's men will start taking it apart this afternoon."

Cameron confronted the woman. "Do you understand the seriousness of the charges, Mrs. Vasilivich?" His voice was patient. "Last night an American vessel was blown up in this harbor. There were several people aboard that craft when it happened. Most of them died in that explosion. Based on what we've uncovered about your vessel so far, we have every reason to believe that you and the two men Commander Stone referred to are involved. And I can assure you that the longer we dig, the more we'll come up with. In other words, we're building a case against you, Mrs. Vasilivich, and at the moment you are well on your way to being implicated in a matter that is likely to result in murder charges. You can help yourself and your son by cooperating with us."

Olga Vasilivich's eyes darted momentarily to her son. Like his mother, the boy remained silent.

"You do understand English, don't you?" Stone asked.

The woman looked at him, still refusing to answer.

"Very well." Langley shrugged. "We'll start with the kid. Have someone escort Mrs. Vasilivich down to D Deck until we're ready for her."

Olga's eyes narrowed. "Leave my son out of this. What is it you want to know?"

"Okay," Langley sighed, "now we're getting somewhere. Apparently Mrs. Vasilivich does understand English." He offered her a cigarette which she declined. "This is the way it works. I ask the questions and you answer them. The first time you refuse to answer a question or I think you are lying, we separate you and your son and you don't see him again. Do I make myself perfectly clear?"

Olga Vasilivich hesitated again before nodding.

"Commander Stone here has three different reports of two different men who were seen aboard the *Cuboc* in the last three days. Where are they?"

The Vasilivich woman averted her eyes, looking down at her hands. "They . . . they did not return." Her voice was small and defeated.

"Return from where?" Stone demanded.

"A mission."

"A mission? What mission? Blowing up the *Codicile*?" Langley shouted.

"I know nothing of any plans to blow up anything. They had another purpose."

Bogner stepped in. "Was that a plan to assassinate Sergei Zhelannov, Mrs. Vasilivich?"

Olga's expression was stoic. Then she chewed her lip.

"What Commander Bogner was about to tell you, Mrs. Vasilivich, is that they failed. President Zhelannov is here aboard this vessel—and he is alive."

Cameron's voice had the stinging ring of a slap. The wife of Ilya Vasilivich looked at him and tears began to furrow down her face again.

Bogner looked down the table at the boy who was watching his mother.

"That yacht of yours is rigged to accommodate some sort of submersible, Mrs. Vasilivich. What kind? A sled? A PS? What kind? We know a vehicle of some sort was launched from the *Cuboc* last night," Stone insisted, "and we believe the operator of that submersible is the one who attempted to assassinate the Russian President."

Olga looked slowly around the table. There was no compassion or sanctuary in any of the faces. She was alone with her son, and more than the secrecy of the mission, she was worried about Ilya. "It was a Mala," she said softly. She leaned her head on the table and began to sob.

Langley looked at Cameron. "Bingo. Mala—Yugoslavian, two classes, both two man versions. The Russians used a ton of them in their midget

submarine fleet. Now we know what we're looking for."

Olga Vasilivich reached out for her son, but he
recoiled from her.

*Datum: 10:6 . . . Wardroom K, USS Black River,
1155NLT*

Langley was crouched over his coffee. "You
mentioned something called the Jehovah Hole.
Tell me about it."

"Graveyard of ships," Bogner said. "It's down
there all right."

"Tell me about it."

"Don't know that there's much to tell. Supposedly the people around Negril call it that because
of the lost souls that are trapped down there."

Langley squinted as Bogner took a long sip of
coffee.

"I came down here for a couple of weeks after
Joy and I split. I was trying to get my head screwed
on straight. I fished the reef all day and hit the
bars up and down the beach all night. One night
a friend of mine told me if I didn't change my
ways I'd end up in the graveyard of ships. He
went on to tell me that in the closing days of
the war three German ships, nomenclature never
discussed, were chased inside the reef by a couple
of American destroyers. The way he tells the story, the Americans hammered the Nazis for three
days, and when the Germans figured they didn't
have any other alternative, they scuttled all three
vessels and set them on fire. The problem is, they
left the wounded on board; several hundred men
went down with those burning hulks. Those that

could make it swam to shore and disappeared into the hills. But the Jamaicans thought the place was haunted because of all those bodies down there. Thus—the Jehovah Hole. The locals wouldn't fish it for years."

"True story?"

Bogner nodded. "Fate played a hand in it. They went down in the deepest part of the harbor, which adds a bit of mystery to the story."

"How deep is this harbor?"

"Varies. Most of it isn't much more than a couple of hundred feet. The main channel runs almost three hundred feet deep, but it's narrow. It's completely natural, never been dredged or worked. We've always considered it too small to be of any strategic value."

"But what about this hole?"

"I said most of the harbor. The hole portion runs deep, depths no one has ever really probed. It runs parallel with the reef inside the harbor and extends out. I've heard theories that it extends all the way out to the Cayman Trench."

"Under the reef?"

"Possibly. But because of the local superstition about the place no one knows for certain."

"I'm told you've done some diving in this area," Langley said.

Bogner nodded. "If you're asking me if I've done any diving there, the answer is no. It's not exactly a friendly place with giant kelp beds and some of the biggest goddamn sharks I've ever seen."

Langley slumped back in his chair and rotated his cup between the palms of his hands. "Let me ask you a hypothetical question, Toby. Taking into consideration what we learned from that woman in there, could a Mala sneak out of the harbor at either end of the reef?"

"Doubtful." Bogner shook his head. "Not enough clearance. Besides, Stone's boys would have picked it up. A Mala's diesels would make too much noise."

"But they were able to launch it from that Swath, work their way to the *Codicile* and then get away without getting detected. So why not through the reef?"

"Battery life. If they accomplished the first part of their mission on battery power to avoid detection, then discovered they couldn't rendezvous with their mother craft and went some place to hide, more than likely they've pretty much drained their batteries."

"Good. Good." Langley grinned. "We're both following the same train of logic. Wherever they are, they can't maneuver because they can't use their diesels. The minute they fire those diesels, they know we'll pick up the noise on our sensors, right?"

"In theory at least," Bogner confirmed. "If Stone's units had been trailing sonar inside the harbor last night, even their batteries wouldn't have enabled them to pull this off."

"Let's take it a step further. They can't return to the mother ship and their batteries are low. They can't fire their diesels because they know we can pinpoint their location with our audio sensors. They can't go through the choke points at either end of the reef and they can't go through the main channel because the *Black River* is blocking their way. Now what do they do?"

"They sit and wait."

"How long and where?"

"If they are relying on those batteries for air, they're in trouble. If they have other air capabilities on board without running the diesels, they've got awhile longer. As to where—anywhere along the reef."

"In this so-called Jehovah Hole?"

"How would they know about it?"

"Maybe they did their homework better than we did, Toby. Let me take my hypothesis one step further. Remember Steinmetz, the famous Nazi U-boat commander?"

"Sure," Bogner said, "he's the one that hid in the hulk of the *HMS Dover* for six days while half the British fleet conducted a search and destroy operation right over his head."

"Exactly. Why couldn't our killer be hiding down there in those giant kelp beds you were describing or cozied up to one of the hulks of those German ships waiting for us to drop our guard?"

Bogner picked up the scenario and continued. "By now he has to be thinking we've figured out how he pulled it off, and he is probably thinking we've got his battery problem noodled out as well. The way I see it, our friend thinks he has two alternatives. He hides and waits, hoping that we think he took the tube for lack of air, or he knows that trench at the bottom of the Jehovah Hole does lead out under the reef and figures that's his way out. But that raises a whole new set of problems. How do we flush him out?"

"Toby, what about your ISA buddy, Zack Koorsen? I hear he is a former SEAL."

"That's what it says in his fitness report; we've never talked about it."

"And you've logged some time in a couple of deep sea recovery vehicles, right?"

Bogner straightened. "That was a hundred years ago, Peter, when I was still running seven to ten miles a day. I'm getting too old for that kind of thing."

Langley was musing aloud. "I think Colchin was right. There are only two ways to prove to the Russians that we aren't the ones who tried to knock Zhelannov off. Either the old boy pulls through and tells us who pulled the trigger, which Forsythe thinks is a long shot. Or we have to come up with the trigger-man and make him talk, another long shot. But maybe not as long as hoping that Zhelannov pulls through."

Bogner got out of his chair and studied the map of the harbor. "Assuming all of our assumptions are correct—that the sub didn't make it out of the harbor, that its batteries are about shot and that it's hiding down there somewhere—how are we going to find him? And after we locate him, how the hell are we going to force him to the surface? If this guy is wired like I think he is, he's enough of a zealot to burn his own ass if he thinks we're on to him."

Langley persisted. "First question, T. C.: given the right equipment, do you think we could find him down there?"

"All right, suppose we did find him, then what?"

"That part of it I haven't got worked out yet, but I think there is a way to ferret him out. After the Vasilivich woman let the cat out of the bag about the Mala, Cameron informed me the *Arca-Dino* is still on board. He claims they were transporting it back to Scripts after it was used on the Hogshead Shoals project off the Carolina coast a few weeks back. Colchin ordered the *Black River* down here before they could deliver it."

"The *Arca–Dino* is a research submersible," Bogner reminded Langley. "There's a big difference between the two. Suppose this Mala is armed. Who ever takes the *Dino* down will be a sitting duck."

"On the contrary, the *Dino* has some advantages; it's quiet, quick and highly maneuverable."

Bogner was still shaking his head when the blue intercom light began blinking. Langley picked up the phone. It was Cameron.

"Tell Bogner we've got a code 77 ident in the COM CEN on C level, secured transmission."

Bogner recognized Packer's code. The only thing that amazed him was how long it had taken Packer to hunt him down. Three minutes later he had scaled the summit to C level where a seaman second handed him the phone.

"What's the latest?" Clancy growled. "Cameron claims you located the mother boat for the Mala."

Bogner checked the blue light to make certain the line was secured. "And Langley thinks we've got it trapped in the harbor. We're trying to figure out how we can flush him out."

"Where's Koorsen? This is right up his alley."

"Zack is standing by on one of Stone's cutters. We're seeding the harbor with some broad band hydrophones. We'll be able to monitor and isolate every damn noise in the harbor."

"Are you deploying any non-acoustic sensors?"

"I'm telling you, Clancy, if that Mala is down

there, he won't be able to blow his nose in another thirty minutes without us knowing about it. Langley assures me we can detect any magnetic anomalies, even changes in seawater chemistry resulting from variation in seawater electromagnetic fields."

"Good," Clancy said. His voice was suddenly paternal. "Something else I think you better know, T. C. You're getting company."

"Company? What the hell are you talking about?"

"Within the last hour I've approved the security clearance on four names for the press pool that's coming down to cover the story. Joy is one of them."

"Joy?" Bogner repeated.

"She broke the story from Los Angeles. NBC says she deserves a shot at it."

"Damn," Bogner muttered as he slipped the phone back in its cradle. He was halfway through the door before he realized he had hung up on Packer.

Base Hour
Three-Three:
ZERO ZERO . . . 1500ZULU

Datum: 10:6 . . . Montego Bay, Jamaica, Noon
MBLT

Boris Andrakov began moving the books to one side on the shelf in the alcove and pulled out the concealed meter-long compartment hidden behind them. The small blinking light on the telephone indicated that there had been a transmission, and the hidden facsimile machine would contain a communiqué.

To his surprise, he had received two documents. The first one was the one he had anticipated. The second document utilized the 72XB code designation—highest priority. It was the first time that he had ever received a message of such importance. It would require a long and arduous decoding session.

Nestled in the same compartment with the fax machine was the Ministry of Intelligence Communication's blue code book, numbered, tattered, its spine broken from repeated reference. Andrakov took it out and opened it.

Slowly and with a degree of patience known only to the most methodical of men, he worked and rechecked the complex mathematical equation required to reduce it to a single code key. Then he laboriously translated the clusters of seemingly meaningless numerals into words, matching the words with their antithetical meaning in the English dictionary. Finally, he drew two columns and penciled the word *vashniy* across the top of the paper. Then he carefully printed *'spye'shit nye'mye'd lyenna sye'st*.

The message decoded, he turned to the instructions, reading them a second and finally a third time, until he could repeat them aloud, verbatim.

"Place the instructions in a sealed envelope and placed the envelope inside a menu at Le Chamanade. Leave the menu on the brick retaining wall of the shark tank at the south end of the dining room. Next to the menu place a partially consumed liter of red wine and an empty wine glass."

Satisfied, Andrakov destroyed the written instructions, placed the envelope in the inside pocket of his seersucker coat and repositioned the facsimile in the container behind the books. Then he hurried to his car. With any luck at all, he could get to the bank and be in Negril before the dining room was closed for the afternoon.

As he closed the door, he was momentarily tempted to try to break the code name of the recipient of the communique. Then he would know the identity of General Denisov's personal illegal.

But Boris Andrakov discarded that idea before he had driven beyond the city limits of Montego Bay; some things, he decided, were best left alone.

Datum: 10:6 . . . Moscow: 47-3-7 Novogorod, 2115(a)MLT

Konstantin Nijinsky trudged wearily up the three flights of wooden stairs, his hands thrust deep in the pockets of his raincoat and an unlit cigarette dangling from one side of his crooked mouth.

The offensive odor of mildew, decaying plaster, urine and lye soap assailed him with each step.

At the top of the stairs, an aging former militia man blocked his way. *"Vash dakoo my'ent pasha loosta,"* the man said.

Nijinsky, rather than brush the old man aside, displayed his badge and the man pointed to an open door down the hall.

In the room, a younger man, wearing a military coat without insignia and a pair of American blue jeans, stood by the open window, inhaling the chilly air. When he turned around, Konstantin realized that the man had been throwing up.

"Zdrast vooytye'."

The man tried to straighten himself. "I heard a noise," he started to explain. "I knew Modesta had been having trouble with hooligans, so I came up to investigate. This is what I found and I called the police."

Nijinsky threw away his cigarette and studied the carnage. He recognized the work but said nothing to the younger man. The older one was standing at the door now, watching him.

"You are an inspector?" the man in the jeans asked.

"*Da*. Have you touched anything?" Konstantin took note of the fact that the woman's purse was open. "What is your name?"

"Nadezhada Orlov. I have touched nothing," the man lied. Nijinsky knew he had rifled the woman's purse.

The woman, 45, perhaps a bit older, was naked, face down across the bed. A cheap red wig was tilted to one side, giving her distorted face a comical dimension even in death. Her open eyes appeared to be staring at the wall for one last look at a cheap reproduction of a Seurat print.

Nadezhada saw him looking at it.

"Pointillism," Nadezhada said, "a sign of decadency." He assumed that the officer was a former KGB agent simply because most of them were.

Nijinsky looked at the painting for a moment. "I like it. It speaks to me," he said.

He turned his attention back to the dead woman. Her breasts were tatooed with flowers and the pubic area decorated with multi-inked tatooes issuing obscene invitations. "I like most art," Nijinsky added.

Nijinsky wondered if the woman actually believed that her profession was apparent only when she disrobed. Another prostitute! There were so many of them now. Times were hard.

"Modesta?" Konstantin asked, pointing at the woman's body.

"*Da*," Orlov confirmed, "but him I have never seen before." He was looking at the man's body on the floor beside the bed.

Nijinsky knelt and touched the body. Obviously, an American. You could tell them by their clothing. This one was short and plump, and there was a bullet hole between his eyes. The hole twisted the putty face into a mask of mismatched eyes and a gaping blood-crusted mouth. The body was still warm.

As an afterthought, he removed the leather pocket secretary from the inside pocket of the man's coat. Nadhezhada had been a busy boy; the money had been removed from it as well.

Nijinsky studied the man's identification papers for a moment and sighed. "Are you certain you have not seen him before?"

Nadezhada shook his shaggy head and rubbed his hands together. "Never," he professed.

"Were you her pimp?" Nijinsky asked. He recognized Orlov now. He had seen him standing along the Esplanade selling used auto parts. He was a black marketeer.

Nadezhada hesitated. "She was my sister," he finally admitted. "Life was difficult but up until this we had survived."

Nijinsky took out another cigarette, went to the window and stood there for a moment. Finally he turned back to Orlov. "*Vestuka?*" he asked.

"At the end of the hall."

Konstantin Nijinsky walked past the bed, looking briefly at the woman but paying more attention to the Markarov semiautomatic. The 9-mm round had entered her head just below the left temple and was no doubt the reason for the crooked wig. The gun was locked in her left hand, apparently to give the illusion she had shot the

American and then taken her own life. Curious, he thought to himself, that she would use her left hand to pull the trigger when she was right-handed. The nicotine stains on the first and second finger of her right hand indicated which was the dominant hand.

In the hall, he picked up the public telephone and dropped in the two kopek piece. "Chief Investigator Kolchak, please."

"*Da*, Nijinsky," the coarse voice came on the phone.

"We have a problem, Chief Investigator. There has been a double murder in a third floor walk up at 47 Novogorod. One of the victims is the American Ambassador, Robert Parker."

Kolchak was silent for a moment. "First I must call Kerensky."

Datum: 10:6 . . . Wardroom C, USS Black River, *1239NLT*

On the E Level of the *Black River*, Bogner and Koorsen were getting their first look at the *Arca-Dino*. Even the fatigue lines in Langley's face seemed less prominent now that the plan was beginning to take shape.

"I hope you and Koorsen are fast studies, Toby. I figure we've got just enough time to waltz you through this little lovely one time, then it's going to be up to you to start asking intelligent questions. But the way I see it, any man that's ever piloted a DSRV or a DSSV should be able to catch on to this sweetheart fairly quick."

Bogner *was* a quick study. It was a sixth sense with him. He had learned to utilize it and depend on it. He looked up at the gray-green hull and began to step it off.

"In some ways it's bigger than I thought it would be. What are we looking at? Forty feet or so?"

"Close. Thirty-eight feet, eleven inches and ten-foot-nine athwartship. Maximum speed, five knots, and she can poke that lovely snout of hers along the bottom for twelve hours at a clip. Most of her equipment was conceived and built for something called LOSS, large object salvage system. As she sets, with her upgrades, she is probably one of the best deep-sea salvage vehicles in the fleet."

"So this is your hot button, huh, Peter? I always wondered what turned you on."

Langley managed a smile. "I was a junior at the Naval Academy when the *Thrasher* went down in 1963. I sat in front of that damn television every chance I got. Couldn't sleep I was so damn fascinated. I guess that's when I realized what I wanted to do with my life. Then, during my senior year, one of the officers on the *Thrasher* recovery project came to the Academy to give a series of lectures. Right then and there I decided that if this man's navy ever put a DSSV program together, I was going to be part of it. Six years ago I was able to pull enough strings to get myself assigned to the *Arca-Dino* project. I was there when they laid the beam, and I was second seat on her first shakedown run. Then when I blew the eardrum, Cameron had me assigned to the NSB at NI, but he knew where my heart was."

"Then you know this baby inside and out?"

"They've made a couple of modifications,"

Langley admitted, "but give me an hour with her maintenance chief and I'd be up to speed. Give me another hour and I can have you piloting it."

"You can talk me through down there then?"

"Negative, you'll be running silent. Our prey may have a set of super sophisticated ears. Even you and Koorsen will have to work out a set of hand signals."

Bogner was getting the picture. "Let's get on with it."

Langley climbed the gantry to the conning tower. "You'll be working with the latest ICAD system—sonar, closed circuit television and the very latest state-of-the-art navigational devices." He was pointing out features as he walked along the strakes. "Propulsion and all controls are accomplished by a conventional stern prop in a movable control shroud. The A-D has four ducted thrusters, two fore and two aft. This little lady is so agile you can hover and hold her steady in a two knot current. I heard there was a premature systems shutdown in the Sealab unit assigned to the *Hogshead* project and the pilot of the A-D actually took the last diver out and fought a four mile current drag while he was doing it."

"Battery back up?" Bogner asked.

"Four six packs. You can operate all systems for two hours or at fifty percent for four. You have a load calc on your central control panel. It'll work your reserve out to a tenth of a second."

Bogner held up his hand. "Suppose Zack and I do find this guy, Peter, but what if he doesn't want to come out and play?"

"You've got some options. See that manipulator arm on the bow? You can thread a needle with it. That's the beauty of having the *Black River* in a support role. There's a forty ton crane up there that can jack sixty to seventy thousand pounds right out of the water. And unless this Jehovah Hole you keep talking about is a slip trench, we've got enough wire to get to him. We'll jack his ass right out of the water."

"That's assuming Koorsen and I can find him," Bogner reminded him.

Langley threaded his way through a network of lanyards lashed to the gantry and worked his way back to the conn tower to open the hatch. "From the fantail to the bow sonar, right out through the beak on the manipulator, she has an automatic degassing system. That way, Zack can leave the *Dino* and handle her underwater. There are four PQC accesses so that external personnel can converse with the console jockey without coming aboard. It makes it a hell of a lot easier to communicate down there."

He opened the hatch and descended. Bogner followed, already feeling slightly claustrophobic.

"This is the forechamber where the controls are." Again Langley was pointing them out. "Overhead access, main and auxiliary batteries, port and starboard, variable beam ballast and trim tanks—all controlled from Panel A. Forward thruster, thruster ducts, hydraulic and propulsion controls along with all pumps are worked from panel B. The pilot can work everything, but the manipulator takes a second set of hands; so does the hauldown winch. Depending on the conditions while you're down there, someone has to keep an eye on the hoohah, which is the breathing gas source for connected divers. If Koorsen here is out there in the Newtsuit, he's on his own." Langley looked at Koorsen. "Have you worked in one?"

Koorsen grinned. "I have only one question. Is it big enough? Mama Koorsen spooned a lot of hog jowls in me when I was a pup."

While Bogner listened to Langley and Koorsen, he tried to remember that last time he had worked underwater. He had a sneaking suspicion that snorkeling with the little French gal in Barbados the previous winter didn't count.

They followed Langley into the second chamber. "Everything you'll need if you have to coax him out is right here. Better check it out, Zack, and make sure everything was stowed the way it should be."

He wheeled past them, back through the control cabin, and started topside, still pointing out equipment.

"Access hatch, extensible illuminator and side screening sonar which will probably come in handy if you get yourself into some tight places. And there's the shot ballast solenoid." He looked at Bogner. "And one last very important thing— the way out is up."

"What's our schedule?" Bogner asked.

Langley glanced at his watch. "We're pushing 1300 hours. The crew chief and maintenance crew need a prep hour. If we hustle we can do a little dipping by 1500 local. In the meantime, you need to study the charts."

"Peter, we're playing a long shot here. I know

a man who knows this harbor like the back of his hand. I can learn more talking to him than I can studying charts. Besides, Cameron's boys will program the on-board computers with the latest situation display maps."

"Can you trust this guy, Toby?"

"Completely untrustworthy."

"Good, then you know how to read him."

"He's crooked as hell but he knows this harbor. He can tell me what we're getting into when we take her down in that Jehovah Hole. I don't even have to question his loyalty. He's on record that he sells to the highest bidder."

"Sounds like an entrepreneur to me." Langley grinned. "That means he can't be all bad."

Datum: 10:6 . . . Negril: Le Chamanade, 1258NLT

As Bouderau crossed the narrow strip of beach approaching the veranda of Le Chamanade he was reasonably certain he had been able to dig out everything his cadre of informants knew. They knew he rewarded only those who gave him good information and did not seek information from those he believed to be unreliable.

Despite the gaps in what he could verify, he was now satisfied that he was beginning to piece together a scenario that needed only a small confirmation here and there to validate his suspicions.

As he approached the lobby, the young woman behind the reception desk pointed to a man sitting by himself in the dining room. It was Andrakov. Bouderau was surprised to see him.

"How long has he been here?" Lucian asked.

"A short time," the woman said. "He has not been waiting long."

"*Bonjour*," Bouderau said as he approached the table. Andrakov, startled, looked up from his coffee. To Lucian, the Russian looked even more nervous than usual.

"Monsieur Bouderau," the little man mumbled in surprise. Bouderau found it curious that the Russian had the look of someone doing something immoral or illegal even when he wasn't.

"Did your friend appreciate the little repair job we did on the device beneath his ship last night, *mon ami*?" He did not tell Andrakov that he had just seen the American Coast Guard tow the Swath to a pier at the Negril wharf.

Andrakov looked at him for a moment before he remembered. "Yes. Yes. He was most appreciative." Caught off guard, Andrakov was even less convincing than usual.

"Good," Lucian laughed. "Your friend is happy. You are happy. And I am happy. It is not often that everything works out so well. However, you should have stayed last night. You missed all the excitement in the harbor."

The Russian's eyes darted nervously around the empty dining room to see if anyone could overhear them. "Are you sure it is safe to talk here?" he asked.

"But of course, unless you wish to talk about things that would make even these old walls shudder."

Andrakov swallowed hard, leaned forward and lowered his voice. "I have yet another business matter to discuss with you."

"Excellent," Lucian replied.

Andrakov's head was spinning. So much had happened in the last 72 hours, and now he was actually working directly for General Denisov. The most recent message had not even come through Osipov's office.

"Last night, as you prepared to fix my friend's problem, you mentioned a place called the Jehovah Hole. You know this place?"

Bouderau studied Andrakov's eyes. "And now you want to know more about it, *mon ami*?"

"Tell me about it."

Bouderau thought for a moment. "Well, it is said that there are three ships of some size and perhaps a few smaller ones. It is a graveyard for ships. The larger ones are all German, sunk during the closing days of the war." He saw no reason to burden the little man with the names, lengths and tonnages of the vessels. "I fear that over the years they have become little more than a haven for coral, algae, sponges and darkness."

"I have been told that one of them is very large, perhaps even large enough for another vessel to hide in." Andrakov said.

"An interesting theory, but surely you jest. Who or perhaps what would choose to hide in such a hostile environment?"

Andrakov fidgeted with his linen napkin, dabbing at the corners of his mouth.

"Why do you ask, *mon ami*?"

The Russian cleared his throat. "Merely for the purposes of supposition, you understand, I was wondering if it would be possible for a man, a skilled diver, to go into this place called the Hole and perform a small chore?"

"There are any number of factors that could

cause me to alter my answer. For example, what is the diver supposed to accomplish? Is he supposed to recover something? Or repair something? Where exactly is this something located? Is it buried in the silt? Is there anything on top of it? What is the size? The weight? How long has it been there?"

"The diver must do nothing more than accomplish a small simple chore," Andrakov said bluntly.

Bouderau relaxed. He was pleased that the Russian had finally run out of ways to stall. There was nothing he could do now but be straightforward with him. It was obvious that the matter was out of his hands.

"A small chore, huh?" Bouderau repeated. "Could it be that your need has something to do with the American yacht that so mysteriously exploded in the harbor last night?"

To Lucian's surprise, the bluntness of the question did not seem to catch Andrakov off guard as much as he thought it would. Instead, the Russian picked up his valise, unlocked it and opened it. He extracted a single piece of paper and placed it on the table in front of Lucian.

"It is a bank draft, drawn on the Royal Bank of Cheswick, payable to bearer, authority of the British Exchequer, for the sum of forty thousand pounds," Andrakov said.

Bouderau emitted a small, half-muted whistle. "You said a small chore, *mon ami*. For this sum you can accomplish very big things, very difficult things, perhaps even illegal things."

Andrakov was gaining confidence. He reached into his valise a second time and took out two small drawings of a vessel that appeared to be a hybrid submarine. He laid them on the table in front of Bouderau.

"You are familiar with such a craft?"

Bouderau studied them for a moment. "Perhaps I should remind you that I was a salvage diver in my earlier days, not a submariner."

Andrakov was unwilling to play semantic games with the Frenchman. "In your capacity as a salvage diver you no doubt developed an expertise with explosives, correct?"

"From time to time I handled them," Bouderau sparred.

"In return for the bank draft, Monsieur Bouderau, I want you to place a small plastic explosive device at the designated points on this schematic." The little man's voice suddenly sounded as though it had finally been unburdened.

"One thing a salvage diver learns to do, my Russian friend, is ask all of his questions before he accepts an assignment. After he initiates his dive, it is too late. Failure to ask the right questions can result in unwarranted danger, perhaps even death. As you can well understand, possession of such a handsome bank draft will serve me no purpose if I am not around to cash it."

Andrakov stiffened. "Your only concern is the placement of the explosive device." His eyes had narrowed into hard slits.

"My only real concern is my life," Lucian corrected him. "Either you tell me why, or you will have to find someone else to handle your assignment."

Andrakov flinched. There was little doubt in Lucian's mind that Andrakov had been carefully rehearsed to handle a demand for more money, but not the Frenchman's insistence on knowing the reason for the clandestine venture. Andrakov looked around the room again and leaned closer to the table.

"We have a delicate situation, Monsieur Bouderau. You have no doubt heard the persistent rumors that a high ranking Russian official was aboard the American yacht that was destroyed last night?"

"I have heard the rumors," Bouderau admitted.

Andrakov did his best to look embarrassed. "The discussions taking place aboard that vessel were very sensitive. My government deemed it prudent to monitor those conversations. A week ago, an unmanned Yugoslavian submarine, outfitted with the latest surveillance equipment, was positioned in the place known as the Jehovah Hole. My government had planned to electronically detonate a device and destroy the evidence of our eavesdropping after the craft had served its purpose. It would be a source of extreme embarrassment if the Americans were to discover that those conversations had been monitored."

"What you are telling me is that something has malfunctioned and now you are not able to destroy the evidence, correct?"

"That is correct," Andrakov acknowledged. He was relieved that Bouderau appeared to be buying his story. "Our consternation grows by the hour."

Bouderau looked at the drawings. "I will have to think about it," he said.

"There is not time to think about it," the Russian bristled. "My superiors attach the utmost urgency to this matter."

Bouderau held up his hand again. "Wait a minute, my friend. We are not speaking of a mere casual excursion into a magazine world of pretty fishes and pillar coral. What you are seeking someone to do is in fact quite dangerous. There are risks involved. I will need time—and there are no guarantees. First, this unmanned vessel must be located, and I will have to understand the nature of the explosive device you expect me to use. I have many questions. How much time do I have? Some devices are safe when the diver is no more than fifty meters from the explosion. With others, that could be a deadly distance."

Andrakov looked at his watch. "I must have your answer."

"How do you know that I will not dupe you and simply attach your device to one of those old rusting hulks and tell you that I have accomplished the mission?"

The expression on Andrakov's face indicated that Lucian had finally asked him a question he was prepared to answer. "There is a small metal capseal on the vents that I have circled on the drawing. If you return with them, I will know that you have located the Mala."

Bouderau turned the drawings around. "It is a mission that can be best accomplished with the aid of daylight."

"You must not be discovered," Andrakov emphasized.

Bouderau paused for a moment, pushed himself away from the table and started to laugh.

"All right, my Russian friend, we have a deal. Tell your superiors that you are a strong negotiator and that I have accepted. The mission will be accomplished."

"Will you contact me when you have completed your task?"

"Most assuredly. Now please hand over the bank draft."

"You will receive the bank draft when you hand over the capseals," Andrakov said as he got up from the table.

As the Russian walked out of the room, he noted that the envelope he had left on the brick wall of the shark tank was gone. The signal that it had been picked up by the proper person was there. The wine glass was full.

Base Hour
Three-Two:
ZERO ZERO . . . 1600ZULU

Datum: 10:6 . . . Negril Harbor: Aboard the Mala, 1303NLT

At the control panel of the Mala, Ilya continued to maintain his vigil, monitoring both the sporadic and confusing transmissions of the Americans on the surface and the reserve indicators on the batteries. As Ilya saw it everything now depended on the accuracy of Vsevolod's premission calculations and the infrequent data they could get from the Mala's 100kHz Side Scan sonar.

If the calculations were correct, there was reason for Ilya to be confident that the Mala was situated close enough to the largest of the three ship hulks that any active sonar deployment by the Americans would not reveal their location. Active was one thing; passive sonar however was an altogether different matter.

Zhukov, meanwhile, unfamiliar with the sounds of deep water, continued to listen to the Mala's hull protest and groan with every disturbance on the surface.

Red Tide

Ilya had made two more attempts to engage the retrieval device on the bottom of the *Cuboc* and failed. The proximity of the Coast Guard patrols had made any further attempts too risky.

Now they had sought the refuge of deeper water in the area known as the Jehovah Hole.

The fathometer indicated that the Mala was resting in 47.5 fathoms of water. Since Vsevolod had calculated the largest of the three German ships was resting at 45 fathoms, Ilya now believed that the Mala was resting on the upslope of the trench on the starboard side of the largest section of that wreck. If he was correct, they were safe until the Americans launched a search with coax commanded submersible robots trailing remote controlled imaging pods. Such a device would be able to generate a computer-enhanced profile of the wrecks and the debris surrounding the hole. When that happened, unless they were close enough to the wreck, Ilya knew that the Mala would be the obvious anomaly.

The inclinometer indicated that the Mala had come to rest with a five degree port list, a posture that was resulting in a slight yawing motion from the persistent nontidal current. From his infrared SD, Ilya calculated that the bow was pitched out slightly over the downslope, an attitude that would contribute to and accentuate the yaw phenomenon.

Throughout the long hours of the night and into the day, the Mala had been rigged for red, confining them to a macabre world of half-darkness for well over 18 hours. Ilya's legs throbbed continuously now, and there was a dull, persistent aching sensation throughout his body.

Each time he glanced up at the faintly illuminated chronometer he was dismayed to learn that only a few minutes had passed since his previous check.

Unlike Ilya, Zhukov still gave no visible signs of discomfort. Through his headset, he listened to every transmission picked up by the Mala's antenna.

The two men now knew of the *Cuboc*'s plight on the surface and the American belief that the unmanned *Rozhko* was inoperable. Zhukov's expression had changed only once, when the captain of the *Madison* had indicated that the SUR-COM satellite on three successive passes had indicated no reactor activity on the downed 615.

"Could it be that there actually is a malfunction aboard the *Rozhko*?" Ilya had asked.

Zhukov did not reply.

The conversation between the two American captains had gone on for some time with both Zhukov and Ilya listening intently.

It had become a chess game. The Mala had hoped to reberth with the *Cuboc* and then be jettisoned as the *Cuboc* departed the harbor. But, if for some reason, that failed, the Mala was prepared to wait until the Americans lifted harbor security and then rendezvous with the *Rozhko* at a later time. Ilya viewed both plans as practical. Zhukov had been told that, because of excessive cavitation with the 615 unit, it would be impossible to conceal its location, and the ruse of having it appear to be disabled while it waited in backup would only serve as an added distraction to the events unfolding in the harbor. Even now,

Zhukov still had not come to the realization that Viktor Denisov, from the outset, had no intention of having Zhelannov's assassin return to Russia and assume a role in the revitalized Party. To Zhukov, the presence of the Kiev over the downed *Rozhko* and its apparent unwillingness to allow the Americans to assist in its recovery was simply part of Denisov's brilliant plan—another example of Russian theater.

It was obvious now that Ilya understood their plight better than the man in the second seat of the Mala. He constantly monitored battery reserve and air supply. The batteries continued to drain, and four times now he had found it necessary to adjust the air quality level, further depleting their battery reserves.

The purpose of their mission weighed heavily on Ilya Vasilivich. He recalled the night he had been surprised by the illegal's unexpected approach in a small Orange County bar where he and Olga had gone for a drink. The contact informed him only that he would soon be activated.

Three days later he received a call instructing him to dispose of his personal effects.

A week into those preparations, his schedule was moved up a second time.

And then came the rapid deployment from Havana without the opportunity to conduct a thorough shakedown cruise of the modified Mala. Even the crossing from Havana to Negril had been touch-and-go.

He had learned the true nature of his mission in the sanctity of his cabin on the crossing from Havana. Even if he had wanted to turn back, by then it was too late.

Neither Olga nor Tomas knew the true nature of the *Cuboc*'s mission. She believed what Ilya had told her, that they were there to conduct a clandestine monitoring operation for the GRU of the conversations between the American president, Colchin, and the Commonwealth president, Zhelannov. Olga was the wife of a GRU illegal and a former Spetsnaz midget submarine commandant. She knew where Ilya's loyalties lay, and it was her duty as a member of the Party to accept them.

Ilya was jolted from his moody reflections by a blast of static from the American emergency frequency. He looked into the rearview mirror to test Zhukov's reaction.

"Why are they transmitting in such a fashion?" Zhukov seethed. "It is almost as if they want to alert us to the fact that they are about to communicate."

"But they are not even certain we are here," Ilya reminded him.

"Do not be so certain, Comrade. They have taken the *Cuboc* to the wharf, and by now they know how we accomplished our task. It puzzles me why they do not discuss what happened aboard the American yacht last night."

"I do not understand either," Ilya admitted.

"Think about it, Comrade. The President of the Commonwealth is dead, and these Americans do not discuss it. Why is that?"

"I do not know, Comrade Marshal."

"That is almost as perplexing as the fact that they alert us to each and every one of their transmissions. It is as if they want us to monitor their conversations so that we will know what they are doing."

"Perhaps they are trying to get us to make the first move, to take flight, so that they can isolate our position," Ilya theorized.

Zhukov nodded. "They do not talk about the explosion because they are plotting something. The Americans are pompous and self-centered, but they are not stupid. They know they have the harbor secured, and they are quite confident that their superior hardware will not fail them. You can rest assured they have done more than just seed the harbor with hydro detection devices."

Ilya fell silent, turning his thoughts again to Olga and his son. He was concerned about how the Americans were treating them, far more concerned than he was about his own situation.

Datum: 10:6 . . . Washington: ISA Offices, 1323EST

"Jaffe on three," Miller shouted. Packer picked up the phone.

"We've just been informed that Robert Parker is dead," Jaffe said.

"Holy Christ! When? How?"

"Their version or ours?"

"Both. What the hell happened?"

"Less than fifteen minutes ago we received a relay from the State Department. Apparently Parker delivered the President's message to Churnova and left the Kremlin with their official response around 1700 hours, Moscow time, 0800 Washington time. Then we lost track of him. Four hours later, a homicide investigator reported finding him with a bullet hole between the eyes in some gal's apartment."

"Parker?" Packer repeated. "Impossible."

"Obviously we're not buying it either. Parker probably saw or overheard something that he wasn't supposed to, and it alarmed someone enough to want to keep him from reporting it."

"But—an ambassador? That's playing with fire."

"Not half as risky as blowing up a damn yacht with Zhelannov on it," Jaffe reminded him.

"Then, as of this moment, we don't have an official response to Colchin's invitation?"

"No, but we'll be getting a backup confirmation from the Russian Embassy any minute now. The problem is, it'll be so damned carefully worded that we won't know any more after we log it than we do now. Churnova got his training in the Ministry of Foreign Information. He's a goddamn walking propaganda machine."

"What are your analysts guessing?"

"They've got a theory all right. It's convoluted as hell, Clancy, but I have to admit that it's starting to make sense. Our guys think this whole assassination attempt has misfired in a big way. They think whoever is behind it is playing his cards one at a time and even his own cohorts don't know how he's going to play the next one. This seems to be pretty much supported by Complexity's latest input."

"What input?"

"Complexity has been able to confirm that there is a heavyweight illegal in Jamaica for this operation to clean up the mess if it gets botched. Better tell Bogner and Koorsen to be on their toes."

As Clancy Packer started to hang up he was shouting for Miller.

Bob Miller's cherubic face appeared at the door

of his office before the receiver was nestled in the cradle.

"Have we come up with anything on this other illegal we keep hearing about down there?"

"I've got Morganthaller on it," Miller replied.

"Tell him to get his ass in gear," Packer growled. "We're running out of time."

Datum: 10:6 . . . Negril Beach: Le Chamanade, 1358NLT

After his meeting with Andrakov, Bouderau headed for his office on the second floor of Le Chamanade. Even before he had finished his conversation with the Russian, he had already begun to inventory what he would need and how he would go about it.

Lucian Bouderau knew the treacherous and convoluted floor of the harbor as well as anyone. His repeated salvage assignments for Parant had made him an expert. His efforts had taken him into every coral-infested recess of the reef and frequently into the infamous graveyard of ships as well. On several occasions he had threaded his way through the corroded steel passageways that networked the rusting remains in search of Parant's gold.

As a consequence, he had even attempted to chart the best places for the Colombian to make his drops. Their operation had become so efficient that Parant was virtually assured of recovery anywhere inside the reef.

The sea sled used in these recoveries, along with the rest of Bouderau's gear, was stowed in a rusting steel shed hidden in the mangroves near the water's edge at Apostle Point.

Bouderau had become the harbor's master. On two occasions, he had actually launched the sled and recovered drops while the American Coast Guard units searched the *Broward* on the surface over his head. He had told no one about the unusual combination of thermal and plankton layers extending out from the reef that served as a natural sonar barrier by diffusing the signal.

He unlocked a cabinet, removed the harbor charts and spread them out on his desk. The maps pinpointed the exact location of the downed German vessels resting on the western slope of the hole.

Andrakov had indicated that the monitoring unit used by the Russians had been positioned there, so that was where he would look first. He did not, of course, believe the little man's story, but that was of no concern. His job was to locate the Mala, plant the device and deliver the capseals.

Bouderau located the approximated position of the remains of the *Codicile* and plotted a straight line to the wreck of the *Kleinmagen*, the largest of the three wrecks in the hole. The *Kleinmagen* had weighed in at 9000 tons at the time it sank. Because of the location of the final explosion, it had settled on the shelf adjacent to the deeper recesses along the reef. Judging from the way the debris littered the bottom, Bouderau believed that the explosion occurred in the ship's boilers, snapping the beam and bringing the bow to rest in about 245 feet of water on the downslope of the trench. The stern section, which comprised nearly a third of the hull, was several hundred yards east and buried much deeper. One of the smaller vessels had come to rest beside it and was now wedged stern first in the darkest recesses of the hole.

The entire area was camouflaged by a choking forest of undulating giant kelp. Beyond it lay the underwater maze of trenches and coral-crusted caves that the locals referred to as the den of sharks. Bouderau had long ago determined that it was unwise to venture there. He suspected that because of the strong currents and decidedly colder water there was an as yet undiscovered natural void in the reef somewhere below the 200 foot depth. He suspected it but had never confirmed it.

He had explored the interior of the exposed stern of the *Kleinmagen* on numerous occasions, primarily because of the rumor that the ship was on its way to Argentina with its hold choked full of both gold and stolen religious artifacts at the war's end.

His research into the matter had resulted only in obtaining conflicting reports from the various Nazi war records. Another report, decidedly less intriguing, indicated that the great ship was berthed at Harve at war's end, abandoned by her crew. Neither report was verifiable. Several dives had yielded nothing, and for the most part Bouderau had given up his quest.

If the *Kleinmagen* contained treasures, Bouderau was convinced that those treasures now lay at the bottom of the hostile Jehovah Hole. And there they were likely to remain.

If the Mala was in the area where he expected it to be, hiding among the sunken German ships, it would take him no more than one or possibly two dives to locate it. By the charts, it was three point four kilometers from the site of the explosion. Even considering the depth at which he would be conducting his search, the speed of the sled, the capacity of his air supply, and the risk inherent in his mission, Bouderau was pleased.

The Frenchman checked his watch; he still had approximately seven hours of daylight to work with. Filtered daylight, no matter how muted, was better than total darkness. But the real determining factor would be the movement of the patrol boats in the harbor. The less he had to rely upon any kind of artificial light, the less likely he was to be discovered. Even if he had to use the downshielded halogens with directional beams only when necessary, he still had a good chance of avoiding detection.

Again, by staying close to and descending in the immediate proximity of the reef, using the undulating kelp beds for cover, and descending in a random circular pattern not unlike the movements of the large six gillers, he believed the American sensing devices would mistake him for one of the area's notorious sharks.

With that much of his plan formulated, he poured himself a brandy, lit a cigarette and started to calculate his timing.

The unexpected knock on the door startled him, and he hastily folded the harbor charts, shoveling them into a desk drawer. "*Entrez*," he said, measuring his voice.

Bogner opened the door.

"Ah, *mon ami*, Lucian is psychic, no? Why is it

I expected to see you and your large friend Mr. Koorsen today?"

"Sorry we didn't disappoint you," Bogner said. Both Koorsen and Bogner entered the room. Koorsen went to the window and studied Bouderau's view of the beach. Bogner stood across the desk from him. His face was drawn.

"Well, *mon ami*, from the look on your face I would judge that your vacation is not going so well." He opened his silver cigarette case and laid it on the table. "Smoke?"

Bogner declined the ganja.

"Did the noise in the harbor disturb you last night?"

"It wasn't what I had in mind when I came down here," Bogner admitted.

"I am given to understand that the timing of the explosion was most unfortunate. Even more unfortunate for some than others, wouldn't you say?"

Bogner ignored the question. "I need some information, Lucian."

"What would you like to talk about, my intense friend?"

"The Jehovah Hole," Bogner said.

Lucian leaned forward. "Which part? The myth or the decidedly less colorful real world version?"

"The straight skinny, Lucian. What's down there?"

"Ah, we are being evasive. I have always believed that skillful evasiveness was rapidly becoming a lost art form." The smile faded. "But you are being evasive for a purpose, no?"

"For a purpose," Bogner admitted.

Bouderau looked at Koorsen and propped his

feet up on the desk. "The fact of the matter is, being an old man I no longer choose to dive in the area known as the Jehovah Hole. The sea means only one thing—constant change—and change is far too risky for a man with diminishing skills."

"I'm not asking you to dive, Lucian. I'm asking you what I can expect to find down there."

"Ships. Or perhaps I should say, what is left of them. The sea is not kind to intruders. Besides, why do you ask me? I know for a fact that you have explored the area."

"Not the bottom," Bogner said. "I haven't gone all the way down."

"Who has?" Bouderau said. "I'm not certain anyone has ever been to the bottom of the trench or that anyone can tell you what to expect if you do go—except for the very large sharks that are supposed to be down there."

"Is that suppose to scare me off?"

"On the contrary, *mon ami*, it assures you of almost complete privacy."

Bogner stood up, and Koorsen turned to face the Frenchman as well. "I'm curious, Lucian. Has your Russian friend, Andrakov, been asking questions about the Jehovah Hole this morning?"

Bouderau smiled, he lit a cigarette and watched the smoke create a hazy, silver barrier between his American friends and himself. "As a matter of fact, he has."

"Did he try to hire you?"

Bouderau smiled again. "He did, but I told him the same thing I told you, *mon ami*. I am much too old and my salvage skills are far too rusty."

"Then you won't mind if I ask to borrow your charts."

Bouderau opened the drawer and handed them to him. "You will of course see that they are returned? I am—how do you Americans say it?—nostalgic about them."

"You'll get them back," Bogner said and started for the door with Koorsen following.

In the hallway outside of Lucian Bouderau's office, Koorsen looked at him. "What the hell was that all about?"

"That was all about being on the right track. That was Bouderau's way of telling me the Russians think their man is still down there, too. Now all we have to do is find him first."

"First?" Koorsen repeated.

"First. The way I've got it figured, now that the Russians have been informed that Zhelannov is still alive, they've got two more problems. One, they have to find some way to finish the job and still make it look like our fault. And two, they don't dare let their would-be assassin fall into our hands alive. I've got a pretty good idea who's handling the first part, but the thing that is bothering me is the identity of the one who makes certain the latter doesn't happen."

Koorsen looked at him.

Bogner shook his head. "We're going to have to be alert. Clancy keeps warning me that they've got a heavyweight illegal down here—someone that can handle the tough ones."

"And you think it's Bouderau?"

Bogner stopped. "Think about it. Andrakov pays Lucian Bouderau for information, and Lucian feeds the system. It's the perfect front. Everyone has Lucian pegged as a beach front gossip. They know his past, and everything is right out in the open. Contact between the two goes on all the time, and no one thinks anything about it. And one more thing, Lucian Bouderau will never live to see the day that he is too old to dive into that damn Jehovah Hole."

"But why was he willing to tell you the Russians had already contacted him?"

Bogner started across Le Chamanade's flagstone veranda and down toward the beach. "Lucian doesn't want to play this game alone, Zack. If you and I are poking around down there at the same time, it makes it more interesting for Lucian."

Koorsen nodded as though he understood. He didn't.

Base Hour
Three-Zero:
ZERO ZERO . . . 1800ZULU

Datum: 10:6 . . . COM-CON, USS Black River, *1501NLT*

The radioman looked up from his SDB with a relieved expression. "We got him, sir; Captain Peel from the *Madison* is on S-2. He's standing by."

Cameron loosened his tie and unbuttoned his collar before slipping into the seat in front of the console and picking up the radiophone. "You on, Charley?"

Peel's baritone voice crackled in the static.

"I'm here, Admiral, and it looks like we've got our boarding party identified. We received a garbled message from the Kiev about ten minutes ago. We asked them for a reverification and they got right back to us. They seem to be pretty eager. They've given us the names of the two officers that are being sent over to the *Black River* to act as observers until their medical contingent gets there."

"Ready to copy," Cameron said.

"The senior officer is one Aleksei Potapenko. His rank is shown as Commandant but doesn't say of what. The junior officer is a Lieutenant, a guy by the name of Anatoli Borodin. Bellinger suggests that we have Langley run it through his computers on the outside chance we might be able to learn something before these two board."

"Academic," Cameron blustered. "We know Churnova isn't going to send anyone over without instructions to snoop around as much as they can when they aren't keeping an eye on their President."

"You may want to tell Langley that we can back him up if he runs short of hands," Peel offered.

"Roger, Charley. I'll relay. What are they bringing aboard?"

"Campos informs me it's a modified Hormone B. He says it looks as if they've stripped all the armament off of it. They've been removing gear for the last hour or so. From the looks of things, they're as nervous about you getting a look at their Hormone as you are about them wandering around the *Black River*."

"Did they file an ETA?"

"That's not the way the Russians do things. They give you an ETD and let you guess the rest. Their departure is scheduled for 1900Z, 1600 Negril local. Campos estimates an 'in route' of about forty-one minutes. That should put them on your pad no later than 1941 to 1945Z."

Cameron grunted. "Good. That gives us just about enough time to figure out how to get them from the helo pad to the crew hospital without them seeing anything. Thanks for your help, Charley." He started to push himself away from the console. then, as an afterthought, he asked, "What about the downed sub?"

"Not a thing, Admiral. The Kiev is just sitting there. Hell of a good time for everyone to get a suntan. We're just parked out here looking at each other."

"Stay in touch," Cameron said.

He left the COM-CON and headed for the crew hospital one deck below, arriving just as Forsythe was emerging from the IC unit.

The *Black River*'s chief medical officer and surgeon managed to look even worse than he had earlier. His scrubs were soiled, his hair uncombed, and he needed a shave. Cameron intercepted him just as Forsythe started into the galley.

Thirty-one years of naval command had taught Cameron there was no way to make bad news palatable. "The Russian observers are on their way," he said.

Forsythe poured himself a cup of coffee and slouched back against a stainless steel steam table. He took off his glasses and rubbed his eyes.

"That's what I like about you, Al. You don't waste any time on small talk. Why the hell couldn't you have said they said something like, 'We trust your man implicitly, Admiral. We know he's doing an outstanding job, but we would like to send our own men over just to watch this medical marvel's techniques?' Then I might have felt good about those assholes watching my every move."

Cameron smiled, grunted and poured himself a cup of coffee.

"That's exactly what I intended to say, Frosty, but then I said to myself, 'No, if you do that, Cameron, you'll be passing up an opportunity to be a prick'—and you know how my men enjoy me being a prick."

Forsythe's tired face still managed something of a smile. "How long before they get here?"

"Less than forty minutes according to Peel on the *Madison*. There will be two of them. They're off that Kiev that's been babysitting the downed Soviet 615."

"A couple of real humanitarians, huh? Next thing you're going to tell me is they are both medical experts."

"Fact of the matter is, we don't know what they are or what to expect. I'd be willing to bet they both read and speak English though. They'll be all over Zhelannov's medical charts like a couple of piss ants."

"Which one do you want them to see?" Forsythe asked bluntly.

Cameron grinned. "Don't tell me you fixed the old boy's medical charts?"

"You bet your sweet ass I did. When you said the President wanted us to try to buy him some time until Langley's people could figure out what happened, I knew the jig would be up the minute one of their observers discovered the old boy had half his stomach blown away and was hanging on by a mere plug."

"We're down to that, huh?"

Forsythe nodded. "We may not even have to pull the plug. There isn't much to work with."

"How long can we conceal that gunshot wound?" Cameron asked. He was trying to determine how long he had before he ran out of cards.

Forsythe shrugged. "If these observers aren't medics, they won't know what to look for unless they've been tipped off. It won't take long to figure out what they do and don't know. When their medical team gets here, they'll figure it out right away. The way I've got it calculated, someone out there shot the old boy and he's probably trying to figure out why the hell we haven't talked about the gunshot wound. We're walking a tightrope, and the guy holding one end of that rope, Zhelannov, could cash in and walk out on us any minute."

Cameron sighed and closed his eyes. "This whole thing reminds me of the night I bet my last ten spot on a seventeen to one shot at Washington Park. There were six horses in the field and the other five went off with shorter odds. Do you have any idea how much praying you can do while a nag runs a mile and an eighth?"

"What happened?"

Cameron ignored the question while he reflected. "That's what we're doing here—we're playing long shots. If Zhelannov isn't able to tell us who pulled that trigger, we better hope to hell that Bogner can find that son-of-a-bitch down there in the harbor."

"Do you think he even has a chance?"

"Finding him is one thing. Getting him to the surface alive is another, and making him talk is still another. Put it like this: I hope to hell I have better luck with this than I did my last long shot."

Datum: 10:6 . . . Launch Area, Arca-Dino, 1515NLT

Bogner synchronized his watch with the *Dino*'s chronometer, buckled himself into the pilot's seat and punched the DT into the *Dino*'s computer. It was 1815Z, ops hour 3:00 and counting. The first pass would be a three hour maximum mission.

He watched while Koorsen secured the dog hatch, heard the seals engage and felt the instantaneous change in pressure. Through the *Dino*'s obs ports he could see the launch crew scurrying through their last minute preparations. Their modulated voices filtered into the control cube through the launch com feed; it was a jargon Bogner hadn't heard in years.

The barely perceptible bottoming sensation was the first indication that the sling had been disengaged and that their high tech tubular cocoon was being winched forward on the dolly affixed to the two magnetic rails.

"Ready room to arena," the launch chief alerted him. "You're going to get some buffeting, sir. We're opening the sea valves."

Bogner watched one of the crew inch the *Dino* into a precise position, give the cut signal to the tow motor operator and press the disengage button on the cable.

Koorsen slipped into the copilot's slot, and Bogner began reciting the items from his check list.

The latest surface weather information appeared on the monochrome monitor directly over the pilot panel. He snapped on the voice actuated cabin recorder and began to record the data.

"1831Z launch conditions—sea calm, horizontal visibility 5 to 7, vertical unlimited, surface winds variable to W-3, water temperature 72.2 F, no turbulence." He looked at Koorsen. "Bring back memories?"

Koorsen nodded. "It's been awhile, but I guess I'm as ready as I'll ever be."

Bogner's hands hesitated momentarily at each switch as he double-checked. "Give me a confirmation. Dive trim indicator, on. Diving planes, bow and stern, vertical and off. Encoder, on." Bogner swallowed hard. He could feel perspiration on his forehead as Koorsen confirmed the sequence.

The COM-CON began relaying the COM-SAT info through the feed. "Forecast, 1500 to 2100LT; 1800Z to 0000Z (ND), 06-07. Swells: two. Winds: 5 to 7K, gusts: 10K, barometric: S to F."

Koorsen nodded. "Looks like we're clean and green."

The two men braced themselves as the *Arca-Dino* was subjected to a slight oscillation that felt and sounded like one long continuous roll of thunder. There was another buffeting motion, this one more violent than the first, and they watched as sea water began gushing over the obs ports.

"2:55.31," Bogner recited, "mark DT actual. She's all mine, launch control. Do you read?"

"Sealed and sounded, Commander. You're watertight and lookin' good from here. Is your encoder activated?"

"Affirmative," Bogner said. He checked twice.

"Have a nice trip and bring me something when you come home, daddy." The launch chief laughed.

Bogner secured the *Dino*'s controls. There was a sudden lurch and a feeling of buoyancy. He watched the control panel react to freedom like the backboard of a pinball machine. Lights flashed, gauges began to function, and the contents of his stomach played tag with his mouth before it settled down again.

There was a grating sound in the doors of the *Black River* directly over them, and the hull of the *Dino* began to vibrate as its titanium panels adjusted to the water pressure.

He depressed the first phase button on the auto pilot and a computer-generated voice began reciting sequencing instructions. "All systems control configuration engaged; dive trim actuator on. Please check air mixture."

Bogner looked at Koorsen. "The computer thinks you're breathing too fast."

"The computer ain't scared, Commander. I am."

The *Dino* yawed slightly, and the two men had the sensation of the floor giving way under them. There was a new series of structural protests, and Koorsen wiped the sweat off of his forehead.

"Langley claims we'll be in love with this little gem by the time we've made a couple of sector passes. He swears it's safer than a Sunday afternoon drive down the coastal highway from Oceanside to San Diego.".

"Did you tell him I hate California?" Koorsen grumbled.

Bogner scrolled through the HSD's harbor bottom reference grids. They were superimposed over a series of digital readouts. "Mission monitor on C panel?"

Koorsen acknowledged. "Affirmative."

The CABIN SILENCE light began to flash over the control panel.

There was a reassuring forward thrust as the auto pilot took over. Koorsen monitored the port and down port panel as his eyes danced from a position just over his left shoulder to the one in front of his left knee.

The center port was the largest of the three, a six inch thick carsdan acrylic lens a full 15 inches in diameter. Beyond it, both men could see a world rapidly evolving through a spectrum of yellow-green to green to a murky green grayness.

"Reading?" Bogner asked.

"Fathometer, 15.6. I'll mark at 20.0"

"Good. We'll engage slope at 20.5. In another couple of minutes we'll be in the first grid, 1-C-1 on zone KK. We'll be on the downslope of the reef at that point." Bogner altered the magnification of the display, and Koorsen noticed the small flashing cursor in the upper left-hand corner of the display.

"Anytime you see something that you think looks the least bit out of the ordinary, Zack, mark the grid and we'll go down and take a look."

"If this guy is still down here, Commander, and he's got his ears up, why won't he hear our sonar?"

"According to Langley, we're sending out an absorption beam, no bounce back. It was designed for topographical sounding. It measures the density of the earth. The length of time it takes the signal to be totally absorbed gives us a geological density factor. He claims they've never used it on another submarine before. In theory all they should hear is a deflecting kind of noise similar to something bouncing off the hull that was dropped from the surface."

"In other words, we get a ping only when we hit something the signal won't absorb."

"That's the theory. Let's hope to hell it works."

"But even if we locate him, how do we get a look at him?"

"That's when you don the Newtsuit back there and case him out."

The cabin lights went red, and Bogner activated the bow and port illuminators.

An eerie greenish red light splayed out over the coral buildups on the crusted vertical walls of the reef. Objects that were at first little more than ill-defined and brooding shadows suddenly sprang to life in a montage of color and movement.

"Mark 20.0," Koorsen said. "We're over sector 1-C-1, bearing 0.093, coming around and correcting to 0.090, speed 1.5 knots."

Both men could feel the *Dino* groan as she encountered a strong crosscurrent.

Koorsen gave him a hand signal when they hit the mark.

"We'll sweep to 1-J-1," Bogner said, "and do a 180. That should line us up directly with the hole."

"Hold it," Koorsen whispered. "Off your shoulder. I caught a glimpse of something out your port."

Bogner looked but it was already gone. "What the hell was it?"

Koorsen had activated the starboard illuminator and was swinging it in a wide 180 degree arc. "I don't know what it was. But whatever it was, it was big—damn big."

Bogner turned off the illuminator and activated the side sonar. "We'll see if we can locate it with a pulse."

Bogner brought the *Dino* around, and Koorsen dropped to his knees with his face plastered against the lens. "Damn it, Skipper, I know I saw something. It was moving from bow to stern, elevated starboard port."

"Nothing so far," Bogner muttered, scanning the monitors.

The *Dino* moved into a slow and easy 360. They were suddenly in a world of giant coral outcroppings and undulating strands of kelp. The muted surface light filtering into the underwater jungle created an ethereal universe that defied description. A school of grunt darted in front of the port and startled Bogner. He blinked and leaned his face against the lens trying to see more clearly.

"Whatever it was, we lost it," Koorsen hissed.

There was a momentary grinding sound and a pronounced shudder ran the length of the *Dino*. It was punctuated by a large popping sound near the propeller shroud. Bogner grabbed the controls and switched off the autopilot.

"What the hell's going on?" Koorsen complained.

"Check the absorption beam," Bogner said.

"Either we've got a malfunction or we've hit something," Koorsen said. "There's nothing on the monitor, so there must be something in the water. What the hell was it?"

Bogner watched the *Dino* drift port from centerline. "I think something hit us. Give me a reading."

Koorsen scanned the displays. "Fathometer 23.3, water temperature 59.6F. Suddenly it's a hell of a lot darker and colder out there, Commander."

"We're under an outcropping—and there's your culprit."

Bogner was pointing out of the starboard lower port.

Koorsen's eyes widened. "Holy mother of Jesus!"

It was coming from the depth, straight at them. Bogner switched on the illuminator and they watched in silence as a massive six-gilled shark cruised within feet of the *Dino*, brushed against them, wheeled and made a second pass. It circled, made a third pass and then a fourth.

"They feed just below the thermal barrier," Bogner said. "In these waters the shallows are too warm for them. That's what the jolt was. We stumbled into his territory."

"Let's get the hell out of here then," Koorsen said.

Bogner realigned the *Dino* and corrected his heading. "I'm taking us back up above the thermal layer. Keep giving me readings until you see the temperature start to climb."

Datum: 10:6 . . . USS Black River, 1558NLT

The Kamov Ka-25 'Hormone B', as Peel had reported, had been stripped prior to its arrival on the *Black River*.

The familiar long cylindrical container under the rear of the cabin had been removed and the ventral used for the wire-guided torpedoes was also missing.

Smaller than Colchin's Sikorsky, it gave the impression of cowering at the far side of the helo pad while two fatigue clad Russian airmen hopped out and took up sentry positions. It struck Langley as curious that the sentries carried no weapons.

Langley waited until the pilot shut down the two 990-shp Glushenkov engines and approached the aircraft. Potapenko lumbered off first and Borodin followed.

The senior Russian reminded Langley of a medieval icon. He was squat and heavy featured with unusually shaggy eyebrows that all but concealed his gray, empty eyes.

Alexsei Potapenko was quickly assessing the *Black River* and the rotating radar scanners aft of the pad, no doubt just as quickly deducing that the host ship was a hybrid that concealed something far more ominous than the standard array of air-defense and long range surface missiles.

Langley guessed Potapenko to be in his late forties. He was wearing an often laundered green field combat uniform and the cluster rank of the Commandant. He was an unsmiling, homely man with full fleshy lips and yellow, tobacco-stained teeth. The bulge of his sidearm was obvious.

Borodin wore the rank of Lieutenant and the same type of uniform. In addition, he wore the silver embroidered wings and the gilcha white and yellow crest over his jacket pocket. It was the reconnaissance insignia of the former Soviet helicopter pilots in the Baltic command. He was blond, good-looking and, Langley judged, about the age of his son.

The salutes were perfunctory and the introductions brief. "This way, gentlemen," Langley said.

Borodin quickly demonstrated an inclination to speak to his hosts in English. Langley walked along beside him, leaving the senior Potapenko to bring up the rear. At this point he wasn't certain whether Potapenko didn't understand English or simply refused to make conversation.

When the elevator door opened to the ward deck, they were greeted by Cameron and Stone. Forsythe had chosen to remain in the background.

Despite his junior officer status, Borodin did most of the talking. "We will try not to disturb your routine during our visit, Commander, but Commandant Potapenko has been instructed to remain with our President while I have been ordered to confirm the identification of our fallen comrades to the Bureau of Defense and Manpower. I trust you will be able to accommodate us?"

Cameron nodded and motioned for Forsythe to join in the discussion.

"This is our senior medical officer, Captain Forsythe. He has personally been tending to President Zhelannov since he was recovered from the site of the explosion."

Forsythe motioned for the entourage to follow him and led them to the clinic by way of the empty surgical ward into the ship's cramped IC unit. Zhelannov's area was posted with two of Langley's security men.

The Russians could see their President for the first time. Everything but his face was covered with a sheet. The exposed areas were heavily bandaged, and he was connected to a convoluted series of plastic tubing and electrical wiring.

When Potapenko spotted Zhelannov's medical charts, he picked them up and handed them to Borodin.

Forsythe breathed a sigh of relief. Not only was the taciturn little bastard unable to read English, he was equally unable to determine anything from the graphs on the charts.

"I can assure you," Cameron said, measuring his words, "your President has access to the finest medical treatment the United States Navy has to offer."

Borodin scanned the bogus medical report and nodded reassurance to Potapenko. Forsythe retrieved the charts just as the senior Russian stepped toward Zhelannov's bedside and the guards started to challenge him. Langley nodded his head, and the two men stepped back.

Cameron looked at Borodin. "Please assure Commandant Potapenko that he is welcome to stay with the patient," Cameron said.

As he spoke, the scene behind the curtain at the side of Zhelannov's bed was changing as well. The surveillance cameras were being repositioned from the bedside to the Russian officer. Neither Potapenko nor Borodin were aware of Langley's earlier order: "If either one of those bastards makes a move toward President Zhelannov, ram the butt of your rifle down his damn throat and then ask questions."

"Ready, Lieutenant?" Langley asked.

"*Da*," Borodin replied.

Ten minutes later and one deck lower, Langley opened the vault-like door to the auxiliary cooler and turned on the lights. When he did, he heard the young Russian suck in his breath. It was a sight Anatoli Borodin wasn't prepared for.

The bodies had been arranged in two rows along the north and east walls of the unit. Six of the nine bodies were covered by stiffly starched white sheets; three of them, the bodies of the

R. Karl Largent

Codicile crew, had already been identified by Bogner. The fourth body was that of the Jamaican harbor launch pilot.

The remaining four were grotesque mannikins, charred and mutilated by the force of the explosions. A tag attached to each individual medical gurney indicated the American's tentative identification.

"President Zhelannov and one of your airmen were the only ones who were still alive when they were recovered," Langley said. "The airman later died."

Borodin shivered involuntarily and began to thread his way through the maze of bodies. As he did, Langley handed him a clipboard with gurney numbers that corresponded to the tentative identification.

Borodin lifted the sheet of the body of one of the airmen and recoiled. His voice quivered. "I know him. Like me he was assigned to the crew of the attendant *Hormone*."

Langley made a check mark and scribbled the word "confirmed" in the margin.

At the second gurney, Borodin paused again. He lifted the sheet, peered into the exploded face with its crop of mocking reddish brown hair and checked the number against the identification on the chart. "Your people have made an error, Commander. This is not Marshal Zhukov," he said.

Langley stepped toward the gurney. "Better check again, Lieutenant. He's wearing a Field Marshal's tunic."

"There is perhaps a feasible explanation for this," Borodin said, "but I am most positive. This is not Marshal Zhukov."

Langley nodded.

It took Borodin another 30 minutes to complete his grisly inspection. When he finished his youthful face betrayed his consternation. "I have identified Comrade Techka, and I feel quite certain that I have verified the identities of the others. I am equally convinced that Marshal Zhukov is not among them."

"You are certain?"

Borodin managed a boyish smile. "I knew Comrade Zhukov. He was my instructor in Pyatigorsk. I recall him well. He used metaphors from poetry to describe tactical maneuvers. One does not forget such a teacher so readily."

Borodin could tell by the expression on the Commander's face that Langley still wasn't convinced. He returned to the body that had originally been identified as Zhukov and lifted the sheet again. "This man is somewhat smaller than the Marshal. Perhaps the Marshal's body has not yet been recovered?"

"It's possible," Langley stalled, "but we had eight divers combing that wreckage for over seven hours. All of the bodies were recovered in the first two hours. We found nothing after that."

Langley followed the young officer out of the cooler and reached for the intercom. "Security one, code five. Find Cameron."

The Admiral was on the line in seconds. "What's up, Peter?"

"Borodin just finished checking the bodies. He thinks we've got all of them correctly identified except one. The body we identified as Zhukov apparently isn't Zhukov."

"Could he identify which one was?"

"That's the problem, Admiral. He says none of them are Zhukov."

Cameron, one deck above, couldn't see Langley's contrived shrug. The continued silence on the other end of the line answered his question. "Are you thinking the same thing I am, Peter?"

"Very likely, sir." Langley had measured his response.

Cameron thought for a minute. "Okay. Let's get everybody assembled in Ward C-5. Better tell them we think we now know who pulled the trigger on Zhelannov."

Cameron placed the intercom back in its cradle and looked at Forsythe.

"I think we just solved a major piece of our puzzle. I think we now know who and how. But *where* the hell is he?"

Datum: 10:6 . . . Apostle Point, Negril Beach, 1555NLT

Lucian Bouderau moved with the grace of a man half his size and age. Every move around Parant's artfully engineered sea sled was practiced and efficient.

The procedure for launching the 20-foot-long underwater vehicle had been reduced to a chore of uncompromising ease.

The ten-year-old *Chambeau IV* was a French design with a shrouded cockpit. It was maintained in a shed sheltered by a dense grove of coconut and banana trees less than ten meters from the water's edge. The shed, situated on land owned by the Columbian, Parant, was protected by a high security fence and had been constructed for the sole purpose of recovering Parant's drops inside the reef.

Parant had commissioned the *Chambeau IV* with design features specified by Bouderau. All instrumentation, including an auto pilot and scanning sonar plus batteries, were encased in a tubular-shaped watertight compartment. To enable Bouderau to leave the sled at depth, the closed circuit breathing apparatus was not source dependant. Bouderau was thus able to park the sled and retrieve articles in places too small for the sled itself.

Bouderau, from years of salvage experience, had learned to burden himself with only the barest essentials on his dives. In addition to his Nikonis, a nitrogen-charged spear gun and a chest-mounted halogen, he carried a miniaturized LSS that enabled him to sustain an additional 20 minutes at depth in the event of an emergency.

Hidden by the trees, he opened the door to the shed and carefully lowered the aluminum hulled *Chambeau* onto a small dolly with wide pneumatic tires. Then he released it into the sheltered alcove and watched it submerge in six feet of water. He disconnected the cables and freed the sled, then went back up on the beach and carefully obliterated the tire tracks between the shed and the water. As a final precaution, he checked his suit and gear one final time, donned his fins and entered the water.

Impulsively he had given the harbor charts to Bogner and in so doing had created within himself a renewed sense of exhilaration.

Now with Bogner conducting his search for the Mala at the same time, Lucian had assured himself of a new and exciting dimension of chance that added a sense of adventure to Andrakov's mission. Without the presence of Bogner in the equation, the assignment was too much like child's play.

Andrakov would have him believe that the Mala was merely a surveillance tool, but Bouderau knew better. He had little doubt now that the occupants of the submarine were the men who had engineered the explosion aboard the American yacht. He wondered if Andrakov really believed that he was so naive as not to have figured it out.

Also he knew the occupants of the Mala had to be terrified and helpless, captives of a world few men knew as much about as Bouderau.

These matters were not moral issues for Lucian Bouderau. He had long ago decided that no issue was black or white, just as there was no absolute right or absolute wrong. The Frenchman's philosophy had been reduced to the simple belief that the real value of an object was only worth what the possessor chose to bestow upon it—even life. And life, therefore, was nothing more than one long continuum of arbitrary values in light to dark gradations.

In the final analysis, matters were either practical or impractical, worth doing or not worth doing.

Now he had introduced an element of risk. Even with the aid of his charts and his superior equipment, Lucian Bouderau doubted if Bogner could locate the Mala first.

But if Bogner did, the excitement in completing Andrakov's assignment would only be intensified.

Behind his mask, Bouderau could feel the smile of anticipation spread over his face.

Base Hour
Two-Eight:
ZERO ZERO. . . 2000ZULU

*Datum: 10:6 . . . Washington: ISA Headquarters,
1700EST*

The pastrami was old, the rye tasted like cardboard, and the deli had only compounded the
problem by putting too much mustard on something that was already a lost cause.

Still, it was the only thing that Clancy Packer
had to eat since Sara stuffed a bagel in his pocket
as he left the house after Miller's early morning
call. He took a second bite, washed it down with
a mouthful of tepid coffee and pressed Miller's
button on the intercom.

"I've got NI on the line, Chief. I'll be in as soon
as I hang up," Miller said.

Packer got up from his desk and checked the
fax machine; there was still no response from the
State Department.

For the past hour, he had been trying to get a
copy of Churnova's response to Colchin's invitation. He looked out the window at the October

afternoon sun filtering through the orange leaves clinging to the oaks and wondered if it was an equally beautiful day in Vermont.

His momentary reverie was interrupted by Miller.

"That was Sannon's office. Some guy by the name of Bertram said we should stand by for a secured transmission on the red fax; he says their crypto team has already verified the text."

"How the hell did NI get a copy of Churnova's response before we did?"

"I get the feeling this isn't about Churnova," Miller said.

Packer forced down another bite of his sandwich and chased it with a swallow of coffee. As he did, the buzzer sounded and Clancy punched in his security code authorization.

"What the hell do you suppose this is all about?" he muttered.

"It's a code 5," Miller said. "That's all they would tell me." Then, as always, he reminded Packer to enter the acknowledgment code or he would set off the security alarm.

"It's a dupe from Cameron aboard the *Black River* to NI with Sannon's approval. It's cleared to ISA." Packer scanned the transmission, arched his eyebrows and hit the intercom. "Cornwell," he shouted, "get everybody in here on the double."

The ISA field staff was assembled in a matter of minutes. Only Oskiwicz was missing.

"Pete's still on the phone to that press pool," Cornwell informed him. "They just landed in Montego Bay and are on their way to Negril."

Miller reached across the desk, picked up the NI fax and read it. "Zhukov?" he repeated. "Wasn't he one of Zhelannov's entourage?"

Cornwell appeared at the door, steno pad in one hand and a pot of coffee in the other. She was wearing a sweatshirt with the word "Hoyas" emblazoned across the chest. Oskiwicz had come into the room and was taking a seat as Packer cleared his throat.

"According to Langley and Cameron, the Russian officer aboard the *Black River* has confirmed the identification of all the bodies but one. The one we had pegged as Zhukov isn't Zhukov."

"Are they certain?" Mildred Ploughman asked.

"According to Cameron and Langley, the identification was made by an officer who had Zhukov as an instructor."

Mildred Ploughman was still skeptical. "Is this guy absolutely certain?"

"He should be. He claims he served under Marshal Zhukov. Cameron is buying his story. At the same time, I'm sitting here wondering what the hell the Russians would have to gain by lying about it even if it was Zhukov?"

"Maybe they just haven't recovered Zhukov's body yet," Miller speculated.

"Cameron says he's buying this guy's story because one of the bodies we recovered was wearing Zhukov's tunic. The papers in the pocket of the tunic was the way our guys identified him. According to Langley the body was so mangled there wasn't much else to go on."

The buzzer sounded a second time and Packer reached around to tap in his code. He began reading as soon as the fax started to spew out the message. "This is the NI analysis of Cameron and Langley's situation report." He tore it off and handed it to Miller.

"Actually it's a compilation of related background material as well. The troops over at NI are trying to develop some kind of dossier on Zhukov and a workable scenario."

Cornwell didn't wait for instructions. She sat down at Packer's computer and began searching for the access file. The name Zhukov sounded familiar to her.

"Didn't he attend the first summit between Colchin and Zhelannov?"

The screen promptly displayed a recognition profile and a biographical capsule. Then it began issuing a list of educational and international seminars where Zhukov had been in attendance along with known American contacts.

Cornwell's nimble fingers plodded the keyboard a second time and a series of photographs came up on the screen. Each was a picture of Zhukov along with another Party dignitary.

Packer looked around the table at his staff. "Anyone got a gut feel about this?"

Mildred Ploughman was the ISA's acknowledged authority on the Kremlin's inner workings. "Well, prior to showing up as part of Zhelannov's contingent at the Oslo summit a year ago, the guy was pretty much a nonentity. He gets around, but he's never been in the headlines."

Cornwell continued to scroll the data on the screen. "Here's something interesting," she said, looking at Mildred Ploughman. "He attended the war college at the same time Parlenko, Churnova and Denisov did."

"All one-time GRU heavyweights," Ploughman assessed.

"I think maybe you've just identified another member of the plot," Miller said. "It could explain a lot of things. Parker talks to Churnova, tells him Zhelannov is still alive, and a couple of hours later Parker's body is discovered. I wonder if there is any way to determine who else attended that meeting between Parker and Churnova? If we knew that we might have more of the right names."

Packer began ticking them off. "Parlenko, Aprihnen, Osipov, Denisov, Zhukov—holy shit, we're talking Party hard-liners and big wigs."

"Let's see what else I can find." Cornwell was orchestrating more data.

Packer was looking over her shoulder. "Check the military files as well."

Henline leaned back in his chair. "How much stock can we put in what this guy Borodin is telling us? Is there any reason he could be trying to throw us off, like a personal vendetta against his old mentor?"

Packer scowled and rubbed his forehead. "I been asking myself the same question, Mike, and I come up with just the opposite. If this guy Borodin was part of the plot, he wouldn't have let us know that we had misidentified Zhukov's body. If the truth were known, he probably let one slip—which can also be interpreted that he doesn't know anything about what's going on. By the same token, it confirms that someone went to a helluva lot of trouble to make us think we had recovered Zhukov's body in the first place."

Miller leaned forward with his arms on the conference table. "Okay, let's put it together. We know that Zhukov was there when the meeting started. We know only Colchin's party left, and Zhukov didn't leave with them. The fact that we haven't recovered his body can mean only one thing. He could be the one that pulled the trigger and somehow substituted another body, so we would have the right body count."

"Tie this back to Bogner's theory about the assassin still being somewhere there in the harbor. Does it work?" Taggert asked.

"According to the computer files, Zhukov hasn't had any sub training," Ploughman countered.

"But there are two men missing from that *Cuboc* Langley had towed into the wharf area to be stripped. The body wearing Zhukov's tunic could be one of them," Packer said.

"And the other is piloting the Mala," Ploughman concluded.

"It's a hell of a theory, Chief," Miller said. "Now, what the hell do we do with it?"

Packer picked up the phone. "The first thing we do is try it out on Jaffe. If it sounds as good the second time as it did when we heard it the first, we'll know we're on to something."

Mildred Ploughman's expression continued to be skeptical. "Another thing we may be overlooking is the role of this heavyweight illegal we keep hearing about."

Base Hour
Two-Seven:
ZERO ZERO. . . 2100ZULU

Datum: 10:6 . . . Negril Harbor: the Arca-Dino,
1802NLT

"There she is," Koorsen whispered. "Look's like
your buddy, Bouderau, was giving you the straight
skinny, Skipper. It's right where his charts said it
would be."

Bogner played the searching beam of the forward extensible illuminator back and forth over
a coral encrusted irregularity in the ocean floor
that according to Bouderau's charts was supposed
to be the aft section of the rusting *Kleinmagen*. It
was 30 to 40 feet below them off of the *Dino*'s
starboard.

At first sighting the corpse of the German
freighter appeared to be little more than another
in an endless series of the ill-defined, shapeless
anomalies on the slope of the hole, but gradually
Bogner began to see it for what it was, the outline
of the fantail.

He played the light systematically over the aft

cargo hatches and down to the gaping hole where the beam had snapped before tearing away from the bow.

The deck was littered with debris, and an unexpected void in the giant kelp beds enabled him to see a section where he could aim the beams of the *Dino*'s illuminators to check small sections of the interior.

"It agrees with the charts. She's perched right on the edge all right," Koorsen said. "Another hundred yards or so and the old tub would have slid right on into the hole." He looked at Bogner. "What do you say? Let's go down and have a look at her."

"How much time do we have left?"

Koorsen checked the mission log. "We're 2:03:58 into it. That gives another fifty-six minutes."

"That's cutting it too close," Bogner said.

"At least we can take a peek," Koorsen said. "I've got the coordinates plotted." He began reading them off.

"Fathometer 36.66 and mark. Hey, this is kid's stuff. She's only in 220 feet of water. Give me the grids."

Bogner scanned his instruments from the HSD to the digital read out and back again. "Sector 1-M-1, quadrant 14. How deep to you suppose that damn hole is?" He was looking down the barrel of it through the starboard lower lens.

"Time check and water temp reading coming up, Commander," Koorsen said.

Bogner was just glancing up at the A panel chrono when he felt the *Arca-Dino* shudder for the first time. Suddenly they were yawing wildly to port as though there had been an on-board explosion, and he heard Koorsen shouting, "What the hell was that?"

The *Dino* pitched abruptly in the opposite direction and began a violent roll. Out of the corner of his eye Bogner saw Koorsen's head snap backward and then jerk violently forward, slamming against the stainless steel support beam of the control panel.

Koorsen's head lolled backward, rolling helplessly from side to side. There was a deep laceration extending across the ridge of his forehead and blood poured out, covering the B panel's array of switches and indicator lights.

The aluminum and titanium cocoon was spinning wildly, buffeted first in one direction and then another. A series of small phosphor fires broke out in random patterns behind the A panel, and a mist of salt water jetted in through a rupture in the seam over his right shoulder.

The cabin was instantaneously filled with a fog of acrid fumes from the burning wiring and the sounds of the *Dino's* air system struggling to regulate the air supply.

Bogner slapped at the air supply mixture switch to cut off the oxygen. He was all too aware that the deadly combination of flash fires and oxygen could result in an explosion at any second.

The cabin plunged into darkness, and Bogner felt his body being pinned to the back of his seat by the ship's violent rotation. Then, just as quickly as it had started, it stopped. He was momentarily suspended in some kind of sense warp where all of his references were purposeless.

The *Dino* felt as if it was standing on its fantail,

undulating wildly as though giant hands were rolling it back and forth like a pair of casino dice.

He saw a fire break out behind the life support panel, and even though he was pinned to his control seat, he managed to shut the system down by kicking at the switch.

The high starboard viewing port had been damaged and sea water was beginning to seep in around the ruptured casing. Then he spotted two additional violated seams, one above the port bulkhead and one directly over his head. He managed to squeeze his hand out from under his safety harness and retrieve the small survival light from his uniform pocket. He stabbed the narrow beam of light around the cabin to assess the damage.

Then the buffeting motion stopped, and the *Dino* toppled to the starboard, bow down, inclinometer reading .099.

Still pinned in his command chair, he cleared his head and started looking for Koorsen. He found him wedged directly beneath the support structure for the console and the bulkhead. A pool of water had started to form under Koorsen's shoulder. It was mixed with his blood and his face was no more than six inches from the rising water.

"Zack, damnit, can you hear me?"

Koorsen didn't move.

He tried again, but there was still no answer. There were two sheared bolts in the port bulkhead and a thin wall of sea water was washing down the cabin interior, shorting out the few remaining functioning systems.

With his free hand he managed to get his harness unbuckled and his arm free from the safety harness, wedging it against the console. Then he wiggled his leg loose and propped his knees against Koorsen's command chair until he could extricate himself.

A searing pain raced down his right leg, and he looked down to find a four-inch-long gash in the meaty part of his thigh. His pant leg was already soaked with blood. Bogner grabbed the console, peeled back an access plate and ripped out a section of wiring harness to make a tourniquet.

When he started to lower himself toward Koorsen the *Dino* gave another lurch. He heard the hollow, grating sound of the titanium hull as it slid closer to the lip of the hole.

He aimed the thin beam of his light at the inclinometer. It was still functioning and was reading .109. He had a mental picture of the tiny craft teetering on the edge of the hole as the bow bobbed in the turbulence. By now he knew that anything sudden—a shift of current, a movement inside the cocoon, taking on more water—could plunge the *Dino* down into the trench.

He breathed deeply, steadied himself and supported his weight on the handles of the metal stabilizer bar until he could get his feet under him. He had to turn on the pumps which were in the bow, and the bow was heavily damaged. Even if he could get to them, he wasn't certain the pumps would work.

Through the upper port and upper starboard lens he could see the sediment in the water starting to settle. There were still the disconcerting sounds of the sand abrading the craft's exterior as it continued to inch its way toward the precipice.

His hands grasped underwater for the controls to the first reserve battery on LS. He located it, pushed the switch into the up position and heard the electric air pump activate. He jammed his face close to the valve and inhaled.

Then he reached for Koorsen. The left side of the big man's head was partially submerged, and the water was starting to find its way into his mouth. Bogner pulled Koorsen into a sitting position while he reached for the first-aid kit in the emergency panel over the access door to the second compartment.

At the same time the first wave of dizziness hit him, and he jabbed the beam of light at the air supply mixture gauge. He was breathing too quickly and too deeply. He tried to regulate his breathing, but he was already disoriented. He felt his legs get rubbery and felt himself slumping against the bulkhead. Bogner closed his eyes in an effort to regain his equilibrium and shut out the pain. Before he realized what was happening, he had spiraled into a world of darkness and sharks and fear and panic.

Datum: 10:6 . . . Negril Harbor, 1807NLT

The DM combination depth gauge and chrono indicated it was dive minute 57.1 and a depth of 187.00 when Bouderau felt the first tremor.

The divers called them swarm quakes—small, repetitious clusters of minor earthquakes, none of which were overly dangerous unless they were precursors to a quake of larger magnitude.

The first tremor sent a shock wave through the water that slammed broadside into the *Chambeau* and caused the frame to vibrate. The second came less than 30 seconds later, after Bouderau had started for the surface. He had not hesitated.

Twice before Bouderau had been caught by the dreaded swarm quakes. The first time he had watched the heaving floor of the harbor buckle violently, shifting, dislodging massive chunks of rock and creating a rolling underwater tidal wave of turbulence that nearly knocked him unconscious.

The second instance had occurred right there in the shadow of the great Negril reef as huge fragments of coral and rock had splintered off and rained down on him, almost crushing the sea sled.

Now, older and more prudent, Bouderau headed for the surface until he could be reasonably certain that there would be no more quake activity. He corrected his course to 335 degrees and watched what was left of the daylight struggle to penetrate the murky water.

He brought the *Chambeau* up to within 50 yards of the beach and the submerged dolly. He swam to the surface, scanned the horizon to check the location of the American Coast Guard units, submerged again to a depth of ten feet and propelled himself toward the shore.

He docked the *Chambeau* in its underwater slip, tethered it and swam to a point on the shore where he could come up in the alcove sheltered by the jimba trees. He kicked off his fins and headed for the shed to change air tanks.

The unexpected seismic activity would necessitate a change in plans. The first wave of sediment had obscured most of the downslope east of the stern section of the *Kleinmagen*.

Red Tide

He rebuked himself; the signs had been there. The activity of the agitated sharks had been a sign, but he had ignored them thinking that they had simply blundered into the warmer waters under a somewhat elevated thermal layer where they normally fed.

The danger after the first shock had been apparent. The turbulence had dislodged debris and kelp, both of which could have fouled the unshrouded propeller.

But now he was back on the surface again and he paused to assess the harbor. It was still too soon to be certain. He would have to wait another several minutes.

The last rays of the sun clawed their way from the western sky to the reef, and he began to mentally grapple with the urgency of his mission. He had already decided that the game with his friend, Bogner, would have to be waged another time and perhaps even another place—if, that is, he decided to return to complete his mission at all. Even that was not firm in his mind.

As he stood there he considered telling Andrakov that the Mala had ventured too far into the hole and was now beyond recovery, a condition that Bouderau had begun to believe was a distinct possibility. It had been more difficult to locate than he had anticipated it would be.

If the Americans still wanted to try, let them; there was a difference between courage and foolishness. The Jehovah Hole was deep and treacherous, guarding its treasures jealously.

Or was there wisdom in telling Andrakov that the task had been completed prior to the disturbance and that the capseals had been dislodged from his grasp by the violent turbulence? Under such a scenario he wondered whether Andrakov would pay him—or would he have to resort to other means to get his money?

For the moment, he was willing to set aside his mental turmoil and turn his attention back to the harbor.

The gulls, ever the alarmists, were returning. The waters were again tranquil. He knew that he could no longer delay a decision.

Just as he was about to reenter the water, he was distracted by an unexpected set of car lights. Finally there was the sound of an automobile engine which he recognized as Andrakov's aging Toyota. He reached down, picked up his speargun and started for Andrakov's car.

Datum: 10:6 . . . USS Black River, *1839NLT*

Cameron, Stone and Langley had congregated in the computer positioning room on the E deck to assess Sannon's latest situation analysis. The *Dino's* progress was being reflected in a digital display over the mainframe of the G-1. The mission monitor indicated that the *Dino* had now been down 2 hrs. 28 mins. It also indicated that the craft was still exploring sector 1-M-1. The sonarman reported the last random ping, the *Dino's* all functioning signal, had occurred at mission time interval 2.13.15. The next signal, he informed them, could occur anytime in the next 20 minutes.

Langley felt the first jolt. There was a barely perceptible shudder in the big ship, and it caused a slight port to starboard heave only to settle again.

Red Tide

On the second, Cameron's coffee cup slid across the table and crashed to the floor. Stone, standing next to the mainframe of the G-1, momentarily lost his balance.

"What the hell was that?" Langley growled.

"Feels like we ran aground," Stone said.

"Aground?" Cameron glowered. "We're at anchor. How the hell could we run aground?" He was already hammering on the com button to the bridge. "Fuzzy, what the hell is going on up there?"

Lieutenant-Commander Collins, or Fuzzy to the rest of the crew, was the OOB.

"Hang on, Admiral, I'm getting a DR from the reactor room. Majors says it sounded as though we took a direct hit down there. I'm getting a 'no apparent damage' signal from both the arena and the staging arena. Damage control is getting hot wires from all over the ship though."

Langley had bolted out of his chair after the first jolt and was monitoring the auxiliary channel. The computer was spewing out the same report Collins was getting from the bridge.

"Find out what the hell happened," Cameron fumed.

The light on the intercom began blinking and Langley snatched it up. Forsythe's voice shot through.

"Get your security boys down here, Peter; we got big problems."

Langley raced for the door with Cameron and Stone behind him. By the time they arrived at the crew hospital two of Langley's men were already there and two more were in the corridor outside the IC unit. Langley elbowed his way past a dazed

311

looking petty officer to find Forsythe bending over Potapenko. The Russian's face had been hammered to one side, and his unhinged jaw hung down like a broken trap door.

A young marine corporal was towering over them.

"What happened?" Langley demanded.

Stone raced around to the other side of the security curtain and ripped it back. "Holy shit, somebody unplugged the President's LS system."

"That's why I cold-cocked him, sir," the corporal was admitting.

Forsythe looked up from the fallen Russian officer. "Corporal Kendrick here saw Potapenko slip behind the curtain, and when he went for the plug, the corporal nailed him."

"What the hell did you hit him with?" Stone asked.

Kendrick held up his fist. "This, sir."

Cameron looked at Zhelannov. "How is he?" Forsythe was still checking him with a stethoscope. Meanwhile Langley was motioning Stone into the hall outside of the IC unit.

"You know what this means, don't you?"

Stone nodded. "Hell, yes, I know exactly what it means, Potapenko is part of the damn plot. Those bastards sent him over here to finish the old boy off. He must have figured that noise and commotion was enough of a distraction to try it."

The intercom light was blinking again. Collin's voice boomed through from the bridge. "Get Cameron and Stone up to the B deck. Rawlins is on his way down."

In the B deck COM-CON, Cameron and Stone found Rawlins bent over the crypto message center. He looked up at them and handed them Sannon's transmission. His voice was shaky.

"FLEET COM indicates our Russian friends are starting to do a little saber rattling. The eye in the sky reports that everything that floats from Murmansk down is being upgraded to a level 2 stage. They say the messages are flying back and forth between the officers in the Kremlin and Fleet Command. Not only that, our Kiev friend sitting over that downed 615 is showing signs of life as well."

"Any directives?"

"Not as yet," Rawlins confirmed. "I've already checked to see if Seventh has fired off a readiness advisory, but so far nothing."

"What are they waiting on?" Cameron fumed.

"Us," Langley said. "I'll give you odds they're waiting to see what the *Dino* finds down there."

Rawlins shook his head. "Ready room reports we haven't received the latest random signal from the Dino. Two of the operation officers are afraid those swarm quakes may have damaged some of their equipment."

"Were those the foreshocks or the main course?" Cameron asked.

"You mean there could be more to come?" Stone said.

"Been going on most of the night," Rawlins confirmed. "PAC FLEET confirmed four last night—in the Kurils, the Solomons and two in the Philippines. They seem to be everywhere. This morning there were reports of low level activity in Santo Domingo and some heavy damage in Baraliona in the Dominican Republic. The Seismology Center seems to feel we're in for two or three days of minor magma shifts."

"No big ones?" Cameron pressed.

"They say there is no way of knowing for certain, but they're not looking for one."

"Think we better hold the *Dino* on the surface when she comes up?" Stone asked.

Rawlins looked at his watch. "I imagine that first cluster probably shook them up enough that they are already on their way back. That's probably why they didn't transmit during the fourth scheduled window."

Base Hour
Two-Six:
ZERO ZERO . . . 2200ZULU

Datum: 10:6 . . . Apostle Point, Negril Beach, 1907NLT

Andrakov turned off the lights of the Toyota and stepped out of the car. In the moonlight he reminded Bouderau of a repugnant little toad with a corpulent face trying to prove he was a man by wearing a suit. From the expectant look on his face, Bouderau knew that the Russian illegal believed that the mission had been accomplished.

"It is done?" he asked.

Bouderau made his decision. "It is done," he lied.

The Russian walked toward him, his hand extended. "You have the capseals?"

Bouderau shook his head. "The proof you want cannot be obtained."

Andrakov arched his eyebrows. His mouth twitched anxiously to one side.

"Your so-called clandestine monitoring device is buried at the bottom of the Jehovah Hole, Comrade Andrakov. You can assure your superiors that their worrisome Mala is in no danger of ever being discovered by the Americans—or anyone else for that matter."

"You did not retrieve the capseals?" Andrakov asked flatly. The Frenchman was surprised by the lack of emotion in the man's voice.

"I could not," Bouderau said. "As I approached the Mala, the swarm quakes began. The water became very turbulent. Large chunks of coral began to shake loose from the reef, and soon your listening device, even as large as it is, was partially covered by rock, coral and other debris." Bouderau contrived a smile. "It is a good thing that there was no one in your submarine, *mon ami*, or they would have perished, don't you agree?"

Andrakov studied the Frenchman as though he was assessing what he had said. Finally he surprised him with an uncharacteristic shrug of his shoulders, turned and started for his car.

"One moment, *mon ami*, have you forgotten something? There is still the matter of the money."

"There was also a matter of capseals, Monsieur Bouderau. No capseals, no payment."

It had occurred to Bouderau even as he struck his bargain with Andrakov that proof in form of the capseals was an unusual request for the Russians; they had never insisted on proof before. Was it simply Andrakov's added little twist?

"But the effect is the same," Bouderau protested. "I attempted to retrieve them and in so doing witnessed what happened. I can assure you that you and your comrades need never be concerned about your device's discovery. Is not that news worth the price of our agreement?"

To Bouderau's amazement, the disquieted little man shrugged his shoulders again. It was an uncommon gesture for Andrakov. Instead, he reached into his pocket and his hand emerged with a small handgun, a Korean semiautomatic. There was an alarming casualness about the manner in which he hefted it.

"You still do not understand, Monsieur Bouderau. Even if you had courageously retrieved the capseals, your fate would have been the same."

"You did not bargain in good faith, *mon ami?* Are you saying that the money is not good?"

"On the contrary, my greedy French friend, the bank draft is genuine. What I am saying is that even if you had handed over the capseals, I would have shot you anyway."

"This is hardly the settlement I would have expected from a long time business associate," Bouderau said.

Even as he spoke, his own finger was curling through the trigger housing of his speargun. He took a step toward the Russian, moving himself into the indefinite shadows and within range of his newfound adversary.

"What will you do with so much money? Because I am certain you have no intention of returning it to your superiors."

Andrakov actually appeared anxious to discuss his plans.

"There is an island," he said dreamily, "called Calittie in the Leewards. You have heard of it perhaps?"

Bouderau shook his head and moved a step closer.

"It is just as well. It is small and out-of-the-way. The winds are fair and the fruit is sweet. A man with a sum of money such as this can live quite handsomely in such a place. No one, not even my comrades, will think to look for me there. I have planned long, and I have said nothing of my plan.

"The spider is a remarkable creature, Monsieur Bouderau. He sets his trap and waits. He is rewarded handsomely for his patience. I have been patient, and now my time has come. You were simply unfortunate enough to become ensnared in my web, and now you must pay the price."

Bouderau decided he could risk waiting no longer. He squeezed the trigger. The CO2 cartridge discharged and the spear ripped through the darkness.

Andrakov's body rocketed backward with the spear lodged in his side. For the briefest of moments, he stood there, then he toppled backward against the fender of his Toyota and slumped to the ground in a sitting position. His eyes remained open and his mouth tried to form a denial.

Bouderau walked slowly toward him, bent over and searched through his pockets until he found the bank draft. He folded it, carefully tucked it in the flap of his wetsuit and began to consider what he would do with the Russian's body.

Would he report to the West Mathews police that he had discovered Andrakov snooping around Parant's property on Apostle Point? The police were aware of Parant's operation and his importance; they would cooperate. No, it was too risky, he decided. Perhaps he should simply dispose of the body, a mere matter of weighting the body and dumping it at the reef. The fish along the reef, he was confident, would do the rest. Or . . .

Lucian Bouderau did not have the opportunity to explore other options.

Andrakov, like the spider he admired, had patiently waited until Bouderau's back was turned. He fired twice. The first 9-mm round blew a hole in the Frenchman's shoulder and the second shredded his kidneys. A vomit of thick, black blood erupted from Bouderau's mouth as he pitched face forward in the sand.

The sound of the shots ricocheted out over the harbor while Bouderau fell to the sand and experienced a fear he had never known before.

He felt the man's hands on him, rolling him over and searching. Then he heard the sounds of gulls and the surf searching its way in a kind of primitive rhythm to the shore. He heard the voice of Bob Marley and a distant laugh—and then the sound of someone struggling.

Finally a car door slammed and a tired engine sputtered to life.

Powerless to move or protest, he watched as the beams from the car lights flooded the beach, arced around, searched him out and propelled themselves straight for him.

And in the end, he thought he could hear Andrakov laughing.

Datum: 10:6 . . . the Arca-Dino, *1931NLT.*

Consciousness crept over Bogner with a terrible and icy reality. The stinging bite of the salt water lapping at the hole in his leg created a painful corridor back to a wary acceptance of his surroundings.

Despite it all, he managed to force his eyes open to assess the damage.

The cabin was a scene of destruction, littered with smashed electronic gear and a tangle of disgorged wiring. It was eerily quiet except for the thin veil of water washing down the violated titanium wall of the control cabin.

Koorsen was lying beside him in the water, his huge body undulating in the gentle buffeting motion created by the undersea current. The big man's unseeing eyes were fixed on some part of a universe that no longer functioned and no longer mattered.

Bogner spent minutes trying to clear his addled brain and orient his thinking. From where he had slipped into his unconscious world, wedged against the bulkhead near the lower port lens, he could see the ghostly hull of the *Kleinmagen*, half-concealed by a ballet of gently rising and falling giant kelp.

The forward extensible illuminator was still operating, its probing beam bathing the decaying hull of the German freighter in a mocking and surreal half-light. For a brief moment, he was transfixed by what he was witnessing.

Strangely, there was an ethereal calmness about the scene, as though he had been placed among objects permanently discarded, things of no apparent further value to anyone.

The pale wash of light emitted by the few functioning gauge dials on the *Dino* created an environment that was void of any semblance of reality.

320

It was, he decided, like being trapped in a subtle yet garish nightmare.

He tried to move his leg and the pain shot up, knifing into his brain and bringing his palpability into clearer focus.

He began to carry on a conversation with himself. "Bogner, old buddy, this time you're in some deep shit. You better keep yourself planted right where you are until you can get your head screwed on straight and formulate some kind of plan. Save your energy, and above all save your oxygen."

He retrieved his flashlight, shook the water from the lens and stabbed the beam of light around the cabin.

The A panel was gone, a mocking montage of shattered displays with disgorged circuitry. Dials dangled in space, hanging precariously by three or four strands of multicolored wiring. He tried to remember exactly what the A panel gave him access to. For certain all COM-CON capabilities were out and contact with the surface was no longer possible. The fathometer was smashed and the inclinometer was awash in sea water.

The B panel was still partially intact, but that was mostly external controls and some interior television equipment. He studied the camera and the position of the extensible illuminator. It occurred to him that if the camera worked, he could aim it at the *Kleinmagen* and transmit the image to the receivers on the *Black River*.

At least they would know that he had located the wrecks and someone might put two and two together. Slowly he began the arduous process of getting to his feet.

He momentarily released the pressure on his makeshift tourniquet, felt the surge of blood race into his lower leg and watched it belch through the laceration in his thigh. A crimson colored pool quickly swirled through the murky salt water.

He tightened the tourniquet again, continued to explore what was left of the control module, and saw the main chronometer was smashed. He checked his watch. Elapsed mission time now stood at 3:37:08—37 minutes past the docking ETA with the *Black River*. He wondered if the crew of the mother ship had any idea what had happened.

Logic kept telling him that if the *Black River* had supported the *Arca–Dino* on the Shoals Project, they were prepared to handle a mission malfunction and the subsequent retrieval—but how long would it take them to recognize that they had a problem?

He remembered reading about a pilot who had crashed on a remote island and simply waited for the rescue team. The downed flyer diligently kept a daily log of his ordeal but made no attempt to enhance his chances for recovery. The bottom line to the story was when the ASAR teams finally located his downed plane, they found one very detailed diary and one very dead pilot.

With that thought to spur him forward, he pushed on. He was dizzy, he was weak, and he was having difficulty breathing. The word "anoxia" rattled around in his brain like a marble in an empty barrel, and he began to search for the submerged AQSG controls. Each step was spiced with a biting pain that searched its way up and through his body.

When he located the controls to the air quality supply gauge, the needle was already in the red zone and read critical. He managed to pull the insulation away from the instrument and check the connection to the auxiliary supply pod. The *Dino* was already operating on standby. In some short space of time, and Bogner had no idea how long that was, the *Dino*'s air supply would be completely depleted.

By the time he had sloshed his way through the debris of the command module, he had his situation inventoried. The *Arca-Dino* was going nowhere, unless it was on the end of the cable leading to the crane on the *Black River*—and the odds were that wasn't going to happen in time.

He stopped long enough to study the ravaged hull of the *Kleinmagen* bathed in the light of the illuminator. He grabbed hold of the control, switched it from automatic to manual, heard the gears engage and slowly rotated the light first to the left and then to the right.

On the second sweep, he saw it—a clumpish mound of gray-black with no coral. It was dwarfed by the decaying hull, laying low on the starboard side of the wreck, perched on the downslope of the hole. It was backdropped and almost concealed by kelp and upward thrustings of coral.

"I'll be damned," Bogner hissed. "There it is and there he sits."

He studied the scene for several seconds, wondering what he could do about it. He couldn't contact the surface to let them know, and he had no way of getting to the Mala—or did he?

He thought for a moment. Maybe, just maybe there was a way. But he would have to open the door to the second module to be sure. If it was flooded, if it had been ruptured in the swarm quakes and was full of sea water, he was only hastening the inevitable.

He thrashed his way back through the wreckage and examined the seal around the hatch to the second compartment. In training they had taught him to examine the lower third of the hatch for moisture buildup. Unfortunately, no one had told him what to look for when the hatch was partially underwater.

Still, if there was any hope of getting out of the *Dino* alive before the air supply gave out, that hope was in the access module.

Bogner held his breath and began to rotate the dog wheel on the pressure lock.

Datum: 10:6 . . . Aboard the Mala, 1940NLT

While Ilya dozed fitfully in their world of thin air, Zhukov continued to stare at the Mala's darkened control panel; motionless and stolid, he scrutinized each American transmission for content.

He said nothing to the Mala's commandant as he continued to weave together the fragments of information passing back and forth between the vessels on the surface.

Zhukov now knew that the Hormone had landed on the *Black River*, delivering two officers. He had long since accepted the fact that something had gone drastically wrong with their operation. The question was—what?

Among the many possible scenarios Zhukov now had to consider was the fact that Zhelannov had somehow managed to survive. Over the past several hours he had replayed those final minutes aboard the American yacht over and over in his mind. He could still see the look of confusion and terror on Zhelannov's face as the man realized Zhukov's intent.

Zhukov chastised himself now for not having made absolutely certain the man was dead. Yet how could he have survived both the gunshots and the explosion? Hadn't Vasilivich, through the Mala's periscope, described the carnage on the harbor's surface and applauded their effort?

Or was it possible that the arrival of the Russian naval officers was nothing more than a display of Viktor's flare for the dramatic? Were they mere window dressing, noble comrades standing guard over the body of the fallen leader? It was the kind of flamboyant gesture he would have expected from his old political combatant.

Waiting, he weighed each American word like a semanticist, groping for every conceivable couched innuendo in the Americans' speech patterns. He did not speak even when Ilya stirred, and he continued to somehow ward off the drowsiness and the dull headache brought on by the Mala's increasingly fouled air supply.

Even the cluster quakes had not alarmed him. The Mala had been protected by the hulk of the great German ship and suffered no damage.

Ilya, meanwhile, shifted uncomfortably in his seat, massaging his neck and flexing his arms to increase his circulation. Their eyes locked momentarily but nothing was said until Vasilivich suddenly broke the silence. He had been looking into what constituted the Mala's single viewing port, through the oblique lens in the downed scope.

"What is wrong?" Zhukov demanded.

"A light. I saw a light," Vasilivich insisted.

"Impossible." Zhukov's vigilant eyes checked the Mala's fathometer. "There is no light at this depth."

Ilya twisted the mirror so that Zhukov would be able to pick up the refraction of the light if it flashed by again. "It is not the bio-luminescence about which I have read" Ilya said. "It was a light."

Zhukov waited, his eyes fixed on the mirror.

Ilya studied the illuminated dial of his watch, timing the interval. "If the Americans are looking for us with one of their underwater salvage vehicles, it is altogether possible, Comrade."

Despite the choking closeness in the Mala's tiny control center, Zhukov lit a cigarette and waited. As the smoke curled upward into the cabin's stagnant air the light flashed again, briefly casting a milky yellow wash in their otherwise darkened red world.

Zhukov straightened.

Ilya was again timing the sweep. When it passed again, he realized that a shorter time interval had elapsed, which he knew could only mean that the light was being manually operated. If that was true, it was not a remote unit tethered to some vessel on the surface.

Zhukov's voice betrayed his irritation at being discovered. "How far away are they?"

"Not far," Ilya assessed. "At this depth the light would be quickly absorbed. The fact that the light is so bright means that they are very close."

"Are they blocking us in such a way that we could not get past them?"

The question surprised Ilya. "There is no way to tell, Comrade Marshal."

"This Mala, it is faster than the American machine?"

Vasilivich considered the question. "In all probability we are faster," he said. "Their machines are built for specific types of research and salvage missions. As a rule, they are not swift."

"Then we will outrun them," Zhukov decided.

"Outrun them? Where will we go? The Americans have the harbor blocked off, and now that they suspect that we are trapped in here they will have intensified their blockade. Emerging from our cover will only make us more vulnerable to their detection devices, Comrade Marshal."

Zhukov continued to study the pattern of the passing light.

"How long have they been monitoring us?"

"Seven minutes now," Ilya confirmed.

"Why do they not come in after us?"

"I do not know."

"I have heard no transmissions," Zhukov insisted.

If Zhukov had asked him, Ilya would have admitted to being equally perplexed by the American's lack of action. If the Americans had located them, why did they not ask for assistance from their surface support units? Unless the American DSSV had already deployed divers who were in the process even now of rendering the Mala's escape impossible. If he told Zhukov of his suspicions, he knew Zhukov would insist that the Mala make an attempt to escape before the American divers disabled their vessel. But flee? Flee to where? Deeper into the graveyard of ships? Such a maneuver would only compound their problems, further depleting their air supply and necessitating the use of the Mala's diesels. If they used the diesels there was no way they could escape the American sensing devices.

"It is curious," Zhukov said, "that they neither transmit to ask for help nor make an attempt to come in after us."

"Perhaps they are planning how to take us," Ilya said.

"Or," Zhukov countered, "the series of quakes somehow rendered them less mobile than they need to be to close the void."

The light swept past them again, stopped, swung into position and fixed directly on the Mala.

"There is no doubt about it now, Comrade Marshal. They know we are here."

"We will take our chances," Zhukov said. "We must strike them before they can betray our location to their support vessels on the surface."

"Strike them? How?"

"We will ram them with our bow," Zhukov said coldly. "I have seen schematics and pictures of their salvage vehicles. They are not substantial."

"Such a maneuver is madness," Ilya protested.

"It is our only hope. We will strike them and then seek refuge in the deeper recesses of the place known as the Jehovah Hole."

Ilya began to protest, but the words froze in his mouth when he realized that what he felt was the cold steel of Zhukov's gun. The barrel was pressed against the base of his skull.

"In case there was any doubt about it before, Commandant Vasilivich, I have just taken command. You will prepare us to attack."

Ilya's hands moved with reluctance, opening the current to the pre-ignition on the Mala's diesels. It would take several minutes before he dared to risk an attempted ignition. He knew that the moment he did, every hydrophone in the harbor would pick up the sound, and within a matter of seconds the Americans would have their position isolated.

He activated the bow sonar and determined that the DSSV was less than 200 metres directly in front of them and stationary. Ilya knew that the DSSV could pick up the ping, and the moment they did, they would be aware that the Mala now knew they were out there.

It was a deadly game. Suppose, Ilya thought to himself, the DSSV is capable of moving. Could it be nothing more than a ploy to get the Mala to reveal its position? He leaned forward, the gauges now indicating a 20 percent purge in ballast. The batteries were on reserve; two of the packs indicated readings in the critical range. It was now five minutes until he could begin the ignition test. He watched the temperature in the cylinders climb and glanced in the mirror at Zhukov.

Zhelannov's assassin glowered back at him. "Now," he said. Ilya could feel the hard steel press deeper into the hairline at the back of his skull.

Datum: 10:6 . . . the Arca-Dino, *1950NLT*

Bogner had already calculated his odds at somewhere between slim and nonexistent. He had rigged a wire to the manual control handle of the extensible illuminator, moving it from time to time to give whoever was in the Mala the impression that the *Dino* was monitoring them.

Now the door to the second module was closed, the beam was fixed on the submarine, and he busied himself putting on the air tanks while he increased the dive pressure in preparation for leaving the personnel cocoon of the *Dino*.

The plan he had formulated was simple and risky, at best a long shot. But any odds at all were better than none, and he knew his options had been played out.

The *Dino*'s air supply was gone. If he could find some way to disable the Mala and somehow get to the surface, there might be a chance. They would know the location of the Mala, and there was still the slim hope that they could crank her to the surface. The fact that the Mala had activated her sonar, on the other hand, was a sign they were getting nervous.

Everything was in place except for the mask. Bogner went through his pre-dive check list for the second time. As part of his plan he had removed two of the stainless steel ballast bars and inserted a handful of CO_2 cartridges along with two packets of 41DR plastic explosives, just in case. He had no real plan other than to find some way of fouling the shrouded prop of the Mala. From that point on it was survival time.

There was still 30 seconds to go. As he watched the needle on the pressure gauge creep toward the 37 fathom equivalency mark, he pulled his mask down on his face and opened the air valve on his tanks.

Everything Toby Bogner never wanted to think about now muscled its way into his brain. His leg throbbed and there was a parched dryness in his throat from breathing the *Dino*'s fouled air. There were disturbing thoughts of Joy and Kim and faces and places either without names or long ago forgotten.

As the needle continued its methodical creep to the mark at the 37 fathom level, the safety light indicators in the personnel cocoon began to flash. He turned on the halogen as the cocoon lights began fading into darkness and took one final look around at the interior of the *Dino*.

In the control cabin, Koorsen's lifeless body undulated in sea water amidst the ruble of the swarm quake's destruction, and outside was the uncertainty of his mission.

He pulled the valve pin on the sea gate, rotated it to the open position, and the sea water began to flood in.

Datum: 10:6 . . . Negril Harbor, 1959NLT

There was a nearly imperceptible shudder in the hull of the midget Mala. The submarine creaked in protest to the abrupt change in pressure as the diesels began to take over.

Light spilled out from the clusters of dials and gauges, and Zhukov's unaccustomed eyes squinted, adjusting to the harshness. The Mala surged restlessly as Ilya listened with the trained ear of a commandant to the reassuring sounds coming from the cramped engine room.

Zhukov glared at the sudden illumination on his panel after so many hours of darkness and

R. Karl Largent

leaned forward exerting pressure on the barrel of the Makarov pressed against Ilya's head.

"I will tolerate no further delay, Comrade."

"This is an act of madness," Vasilivich protested.

"It is the only way," Zhukov insisted, "Do it. Now."

The plates of the *Dino*'s access panel opened and Bogner drifted down to the sand and rocks on the ocean floor.

He settled, oriented himself and began swimming toward the Mala just as its engines came to life. Reacting instantly, he altered his course and swam straight for the hole in the stern of the *Kleinmagen*.

The Mala was beginning to plow forward, emerging from the deeper shadows of the rusting hulk of the freighter, heading straight for the helpless *Dino*, leaving a trail of shifting silt and sand in its wake.

Bogner watched in disbelief. The intent of the Mala's skipper was now apparent; it was going to ram the *Dino*. Stop, it's suicide, Bogner wanted to scream.

The bow of the Yugoslavian submarine speared the helpless *Dino*, sending out shock waves accompanied by the shrill high-pitched squeal of tearing metal and the more muted symphony of other smaller explosions. The DSSV hurtled sideways like a mortally wounded medieval warrior, leaving its extensible illuminator imbedded in the hull of the Mala.

The beam of the tiny *Dino* snapped and it began breaking apart.

The impaled Mala was equally devastated by the impact. The shielding on the fore hull began peeling away, and it somersaulted up on its bow, spinning out of control on its sonar heavy nose, grinding itself into the coral crevices and the spongy, rocky terrain of the harbor bottom.

The Mala bucked violently for a moment as its diesels drove it deeper into the sand. With its fantail elevated, it pitched and began to topple to its side, grinding against the coral and rocks.

Inside the Mala, the bulkhead shields were crushed and Zhukov could hear the exterior plating being shredded away. The steel arm of the *Dino*'s illuminator had pierced the Mala's bulkhead, sliced through the fore cabin and ravaged its way through the body of Ilya Vasilivich.

Zhukov watched helplessly as the heavy, stainless steel angle rod raped its way through the control cabin with a terrifying kind of vengeance.

Ilya Vasilivich saw none of this. His disemboweled body was pinned to the port bulkhead, his eyes frozen straight ahead, centerpieces in a florid death mask. What was left of his life was rapidly ebbing out of him.

Sea water gushed into the fore cabin and control pod, spinning the Mala into a series of violent rolls and snapping off the *Dino*'s deadly lance-like illuminator. Zhukov was being thrown about the control room like a discarded toy, his semiautomatic still clutched in his hand.

When the Mala finally crashed over on its side, the aft section began flooding. Zhukov managed to claw his way through the devastation to the conn tower and started to climb the ladder toward the escape hatch.

As the midget submarine continued its slide toward the ridge of the abyss, he struggled to break the air lock on the dog wheel and heard the electric motor struggle to open the steel hatch against 200 feet of depth pressure.

Zhukov gulped his lungs full of the Mala's fouled air and tried to force his way through the partially opened hatch before it closed again.

He had made it only halfway out when the motor shorted out, pinning him.

Bogner swam from his sanctuary in the *Kleinmagen's* super structure and headed for Zhukov. Zhelannov's assassin was less than 30 feet from him when the halogen finally searched him out. He could see the man's face.

It was a montage of rupturing and oxygen-heated blood vessels that could no longer be concealed by the layers of ravaged flesh. Zhukov was caught in a terrifying limbo between life and certain death. His mouth was open, silently screaming his final protest against the agony of the crushing pressure.

There was nothing Bogner could do.

He watched as the Mala teetered on the rim of the precipice, the rocks and sand that embraced it slowly eroding away from beneath the desolated hull. Then, as if its fate had been ordained by some terrible proclamation, the dying Mala toppled over the edge and plummeted downward, spiraling into the yawning blackness of the hole.

Finally, Bogner lost sight of it.

There was an unmeasured period of time when he was too stunned, too overwhelmed, too overpowered to move—and then came the terrible and inexorable realization that there was absolutely nothing he could do.

Still dazed, he struggled to regulate his breathing apparatus, and then slowly and methodically, Bogner began to claw his way through the murky water toward the surface.

PART THREE

BASE HOUR
TWO-THREE
2200 NEGRIL LOCAL 10:6
0700 MOSCOW LOCAL 10:7
0100 GREENWICH (Z) 10:6

Base Hour
Two-Three:
ZERO ZERO. . . 0100ZULU

Datum: 10:7 . . . Moscow: Chesnakov Compound, 0713MLT

Viktor Denisov shaved, savoring the little time he had left before his meeting with Vitali Parlenko. In the mirror he could see Corporal Achina setting the table in his quarters for his breakfast with Vitali.

Parlenko had insisted on the early morning meeting when he heard the news that Zhelannov was still alive.

Viktor had slept fitfully since the early hours of the morning. He had awakened and watched Achina get dressed in the middle of the night and then had drifted back into his troubled sleep until she again awoke him with the latest communiqué from Osipov's Naval Directorate.

The message was from Andrakov, who reported that the assignment in Sector IV was a success. By simply having the Negril salvage diver remove the two capseals, Viktor was now assured

339

that Zhelannov's would-be assassin would never be captured—at least not captured alive. He was also now in a position to assure the worried Parlenko that their plan was back on schedule, awaiting only the confirming report of Commandant Potapenko's success aboard the American cruiser.

As he walked back into his quarters, he stopped to assess the somber Sunday morning unfolding outside his second floor window.

A fresh blanket of snow quilted the compound's parade grounds, and the tracks of the domestic workers on their early morning trek to the compound's kitchens were the only thing that marred the pristine military landscape.

He picked up his glass of berry juice, sipped it and watched Corporal Achina's supple young body shift suggestively under the harshness of her uniform. As she started past him, he reached out to capture her.

"You are very appealing this morning, Corporal Achina," he said.

"And you were very appealing last night, my General." Her voice was still husky, and Viktor wondered if the overly suspicious Vitali would wonder about his attractive new aide.

He bent to kiss her, and she reproached him.

"What if Minister Parlenko should find us this way? Would this not be an embarrassment?"

Viktor stepped away, releasing her. When he did, she frowned but quickly regained her composure.

"What are we having this morning?"

"*Yan,*" she said pointing to the samovar. "You said it was the Minister's favorite along with *sm'odahn* and *abhbreekos*. And to sustain my general, *sahseeskee* and *ch'orniy khl'ehp*."

Pleased at her thoroughness, Viktor walked slowly around the small neatly arranged table, picking up one of the finger-sized sausages as he went. He indulged himself in one swallow.

When he looked up, Vitali Parlenko was standing at the door of his quarters taking off his coat. Achina nodded to the old man, excused herself and left, closing the door behind her.

Parlenko's expression was doleful. "You look rather pleased with yourself for someone who has had so many difficulties in the past two days, Comrade."

Viktor Denisov never responded to what he considered trite observations.

"I assume you have heard about the American Ambassador Parker?" Parlenko asked.

Viktor motioned his guest to a seat at the table. "*Da*, I have heard. Most unfortunate."

Parlenko sat down and spread his napkin in his lap. He was the antithesis of Denisov—gentlemanly, almost courtly. He reached for his cup of dark tea.

"If I were the Americans, I would be asking many questions. There is nothing in Parker's dossier to indicate he was given to such lascivious appetites."

"I fear the capitalistic veneer conceals many things about the darker side of our colleagues," Viktor sighed.

Parlenko picked up a slice of the black bread and spread it liberally with the apricot preserves. "And our situation in Jamaica?" It was an open question. Viktor knew he could address himself to any part or all of it.

Out of habit, he leaned forward and tempered his voice. "As well as can be expected under the circumstances. Admiral Osipov has sent two of our officers to monitor President Zhelannov's progress until our medical representatives arrive."

"Do I know these men?"

"A Commandant Potapenko, sympathetic to our cause, and a junior officer whose name escapes me."

Vitali Parlenko looked disappointed. "Osipov could find none better? I know Potapenko. He is a dolt, incapable of complex problem solving."

"This is not a complex problem, Comrade. He has but one assignment—to see that Comrade Zhelannov is not alive when our medical contingent arrives. Moshe assures me the task will be no more difficult than perhaps removing a plug."

Parlenko's expression continued to deteriorate.

"You must change your frame of reference," Viktor said. "The Americans now know of the assassination attempt, but they do not know who and can prove nothing. A dead Zhelannov is a dead Zhelannov—nothing more, nothing less. He cannot talk. Potapenko will not fail. I have Osipov's assurances. And remember, there still is the matter of the gunshot wound."

"There is more to report?"

"I have just had confirmation from the GRU resident illegal in Montego Bay that Zhukov's recovery alive is no longer a possibility. That matter has been sufficiently taken care of as well."

"And the man that did the task for Andrakov?"

"Dead," Viktor said. "Of all of life's many vagaries, there is one certainty. Andrakov will follow his instructions to the letter."

Parlenko sighed. "It is a never-ending chain, Comrade. Now we must worry about Andrakov being discovered."

"If the Americans discover the loose thread that leads them to Andrakov, that can be handled as well. I still have resources."

Vitali shook his head. "In the meantime, we must continue to convey the impression that we know nothing of all of this and insist that there has been some insidious plot by the Americans to destroy the new Russian Commonwealth."

Denisov nodded. "At noon, national radio and television will announce that we have grave concerns about certain factions of the Colchin administration and question why they are handling this affair in the manner they have. To give our concern impetus, we will also announce that Ambassador Yerrov is being recalled for consultations. The Americans will get the message. They will recognize that Yerrov's recall is the first step in breaking off diplomatic relations."

"Need I remind you, Comrade, we are playing a very dangerous game. If just one of the dominoes does not topple on cue, there will be grave repercussions."

Viktor Denisov settled back in his chair. If he was worried, Vitali Parlenko could not read it in his eyes. The General selected a sausage, wrapped it in a slice of bread and devoured it. Then he washed it down with a glass of berry juice. He looked at Parlenko and allowed his face to manufacture an indolent smile.

"You will see, Comrade. Tomorrow morning at this time a new Socialist Republic will emerge from this dark hour."

Vitali's face, as Viktor could have predicted, had grown darker with doubt.

"I hope you are right, General," he said.

Datum: 10:6 . . . Crew Hospital, USS Black River, *2222NLT*

Toby Bogner was being prodded back into a level of awareness by Peter Langley's strident voice:

"Look, Doc, this is important. The only thing that will keep me from insisting is if you tell me it might do some permanent damage."

Forsythe folded his arms and glanced down at the man they had pulled from the harbor less than two hours ago.

"All I can tell you is, he's lost a lot of blood, Peter. He's weak, but it won't kill him."

Langley walked to the side of the bed and leaned over. "How about it, Toby? Feel good enough to answer a few questions?"

Leave me alone, Bogner thought to himself, but he managed to open his eyes and roll his head in Langley's direction.

The room was bathed in a discreet half-light, and Cameron stood at the end of the bed with his arms folded. A nurse and corpsmen stood next to him. Only Stone was missing. His eyes drifted shut again.

"It's the painkiller," Forsythe acknowledged. He placed his hand on Bogner's arm. "We gave you a local, Toby, while we repaired that hole in your leg. If you think you feel like a piece of shit now, wait until that sedative wears off. Do what you want, but my advice is to stay right here and get some rest."

On the second try, Bogner was able to open both eyes. He moved his leg and felt a sharp pain. He peeled back the sheet and assessed the bulky bandage that extended from his crotch to his knee. Forsythe was wrong. He was still groggy so the painkiller hadn't worn off, but the leg hurt like hell anyway.

Cameron came around to the side of the bed. "Think you can handle some of Peter's questions?"

"If he can handle half-answers," Bogner managed.

Langley bent over him again. "When Stoney's crew hauled you out of the water, they said you told them you had located the Mala."

Bogner nodded. " 'Had' is the right word." In a raspy voice he managed to repeat the story of the final minutes on the bottom of the harbor.

"You're certain—no survivors?" Langley was trying to clarify.

"None on either side. The swarm quakes caught us off guard. They wadded the *Dino* up like a spitball. I don't think Koorsen knew what hit him. As for the Mala, I saw it go over the edge and slip on down into the hole. She was breaking up and taking on water. Even if there was a way to get to it and we could bring it up, we wouldn't learn much."

"We'll bring it up," Cameron confirmed. "There may be something aboard it that corroborates our story. It may be our only chance."

"Unless Sam Forsythe can pull Zhelannov through," Langley added.

"We're running out of possibilities and options," Cameron said. "Colchin wants a progress report, and the boys at NI tell us the Soviet fleet is coming together and darting in and out of port taking on added armament. Even the boys at the state department are starting to get a little nervous. They say the rhetoric coming out of the Kremlin sounds just like it did back in the days of the cold war."

"How about Zhelannov?" Bogner asked.

"I think we can hold on to him now as long as the generators keep working," Forsythe said. "But the minute that Russian medical team gets here they'll know it's a mere formality, and it won't take them long to discover that the old boy was shot before the explosion. Any pathologist worth half his salt will know what happened the minute he examines him."

"While we're dumping on you, Toby, we've got another problem," Cameron said. "Ten minutes ago one of Stoney's patrol boats picked up four members of the press pool at Le Chamanade. The briefing session is scheduled for 2330 local. If you're up to it, T. C., I want you down there."

Bogner wondered how many of them knew that the one called Joy Carpenter was the former Joy Bogner. He looked at Cameron.

"If you want me down there, you better brief me first."

Cameron studied him. "Curious you would indicate a willingness to attend, Toby. I know how you usually shy away from these things. At any rate, one of the members of the press pool has already requested permission to talk to you in private."

"We use to be friends," Bogner said, choosing

his words carefully. "What did you tell her?"

"I told her it was up to you, that you had been in an accident. No details of course, just an accident."

Datum: 10:6 . . . Washington: ISA Offices, 2231EST

Clancy Packer slammed the phone down and shouted for Miller. "Grab Taggert and bring him in with you."

The two men appeared at the door. Taggert was still carrying his notes from his earlier briefing with NI.

"Sounded like that was Jaffe," Miller said.

Packer nodded. "He just heard from Complexity. The Russians are planning to air a broadcast at noon Moscow time that announces to the Commonwealth of Independent States that the GRU has confirmed a plot by the United States government to assassinate their President and overthrow the government."

Miller let out a whistle. "The plot thickens. The GRU, huh?"

"That's what we're being told. The broth may be thickening but at least we now know who is stirring the pot. Miller, get in touch with Millie Ploughman and Cornwell and tell them we need them both in here. The way I see it we've got less than five hours to defuse this thing. I want to dig up everything we can on any recent GRU activity. Nothing old, just data that has been fed in over the last six months."

"We already know most of the names," Miller reminded him.

"You're right, but we've heard a lot of new names in the past forty-eight hours. I want to know who authorized this guy Zhukov to pull the trigger."

"According to what Cornwell dug up this morning, a guy by the name of Vitali Parlenko is the current Chief of the Second Directorate," Taggert said.

"That's the trouble with the damn Russian intelligence network," Packer growled. "They've got Generals reporting to Marshals and Marshals reporting to Commandants. Rank doesn't mean shit, and it doesn't necessarily hold that the head of the GRU is the man masterminding this escapade. For all we know, it could be someone from their damned Operational-Technical Directorate or the Chief of Information."

"Five hours isn't much time," Miller said. "We're looking for a tack on an expressway."

"I talked to Peter Langley aboard the *Black River* before I talked to Jaffe. Apparently Bogner located the Mala that Zhukov supposedly escaped in. It tried to ram Bogner and Koorsen and they lost it. The only one that got out alive was Toby."

"What about Zack Koorsen?" Miller asked.

Packer didn't answer. He didn't have too. Miller knew.

Datum: 10:6 . . . Waiting Room, USS Black River, *2249NLT*

When Joy Carpenter appeared in the doorway of the C deck waiting room, she lived up to Bogner's expectations. She hadn't allowed something like the better part of 48 hours without sleep and being in an out-of-the-way place like Negril play havoc with the famous Joy image.

Her sable-colored hair was knotted in a business-like bun and she was wearing her glasses—probably, Bogner figured, her only concession to the lack of sleep. She looked exactly like he expected her to look. She was wearing a taupe two piece field suit that smacked of the military, complete with patch pockets, two button cuffs and epaulets. Just right, Bogner decided, for the occasion.

"I'm surprised," she said. "You look like you'll live. I figured with Admiral Cameron's reputation for understatement that you'd be in a complete body cast."

She walked to the side of the bed, bent over and kissed him. She lingered longer than he had expected her to. "Are you all right?"

When Bogner tried to stand up, his legs wobbled and he sat back down.

"Sorry I can't greet you properly."

He wondered where the conversation would head after the formalities.

Joy was studying him in much the same fashion that he believed she contemplated the purchase of a new dress, with a critical eye for the smallest detail.

"Keep sitting," she said. "You can impress me with macho posturing some other time." She looked around the room. "What, no Scoresby? You're slipping."

"I can offer you a beer," he said. After he said it he realized it sounded frivolous.

"So what happened?" she asked, pointing to the bulge in his thigh. "Looks like it came a little too close to the important parts, didn't it?"

Bogner shrugged.

Joy sat down beside the bed. "I'm serious, Tobias. What happened?"

He shrugged again, suddenly feeling bitter. Why the hell did he expect her to really care what happened to him? He just happened to be part of the story—a story that was happening in Negril—and she was a reporter.

"I understand you're here as part of the press pool," he said weakly.

"I am the press pool. Those other clowns turned green with envy when they found out I actually knew someone aboard the *Black River*. They're all convinced I'm in here getting a scoop while they cool their heels waiting for the official briefing."

"Are you?"

"Can't tell yet." She winked. "I haven't asked my questions yet." Suddenly her face sobered. "I'm assuming someone has told you about Lucian."

"You were right there at Le Chamanade. I'm surprised you didn't see him. He's never very far away when there is a beautiful woman around. He asks about you all the time."

Joy turned her head to one side. Her voice caught in her throat. "You really don't know, do you?"

"Know what?"

"Lucian is dead."

Bogner felt like he had been punched.

Joy managed to keep her voice from cracking. "That's the first thing I learned when I got out of the van that brought us over from the airport. The West Mathews police were all over the place.

I was finally able to get someone to tell me what happened. Someone shot him, and then to make certain they didn't leave anything to chance they drove their car over him three or four times."

Bogner had to force out the questions. "Where? When?"

Joy opened her purse, took out her cigarette case, lit a cigarette and handed it to him. There was lipstick on the cork filter tip. It was like old times.

"What little I was able to pick up was a little too sketchy to make anything out of it."

"Try me."

"Well, are you familiar with a place called Apostle Point?"

Bogner nodded. "I've done a little fishing out there. It's close to a break in the reef."

"That's where it happened. The police think Lucian was doing a little recreational diving. The found his sea sled in about twelve feet of water. He was wearing a wet suit and his tanks were lying on the beach. The police theorize that he must have been down, ran low on air, came up, saw someone messing around the shed where he keeps his equipment, confronted him and got shot. Whoever shot him did the car bit for added measure."

Despite his throbbing leg, Bogner stood up. He was unsteady. Forsythe's painkiller wasn't working but the sedative was. He reached out for her hand. "How about a twenty-four hour truce?"

"What for? You wouldn't be any good in bed with that leg of yours." She smiled for added emphasis. "Maybe some other time, sailor. The last time I got all primed for you, you took a look at the traffic and told me you only had twenty minutes until you had to catch a plane."

Bogner swallowed. He knew Joy well enough to know that she was telling it exactly the way it was. Joy meant what she said.

"I need your help," he told her.

"What kind of help?"

"What are you doing after the press briefing?"

She shrugged. "I'm open to suggestions."

"You may get a better story out of what I'm going to suggest than you do at the press briefing."

"Now you've really got my attention," she said. "Work now, play later."

Base Hour
Two-Zero:
ZERO ZERO . . . 0400ZULU

*Datum: 10:7 . . . Apostle Point, Negril Beach,
0114NLT*

Bogner limped from the West Mathews' patrol
car to Bouderau's storage shed and then worked
his way out on the beach, splaying the beam of
the officer's flashlight back and forth in front of
him. Joy and the young Jamaican police officer
in his ill-fitting, stiffly starched khaki shirt and
blue trousers dutifully waited by the car.

Joy watched the beam of light dance from spot
to spot in the sand and said, "I'm impressed,
Tobias. How did you swing this?"

"I didn't. Avery Thomas did. All it took was a
phone call."

Joy shook her head. "I still don't understand. A
man was murdered here, and here you are poking
around. You and I both know they haven't had
time to complete their investigation yet."

"This is Jamaica," he reminded her. "You know
how they think; tomorrow is soon enough."

"But what if we inadvertently disturb something?"

"Thomas is aware of that possibility. I did him a favor and he reciprocated." Bogner turned to the young officer. "Exactly where did they find the body?"

The Jamaican had enormous yellow teeth, crooked and discolored from constant overindulgence in unrefined ganja. He made an effort to look official by walking toward Bogner and pointing out the exact spot.

Tire tracks crossed the depression in the sand several times and footprints obliterated the rest. No one, Bogner thought to himself, could accuse the West Mathews police of being concerned about him destroying evidence.

Bogner turned back toward Joy. "Think back. Just exactly what did they tell you when you heard about this?"

"The man said his tanks were lying halfway between the edge of the water and where the body was found and that he was wearing a wet suit. He theorized that Lucian came up for fresh tanks, surprised the intruder, and whoever it was shot him."

Bogner examined the tanks and retraced a line from the shed to the water, stopping where Bouderau's body was discovered. He limped down to the water's edge again, turned around and shut off his flashlight. The beach was bathed in the glow of a full Caribbean moon. The boats in the harbor were dark except for Stone's patrol units.

"Come here a minute, Joy. Look at the shed from here. Now, assume for the moment that he surfaced and came up out of the water some-where right along through here, intending to go to the shed. Then ask yourself, could he have seen anyone lurking around the shed? Even with this much moonlight, you can't see the shed very well from this point on the beach. So how could he have seen anyone messing around?"

"Maybe they had a flashlight. Maybe they were making noise. How should I know?"

Bogner shook his head. "I don't think so. I think you have to start by asking yourself who would come back here in the first place."

"Come on, Tobias, the police said the gate was open. A gate left open on a security fence is an open invitation. People don't put up fences like that unless they've got something to protect or want privacy."

"But if you don't lock the gate, which Bouderau didn't after he drove in, what does that tell you?"

Even in the moonlight, T. C. could see Joy's eyes flicker with recognition. "You're saying you think Lucian was actually expecting someone."

"Precisely. The question is—who?"

Bogner left her standing at the water's edge and limped back to the Jamaican.

"Think hard. Is there anything you haven't told us?"

The officer pointed to a crusty brown patch in the sand on the path behind the shed. It was less than eight inches in diameter. "We are doing an analysis," he said, "but I can already tell you, *mon*, it is blood."

Bogner studied the patch of ground and then went back to where Bouderau's body was found. It was a clear path.

"How far would you estimate this is?" he asked Joy.

"Thirty, maybe forty feet," she guessed. "Hell, Tobias, I'm not an engineer."

"Let me ask you this then. If that is Bouderau's blood back there on the path, why did the killer drag his body all the way out here on the beach to run over him? The car was right there. Why didn't he just do it there? Lucian would be a load; he was a big man. And there is nothing to indicate that the killer dragged him from one place to the other, no tracks at all."

Joy put her hands on her hips. "All of this may mean something to you, but I don't have the slightest idea of what you're trying to get at," she admitted.

Bogner shrugged. "I'm not sure I know either, but I can tell you one thing. This whole scene is failing the old Bogner logic test. What we're looking at and what the police say happened appear to be two different things."

Joy sighed. "Come on, Tobias, I'm tired of playing detective," she complained. "Can't we find a bar some place and discuss your theories over some Scoresby's? Or," her voice dropped, "let's send your police friend away and you and I can go skinny dipping." The more Joy thought about it, the better she liked the idea. "Hey, we could even swim out to the reef."

"I thought you were afraid of sharks," T. C. teased. His face suddenly brightened. "That's it, damnit. That's what's missing—Lucian's spear gun. No one dives these reefs without a spear gun, and Lucian carried a big one, big enough to slow down some of the six gillers that haunt the waters around the reef. He never went in without it. So if he was diving and surfaced and the intruder shot him, where is his spear gun?"

Joy seldom frowned but was doing so now.

T. C. looked at the officer. "Was there a spear gun anywhere around the body?"

The Jamaican stepped from the shadows near the shed where he had been smoking a ganja.

"It is here, *mon*, by the shed. I retrieved it from the edge of the water myself."

Bogner hobbled back to the shed and picked up the spear gun. It had been fired. "See," he said, holding it up for Joy's inspection.

"Look, Sherlock," she sighed, "take a break and tell me what the hell is going on."

Bogner took her by the arm and led her back toward the water's edge, half-leaning on her for support.

"We're going to carry this little hypothesis of mine a bit further," he said. "I want you to listen very carefully. Tell me if you can hear any holes in this."

As they walked, Joy put her arm around his waist to support him.

"From the outset I didn't buy that bit about Lucian being out here to do a little recreational diving, certainly not at night and definitely not when he knows the harbor is crawling with Coast Guard patrol boats.

"Secondly, Lucian told me his diving days were over. He said he was getting too old for it. But— and this is the one exception—I know for a fact he would be diving if he thought it was going to put something in his pocket."

Joy sat down in the sand and hugged her knees. "Go on."

"Now, because the harbor has been sealed off for three days, we know the Colombian didn't make a drug drop. The planes have been staying away and Parant's *Broward* hasn't budged. That means he was working for someone else.

"We were looking for something down there and somebody else was either looking for the same thing or didn't want us to find it. I saw Lucian earlier in the day when I went to his office to ask him about the Jehovah Hole. He already had the harbor charts out and tried to conceal them in a desk drawer when I walked in."

"No holes so far," Joy said. "You're on a roll, keep going."

"I think someone else was talking to Lucian about the same thing, but in their case they wanted to make sure we didn't find anything."

"Or," Joy countered, "they wanted to find it before you did."

"I like your conclusion better than mine," Bogner said.

"So how do you prove it?"

Bogner moved unsteadily back to the spot where Bouderau's body had been found and picked up the air tanks again. "According to the gauges these cylinders are still half-full. That tells me he came up either because of the swarm quakes or because he was expecting to meet someone here."

"Whoever hired him, right?"

Bogner nodded.

"Then what happened?"

"I'm still piecing it together. But I'm willing to

bet that whatever went wrong, the reason there isn't any spear in Lucian's spear gun is because whoever killed him didn't get off the first shot. Our French friend did."

"Sure," Joy agreed, "it makes sense. The guy hires him, comes to check on his progress, and for whatever reason they end up in a shootout. All of which would explain that patch of blood and the location of Lucian's body, but it doesn't get us any closer to who did it."

"On the contrary, it puts a guy by the name of Andrakov right in the middle of all of this."

"Andrakov?" Joy repeated.

Bogner hesitated. He was telling her more than he had intended. "Sure, it makes sense. Andrakov is the former Soviet GRU illegal stationed in Montego Bay. He had to know what was going on here the last couple of days and probably knew about the attempted assassination. In fact, if Packer is getting good information about GRU involvement, that little twerp probably knew everything that was happening."

"So what do we do now?" Joy was standing up again, brushing the sand away.

Bogner looked around to see if the Jamaican was listening. He wasn't.

"First, we get Marshal Dillon there to chauffeur us back to Le Chamanade and you help me get to a telephone. I'll call Morganthaller and tell him to put our boy Andrakov under surveillance. Then I can get a car and head for Montego Bay. If I can get my hands on Andrakov and make him talk, we still may be able to prove we weren't the ones that pulled the trigger on Zhelannov."

Joy's hand darted out and grabbed his arm.

"What do you mean 'pulled the trigger on Zhelan-nov'?"

"Figure of speech."

"Bullshit! You don't use figures of speech, Tobias. What you're really saying is we didn't get the whole story back there at that press briefing, did we? There's more to this than just Sparrow's damn yacht mysteriously blowing up, isn't there?"

"Never mind that. Get me to a phone. As soon as I get in touch with Simon I'm heading for Montego Bay."

"Not until you tell me what the hell is going on."

Bogner hesitated. "Off the record?"

"I don't like off-the-record qualifications, Tobias, and you know it."

"Trust me, Joy. Play along with me now and you'll have one helluva story to tell your viewers."

Datum: 10:7 . . . Kremlin, Council of Ministers, 1047MLT

Churnova's tone was angry. "Why was I not told of this?" he demanded.

Parlenko, standing at the window overlooking the barren courtyard, lit a cigarette and studied Denisov while he waited for the General's reply.

"It would appear," Moshe Aprihnen appraised, "that our esteemed Comrade has made a number of moves without our knowledge in the last forty-eight hours."

Viktor was defiant and leaned back in his chair. "I do not share your concern, Comrades. And I do not agree with you that I must consult with you before taking action. Besides, it is a small matter."

"I do not consider your decision to dispose of Marshal Zhukov a small matter," Moshe lashed out.

"The man failed his mission," Viktor replied. "It is as simple as that."

"The plan was too convoluted from the outset," Vitali complained. "There were too many elements."

Denisov continued to smile. "I have said it before, Comrade, and I will say it again; you are an old woman. You worry too much."

Parlenko stepped away from the window with his hands in his pockets. He looked tired. "Perhaps all of this is a bit premature, but I caution you that Commandant Potapenko has not yet reported in. He was instructed to find cause to have the young lieutenant sent back to the Kiev as a signal that his mission was accomplished. Let me remind you, Comrades, so far we have a dubious record."

Churnova cleared his throat. "I, too, question aspects of Viktor's judgment, but there is still much that we do not know. If Comrade Zhukov followed the plan to the letter, then we know the Americans cannot conceal much longer the fact that our beloved President was shot as well as suffered whatever damage was inflicted by the explosion. Are we not confident that our medical team will discover what the Americans have been concealing?" He paused and cleared his throat. "Then, as they like to say, the ball will be back in their court and they will be forced to come up with an explanation."

"If," Moshe sniffed, repeating Churnova's qualifier.

"Moshe is right," Vitali said. "Whether or not Zhukov followed the plan is not the issue. If Zhelannov recovers, he will be in a position to explain the gunshot wound and identify his attempted assassin. Then what?"

"If that much happens," Vitali added, "then surely our duplicity in this matter will be discovered as well."

"How?" Denisov slapped the table. "No one outside of this room knows the totality of our endeavor. Who is to reveal it?"

"What about your illegals, Comrade? Would you not agree that they are suspect? You have received communiqués from them that are wholly inconsistent with the information we are receiving through other channels."

"You are bigger fools than I thought if you take everything the Americans say as the absolute truth," Viktor snarled.

Churnova pushed himself away from the table and stood up. "Perhaps we should delay our announcement until our medical staff arrives on the American cruiser and makes their assessment. Perhaps we are being hasty."

"Now is not the time to appear indecisive," Denisov thundered. "It will be construed as weakness. Consider what we do know and recognize that we must think like the Americans. The Commonwealth President has been seriously, perhaps even mortally wounded. They do not know the cause of the attack and have bungled what few actions they have taken. In the eyes of many Russians, their delaying tactics have only acerbated the situation. The world is watching to see how we react to this transgression.

"We have not been imprudent. I assure you, our Comrades, even those of less conviction, would not have been as judicious. Right now, the rest of the world is watching the Americans mishandle the situation. If we protest with the appropriate action, not a mere demonstration of strength, the world will understand."

"The question remains," Churnova insisted. "Do we or do we not proceed with the recall of Ambassador Yerrov in our noon message? It is a gesture that the diplomatic world will rightly interpret as the forerunner to increasing hostility."

"Are you saying that we do not have cause?" Viktor said.

"I said nothing of the kind. I am simply saying that we have been making too many singular and unilateral decisions. On the matter of Yerrov we must collectively agree."

"We should proceed," Viktor said. His anger was evident.

"And I concur," Parlenko said, "but we should take no action beyond that until we have heard from our medical contingent when it arrives aboard the American ship. To do more than that will make our actions appear rash and ill-advised."

"I would accept the word of Potapenko as well," Moshe added.

Viktor stood up. His face was flushed.

"Can you not see that the Americans are gullible? Our timing is perfect. We move a few ships, the American satellites determine that the reactors on our fleet are now active even on long dormant craft, and we recall our Ambassador. They will appear nervous and inept while we exhibit strength and control of the volatile situation. This is a rare opportunity, Comrades. These are the circumstances under which the people of the independent states will see the Party take control again. The Russian people will no longer be in control of men who are willing to negotiate away our heritage to the decadent precepts of democracy."

"You are forgetting something, Comrade General," Moshe hissed. "The President is not yet dead."

"Of that I am not so certain," Viktor finally replied. "There is something very peculiar about the way the Americans have handled the entire situation."

Churnova nodded. "On that point I am in agreement. Their responses have not been as we predicted."

Datum: 10:7 . . . Washington, 0152EST

Even in the dim streetlights, Packer recognized the CIA car while it was still a block away. It was the same dark brown LTD he had seen in back of the hotel.

Burnsy was driving. The dirty navy pee coat was gone and he was wearing a white shirt and tie. A raincoat with the collar turned up concealed the rest of his sartorial trappings.

He glided to the curb, and Jaffe opened the back door. Packer got in, leaving the cold, irritating mist behind him.

Jaffe was surly. "Jesus H. Christ, Clancy, don't you ever sleep?"

Packer strained to see the CIA man bundled and huddled in the far corner of the rear seat.

"Sorry," he said. His apology didn't sound sincere. "This couldn't wait until daybreak. We just got word that the Russians are going to make a big announcement at noon, Moscow time. Word is that they are going to pull Yerrov."

Jaffe looked at his watch. "That's an hour from now, Washington time. Yerrov is probably already on his way to the State department with a copy of the text. If what you say is true, he'll be on his way to the airport by the time they make the announcement."

"Have you talked to your office in the last hour?"

Jaffe had a cigarette and a cup of coffee. While Packer could not remember ever seeing Jaffe smile, he also could not remember seeing him without the trademark cigarette and coffee either.

"Cold," Jaffe scowled. He rolled down his window and dumped the coffee, disposing of the cigarette at the same time. He lit another.

"If you are asking me about Potapenko, I've heard. If it was up to me I'd give that marine a commendation."

"They're serious," Packer said, "and I think this points out just how serious. Two attempts, both of them right under our noses."

Jaffe grunted. "If you ask me, they've fucked this thing up royally. They've had two shots at it and Zhelannov is still alive."

"I talked to Peter Langley aboard the *Black River* less than an hour ago. He says our man located the Mala but wasn't able to get to it. The sub and the would-be assassin are both at the bottom of the Negril Harbor under several hundred feet of salt water."

"Which means there's no hope of getting our hands on the son-of-a-bitch to make him talk."

Packer nodded. "We're running out of options."

"Save your prayers for Zhelannov, huh?"

"According to what we're hearing from the *Black River*, those are the longest odds in town."

Jaffe somehow managed to give the appearance of slipping deeper into the folds of the LTD's plush rear seat. "So what did you call me for, Clancy? You don't drink, you don't smoke, and you're not the kind of guy I hang out with. So I know you didn't call me to go bar hopping with you."

"Talk to me about Complexity."

"I don't talk about Complexity. As far as I'm concerned that's the biggest secret in town."

Packer continued. "Based on everything we've been able to come up with, the GRU is still functioning and they're behind this. And from what we've been able to determine, when you're talking about the Chief Intelligence Directorate of the General Staff, the same small handful of names keep popping up—Moshe Aprihnen, Vitali Parlenko, Felix Osipov, Vyacheslav Churnova and Viktor Denisov. There are two or three other heavyweights such as Gontar, Zimin and Borovinski, but they don't seem to get as much of the ink as the five I mentioned."

"Aprihnen, Osipov, Churnova, Parlenko and Denisov—you've just named the top five Party hardliners. They didn't do Yeltsin or Gorbachev any favors either. These guys all cut their teeth in Krushchev's politburo. Concepts like free markets and democratic forms of government make them puke."

Burnsy slowed for a stoplight, and his eyes met Jaffe's in the rearview mirror. Packer knew that a signal had passed between the two men but he didn't know what it meant.

From his window he could see that they were crossing the Potomac into Maryland.

"Who is the strongest?"

"Churnova carries the biggest title. Parlenko is the brains, and Denisov is the balls. Osipov cools his heels in Murmansk most of the time. Aprihnen is a Marxist philosopher. The real son-of-a-bitch in the lot is Denisov. He's a Lieutenant-General, used to head up the Fifth Directorate. I told Complexity the way to get rid of him was to get him lined up with some hooker and dose him up with the clap. So far, no luck. We'll get him though. He can't keep his fly zipped."

"How close is Complexity to the situation?"

"Close enough."

"That doesn't help me."

"You know all you're going to know," Jaffe said.

"Do you think Denisov or Parlenko is running the show?"

"Odds are, if the hardliners are making a power play, Parlenko engineered it and turned it over to Denisov to implement. Our boy Viktor loves the spotlight almost as much as he does pussy."

"Suppose I told you I wanted to defuse this situation."

"Then I'd say you had to make certain one them doesn't show up for work."

"Can that be arranged?"

"You're talking some risky shit, Clancy. Guys

like you and I don't call that shot. People in sound-proof rooms with no tape recorders call those shots up on Pennsylvania Avenue."

"If you had the authority, could it be arranged?"

"My daddy always told me that anything was possible."

"That's all I needed to know. Tell Burnsy to drop me off back at the ISA offices."

"Hey, wait a minute, Clancy. You call me out in the middle of the night and don't even offer to buy me a cup of coffee for my trouble?"

Packer leaned forward and tapped Burnsy on the shoulder. "Pull in at the next place that sells coffee and has a telephone," he said.

Datum: 10:7 . . . Negril Beach: Le Chamanade, 0159NLT

Bogner heard Simon Morganthaller fumbling with the phone before he could get it up to his ear. "Yeah," he wheezed, pushing his mouth up close to the mouthpiece.

"Simon, Bogner here. Does the name Andrakov mean anything to you?"

There was a gap of several seconds while Morganthaller coughed and juggled the receiver again. "Yeah, he's the little Russian turd that's been firing off all those messages Packer has had me monitoring for the past week or so."

"Do you have any idea where to start looking for him?"

"The question is when, not where, Bogner. It's the middle of the goddamn night."

"The when is now, Simon. We've got to find him right now."

"Can't it wait till morning?"

"Simon, Zack Koorsen is dead and so is Bouderau. I'm convinced Andrakov is involved."

There was a prolonged silence on the other end of the line. Finally the voice came through. "How could Andrakov be involved? He's nothing but a shit-faced messenger boy."

"Are you up to speed on what's happening down here?"

"The way I hear it, you're up to your ever lovin' ass in hot water." When Bogner didn't reply, he added, "Hell yes, I'm up to speed. I talked to Packer less than two hours ago. I asked him if you needed backup but he said to stay here and keep tabs on the message center."

"A lot has happened in the past several hours. I'm convinced your messenger boy is one of the few people we can get our hands on that knows what happened here in the last forty-eight hours."

There was another pause, and he could hear Simon's heavy breathing. "After I find him, what do I do with him?"

"Sit on him. I'm on my way."

"How will you find me?"

"You get Andrakov and hold on to him, then get in touch with Avery Thomas over at the Foreign Affairs Bureau. Tell him where you're holding Andrakov. When I get to Montego Bay, I'll call Thomas."

Bogner hung up the phone and looked around the lobby of Le Chamanade. Except for Joy, it was deserted.

"Where to now?" she said.

"Montego Bay."

"I'm going with you. You'll never make it on that leg."

Bogner shook his head. "Not this time."

Joy's face twisted into an angry mask. "Look, damnit, I came down here to follow a story."

"The story you came down here for is out there on that ship anchored at the mouth of the harbor. This is where we part company."

"Again," she added bitterly.

Base Hour
One-Seven:
ZERO ZERO . . . 0700ZULU

Datum: 10:7 . . . Montego Bay, 0404MBLT

Boris Andrakov's injury had proven to be more painful than devastating. Despite his discomfort and the loss of blood, he was able to manage the drive from his encounter with Bouderau straight to Chinatown in Montego Bay and a doctor who specialized in not asking questions.

The wound inflicted by the Frenchman's speargun, as it turned out, was proving to be little more than a distressing inconvenience. The taciturn little oriental had not even cautioned Andrakov to scrap his plans to leave on the morning flight. As it was, he had a hole in his left side and an uncertain number of stitches holding it together. A liberal dosage of morphine enabled him to stay on schedule.

Slowed, but able to continue, he gathered his meager belongings with the graceless lack of precision men embrace when they are casting aside one lifestyle for another.

Andrakov's only real precautions were exercised in making certain he left nothing behind that would give any clue to his whereabouts. He had already made two arduous trips to the burning trash barrel in the cluttered alley behind the house where he had lived for the past 11 years.

Copies of communiqués had been destroyed, his files burned, and his correspondence shredded. Selected items from his meager wardrobe had been wadded up and carelessly packed in a cheap cardboard suitcase, and both the electric and telephone bills had been paid accompanied by terse notes to discontinue the service.

Andrakov went about his chores with both a certain sadness as well as a pervasive elation. Documentation was his life. He was a man who validated his importance in the orderliness of his meticulous files.

He looked through the closet one final time, then went into the tiny kitchen and drained the last few drops of a disappointing chardonnay from the bottle he kept by the kitchen window. As he drank it, he again experienced the bitter aftertaste of the morphine and checked the time. Then he washed out the bottle, peeled off the label and sat it on the drainboard to dry.

He heard a car pull to a stop in the street below, then heard the engine quit and the car door slam. He watched as the man headed for the door to his building.

Andrakov walked from the kitchen into his sitting room and waited with uncertainty. There was the sound of labored steps on the stairs leading to the second floor and hesitation when they reached the landing. He went back into the bedroom and quickly slipped the small Korean automatic into his coat pocket.

The aged flooring in the hallway creaked under the man's weight. There was another hesitation and then a knock on the door—the door next to his.

Andrakov opened his own door slightly and watched as the lovers embraced. There was a muffled invitation, and the door closed behind them. He returned to his packing.

Moments later he checked his watch again. Over the rooftop of the warehouse across the street he could see an occasional flash of tropical heat lightning and he wondered if there would be a storm. If there was a storm, would it delay his flight?

He latched the suitcase and set it by the door.

Andrakov had decided to leave the fax machine right where it was. Disposing of it would only call attention to the fact that he had one, and if he left it in the concealed compartment behind the books it could well be a long time before it was even discovered. He reasoned that it could be months before the apartment was even rented.

As a final and typically cautious gesture, he wiped off any last minute fingerprints and disconnected all of the lamps and electrical appliances.

Then he picked up his suitcase and stepped into the hall, closed and locked the door and dropped the key into the garbage chute at the end of the hall. Through the paper-thin walls he could hear the lovers.

At street level he put his suitcase in the trunk of the Toyota and started for the airport. He had already considered where he would park and how he would effect his departure.

Thirty minutes later he slipped the nondescript car into a space between two larger ones, opened the trunk, removed his luggage and a small parcel wrapped in butcher paper. He put the parcel on the floor of the front seat under the steering wheel, connected the two wires to the cheap kitchen timer, set it for 20 minutes and walked into the terminal.

By the time he had checked in at the ticket counter, cleared customs and purchased a morning paper, there were nine minutes left until his flight was scheduled to depart.

When he reached the CIL boarding area, he selected a seat, opened his paper and checked his watch. Now there were only eight minutes to go.

There was only one other passenger in the boarding area, a man, heavy-set and unpleasant looking. The man had obviously been drinking. He watched Boris with the vacant, bored eyes of a man who has overindulged and gone without sleep.

Andrakov, wishing to maintain anonimity, avoided conversation. The man's eyes drifted shut, and his head tilted lethargically to one side.

Andrakov turned his attention to the window and the ground crew. There was an unhurried air about them as they milled about the ancient DC-3, preparing it for its three island journey from Montego Bay to Banja Gore to Ariba San Luan and finally Calittie.

Moments later there was a distant rumble, not unlike thunder, but solitary and without reverberation. The young woman at the passenger service counter looked up briefly from her paperwork and then went back about her business.

"The storm will delay us?" Andrakov asked.

The woman shook her head without looking up. "I have heard nothing of bad weather," she said. Andrakov noted that her voice had lost some of the musical quality of the Jamaican countryside. She was citified, her jewelry and makeup indicating her preference for a more modern culture.

Andrakov returned to his paper again, pretending to read it.

"They just blew up another one," a young man said as he entered the area. He was wearing a tattered tee shirt with the barely discernable words "Hard Rock Cafe" bleeding from the front. "That's three this month."

The girl shrugged. Her expression was one of distinct disinterest.

Andrakov had hit upon the idea from an article in the newspaper. Cars being used to transport drugs were being left in the Montego Bay airport, and the last order of business for the driver was to place a small, timed explosive device in the car—no fingerprints, no inadvertent evidence left behind, nothing to trace.

The late arriving and inept police would swarm the terminal, looking for someone with a courier's profile. Everyone would be distracted. They would not, Andrakov was confident, be suspicious of a middle-aged man carrying a Russian passport on his way to Calittie. After all, what market was there for drugs in Calittie?

He got up from his seat and slipped the Toyota's ignition key out of his pocket, wrapped it in a piece of paper, wadded it up and dropped it into the trash receptacle.

The fat man was awake again, watching the animated conversation between the young man and the girl at the counter. The girl was laughing now. The youth had changed the conversation from exploding cars to matters more to her liking.

There was a distant wail of sirens, and Andrakov saw two airport fire fighting units slither through the first rays of light appearing on the eastern horizon. As they did, another passenger entered the area. A bureaucrat, Boris thought, young, well-dressed, bored, impatient with the way the CIL operation was being handled.

Andrakov checked his watch.

A fourth passenger came into the area, an old black man with snow-white hair, and then a fifth, another black with his long braided hair stuffed into a stocking cap. He was carrying a small crate with two chickens. He eyed Andrakov and sat down two seats from the fat man.

By now a slash of orange encompassed most of the horizon to the east, and the young woman made her announcement. The flight for Banja Gore, Ariba San Luan and Calittie was ready for boarding.

Andrakov, still feeling the nauseating side effects of the morphine, got on the plane first, selecting a seat over the wing where he would feel the least amount of turbulence. The bureaucrat selected a seat up the aisle toward the front of the plane. The black man with white hair sat across from him and up one seat. He promptly pulled the shade down and prepared to sleep.

The fat man selected a seat directly behind Boris, bumped Andrakov's chair back, abruptly excused himself with an impatient voice and dropped his bulk down after lifting the center arm between the two seats.

Andrakov watched the crew go through their pre-flight check list, heard one engine sputter to life and then the second. He patted the envelope containing the bank draft, leaned his head back and closed his eyes.

The fat man got up, bumped Andrakov's seat again, this time harder than the first, offered another apology, walked back down the aisle and spoke to the flight attendant. His voice was still slightly slurred.

"I . . . I have forgotten some very important documents. Will you hold the flight until I go out to the parking lot to get them?"

"We must leave on schedule," the woman informed him. "How long will it take?"

"No more than ten minutes,"

"I am sorry," she said. "We must leave on schedule. It is regulations."

The fat man looked dismayed. "It is pointless for me to go to Ariba San Luan without my papers," he sighed. "I . . . guess I will have to catch the afternoon flight."

The man with the chickens began to smile and hum a small tune. He was happy, he was going home. The black man with the white hair had managed to slip into a long overdue sleep. The bureaucrat, briefcase open, was already engrossed in his paperwork. If events went according to plan, the fat man was confident that no one would notice the steel pin that

R. Karl Largent

he had driven into the base of Boris Andrakov's skull until the plane landed at Calittie.

Datum: 10:7 . . . Ward Room C, USS Black River, *0444NLT*

Vice-Admiral Albert Cameron sighed and pushed himself away from the conference table. "Murphy was right," he muttered. "If there was any possibility it could go wrong, it has. First the goddamn Mala and now this."

He unwrapped his cigar, bit off the end and wedged it in the corner of his mouth without lighting it. Then he went to the port overlooking the massive crane on the aft deck and stared out.

"Look, I know you did all you could, Sam. We all knew it was a long shot."

Forsythe, at the far end of the table, stared blankly into space, allowing his long angular face to reflect the fatigue that now encompassed his entire body. He had the look of a man who had put up a noble fight and lost.

"We didn't have a hell of a lot to work with, Admiral."

"Cause of death?" Langley asked.

Forsythe leaned forward with his arms on the table. "He took one slug in the upper left quadrant of the chest. That bullet severed the right common carotid artery and the right internal jugular. There was extreme trauma to both the brachiocephalic vein and the subclavian artery. Which is another way of saying the slug tore off the top of the lung which filled up with blood from the two severed arteries. The other slug—and I should point out that I don't know in what sequence the shots hit him, but a good pathologist will—did essentially superficial damage. It's academic whether or not we could have done anything if we had known about the damage from the gunshots when he was brought aboard. He was burned extensively over the entire upper torso where the bullets hit. Lots of tissue damage."

"Damn," Stone muttered. "For some reason I figured the old fart was too tough to die. If he could have lived long enough to do a little finger-pointing, it sure could have helped us."

"That's the irony of it," Forsythe said. "There was never any real hope for that. That bullet cut off the supply of blood to the brain; ostensibly we were dealing with a vegetable from the word go."

Cameron had crossed to the bank of telephones but hesitated before picking one up. "How long have we got?"

Langley bit his lower lip and looked at his watch. "Not long. According to the latest from the NI office in Washington, the Russian medical team should land in Montego in about another hour. Their Aeroflot flight left Sheremetyeo about seven hours ago. That young Lieutenant that came aboard with Potapenko has already ordered the Hormone to Montego to pick them up. And you can lay your last buck on the fact that he'll have given them a full report by the time they hit the *River*."

"Including how one of our boys punched out their Commandant Potapenko? Speaking of Potapenko, where is he?"

Forsythe was absently drawing abstract designs on a folded piece of paper. "Still in recovery. We had to wire his jaw back together. He'll be sick and tired of straws long before that jaw works again."

"Then that Lieutenant Borodin left here thinking that Zhelannov was still alive?" Cameron clarified.

Forsythe nodded. "They'll come aboard all fired up. Someone has to be figuring there's a hero medal or two on the line in this one."

"So how long does that give us?" Cameron persisted.

"At best, two hours. By the time they land in Montego, board the Hormone, get here and then down to see the President, two hours is my best guess," Stone said.

"And how long before they discover he was shot?"

Forsythe hunched his shoulders, "Not very damn long."

Cameron reached for the telephone. "Priority one. Get me Bullpen."

He could hear the scramble in the radio room. There was a flurry of cross voices and the sound of relays.

"Bullpen," the resonant voice announced.

"Code 44—Lattimere Spitz."

There was another short delay, and Cameron knew that the computer was electronically analyzing a profile of his voice.

"Spitz here," the voice said. "Is that you, Cam?"

"We lost him," he said flatly.

There was a protracted silence.

Cameron was on a shielded line. Still he was reluctant to say Zhelannov's name aloud.

"When?" Spitz asked.

"Frosty is using 0414 local."

Spitz sounded irritated. "Who all knows?"

"Four here—and you."

Cameron could hear Spitz hand the phone over to the President.

Colchin's voice was flat. "How long before they find out?"

"Two hours tops."

"No way to delay them?"

"I think we've played our last trump card, Mr. President."

"All right," Colchin said. "I want the announcement to come from down there. If that press pool is still there, get them together and make the announcement. With Yerrov and Parker out of the picture we've got a problem letting the proper people know before it hits the wires. I'll have Hurley try to get through to the State Department and see if they can notify Churnova. I'll need every bit of that two hours."

"How much do we tell them?"

"As little as possible. If Bogner can get his hands on that illegal in Montego we still have a chance."

Datum: 10:7 . . . Moscow, 1351MLT

Konstantin Nijinsky sat near the end of the bar. While he waited he listened to the dissonance of fragmented conversations going on around him.

At one table an investigator with the Moscow Regional Office carried on a droning conversation with a young informant. At another table a couple of youthful intellectuals debated what it meant for Churnova to call Ambassador Yerrov home from Washington. At still another, a Marxist hardliner was praising the Vice-President's bold course of action.

Nijinsky had heard only one person, a young woman, inquire about how long it would take the President to recover.

Nijinsky ordered another beer and loosened his tie. He was waiting for Kerensky, and when a shadow fell over the table, he knew that Nikolai had finally arrived.

Even before the Internal Affairs Directorate of the RSB sat down, he was asking Konstantin if he had heard Churnova's speech.

Nijinsky nodded. "Now that I know what is happening, I find it fascinating to watch their plan unfold."

Kerensky's smile was indulgent. "You are quite certain of what you told me over the telephone?"

Nijinsky wrapped his large hands around his mug of warm, dark beer and studied his distorted reflection in the amber wash of the glass's reflection. "The people of the KGB had a way of doing things. It was more of a procedural thing that I have learned to recognize. At first that's what I thought it was. I even indicated as much to the Chief Investigator of my section before he called you. That is why I did not point out the discrepancies. But the more I thought about it, I finally came to the realization that they had put the gun in the woman's left hand merely to throw me off."

Kerensky leaned into the conversation, his dark, penetrating eyes hooded by heavy eyebrows. "And now you believe they wanted to be certain you knew it was a setup, correct?"

Nijinsky put his hand on the table and pointed to the nicotine stain between the first two fingers on his right hand. He spit on them and rubbed vigorously.

"At best it is difficult to get off."

Kerensky agreed.

Nijinsky took out his handkerchief and showed it to the officer. There were two brown smudges on it.

"From Modesta Orlov's hand. I obtained this at the morgue. It is makeup, made to look like nicotine stains. When I discovered this, I asked myself, why did someone go to so much trouble to cast suspicion on the KGB, unless of course it was the GRU? Then I traced the American's movements from the time he left the American embassy until he disappeared late in the afternoon."

"You have confirmed that he did meet with them?" Kerensky asked.

"*Da*. He had a four-thirty meeting with Vice-President Churnova and Lieutenant-General Denisov, and I can find no one who saw him leave the building, not even our own people. He did not take his official car and his driver waited until almost six o'clock before going in search of him."

Nikolai Kerensky rubbed his blunt fingers back and forth across his forehead. He signaled the bartender for another round of beers. Nijinsky again contemplated his reflection as Kerensky counted from a stack of kopeks.

"It is a dangerous game we play," Nijinsky said.

"It is not a game," Kerensky reminded him.

"I was using a metaphor. But you are right, it is not a game. You are a practical man, Inspector Kerensky, not a theorizing intellectual."

"You have documented all of this?" Kerensky asked as he stood up. He had known Nijinsky a long time and trusted his work, but he had been hesitant to bring him into the investigation of the rumored GRU plot. Now he was happy that he had.

"*Da*," Nijinsky sighed. He lowered his voice. "Most definitely. It was clearly the GRU that killed the American Ambassador, and it was the GRU puppet, Churnova, that has just called Yerrov home. If you couple that with everything else we have uncovered about their ambitions, it fits."

When Nikolai Kerensky turned to leave, his brooding exterior had lightened perceptibly. Now he had a phone call to make.

A pleased Konstantin Nijinsky allowed a small smile to invade his homely face and ordered another beer. As he counted out the kopecks, his smile broadened.

Base Hour
One-Four:
ZERO ZERO. . . 1000ZULU

Datum: 10:7 . . . Montego Bay Airport, 0711MBLT

By seven o'clock that morning Bogner had listened to the interrogation of the young woman at the passenger service counter of CIL and accompanied Avery Thomas and Montego Bay Police Captain Crompton Chastain back to the cordoned-off wreckage of Andrakov's car.

Two of Chastain's assistants were using steel claws to sift through the smoldering devastation, and Thomas began going over the sequence of events since receiving Morganthaller's call.

"He called at precisely 2:15 A.M., Commander. I recorded the time, knowing your penchant for preciseness. He said quite simply that you had called him from Montego Bay and that it was your desire that we detain Mr. Andrakov until your arrival."

"And?" Bogner pushed.

"I told him that would be quite impossible. To

the best of our knowledge, Mr. Andrakov had not committed any crime. The Jamaican government does not detain foreigners who are merely suspected of being involved in a crime. I must remind you that Mr. Andrakov is a Russian citizen who has, to our knowledge at least, complied with Jamaican laws during his residency. Had the request come through official channels of U.S. Government law enforcement authorities, I might have been able to do something."

"Damn it, Avery, he murdered a man in Negril."

Thomas smiled patiently. "At the time I knew nothing of such a crime. Let me remind you, Commander, I am here only because you were kind enough to see that I got a copy of the report of the explosion aboard the American yacht."

"Then what?"

"I called Mr. Morganthaller back and advised him that I had checked with Captain Chastain and verified my government's position concerning this matter. From what has transpired since then, it would appear that your Mr. Morganthaller decided to drive to Andrakov's house and keep him under surveillance himself."

"Then how the hell did Andrakov get to the airport and on that plane without Morganthaller seeing him?"

Chastain, a tall, regal-looking man in a crisply starched police uniform, sporting a neatly trimmed silver moustache and goatee, spoke up.

"It is possible that your man Morganthaller did not take up his surveillance until Andrakov had already left for the airport, or that the attack on his person came before Mr. Andrakov left and he simply was in no condition to do anything about it when he departed. You already know what our patrol officer found when he investigated."

"How bad is Morganthaller hurt?"

"The wound is quite superficial. Mr. Morganthaller was complaining of dizziness. We thought it best to transport him to Mercy Hospital where his condition could be evaluated," Thomas said.

Chastain folded his hands behind his back. "Following Consul Thomas's phone call last night, I did not sit idly by. Often we hear of crimes in some of the rural areas after the fact. Because of that, I followed the usual procedure and had my men do some checking. We were able to determine that Mr. Andrakov had booked a seat on the early morning flight to one of the outer islands. As a precaution, I booked a seat for one of my own men on the same flight. He is the one who discovered that Mr. Andrakov was dead when the plane made its first stop in Ariba San Luan and Mr. Andrakov did not move."

Bogner, still limping, circled the wreckage of Andrakov's Toyota.

"From the outset we knew," Chastain continued, "that this explosion was not one of the series of abandoned cars being destroyed by drug couriers who no longer have use for them. Unlike the professionals, Mr. Andrakov forgot to remove his license plates. It was an easy matter to trace it to him through the Bureau of Motors."

"The entire matter is most unfortunate," Avery Thomas said. "Your involvement would indicate that this matter somehow ties in to the incident in Negril harbor the night before last. The news is quite disturbing, no?"

"What news?"

"There was a news bulletin some thirty minutes ago on my way over here. The bulletin indicated that the Americans had just held a press conference to confirm that fact that President Zhelannov died in the explosion aboard the American yacht."

Bogner stopped, his face drained of color. He thought about Colchin and then Joy. After he had called Morganthaller from Negril, he had sent Joy back to the *Black River*. She got what she came for all right—probably the biggest story of the year and certainly the biggest one of her career.

He sagged back against the door of Thomas' car. It was hard for him to breathe—first the Mala, then Bouderau and Andrakov, and now Zhelannov. The sons-of-bitches had pulled it off after all.

"Is there anything I can do for you, Commander?" Thomas asked.

Bogner shook his head. "I guess not. I'll try to call Simon and then I better get back to Negril."

As he reached out to shake Thomas's hand, he could see the man hesitate.

"I do not know whether it is important, Commander, but I will mention it anyway. Do you recall the night aboard the American patrol boat when we discussed the call I had received earlier that evening?"

Bogner nodded, "Sure. You said you received the call notifying you that there was an explosion even before you received official word from the Negril authorities."

"I also told you that I made a practice of taping all incoming calls and that I gave the tape to Captain Chastain to see if he recognized the voice." Avery Thomas was the epitome of tact despite the long night. "I believe, Commander, that the caller last night, the one you call Simon Morganthaller, and the man who called me the night of the explosion are one in the same."

"Impossible," Bogner snapped back. "Morganthaller is an ISA agent."

"That may well be," Chastain interrupted, "but when Avery called me last night, he told me of his suspicions. I took the liberty of bringing the original tape with me and we have listened to it several times. I have known Consul Thomas for many years and I can assure you, he seldom makes mistakes about things of this nature. The man's voice he recorded last night and the man who called him the night of the explosion are one and the same. We have verified as much."

Bogner was suddenly alert again. "All right, where is Morganthaller now?"

"He was released from the hospital less than an hour ago," Chastain said.

"One three one three, Avenue of Flowers," Thomas said.

Bogner looked at him.

"You were going to ask me if we knew where Mr. Morganthaller lives, weren't you?" Thomas smiled.

Bogner turned to get in his car.

"You do not wish assistance in this matter, Commander?" Thomas asked.

Bogner turned the key to the ignition. "I can handle this one," he said.

Thomas bowed politely.

Base Hour
One-Three:
ZERO ZERO. . . 1100ZULU

Datum: 10:7 . . . Treptin, Near the Lake, 1725LT

Less than two hours after his meeting with Konstantin Nijinsky, Nikolai Kerensky's silver Volga surged through the countryside near the outskirts of Treptin approaching the Pasnikai lake country.

Kerensky turned on the Fulovic Pasava toward the cluster of housing on the north shore of the lake and entered the first open iron gate. The long drive up to the main structure had been shoveled by hand.

He drove around to the back of the dacha on the circular drive and spotted the long black Chaika limousine. It had been tucked under the cantilevered porch that jutted out over the lake.

Kerensky emerged from his car into the icy mist of late afternoon and permitted himself a moment of reflection.

He gazed out over the stark expanse of frozen

lake with its patchwork quilt of bunched ice and crusted snow, lingering longest when he spied the beguiling and shimmering ice fog on the lake's distant shore.

Nikolai Kerensky loved this place above all others in his adopted Russia. It reminded him of the winters of his youth in his native Bastava in Yugoslavia. Were it up to him, he would remain in this place and never return to the madness of Moscow.

He took a deep breath and entered the house through the rear entrance. As soon as he stepped inside he could hear their voices. They were waiting for him in the sitting room overlooking the woods between the dacha and the road.

Ruta was wearing her blue jogging suit, sitting in a large oversized chair, her face flushed from the afternoon's hike and two glasses of vodka.

A somber-faced Moshe Aprihnen stood by the fireplace, cigarette holder in one hand and the inevitable glass in the other. His unappealing sallow complexion stood in striking contrast to Ruta's.

"Ah, good," Moshe said when he saw Kerensky. "I trust you left our comrades in the city in an appropriate state of vexation?"

Ruta laughed, as did Kerensky. Nikolai kissed her lightly on the lips and fixed himself a drink.

There was the aroma of *chifir* in the room, and Kerensky knew that Moshe had insisted on a cup of the ancient concoction to warm himself against the chill of the October air after his own drive from the city. Moshe seldom ate, drank too much vodka and smoked three packs of cigarettes a day. The British saying, "death warmed over," frequently occurred to Kerensky when he looked at the academic.

"You need to put away your philosophy books and enjoy life," Ruta repeatedly admonished Moshe.

"You are late, my love," Ruta now said.

"*Da*. I received a call from our old friend, Inspector Nijinsky, just as I was leaving the office. There was something he wanted to discuss with me."

As usual, Moshe permitted his expression to ask the question. The Marxist had the kind of face that allowed his comrades to see through his social veneer and into the depths of his soul.

To Kerensky, Moshe Aprihnen represented the prototypical melodramatic Russian intelligentsia.

Kerensky laughed. "I am happy to report, it worked just as we had hoped. It took him awhile to discover what we thought he would find obvious at the outset. Most characteristic of a criminal investigator, don't you think? Ponderous, religiously ponderous."

"Not an intellectual, but tenacious," Moshe assessed. "He is now convinced that it was a GRU plot to make it look as though former KGB elements killed the American ambassador, correct?"

"Indeed," Kerensky nodded, "that is exactly what he believes. Not only that, with my aid he has now very cleverly tied it back to Churnova's recall of Yerrov, and he has further deduced that there is something far more convoluted afoot than a simple assassination plot. Brilliant, no? Nevertheless, you can count on him unveiling his suspicions to his superiors, perhaps even as we speak."

"You supported his conclusions, of course?" Ruta asked.

"Of course."

Ruta got up, walked to the fireplace, took a piece of paper down from the mantle and handed it to Kerensky. He read it carefully, his mind working back and forth between the English words and his Russian way of thinking.

When he finished, he offered it to Moshe who declined.

"I have read it," Moshe said. "Do you not think it is fortuitous?"

Ruta, still smiling, glided back across the room and sat down again, curling her long catlike legs up under her "We could not have planned it better," she sighed.

Kerensky raised his glass in a toast to her. "Ahhh, my lovely Complexity, at this very moment you are doubtless the toast of the American intelligence community."

Moshe raised his hand and put a reflective finger to his mouth. "I cautioned Ruta that their request is a departure from accepted practices. A source such as Complexity is seldom asked to perform such a task."

"Do you think it is a trick?" Ruta asked. "And if it is a trick, why would they be testing me?"

Kerensky's darkly handsome face furrowed. "Moshe is right. Their request is highly unusual. We must think it through before we respond."

Ruta laughed. "Both of you are far too suspicious. Americans are childlike in their openness. Instead of being so serious, we should be savoring this moment. How long have we collectively pointed toward this very night?"

"A long time," Kerensky acknowledged.

"A long time, indeed," Ruta said. "From the moment that Zhelannov was elected, we have known about Churnova and Denisov's ambitions. Now, just as they begin to luxuriate in what they believe to be their moment of triumph, we will slip in and deftly snatch it from them."

Moshe stepped away from the warmth of the fireplace, his thin body now sufficiently warmed by the fire and the vodka.

"The stations in Moscow continue to play the dirge for our fallen leader. I was with General Denisov when the Americans finally announced that President Zhelannov was dead. Viktor, as you would expect, foolishly believes he has already achieved his ultimate victory. He does not seem to realize that he has survived only the initial skirmish. I pointed out that he still must wait for the medical team to discover the bullet wounds and determine that Zhelannov was dead even before the explosion. Only then will he truly be able to prove his contention that it was the Americans who assassinated our glorious leader, and only then will he be able to convince the people of the need to rally behind him in his war with the imperialists."

Both Ruta and Kerensky were smiling.

"We must remember that even now, Denisov and Churnova continue to work toward our, not their, goal. What they have done is to take only the first questionable steps. Yerrov's recall implies much but says nothing. Movement in the fleet portends much but again means nothing until it takes some kind of definitive action. A sword raised and a voice elevated in anger are nothing more than posturing. Militarily there has been nothing done so far that cannot be just as easily undone. Only when the gunshot wounds are revealed will we begin to see people stirring in response to Viktor's typically ineloquent plea for unity."

Kerensky looked past Moshe at Ruta. "How do you interpret the American request?" he asked.

"It is simple. When you strip away their bureaucratic jargon, they simply want to know if I can arrange to have Denisov eliminated. They are merely responding to the information we have given them. The request came through channels and therefore betrays fear at the highest levels. As we expected, by feeding them information in advance of each event, they now believe I am very close to the situation. The only reason they knew about the GRU plot is because we told them. They would not have known about it on their own. What they do not realize, of course, is that Complexity's information comes to them through the benevolence of the RSB."

Ruta paused to smile in Kerensky's direction.

"To put it simply, they know what we want them to know and they trust me implicitly. Therefore the answer to your question, my darling Nikolai, is no. The request is not a test."

"Still," Moshe cautioned, "we must not be cavalier. We must be able to capitalize on the rapport you have built with them when and if it is needed in the future. Like Viktor, we too have options, but we must be cautious. When the news of the gunshot wounds is revealed, we can in turn reveal that an RSB investigation indicates that Denisov and his cronies in the GRU engineered this corrupt deed. By letting the Americans know in advance of the announcement on our own television, we will be further solidifying your position with them."

"Either way we will accomplish our goals," Kerensky admitted. "The GRU will be dismantled when it is discovered that Denisov and Churnova are behind this plot, and the RSB will emerge from the rubble of this black moment in our history as the only police power of the Party and the new Soviet people."

Moshe permitted one of his infrequent smiles. "What is your plan?" he asked, looking at Ruta.

"I will leave for Moscow within the hour. I want to be at the apartment when Viktor arrives."

"And you, Moshe, where will you be? And are you certain your comrades suspect nothing?"

"I am certain of it. When I left Moscow, Viktor was gloating over the American announcement and planning his ascendancy to the Party leadership."

"But we still have not settled how I shall respond to the American request," Ruta reminded them.

"Delay, seek clarification, inform them that it will take time to make the appropriate arrangements," Moshe advised. "That way we keep our options open and Complexity continues to be held in high esteem by the American intelligence community. By then, we should have received the announcement by the Russian medical team. If everything is in place, at seven o'clock tomorrow morning Kerensky will announce that the RSB has uncovered the GRU plot, led by Viktor Denisov, to assassinate Zhelannov and take over the Party leadership. Kerensky will also say that he has issued a warrant for Denisov's arrest.

Churnova, of course, will be implicated later."

"You are a master of words, Comrade Aprihnen," Kerensky complimented. "But what about Ruta?"

"The naive Americans will not suspect that our lovely Ruta is a double agent even if she is discovered with the General. On the contrary, they will simply think that is how she was able to obtain her information. Our official investigation will show that she was not part of their bungled duplicity. As a precaution, however, she will be allowed to leave when my men arrive."

Ruta stood up. "We are in agreement then. Now I must go. My bear will be expecting me to be there when he arrives."

Kerensky walked around the room filling their glasses, proposing a second toast.

"To our lovely Complexity. Tonight she is the pride of the American intelligence community, but more importantly, she is the treasure of the RSB."

Both Ruta and Aprihnen smiled and lifted their glasses

Datum: 10:7 . . . 1313 Avenue of Flowers,
0851MBLT

At the corner of Caneel Street and the 1200 block of Avenue of the Flowers, Bogner edged Bouderau's borrowed Simca over to the curb, tucked it in behind a Red Top Beer truck and walked the last block.

The narrow Montego Bay side street was lined with tourist shops, but because of the early hour most of them were still closed.

He located 1313, a weathered, pale blue, narrow

clapboard that had been squeezed between similar types of structures backing up to the docks on the Bay of Judy. He slipped between two of the houses, going around to the rear.

To his surprise there was a 38 foot Cabo Rico cutter tied up at the pier behind Morganthaller's place.

On the other side of the wharf was a carefully maintained garden with a thick tangle of royal poinciana that flowered all the way up to the support beams for the second deck. The deck itself jutted out over the water and appeared to have been added as an afterthought.

At the foot of the wooden steps leading to the second level was a small pink plaster statue of Neptune astride a dolphin and tucked back in under the deck was a paint blistered dingy. It had been tipped up on its side to protect it from further weather damage.

Between the house and the dock was a row of spindly, wind-whipped palms, enclosed by a stone fence that was an extension of the sea wall. It occurred to Bogner that Morganthaller's hell hole, as he called it, could just as easily have been another man's paradise.

Bogner put his back up against the side of the house and slowly began working his way up the steps. As he stepped up onto the deck proper, he heard an ugly metallic click.

"You're so fuckin' predictable it's pathetic," Morganthaller snarled.

He was sitting in a high-backed, wicker chair at the end of the deck with a menacing .38 leveled directly at Bogner. His index finger was curled around the trigger.

"With that gimpy leg of yours, Bogner, you couldn't slip up on a deaf man. I heard you comin' when you started between the houses."

"I called the hospital. They said you had been released," Bogner tried.

"Come on, Bogner, show some class. I know you know what's comin' down. That little tap I gave myself on the head wasn't all that convincing, was it? You've got it all figured out by now. I know how your mind works because I know where I screwed up. I knew it the moment I heard that Jamaican stiff, Thomas, answer the phone last night. He remembered my voice when I called him that night about the explosion in Negril Harbor. The old boy wasn't too cool, know what I mean? He got real formal, real quick."

Bogner kept his voice steady. "When you took out Andrakov, you took out our last hope of fingering the Russians for their attempt on Zhelannov's life."

"Fuck your last hope, Toby boy. That's how much I care whether you and Packer find a way to wiggle out of this mess." Morganthaller's huge head wobbled back and forth when he laughed. "Damn right I took out Andrakov. Know what that little bastard was trying to do? He was trying to double-cross both sides. He was going to pocket the money that the Fifth Directorate sent him to hire your buddy, Bouderau, to disable the Mala."

"I didn't realize you felt that kind of loyalty to your employer, Simon. I have to admit, you had me fooled, too. I'd be the first to admit it. No one suspected you of being the heavyweight illegal we kept hearing about."

Morganthaller was enjoying himself. "Why not? This way I'm collecting from both sides. First Packer and then Denisov. Packer does this. Denisov does that. One counteracts the other. It's a fuckin' game, Bogner, and I'm the only winner. Packer calls me his man in Jamaica. And Denisov calls me his personal illegal. You get the glory, Bogner, and I get the bucks. The arrangement suits me fine. While you and the rest of Packer's clowns are crawlin' all over each other to pick up the scraps, old Simon is cashin' in on your misplaced sense of loyalty."

"How did you kill Andrakov?"

"That stupid little shit! Four years he's known Denisov had his own personal illegal in Montego Bay. Think he made any effort to find out who it was? Hell no. Now look at him. That's what happens to you clowns that insist on livin' by the rule book; you lose your survival instincts."

Bogner took a step forward, and the .38 came up out of Simon's lap with the hammer cocked.

"Stay right where you are, Toby boy, or you won't be around to hear the end of my story. And that would be too bad. I've handled this whole situation rather well."

Bogner leaned his weight against the siding, taking some of the pressure off of his throbbing leg.

"Hey, all I had to do was wait for the little weasel to cut out for the airport. While he was screwin' around with that sophomoric bomb of his, I went to the passenger area and waited for him."

Morganthaller began to laugh and slipped into a fit of racking coughs.

"Then when he got on the plane, I simply boarded, sat down behind him and wedged a three-inch-long steel pin up under his skull. It was child's play."

"So what happens now?"

"Well, Toby boy, I got two choices. Either I blow you away right here, make a big damn mess and end up finding some place else to hang my hat—or I take you somewhere else to waste you. Either way, you lose. What we're talkin' about is my personal inconvenience. The fact of the matter is, I been thinkin', your buddy Thomas probably knows you came here, and that means I got to be a little more careful how I handle it."

Bogner was growing weaker by the minute and began to sag toward a chair. "Mind if I sit down?" he mumbled. "One leg doesn't seem to work as well as two."

Morganthaller's grating laugh erupted again. "You got it all wrong, Toby, my boy. That leg isn't your problem—I am. You may not realize it but that leg of yours is the least of your worries."

Simon Morganthaller leaned forward as a prelude to hefting his great bulk out of the wicker chair.

Bogner kept his eyes fixed on the barrel of the .38. He half-expected Simon to start shooting right there.

"So when and where does it happen, Simon?"

"Curiosity killed the cat, Bogner, and cats are quick and agile. Exactly what you ain't. With that bum wheel of yours you're no cat; you're a sittin' duck."

Morganthaller started forward with the revolver aimed at Bogner's face. "If I do it here, Bogner, I got all kinds of problems disposing of your body. But if I take you out on the water, the question of what to do with what's left of one T. C. Bogner is solved for me. I simply feed you to the sharks. Unfortunately for you, we've got lots of 'em around here, and I know where they feed."

Morganthaller motioned for Bogner to stand up.

When he did he began prodding his prisoner down the steps toward the wharf. The fat man kept the barrel of the .38 buried in the small of his back.

When Bogner finally conquered the ramp and entered the companionway of the Cabo Rico, Morganthaller crushed the handle of the .38 down just above his ear.

When that happened, the world of Tobias Carrington Bogner exploded. He pitched forward down the ladder of the Cabo Rico into the galley, unconscious before he hit the deck.

Datum: 10:7 . . . Moscow: Council of Ministers, 1758MLT

With the news coming from Negril indicating that Zhelannov was dead, Viktor was convinced he saw an instantaneous change in the mood of his comrades. There was a kind of grim-faced melancholia on the faces of the people in the streets, and the offices in the Kremlin were ablaze despite the hour.

The people, he told himself, recognized the momentousness of the occasion.

He stopped briefly outside of Parlenko's office, straightened his collar, knocked once and entered.

Vitali Parlenko was sitting behind his pretentious desk, smiling. He stood up when Viktor entered.

"You are to be congratulated, Comrade General," Vitali said. He came around from behind his desk and extended his hand to Viktor.

Denisov removed his hat and seated himself at the head of Parlenko's conference table. It was symbolic. He lit one of his American cigarettes and exhaled slowly, savoring the moment.

"You have received the word from our medical team?" Vitali asked.

"*Nyet*," Viktor answered. Parlenko was surprised at the restraint in the volatile Denisov's voice. "No word as yet."

"Churnova reports that condolences to the Russian people are pouring in from all over the world. We have already received many inquiries about the state funeral."

Denisov scowled. "It will be a closed funeral," he said uncompromisingly. "I will not permit the Russian people to be subjected to a circus of visiting dignitaries and irritating journalists in their hour of personal and national grief. Besides, Zhelannov's funeral is an opportunity for us to set the tone of the Party's reemergence from the rubble of the insane policies of Gorbachev and Zhelannov. A new, stronger than ever, Soviet Republic will rise from the ashes of their administrations."

Parlenko sat down at the table across from his comrade. His face had darkened.

"Does it not seem strange to you that we have not heard from our medical team as yet? Do you not think they have had sufficient time to discover the gunshot wounds?"

As far as Vitali was concerned, that was the one unsettled matter. As soon as the Russian people were aware that their beloved leader had been shot in cold blood by the Americans even before the explosion, there would be no question of them rallying behind Denisov's leadership.

That explosion, they would be told, was the American imperialist's desperate effort to conceal the heinousness of the brutal crime.

Vitali smiled; the Party line was well-rehearsed.

"The Americans continue to find ways to stall. They delay everything," Viktor said.

Even though they were alone, Parlenko lowered his voice. "And your own personal illegal, he has tended to the other matters as you planned?"

Viktor reached inside his tunic and retrieved the communiqué from Morganthaller. He had shown it to no one else because he believed it to be disturbingly vague; the American's choice of words confused him.

He laid the message on the table for Parlenko to read. As he did, it occurred to him that much of the precaution of the early hours of their plot was no longer necessary. Now they were in control. His task over the next 24 hours would be one of seizing, asserting and maintaining that control.

Vitali read it and his face darkened further. "What does this mean?" he insisted.

"It means that Andrakov is dead, and further, it states that there is no way to confirm Zhukov's death. He claims that the bullheaded Americans continue their search of the harbor."

"But Andrakov reported that the matter had been disposed of," Vitali said.

"He reported it, but is it true? His source, a salvage diver, reported that the Mala was disabled, at the bottom of the harbor and unable to surface because of damages it had incurred."

"You do not have proof of this?" Vitali bristled.

"*Nyet,*" Viktor admitted, "I do not have proof. I do have the word of a loyal and proven illegal. I show you this to make my point that our information is simply not as conclusive as we would wish it to be."

Parlenko got up and began to pace back and forth. He worried about such things; Viktor did not.

"Why did you not inform me of this earlier?" he said.

"Because I believe it to be a matter of little consequence," Viktor insisted. "Confirmation with such things as the capseal hardware was a mere formality, suggested by Andrakov. I am convinced that the Americans will give up their search soon enough. True, they have the Vasilivich woman in custody, but she knows nothing. Even if she did, she is the wife of a Spetsnaz commandant. Her loyalty is to the Party."

"I do not like it," Parlenko said.

"You worry too much."

Vitali Parlenko stopped pacing. There was a gnawing concern growing within him. He wondered if Churnova, Aprihnen and Osipov knew that they still had no confirmation that the Mala had been destroyed.

"What do you intend to do now?" he asked Viktor.

"I will go somewhere—perhaps home. There I

will wait for further developments. I have made arrangements for the news of the medical team's discovery to be brought to me immediately. When the news comes, I will make a statement."

"But Comrade Churnova has already prepared a statement," Vitali cautioned.

"Need I remind you, Comrade, that when the GRU assumes control of the Party tomorrow morning, I will be at the helm, not Comrade Churnova. It is appropriate that I make the statement."

Parlenko backed away.

Denisov picked up his hat and started for the door. He had no intention of going home or of returning to his quarters at Chesnakov Compound. He would, he had already decided, retire to Ruta's apartment for the night. He had been without her too long.

Vitali's voice was tempered. "We will need to know how to contact you, Comrade General, even at times inconvenient for you."

"You will be able to contact me through my driver, Corporal Achina Moslavoka. She will be at the Directorate dispatcher. She will know where I am."

Parlenko watched the door close and went to the telephone.

Base Hour
Zero-Nine:
ZERO ZERO . . . 1500ZULU

Datum: 10:7 . . . Curacao Inlet, Montego Bay, 1209MBLT

The first thing Bogner became cognizant of was the burning sensation. The awareness came over him slowly, first on his lips, then his eyelids and finally his blistered forehead. The scorching midday Montego Bay sun was hammering down on him.

The pain he was experiencing in his gradual return to consciousness began to spread, creeping down his arms and legs until there was some vestige of pain in every part of his body.

His tongue, swollen and sluggish, tried to snake out between his parched lips, and when it did, he tasted the salty, scaly flecks of crusted blood.

His eyes were still closed, sealed against the tangibleness of his pain as much as the unremitting sun.

All around him there were noises. One of the sounds was unfamiliar, as though something was being shoveled or ladled. Another was unmistakable labored breathing, and then there was the sound of sea water gently lapping against the hull of a boat.

But there was little or no movement, and he reasoned that the surface of the water must be extremely calm.

Slowly the pieces came together, and his addled brain began to make some sense of them.

He managed to squint one eye open, just far enough to make out an outline and a shape, and he was able to get a quick assessment of his surroundings. A man's lower back was to him; an expanse of pinkish fat flesh was exposed below the sweat-soaked bottom of a tent-sized tee shirt and the belt line of his trousers. The latter were soiled and soaked with perspiration.

There was a foul, choking odor, unpleasant and rancid, almost to the point of making Bogner gag. Yet somehow his instincts told him that it was important that the man not yet know that he was awake.

He tried again to trace the tip of his tongue along the tortured line of his lips but he could only reach a small part of them. It was too much of a strain, and he allowed the half-open eye to flutter shut so that he could concentrate.

Where the hell was he? And who was the fat man?

There were no reference points. Above him was a glaring blue canopy that was much too bright to look at. Beneath him was a hard surface with a barely perceptible undulation.

Nothing made sense.

He felt something on his forehead and compromised by barely opening one eye again. Only this time he realized what it was.

The obese thing was bent over him, glaring down with its sweat dripping down on Bogner's face.

Piece by piece, fragment by tiny fragment, the components of the nightmare were starting to come back to him.

He heard the same metallic click he had heard earlier, and this time he knew what it was. Morganthaller pressed the end of the barrel of his .38 against the fleshy part of his lip until the sunburnt tissue ruptured under the force of the pressure.

Tiny rivulets of blood and pus traced their way through the cracks on his lips and into the corner of his mouth.

He could hear the fat man's disgusting half-laugh, half-cough as spittle from Morganthaller's gaping mouth dripped down on his face. To his sun-tortured skin it was almost a relief.

"Welcome back to the ugly world, chump," Morganthaller rasped.

He had slumped his great bulk back against the Cabo Rico's transom, a posture which revealed his enormous and grotesque belly with circular folds of white flesh that clung to him like repugnant ornaments.

He was breathing heavily, and his hands were stained with a foul-smelling, blackish-red oily substance.

"Been mixin' up a little concoction for your friends, Bogner. They call it chum. You know what chum is, don't you, Bogner? Been spoonin' it overboard for the last hour or so, two whole buckets of it. You ought to see it out there, Bogner. The water's damn near black with fish oil and parts. They'll be gettin' the scent of it soon enough."

Morganthaller's voice fragmented and broke off altogether as he fell into a fit of wheezing and coughing.

Bogner closed his eye against the sun's glare but the escape was temporary.

Morganthaller heaved his great corpulence up and away from the transom, stood up and stumbled toward him. When he bent over he entangled his strong, blunt fingers in Bogner's hair.

Bogner, eyes still closed, felt his head being jerked up from the oily deck as his tormentor's surprising strength pulled him into a sitting position and started dragging him across the narrow aft deck toward the stern.

The deck was smeared with chum oil.

He slammed Bogner's head back down against the decking, and for a split second Bogner again teetered on the brink of unconsciousness, at the last second able to gulp in just enough air to retain apperception.

Morganthaller cupped his huge hands, dipped them into the chum bucket and began smearing the slimy substance over Bogner's face, into his hollowed eyes and past his blood crusted lips, making sure it inundated his mouth and his nostrils.

Bogner's stomach revolted, and he began retching up pieces of the chum's crudely concocted recipe of raw fish and entrails.

Morganthaller fell into another fit of laughing. He leaned back to catch his breath and released Bogner while he sagged against the sideboards for support, sucking in more of the foul air.

Several minutes passed before Morganthaller had rested enough to make another effort. He grabbed Bogner again, this time pulling him to a sitting position and bending his head over the cupper so he could see the water.

"Open your eyes, Commander Bogner, and take a good look. Look at the water. See how peaceful and calm it is? They ain't here yet, but they will be. They're comin'.'"

Bogner began slipping in and out of consciousness again, and his eyes fluttered shut.

Enraged, Morganthaller brought his massive knee up, catching Bogner under the line of the jaw. A new wave of intensified pain engulfed him, and his head lolled listlessly back and forth on the cupper.

"Stay awake, damnit. I want you to hear my plan," Morganthaller grunted. "You see, Bogner, I got nothin' to worry about." He clawed through his pockets until his hand emerged with the bank draft he had deftly slipped out of Andrakov's pocket when he bumped into his seat on the DC-3. He held it up for Bogner's inspection.

It was covered with oil and blood from the chum and some of the ink had already been obliterated.

"See how it works, Bogner? I get the money, and I get rid of you—all in the same day. Made myself a hell of a deal, huh, Bogner?"

Despite the fact that his head was throbbing, Bogner was even more aware of the pain in his leg. At this point he wasn't certain he could get to his feet even if Morganthaller presented him with the opportunity.

The fat man was distracted by a noise. He turned to look at the water and his eyes widened.

"Hear 'em, Bogner, hear 'em? They got a sound all their own, Bogner." He looked away again to monitor the brackish waters surrounding the Cabo Rico.

Bogner forced his eyes open again.

When Morganthaller turned back to face him, he was smiling. "They're comin', Bogner, they're comin'. That first one out there is just a little one, but the big ones will get the scent, too. And when they finally get themselves all worked up into a fever, I'll give 'em the main course."

Simon began his rasping, hacking laugh again.

"Main course is you, Bogner. That's funny, huh?"

Morganthaller's breathing was coming in sporadic gulps again, and Bogner slowly began to inch his hand into position so that it could support some of his weight. Morganthaller caught the movement out of the corner of his eye and brought his knee up again, this time crushing it against Bogner's bloody face. Then he crashed the full weight of his heel down on Bogner's hand, exerting a grinding motion until he heard the fingers on Bogner's left hand begin to splinter, snapping like a collection of brittle twigs. As he did, a new, higher level of pain wedged its way into Bogner's brain.

The exertion was too much for Morganthaller who collapsed against the transom again. He was spitting out his words, sandwiching them in between labored searches for sufficient oxygen to continue.

Red Tide

He tilted his great jowled head to one side as though listening to some primitive signal and again searched the waters. He wiped the sweat from his forehead and left a smear of the oily chum across the width of his sunburned face.

"Did I ever tell you about this guy I know, Bogner? The guy that first brought me out here? He's the one that showed me the sharks for the first time. He was good at it. He'd get the water thick with chum and then he'd start throwin' them chunks of horsemeat. Then, when them goddamn sharks got themselves all worked up into a frenzy, he'd stuff the bait with dynamite. He loved it. They'd attack it, and the damn stuff would blow the bastards right out of the water, blow their heads clean off. Damnedest thing you ever saw, Bogner. The rest of the sharks would attack what was left of the ones that had been blown up. Hell of a show, Bogner, hell of a show."

Simon Morganthaller's words were no longer connected. The gaps between the words grew longer as his brain labored to come up with words that were coherent.

Bogner's head sagged to his chest, and Simon jerked it back until his face was pointed to the sun.

"Listen to me, damn you," Morganthaller slurred. "I've gone to a lot of trouble for you, workin' out this elaborate plan. Now when them damn sharks get so thick that you can't see the water, I'm gonna introduce you to 'em, real personal like."

He paused and took out his knife.

"But first I'm gonna make damn sure you look real appetizing to them cold-eyed bastards. I'm

413

goin' to cut off that pant leg and tear out them stitches in your leg, poke around in it some—and when it gets to bleedin' real good, that's when you go overboard. Some plan, huh?"

Bogner began to spiral back into his nightmare world of unconsciousness, and Morganthaller slapped him across the face.

Again Bogner's glazed eyes flickered open.

Now there was a dull, persistent thumping against the hull of the boat. Morganthaller stopped, bent over the stern board and his pig eyes widened. Then he turned back to Bogner.

"Hear that? Feel that? Your wait's over."

As a helpless Bogner watched, Morganthaller cut away the pant leg and ripped off the bandage. The wound and the network of stitches was exposed. Morganthaller began probing it with the tip of his chum knife, flicking away shreds of flesh and systematically severing stitches.

Bogner's scream catapulted him back into consciousness as blood gurgled to the surface and began tracing new patterns down either side of his leg.

As Morganthaller appraised his handiwork, his rasping, throaty laugh gave way to another fit of coughing.

There were repeated jolts now against the wooden hull of the Cabo Rico, and the fat man turned away from Bogner again to count the predators.

Satisfied, he stood up and pulled Bogner to his feet. With his free hand, he reached down and grabbed the handle to the chum bucket. He jerked it up and threw it overboard. The water exploded in the feeding frenzy of the sharks.

Bogner knew the odds, but it was now or never. With every last ounce of energy he could muster, he twisted violently to one side and Morganthaller lost his grip on him. He twisted again, his legs buckled, and he fell backward against the gunnel. He had already lost what slight advantage he had gained with his first maneuver.

Enraged, Morganthaller charged toward him only to lose his own footing in the oily scum of the shark chum. He crashed heavily to the deck of the Cabo Rico and looked around him, stunned and momentarily confused.

Bogner was too desperate not to give it one last try. His hand shot out and grabbed the handle of the metal chum shovel.

From that point on, it was all survival instinct. He brought it up and down, as quickly and as savagely as he could with every last ounce of energy he could muster.

The blow landed flush against the side of Morganthaller's massive head, and his obscene, fleshy face contorted into a mask of outrage.

Bogner was able to hit him a second time, but it was a glancing blow and Morganthaller lunged for the shovel.

Bogner rolled to his right. A poker hot pain shot up his leg and slammed into his brain, but he still managed to get to his feet.

Morganthaller wasn't as fortunate. As he rolled over, Bogner brought the shovel down in a stabbing motion, catching Morganthaller in the fleshy folds of his throat. The hardened edge of steel sliced cleanly through the soft under tissue, and the fat man recoiled with blood squirting down over the endless folds of fat that constituted his throat and stomach.

Now Morganthaller's crazed laughter was mixed with the blood spewing from his violated throat and mouth. The sound wobbled like a wounded animal.

Bogner backed himself against the transom, bracing himself for Morganthaller's charge.

When the fat man lunged and crashed into Bogner, the wind went out of him. What reserve and resolve he had been able to summon up had not been enough.

For Bogner there was a sudden and hopeless realization—the feeling that it was all over.

Bogner staggered, dropped the shovel and waited.

Morganthaller, covered with blood, lunged again. Just as he did, Bogner went down and Morganthaller's charge toppled his body over the transom onto the diver's platform.

The braces held for a moment and then began to tear away. Bogner heard Simon's scream as his flailing, gargantuan body was dragged into the water.

As with Zhukov, Bogner could do nothing but watch.

The turgid waters around the Cabo Rico became Simon Morganthaller's judge and jury. He was tried, convicted and executed all in a matter of seconds.

Finally, a great shark, close to the surface, began to glide majestically away from the Cabo Rico. He plowed through the pinkish waters populated by his lesser brethren, and in the great beast's mouth was the chum-stained arm and hand of Simon Morganthaller.

Bogner teetered involuntarily between worlds of escape and pain. His eyes closed, and he slumped to his knees on the deck. He was trying to hold on, but there was nothing left to hold on to.

Slowly, but inexorably, he escaped back into his silent universe of empty darkness.

Base Hour
Zero-Three:
ZERO ZERO . . . 2100ZULU

Datum: 10:8 . . . Moscow: Zaratsna Towers, 0321MLT

Viktor had arrived at Ruta Putilin's apartment shortly after nine o'clock the previous evening.

His anger and disappointment at not finding her there had been assuaged by a phone call from her just moments after he arrived.

She informed him that she had been waiting for him most of the late afternoon and early evening, and that when he had not arrived, she had decided to go to her office at the Institute of Foreign Languages to pick up some papers for an early morning meeting the following day.

After Ruta's return, they made love. Now she languished beside him in the darkness, asleep. Over the silhouette of her symmetrical face created by the illuminated dial on her clock, Viktor could see the minute hand methodically inching its way toward the bottom of the hour.

He removed his arm from under her head and sat up on the edge of the bed.

The rush of their lovemaking had passed, and his mind had again returned to the turbulent events of the last three days.

Now, more than at any other time since the ordeal had begun, he was confident of the outcome. When Corporal Moslovoka brought him the news from the medical team aboard the American cruiser, the last piece of the puzzle would finally fall into place.

Viktor had not realized how tired he was. The tension of the past three days had taken its toll; mentally and physically, he was exhausted.

Still, he could not sleep.

He got up from the bed and went to the window. With the exception of an infrequent passing car, the street was deserted.

Across the street, through the branches of the barren trees in Savitnisky Park, he could see an occasional light in the windows at the Institute. He imagined the instructors frantically restructuring their lectures to accommodate the potentially explosive situation that had developed in the past 72 hours. In those hours, Negril, a tiny village in Jamaica, had become a name that would be forever entwined into the fabric of Russian history and the new, more powerful Soviet Union that he would create.

The night had turned bitterly cold under a cloudless sky and irregular patches of frost laced the seventh floor windows of Ruta's apartment. He glanced back at the sleeping woman and allowed his thoughts to reflect on his conversation with Vitali Parlenko.

Could Vitali be right? Would Churnova, in the final analysis, pose a problem? If so, Viktor decided, Churnova could be disposed of as well. The new Supreme Soviet did not have to tolerate those who did not support his efforts and policies to the fullest.

In turning back to the window again, he saw a staff Geonanka slowly round the corner and come to a halt at the curb in front of the Zaratsna. The driver did not turn off the motor or lights, and a figure clad in a heavy overcoat stepped from the darkened vehicle into the lobby of the tower.

He felt a tinge of excitement. It could be Achina, and if so, it could only mean one thing; she would have the news dispatch from the medical team.

Ruta had purchased a robe for him which she kept hanging on a small hook on the back of the bathroom door. He seldom used it, but if it was Corporal Maslovoka, he knew he would have to cover himself. He waited for several minutes, and when he heard the heavy door to the top of the steps close, he felt still another aura of anticipation.

He waited for the knock on the door.

Viktor Denisov had not considered how demeaning it would be for the young corporal to be forced to deliver a dispatch to him at his mistress' apartment just a few hours after she, herself, had slept with the General. Moreover, even if Viktor had considered the indelicacy of the situation, he would not have considered it important.

The knock was timid.

When Viktor opened the door, Achina Maslovoka managed to avoid looking at him. Instead, she kept her eyes narrowly focused on the envelope she held in her hand. She thrust the communique at him without speaking. Viktor ignored the young woman's petulance.

"This is from Admiral Osipov?" he asked.

Achina Maslovoka shook her head.

Viktor was surprised. "If it is not from Osipov, could it not have waited until morning?"

"It is coded with the 'U', General." The woman's voice sounded fragile yet edged with anger. "It is from General Meshcheryako of the Second Directorate. The courier from the message center said you had requested a priority security profile on one Nikolai Kerensky two days ago. I thought it best to bring it to your attention immediately."

"Then this is not the news from our medical team?" he clarified. Occupied as he had been for the past several days, he had for the moment forgotten about his concern for Kerensky.

Achina finally looked at him. There was a manufactured dullness in her eyes that Viktor had not noticed before. "*Nyet*, General Denisov," she said. She was being painfully military. "This had been deposited for you in the dispatch files. Do you want me to wait for your response?"

"This was an excuse to come here, was it not?" Viktor asked coldly.

Achina Maslovoka glared back at him and did not answer. There was an air of defiance about the woman.

"There will be no response," he said and closed the door. He went back to the window and waited until he saw her get into the Geonanka and pull away from the curb. Then he went into the bathroom and opened the dispatch.

It was a copy of the official GRU dossier on Nikolai Kerensky. He hurried past the salutation and went to the heart of the report.

NAME: Nikolai Yuri Kerensky

BORN: May 7, 1950, Belgrade, Yugoslavia.

EDUCATED: Prasiston Technical Institute, Borgav.

He scanned the rest of the preliminary data on the first page of the report and turned to the second. It was a copy of Kerensky's former Party card with the vague imprint of Lenin showing through the text. There was also a copy of an already poor quality photograph of Kerensky, and for the first time Viktor knew what Ruta's former lover looked like.

The third page was a chronological history of Kerensky's activities since his graduation from Prasiston. At the bottom of the third page was what Viktor had been looking for—a copy of the number on the red identification book assigned to KGB officers and his current title which was Director-Internal Affairs, RSB.

Viktor felt the blood rush to his face. His suspicions were confirmed; Ruta's former lover was indeed an RSB official.

He placed the report on the top of the toilet, went back into the bedroom, being careful not to awaken the woman, and picked up her purse.

Back in the well-lighted bathroom, he began sifting through its contents. Within moments, his worst fears were confirmed. Tucked carefully in the lining, he found Ruta's red identification book credentials and the small Zimerov revolver issued to women agents.

Not only her former lover but Ruta Putilin as well had at one time been a KGB agent.

Outraged, he went back into the bedroom, turned on the overhead light and shook the woman until she was awake. She sat up with her eyes blinking into the unaccustomed brightness. Her expression was one of questioning confusion.

Viktor threw the identification credentials on the bed beside her.

Ruta Putilin looked at it and without comment reached for her cigarettes on the nightstand. By the time she had lit one and pulled the sheet up to conceal her nakedness, Viktor had demanded an explanation.

"What is there to explain?" she asked. Her voice was brittle.

Viktor had already begun to put on his clothes. "You have made a fool of me."

Ruta laughed. "No, my General, I did not make a fool of you. You have made a fool of yourself."

Viktor bent over the bed toward her. "You will pay for this. I will file a complaint with the MVD and charge you with prostitution. I will instruct them to make an example of you."

Ruta calmly got out of bed and put on her robe. She went to the mirror and checked her hair. Unfolded, it cascaded down over her shoulders, looking almost as carefully coiffured as it had before they made love. She was speaking into the mirror without looking at him.

"And how will it look, my bear, for the man who engineered the assassination of the President of the Commonwealth of Independent States to stand in front of his peers and admit that he has been making love to an RSB officer while his accomplices were carrying out his plan?"

Denisov straightened. "What are you talking about?" he blustered.

"Come, come, Viktor, do you think me a fool?"

"Zhelannov was killed by the Americans. They have been plotting it for months. All of Russia knows it."

Ruta continued to stand in front of the mirror, applying her lipstick.

"On the contrary, my bear, you and your accomplices in the GRU have been plotting it for months. They will ask me how I know of these things and I will say that you told me of your plans in those quiet times after we made love."

"I will insist that you seduced me, that it was all a plot to discredit the military."

Ruta's laugh was both derisive and artificial.

"And I will insist that you forced yourself upon me, that you threatened me with the powers of your Directorate. Think how my charges will be perceived by a tribunal made up of long-suffering babushkas. Viktor Denisov, the power–hungry man who has guile enough to attempt an overthrow of the Commonwealth of Independent States—his word against that of a poorly paid and selfless instructor from the Institute of Languages.

I think," she paused, "my story is more desirable than yours." Again she laughed. "I can hear it all now. The man who believes he is strong enough to rule all of Russia claims he was seduced by a mere teacher from Vladivostok. They will laugh, and when they do, I can assure you, my bear, they will no longer see you in the same light that you wish them to."

Viktor began to sweat. His hands were shaking.

He slipped the revolver out of her purse and leveled it at her.

"You are making a very big mistake," he threatened. "I will not permit your lies and distortions to destroy everything I have accomplished."

Ruta Putilin moved slowly away from the mirror. She was shaking her head.

"You will only compound your troubles if you shoot me, Viktor. My colleagues would hear the shot. They would be at the door before you could escape."

Viktor could feel the chilling sweat begin to trace its way down his graying temples. His palms were wet, and he could detect the stress in his voice. The woman's indolent smile only fueled his anger.

"You see, Viktor, we have known for some time about your ambitious plans. A lust for power is a difficult thing for a man to conceal. We knew all about your plan to assassinate President Zhelannov. We even knew about Marshal Zhukov and who your accomplices were. All we had to do was wait for you to implement your plan and rid us of Zhelannov. Then we could expose you and your conspirators for what you are."

"You are lying," Denisov blustered. "No one knew of our plans."

"Look at the time, my bear. It is almost four o'clock. At precisely four o'clock there will be a knock on my door, and when you open it, four RSB agents will be standing there. It has all been carefully arranged. They will put you under arrest,

I will leave, and they will proceed to interrogate you.

"When you have broken, and you will, Comrade Kerensky will be called in to take your confession. Then, tomorrow morning, when your colleagues are expecting you to make your glorious announcement, they will hear instead the voice of Nikolai Kerensky telling the grieving Russian people that the RSB has uncovered your insidious plot to take over the Russian government after your assassination of our beloved President and reinstall the Party to power. Then Nikolai Kerensky and the RSB, not Viktor Denisov and the GRU, will assume the role of the new leadership."

Viktor checked the time. It was two minutes until the hour. He went to the window and checked the streets below; they were still deserted.

He had made his decision.

"I'm afraid your cohorts are late, my dear Ruta. It would appear that no one is coming to your rescue."

"Do not look for them out there, my bear. I have already told you, they do not have far to come. Moshe has very cleverly arranged for them to be in the next room."

"Moshe?" Viktor repeated.

"Ah yes, your trusted comrade, Moshe, the man you revealed your innermost secrets to, Viktor. You will be happy to know that Moshe will corroborate every charge Comrade Kerensky levels."

"Moshe Aprihnen," Viktor stuttered, "is one of you?"

This time Ruta did not answer; instead she lay down across the bed to watch him. She was still smiling.

Red Tide

Viktor looked at the clock. There was less than a minute. He had started to reach for the pillow that would muffle the shot that killed Ruta Putilin when he heard voices in the hall.

Base Hour
Zero-Zero:
ZERO ZERO. . . 0000ZULU

Datum: 10:7 . . . Montego Bay: Mercy Hospital, 2107MBLT

For the second time in the last 36 hours Bogner found himself swimming upstream against a current of pain killers and narcotics into an uncertain world of reality.

With each stroke came more pain and the realization that he could not be certain if he wanted to break through the final amorphous barrier into the ultimate confrontation with truth.

He had opened his eyes, or at least he thought he had, but nothing had happened.

On the other hand, if they were open, it was a world totally devoid of color and textures and images.

He was confused and disoriented.

The slightest movement of his mouth or the barely perceptible twitch of a finger brought on an inundation of renewed pain.

He found himself mired in a troubled, muddy

world of swirling abstractions even when he was confident that he was holding the world at bay.

There were foreign objects in his mouth, plastic and antiseptic tasting. His mouth was sore and dry but his throat felt even worse. He tried to swallow but there was a constriction. He tried to swallow but nothing happened.

The sounds he heard were all around him, but they were far too muted and too distant to identify.

Voices were at the same time coherent and incoherent. He was coming and going, floating free on water and at the same time confined by oppressive weights.

" . . . and this is Doctor Ramon Pascale," a voice was saying.

The voice was familiar in the sense that a song without a title is familiar, but he was unable to tie a name or a face to the voice.

Then there was a second voice, in some ways even more familiar than the first. The second voice was inquiring, halting and reluctant.

Bogner lay motionless, listening, sifting through names, faces and pieces, trying to make of it some semblance of sanity. One brick at a time, he reminded himself.

"I came as soon as I could," the second voice was saying. The voice sounded somewhat apologetic, and Bogner tried desperately to connect it to someone or something out of his past, to validate it, to give it an identity.

"Do you know what happened to him?" the second voice asked.

There was a void, and Bogner temporarily lost his grip on reality. He had momentarily slipped back into his world of semiawareness, a world where vaporous half-formed images rotated around him, crystalizing one moment and fading the next.

The only thing he knew for certain was that he would have to claw his way back into consciousness again and again until it stayed with him.

He tried to focus on the moment and was able to identify the sound of paper being rustled, of pages being turned, and—the voice of Chastain. That was it—the police officer, Chastain. He was the one who was doing the talking.

"Actually, a fishing boat found him. They were coming in with their morning catch. The captain of the vessel reported that they were just rounding the point at Curacao Inlet when they spotted a Cabo Rico hard against the rocks near Casema Cove. The captain said it appeared as though it had run aground. It had sustained extensive hull damage and was half-submerged in the tidal water. They investigated and discovered Commander Bogner who was unconscious. Unfortunately he has remained that way since. Obviously, because of his condition, we have not been able to interrogate him."

Bogner could hear footsteps crossing the room, coming closer to him. At the same time he was becoming aware of the fact that he was not regulating his own breathing. He was forced to gulp air before he was ready for it and expel it before he could savor it. It was as if his mind was out of sync with his own body.

"What happened to him?" the familiar voice asked.

Suddenly it registered. The voice had an identity and the identity was Avery Thomas. What was Thomas doing here—wherever *here* was?

Bogner tried to say something, to form words, to make a sound, any sound, but the constriction in his throat stopped everything.

A third voice was patiently reciting a litany of medical problems, and slowly Bogner realized that they were talking about him.

The voice was dulcet and gentle but the words were clinical. He had identified two of the voices, that of Thomas and Chastain, so the third had to be the doctor, Pascale. When he was able to retain his tenuous hold on reality the reasoning processes seemed to be working.

"He has a rather sizable laceration on the thigh of his right leg. It would appear that it is a very recent wound that has already been repaired once and traumatized a second time. It was necessary to mend it a second time, the stitches having been ripped out. All four fingers on the left hand have been broken and the rest of what you see is the result of prolonged exposure to the sun. The sunburn was acerbated by his partial immersion in salt water for several hours. In addition to his external injuries, he has had some kind of intensive toxic reaction to something he ingested. We had to pump his stomach. Don't ask me how or why, but it appeared to be chum. Despite all of this and two rather nasty contusions, one at the base of his skull and the other on the side of his head just below the ear, Commander Bogner appears to be in one piece. At this point it is hard to say what is causing his disorientation—the loss of body fluids and blood, the two blows to the head or some combination of the two."

"Permanent damage?" Thomas asked.

"Permanent, no, temporarily impaired, yes. That hand could give him some real difficulties; a forty some year old man doesn't heal quite as rapidly as a man in his twenties. Fortunately, I have treated similar cases of exposure so I know what we are dealing with there. It will be two or three days before we can remove the bandages from his eyes, and it will take several weeks for the tissue to repair itself both on the leg and from the extensive exposure to the sun."

Bogner heard the steps drift away from the bed and the muted voice of Avery Thomas again. He was talking to Chastain. "What have you been able to learn so far? I feel certain Commander Bogner's superiors will want a full report."

"I'm afraid we haven't been able to come up with very much," Chastain sighed. "We have confirmed that the Cabo Rico belonged to a man by the name of Simon Morganthaller. Why Commander Bogner was on that vessel or the whereabouts of Mr. Morganthaller are both unknown at this time. Unfortunately, it's not likely that we are going to know the answers to either of these questions until we either locate Mr. Morganthaller or have the opportunity to talk to Commander Bogner."

Thomas nodded. "Have you notified the U.S. Naval authorities in Negril?"

"Yes, and explained to them that you and I were with him earlier this morning when we were investigating the death of Mr. Andrakov. I explained to them that Commander Bogner seemed to be quite disturbed that this man Andrakov had been murdered. I also informed them that for whatever reason, Commander Bogner would not discuss the matter with us, indicating it was an agency matter."

"About Andrakov?" Thomas interrupted.

Chastain shrugged. "The only thing we know for certain about the man is that he was an accounting clerk and bookkeeper for a local import company. I gathered that Commander Bogner knew quite a bit more."

Chastain cleared his throat before continuing.

"As for Mr. Morganthaller, we are attempting to learn more about him. We do know that Commander Bogner had contacted him early this morning and that Mr. Morganthaller was apparently in turn attacked by an assailant in his car while he conducted surveillance of Mr. Andrakov.

"It would seem, Consul Thomas, that my department is at somewhat of a disadvantage in this matter. At this point in our investigation, we have only disjointed fragments of information. You could assist us by telling what you know."

Thomas nodded, chose not to respond and turned to the doctor. "How long before they will be able to transfer him back to the States?"

"In a few days," Pascale said.

Bogner could hear the footsteps moving further away from the bed. The voices were even more distant and difficult to understand. There was a momentary sense of panic when he realized they were leaving him—or was he leaving them?

He was doing what he could to hold on, but the hold was tenuous. Damnit, there were things he needed to tell Thomas, information that Thomas could relay to Packer and Packer, in turn, to Colchin. Morganthaller had confirmed that it was the GRU Directorate, Denisov, who was behind Zhelannov's assassination plot—or had Packer already put that part of the puzzle together?

He was teetering on the edge of a vast precipice again, peering into an even deeper darkness.

He could hear voices, not talking but screaming.

Into the hole.

Down.

—and then the voice of Chastain yanked him back. "Oh, by the way, if Bogner starts to come around, you can tell him that one of the U.S. authorities at Negril informed me that a representative of the American press pool is on the way to Montego Bay. Her name is Joy Carpenter. I assume she is coming to interview Commander Bogner."

Bogner could hear papers rustle and the shuffle of feet.

A door closed.

There was a howling, whistling silence.

As he again began his retreat into his narcotic world, he was thinking to himself, Joy is a helluva name for an ex-wife.

Datum: 10:7 . . . The White House, 2130LT

David Colchin leaned back in his chair and studied the expression on Lattimere Spitz's face. The aide settled into a chair across the desk from him and laid his report in his lap.

"Any word on Bogner?" Colchin asked.

Spitz nodded. "According to Cameron he's in a Montego Bay hospital. Cameron is sending two members of his medical staff on the *Black River*

434

over to see if they can be of any assistance. The Jamaican authorities inform us he's been worked over pretty good but that he'll make it."

Colchin took a deep breath. "What about the ISA and the CIA? What's the latest?"

Spitz shook his head. "Talked to both agencies less than thirty minutes ago. Jaffe hasn't heard from his contact. Both Jaffe and Packer report that the request was put through a good twelve hours ago."

Colchin turned in his chair and looked out the window. "Nasty business," he repeated absently. "Hell, I don't even know this man, Denisov."

"We're taking all the necessary precautions. I've been assured that we'll have a full situation analysis from the Joint Chiefs no later than 2300. But we're moving ahead. We've even gone so far as to alert our people at the embassies over there. We've told them to expect the worst. With Parker out of the picture it's a little shaky. So far though, all we've seen is a lot of posturing, nothing overt. Sannon at NI admits that he's never seen anything quite like it. He claims that in the past they've always been secretive as hell when they were upstaged. He seems to feel that they are doing an unnecessary amount of muscle flexing."

Colchin stood up and walked to the window. "I keep asking myself if there was something I could have done to avert all of this. Seventy-two hours ago we were on the verge of negotiating an agreement that would have significantly altered the future of—"

Spitz glanced at his watch. "There's still time, Mr. President."

R. Karl Largent

Inspector Konstantin Nijinsky was still half-asleep. Kerensky's call had come shortly after 6:00 A.M., waking him out of a sleep troubled by a recurring dream of a man leaping to his death from a bridge into the icy waters of the Sosenka River.

Each time Konstantin was close enough to grab him, but each time he missed.

Nijinsky had dressed, made a quick phone call, gulped down a cup of hot tea and driven straight to the Zaratsna Tower, all in less than 30 minutes.

In the lobby of the building he discovered that the elevators were not working and he labored up the seven flights to the structure's top floor.

The corridor, as was the case with all state-inspired buildings, was dimly lit. He located unit 72WW and knocked.

Nikolai Kerensky opened the door. His eyes were red and his face was stubbly with a day's growth of beard.

"Konstantin," he said, sounding relieved. "I am glad you could come." It did not sound like Kerensky. This time his voice was void of the RSB officer's usual charm and authority.

Nijinsky stepped into the dark apartment.

With the door to the corridor shut even the feeble illumination from the hall was sealed off, and Kerensky turned on a small light on the table next to the window.

"What is this all about?" Nijinsky asked.

Kerensky seemed somewhat uncertain about what to do or say next.

"Come with me," he finally said. He went to the door of the bedroom, opened it and turned on a light.

Konstantin Nijinsky glanced hurriedly around the room and felt his stomach heave. The harsh yellow light of the single overhead bulb bathed down on a scene of outrage. Ruta Putilin had been strangled and violated. Her naked white body, slender and athletic, was grotesquely transfixed in the posture of a lover. Her legs were spread wide, and a length of cheap cotton electrical cord had been wrapped around her throat, strangling her.

Her finely sculptured face was bruised and ravaged until there was an ugly purple cast to it. It was flecked with minute rust-colored blemishes where the tiny capillaries had ruptured as she struggled for her life.

The fawn-colored hair was in a tangle on the pillow, and a thin trail of dried blood traced down the side of her face over her throat from one of her nostrils.

Her mouth had been savagely hammered to one side, and her underclothes lay on the floor beside the bed.

Nijinsky walked slowly around the death scene, gradually regaining his composure. He stopped, fumbled nervously through his pockets until he found his cigarettes, lit one, exhaled and felt calmer. Then he turned to look at Kerensky who was still staring at the dead woman as though his mind was having difficulty accepting the finality of it all.

"Do you know who she is?" Nijinsky asked.

"Her name is Ruta Putalin. She is an RSB agent."

"She works for you?"

"She was assigned to me, yes."

"Do you know what she was doing here?"

Kerensky hesitated. He had to be careful. He did not want to trap himself into a long and unnecessarily detailed explanation of the relationship the RSB had arranged between Ruta Putilin and Viktor Denisov.

"Some things I cannot talk about. It is a matter of national security," Kerensky finally said.

Konstantin snuffed out his cigarette and lit another. He crossed the room, looked in the closet, then went to the bathroom door and opened it.

Viktor Denisov, only partially dressed, was in the bathtub; the red-black water concealed everything beneath the surface.

The blood bath came from a large open slash that encircled Denisov's throat. His huge head sagged back against the rim of the tub, and Nijinsky could see a mutilated tangle of severed blood vessels and muscles. The mouth was open and a bloated tongue protruded, accentuating the futility of his last gasps for air.

"You know him also?" Nijinsky asked. For Konstantin, it was less difficult to look at the desecrated body of Viktor Denisov than that of the woman in the bedroom.

"He is Lieutenant-General Viktor Denisov, former Fifth Directorate of the GRU," Kerensky said.

Nijinsky pursed his thin lips and shook his head.

"Very interesting, Inspector, a GRU official and a RSB agent. Like the dead American Ambassador, there is more here than—"

"Than what?" Kerensky demanded.

Nijinsky smiled. "I was going to say 'meets the eye.' It is an American expression. But you do not like American expressions, do you, Comrade?"

Kerensky frowned, and Nijinsky cleared his throat.

"Let me make sure I understand what happened here, Comrade. You are telling me that you came here looking for Ruta Putilin and this is what you found?"

"That is correct."

"What time did you arrive here?"

"Shortly before I called you." Kerensky put his hands in his pockets and walked into the apartment's sitting room. He was obviously agitated.

Nijinsky followed, extracting his notebook. "There are questions I must ask."

"And as I have already told you, there are questions I cannot answer," Kerensky said, sitting down. "You must understand that we are dealing with a matter of the utmost security here."

Konstantin went back into the bathroom, dropped his cigarette in the toilet and flushed it. He began talking to Kerensky even before he returned to the room.

"The most obvious question, Inspector Kerensky, is why did you call me? I am a public investigator with the MVD. We are seldom involved in matters where there is a question of security. Why does the RSB not handle the matter itself?"

Kerensky's face colored. "A woman has been murdered and her lover has committed suicide. Is it not proper procedure to call in the police?"

"Then you are saying their relationship was not—how shall I say it?—an arrangement of the RSB?"

Kerensky's face was beginning to mirror his impatience.

"I want you to handle this as you would any other violent crime, Inspector Nijinsky."

Nijinsky was unwilling to accept Kerensky's explanation.

"But it was only yesterday, Comrade, that we discussed the possibility of the GRU involvement in the murder of the American Ambassador, Parker. Now we have this situation. Suddenly you are being surprisingly reticent. In fact, you are being vague."

"I can only repeat what I have already told you. We are dealing with a matter of state security. It is imperative that neither I nor the agency be involved in this investigation."

Nijinsky unbuttoned his coat and sat down. "You are right of course, Inspector Kerensky. You see things on a much larger scale than I do. If you are telling me that the murder of the American Ambassador and this situation are related, I can understand how state security would be involved and will not interfere. How is it that you wish me to handle this matter?"

Kerensky's face softened. "Excellent. I knew I could count on you. I want you to say that you received an anonymous call informing you of a murder-suicide. Report it up through channels as though you do not know who these people are. As far as you know, the woman is simply an instructor at the academy and he is obviously a high-ranking officer, facts that would be immediately apparent to any well-intentioned public investigator."

"Their real identities are certain to come out as

the investigation continues," Nijinsky cautioned. "I cannot control that."

"I am counting on the pieces coming together, just as they would in any investigation, but it is imperative that no one knows I was the one who discovered the bodies. If that fact becomes knowledge, there are those that will suspect RSB involvement."

Konstantin Nijinsky nodded his understanding. As he made notes, he lit another cigarette and allowed it to dangle from the corner of his mouth, enveloping his homely head in a thin veil of smoke.

Kerensky stood up, buttoned his coat and started for the door.

"I am counting on your discretion, Inspector."

Nijinsky nodded as Kerensky closed the door. When he heard Nikolai's footsteps start down the stairs, he went to the window and waited. Several minutes later he saw the RSB officer emerge, cross the street and get into a sleek Volga. When the car disappeared around the corner, Nijinsky signaled to the man standing in the shadows across the street amidst the trees and picked up the telephone.

Moshe Aprihnen answered. He did not wait for Nijinsky's salutation. "It worked?" he asked.

"*Da*," Konstantin said. "He is gone and suspects nothing. I assured him I would handle this as routine until the true identities of the victims were discovered."

Moshe began to laugh. "You have what you need?"

"He was very careless. His fingerprints are everywhere. He will be easy to implicate."

"You are aware of your next step?" Moshe asked.

"I am to call the Chief Inspector and tell him I have found the bodies of a RSB agent and GRU Directorate and that I have a witness who saw Nikolai Kerensky leaving the scene of the crime. Then I will ask him to issue a warrant for the arrest of Kerensky for the murder of Ruta Putilin and Viktor Denisov."

"Excellent," Moshe said.

Nijinsky hesitated. He did not know if it was the proper time to say his carefully prepared speech of congratulations.

"You are to be commended, Comrade Aprihnen. Your plan was brilliant."

Moshe sighed. To Konstantin Nijinsky, Moshe Aprihnen sounded almost sad that it was over.

"We have accomplished a great deal in the last seventy-two hours, Comrade. We have disposed of Zhelannov and effectively castrated the GRU. When Churnova and Parlenko are taken into custody, it will be over."

"And you, Comrade Aprihnen, you will emerge."

Nijinsky could not know it, of course, but on the other end of the line Moshe's sallow, sad face slowly encased itself in a hard smile.

"Yes, Comrade Nijinsky, you are right. Now that Kerensky has been disposed of as well, I will emerge."